BOOK TWO OF THE REFORGED TRILOGY

SWORD OF DREAMS

ERICA LINDQUIST &
ARON CHRISTENSEN

LOOSE LEAF
STORIES

This is a work of fiction.
All characters, organizations, places and events portrayed in this book
are either the product of the authors' imagination or are used fictitiously.

Find more of our books at LLStories.com

For my father, Charles Lindquist,
who taught me how to stand

[PROLOGUE]
WHETSTONES

"Evil perseveres not at the hands of bad men, but by the inaction of good men."

- THE BOOKS OF LIGHT (23 PA)

Fifty-seven years ago.

Gavriel Euvo stood at the edge of a field of withered gray grass that rippled in the cold wind. It was always dark on Zeos, as dark and dry as the inside of a coffin. The low sky churned with brown clouds that blotted out the tiny pair of orange suns and turned the planet's moons into invisible monsters that tugged jealously at the muddy Zeon oceans.

"Gavriel? Are you sure about this? What if things don't work out at the university? Where will we be then? Gavriel...? Love, did you hear a word I said?"

"Hm?" Gavriel answered. He slid an arm around his wife's thin shoulders.

He could feel the sharp angles of her bones through her skin and clothes. Jaissa Euvo was only thirty-seven years old, but a hard life on Zeos had lined her face with worry and streaked her hair in gray. Still, she was no less lovely in her husband's eyes.

"Well?" she asked. "What do you think?"

Gavriel pulled Jaissa close and kissed her furrowed brow.

"I'm sorry," he said. "I heard you, Jai, but I think you're worrying too much."

"And I don't think you worry nearly enough," Jaissa told him, but finally smiled. "Your head's always up in the clouds, love. You're never down here in the mud with the rest of us."

"I'm a philosopher. Having my head in the clouds is my job," Gavriel said. He gave his wife another kiss. "And that's why you fell in love with me."

"On the very first day of class, oh great and wise teacher," Jaissa teased, and then grew serious again. "Do you think they'll approve the transfer this time?"

"I do. The Alliance Education Board likes what they're hearing. It might take some time for the datawork to go through, but then they'll sponsor our move out to Tynerion."

"Tynerion," Jaissa sighed. Now was looking up at the sky, too, as though desire alone could pierce the thick Zeon clouds and see through to the bright stars beyond. "God, I can't wait. Zeos is no planet for Sarru."

"And speaking of our tiny devil..."

Gavriel crouched and held out his arms to the little girl running toward them through the dry grass. It was still early in the morning, but her jumper was already covered in colorless dust. Sarru leapt into her father's embrace with a squeal. The eight-year-old had her mother's graceful build and beautiful sky-blue eyes. Sarru waved a streamer of bright, shiny plastic at Gavriel, too close and too fast to read.

"Come *on*! We're going to be late!" she said.

"Late for what, honey?" Jaissa asked, full of mock confusion. "I don't remember what we're doing here in this God-forsaken chill.

Oh, we must have gotten lost! Maybe we should just go home and get warm."

"No!" Sarru cried. She slid out of Gavriel's arms and stomped her small foot in the grass. "We're going to the fair! Xiv and Dinna are already inside. We have to go soon or they're going to do all the good rides without me!"

"Well, we wouldn't want that," said Gavriel seriously. He took the plastic advertisement from Sarru's hand and picked her up. "Come on, let's go. I think I have some tickets in one of my pockets."

With his daughter giggling and tugging on his beard, Gavriel led his family out across the grassy field. The annual fair was too small for the large venue, with brightly striped tents spaced few and far between. Brilliantly lumapainted rides would have been lonely were it not for the long lines of eager children waiting for their turn to be thrilled.

At the gate, Gavriel handed his tickets to a man who winked at the impatiently fidgeting Sarru and made her promise to have a good time.

"I will," she assured him with childish gravity. She wriggled free of Gavriel and hopped down to the ground. "I'm going to find Xiv and Dinna!"

"We're right behind you, sweetheart," Jaissa said.

They followed their daughter until Sarru found her friends – a small, silver-skinned Ixthian boy and a taller human girl with dark Mirran stripes – already in line for the garishly flashing *Whirly-Swirly*. Gavriel put his arms around Jaissa again and watched Sarru bound over to the other two children, cheerfully ignoring grumbles from the rest of the line when she cut in next to Xiv and Dinna.

"She'll miss them too much," Jaissa sighed. "When we move out to Tynerion, she's probably never going to see those two again."

"Sarru's a sweet girl. She'll make new friends," Gavriel said. He gave Jaissa a reassuring squeeze. "But it's all the more reason for her to have fun with them now."

Dinna's mother had bought her a huge cone of fluffy lavender puff-candy, now proudly shown off and shared with Sarru and Xiv. Sarru managed only a few mouthfuls before the spun sugar stuck to her fingers. She giggled and tried to wipe it off in Xiv's fine white hair. The short Ixthian boy dodged Sarru, but Dinna caught on to her friend's game and dropped a clump of candy onto Xiv's head. It stuck to one of his antennae, making it look like a tiny tree.

"Hey!" Xiv protested. "Stop it!"

"You know, Xiv's a bright boy," Gavriel said contemplatively. "It would be such a waste for him to become a miner like his parents. Maybe when we've been on Tynerion for a while, I can fly Xiv out on a scholarship."

"Really?" Jaissa looked worried again. "You think you could do that? There aren't very many scholarships."

Gavriel smirked. "No, there aren't. But what's the point of power if I can't abuse it a little? Once I've got some clout with the Tynerion universities, I'll see what I can do for Xiv. Maybe Dinna, too, if I can. It would be good for Sarru to have her friends around, after all. Like you said, she's going to miss them when we're gone."

Xiv's hair was full of purple candy now. He fought back against the giggling girls, but to no avail. All three children were screeching and covered in dyed sugar.

Jaissa sighed. "Well, I'd better go save Xiv or else those girls are going to end him long before college age."

She disentangled herself from Gavriel's embrace and went to the children. Sarru and Dinna shrieked and feigned ignorance of their crime, cramming the last of the sweet evidence into innocently smiling mouths. Jaissa just shook her head and picked the candy from Xiv's hair. Her own hands were quickly covered in sugar, too, sticking fingers together and sending all three children off into gales of laughter. Jaissa giggled as she licked her fingers in a vain attempt to clean them. His wife looked no different than the other girls now, Gavriel thought with a grin.

The frozen air shifted as the wind picked up, whipping the low-hanging clouds into sudden motion. They swirled and danced like ink in water. It could almost have been beautiful. Almost. Gavriel squinted up at the sky again. There were stars out there, and worlds better venaformed than Zeos. Worlds like Tynerion, centers of light and learning.

Thank God I can finally take my family there, away from all of this mud and darkness.

Someone screamed – not the mechanical shriek of the rides or children at play, but a sharp cry of absolute terror.

It was Xiv. He was standing over a heaving, thrashing knot of motion on the ground, pointing and screaming. The boy's thin, keening wail cut through the wind and music of the carnival. Dinna fled the scene, weeping and pulling on her green braids.

Jaissa was on the ground, her whole body was twisted in terrible, unnatural convulsions. Her eyes rolled back in her head and her heels drummed rapidly against the rocky ground. Thick red foam boiled up from her mouth and streaked her cheeks in gore. Sarru lay beside her contorted mother. The little girl tore at her own throat with her fingernails as she gurgled and choked. Gavriel ran to his family, scattering frightened fairgoers. He fell to his knees and gathered his wife and daughter into his arms.

"Sarru! Relax, Sarru. Just take slow, deep breaths. Someone call a doctor!" Gavriel shouted.

Jaissa writhed like a worm impaled on a hook. Sarru thrashed in her father's arms and tried to scream, but all that came out was a strangled choking sound. Gavriel pried her hands away from her neck and stroked her hair. There was blood under her nails.

"Everything's going to be fine, Sarru," he said. "No... No, don't fight! Just try to calm down and breathe. Sarru!"

The little girl went stiff in Gavriel's arms as blood erupted from her nose and mouth. Her eyes – so beautiful and blue, just like her mother's – went wide as her eardrums ruptured with a small *pop*.

Sticky red poured down over Gavriel's fingers. He held his daughter to his chest as she died, screaming silently in agony.

When the medics finally arrived at the fair, they found Gavriel still holding his wife and daughter, begging them to breathe.

Sky blue.

Gavriel stared at the painted walls of the waiting room. It was a tiny room, a private place to receive bad news. A prison cell. Why did they call it sky blue? There were no blue skies on Zeos. That soft pastel color was supposed to be calming, Gavriel guessed. He hated it.

A tall Ixthian woman came to tell him what had happened. Her clean lab coat – the same lying color as the walls – was embroidered with the quartered circle of the CWA Medical Corps.

It was the lavender candy, she explained in a smooth, soothing voice. The dye had reacted with deoxylene, an airborne by-product of the mines. The mixture was harmless to most people, but a rare genetic abnormality made it fatal to Jaissa. A trait she had passed on to her daughter.

No one could have predicted it. No one could have known.

That was it. Just a one in a billion random chance. An accident. There was no one to blame. No one would pay the price for their terrible deaths. The mining methods were extensively tested and verified for safety. Nothing would change. Nothing *could* change.

The doctor asked Gavriel to sign the datadex she held, a document that gave the hospital permission to sequence Jaissa's blood so that they could screen other Zeon citizens for the same problem. Gavriel took the datadex, staring at it. He could see nothing but reflections of the blue walls on the shiny screen.

Screenings? Why? To save some stranger from one horrible death, only to deliver them to some other random, terrible chance?

To be crushed by a car as they carry their groceries across the road? Murdered by a jealous lover in a fit of rage? Just to choke to death on a pill meant to save their pointless, pathetic life?

Gavriel flung the datadex across the empty waiting room and it shattered into splinters against the wall. The startled Ixthian doctor jumped and told Gavriel to calm down. Her voice seemed muffled, echoing as though from a great and uncrossable distance.

Why do you live? Gavriel wondered. *Why do I live? We'll only die. We all die, alone and in pain.*

Gavriel grabbed the doctor around her slender silver neck. Her smooth, slightly rubbery skin was so fragile under his strong hand. Her compound eyes shone red with fear. The Ixthian doctor fought against Gavriel, but he was larger and stronger. She could not even scream. Just like Jaissa, just like Sarru, dying in terrible silence... He crushed her throat, choking until she went finally still.

Gavriel held the Ixthian there and stared into her eyes until they went dark. Flat black. Dead.

Dead and free.

[1]

UNDERGROUND

"What's the difference between an evil thought and an evil deed? We all have our evil thoughts, but it takes a broken heart to act on them."

- NOMUSA UDO, CARSAN WRITER (230 MA)

Where are you?

Maeve leaned into the window. The glass was cold and smooth against her cheek, but did nothing to soothe the knots twisting her stomach. It reflected her own face back at her: anxious gray eyes, pointed ears and short black hair, all against the backdrop of her white-feathered wings.

Maeve squinted past the blur of her own features. There was a line of holographic monitors set up at the intersection of two busy city streets outside, broadcasting a live stream of Axis news to millions of passing pedestrians and drivers. Maeve couldn't hear the pretty Mirran newscaster, but she could just make out the ticker running across the bottom of the display: *Union of Light declares Bannon cult heretical.*

"Hey, can I have a drink?"

Across the table, Duaal made a grab for Tiberius' glass. The old Prian pulled it back out of reach. The dark brown beer inside sloshed and foamed.

"Not a chance. You're too young," Tiberius said.

"I'm twenty!" Duaal reached out again. "Come on, captain! I've got a Nnyth of a headache."

"You're nineteen," Tiberius said. He took a long drink and then wiped his mouth with the back of a hairy, scarred hand. "And Prian drinking age is twenty-three."

"We're on Axis!"

"You know, you're right. Legal age here is twenty-five," Tiberius said. "Alcohol isn't medicine, anyway. We'll get you some blockers."

The Blue Phoenix's captain finished off his beer in a few gulps, then replaced his empty mug on the tabletop while Duaal glared. Finally, the boy sighed and sat back, raking long fingers through his bleached hair.

"Fine," Duaal sighed. "Unless you'd like to buy for me, Maeve? You're old enough to be my grandmother."

Maeve turned her attention from the street outside back to her captain and his copilot. The fairy sat in her chair in reverse, straddling the backrest so she could stretch out her wings comfortably behind her.

"If the bartender will even sell to an Arcadian – which I doubt – he will surely notice when I fail to drink my own purchase," Maeve said. She gestured to the corrugated steel bar not far away. "He can probably overhear our discussion even now."

Duaal's gaze followed her pointing finger and he winked at the bald, muscular Hadrian man. The big bartender studiously ignored the oddly dressed young man and set to work reorganizing the bottles behind the bar. Duaal tugged on the embroidered cuff of his black velvet sleeve.

"Not bad at all. I'm sure I could get him to give me *something* interesting," he said. "It doesn't have to be a drink…"

"Don't even think about it," Tiberius told him. "He'll give you a disease or a fight, Duaal. You keep your ass right there in that seat."

The Hyzaari boy rolled his eyes and tipped his chair back on two scarred feet. "Fine. What are you watching out there, Maeve?"

"The news."

"What are they talking about?" Tiberius asked.

"Gavriel's church," Maeve said. "The Alliance Union of Light has named them enemies."

Tiberius furrowed bushy gray brows. "It's about time. Those death-worshipers are a God-damned menace."

"I don't know if that's good news," Duaal said. The Hyzaari boy's dark face had paled a shade. "That means the Union of Light thinks that enough of the Nihilists survived to be a problem. They never did find Gavriel or Xartasia on Stray. That means one or both of them are still alive."

Maeve looked out the window again. The news had moved on to another Starwind press release. But Duaal was right.

Where are you, Xartasia?

Tiberius banged his fist on the tabletop to get the bartender's attention and order another beer.

"We're far away from Stray and Gavriel's cult.," he said when he was done. "We've got problems enough without worrying about the Nihilists."

"If Gripper and Xia can't get anything from Armon, we may *have* to go back to Stray," Duaal said.

Maeve considered that. The idea of returning to Stray was not an unpleasant one. Kessa and her husband were on Stray. And their baby, Baliend. Maeve would have liked to see the child again. Perhaps she could find Xartasia there somehow and... and what?

A human server hurried past, balancing her tray of drinks and not watching where she was going. She tripped over one of Maeve's wings, staggered and fell. Drinks crashed to the floor, spraying glass and alcohol into the air. A man in a dark green CWAAF uniform at the next table jumped to his feet and caught the server before she could follow the glasses down to the ground.

"Don't you worry about that, honey," he assured her. "It wasn't your fault. That bird-back little slat doesn't know where her own feathers are."

Maeve curled her lip and stood, bringing herself eye-to-chest with the much taller Alliance military officer. She didn't recognize the gold rank marked on his collar.

"You fault me for *her* clumsiness?" Maeve asked. "For no reason but my race?"

"Oh look here," the officer said. He didn't speak to Maeve, but to another uniformed man still sitting at their table. "Someone taught this little parrot to talk!"

"My Aver is better than yours, human!"

"Forget it, Maeve," Duaal told her. He smiled and leaned back in his chair again, lacing his fingers behind his head. "The man isn't lying. Someone *did* teach you to speak Aver."

"He is being condescending," Maeve said. "And so are you!"

"That's enough now," Tiberius said in the loud, serious voice that usually quieted his crew.

But the man in the green CWAAF uniform wasn't impressed. He crossed his arms and glared at Tiberius. "You sure you want to get involved in this, old man? Your kid seems to have better sense."

"This guy is Prian, Sanders," said the other soldier. He remained in his seat, sipping at a strong-smelling drink. He gave Tiberius a sly, knowing smirk. "You don't have a problem with the bird-backs at all, do you?"

"Your argument is with *me*," Maeve snarled at the two soldiers. "So let us finish it alone!"

The fairy spread her wings wide and wished she still had her spear. The presence of a sharp blade always seemed to level the field of battle – even verbal battle – between Maeve and her much larger opponents. The first soldier, Sanders, loomed over Maeve.

"Not much good in arguing with pets, even the ones that have learned cute tricks," he said. "But if you're in a biting mood, little beast, then by all means..."

Sanders cracked his knuckles menacingly. Maeve stood up onto her toes and searched for some suitably cutting reply, but another man stepped in front of her, eclipsing her view. The newcomer also wore the CWAAF gold-edged green, with gleaming braids on his shoulders. He was a thick-built, dark-skinned Hadrian, like the bartender. The man stood with his back to Maeve and looked at Sanders.

"The Prian's right. That *is* enough," he announced. "You've obviously had plenty to drink, Lieutenant Sanders. Report back to the Stalwart at once."

Sanders straightened up at once and snapped off a salute. "Yes, Commander Kharos."

With a groan, his friend pushed his drink away and climbed up to his feet. "Well, I guess that's enough fun for one day, then. Come on, Sanders."

The two soldiers threw a couple of white cenmark chips onto the table, then turned away and left. A murmur went through the bar – half disappointed, half relieved. Tiberius nodded respectfully to the CWAAF commander.

"I thank you, sir," Maeve said slowly. "Your aid comes unasked, but is no less welcome."

A thin, gleaming white membrane covered Kharos' eyes, the polarizing filter necessitated by the bright, harsh sun of his homeworld. It was impossible to know exactly what he was looking at, but it didn't seem to be Maeve.

"You should get the Arcadian out of here," Kharos told Tiberius. "You don't want more trouble."

Tiberius made a flustered noise and went quite red in the face.

Duaal jumped up. "You're not going to let him talk to you like that, are you? Captain!"

"What about to me?" Maeve asked sharply, but Duaal ignored her.

"The commander's right," Tiberius said grudgingly. "Let's go."

The white stubble on Tiberius' lined cheeks stood out starkly against his darkened face. Reluctantly, Duaal followed Tiberius outside. Maeve remained, fists still clenched on her hips.

Commander Kharos said nothing to her.

"Maeve! Come on," Tiberius called, standing in the door. "We have to go!"

She stalked out of the bar, muttering to herself. *"Sa'aani shae!"*

Another night.

They found Gripper and Xia a few streets away. It wasn't difficult. Gripper loomed over everyone else on the crowded walkway. He had stopped to stare up at another news display, like the one that Maeve studied from the bar window not long before. The ogreish Arboran's eyes were wide and his mouth hung open.

Other various species and even passing vehicles slowed to stare at Gripper. Some were stunned into silence, but others whispered to each other or shouted at the strange alien. Traffic had ground to a slow trickle and threatened to stop entirely. Nervously, Xia gave Gripper's arm a gentle tug. He blinked his huge brown eyes, shook his head and then followed as the Ixthian hurried over to Tiberius, Duaal and Maeve.

"Hey, did you see that stuff about the Nihilists?" Gripper asked as soon as he neared, falling in beside the fairy. Maeve had to jog to keep up with the longer stride of the taller alien.

Maeve had to raise her voice to make herself heard over the cacophony of echoes ringing back from the city's distant ceiling. "The Alliance church has outlawed their religion."

"And the CWA is putting a bounty on them, too," Gripper said with a nod.

Maeve hadn't heard about that part. She wanted to ask after the details, but Tiberius slapped his fist into his palm.

"That's business for bounty hunters. Not us," he said, and then looked at Xia. "Did Armon have any work for us?"

"No," the Ixthian answered with a shake of her head. Axis' recycled air stirred her short white hair.

"Nothing?" Duaal asked.

"Salvage has been pretty thin," Xia answered. "He's got nothing else to move."

"Bloody hell!" Tiberius growled.

Xia held up her six-fingered silver hand. "I did manage to find us some other work. Armon didn't have anything, but I checked my messages on the mainstream and there was one from an old college friend. I thought you might be interested."

"A job?" Tiberius asked, still bristling but curious now.

"Yes. Carrying passengers and some cargo out to Prianus."

If Xia expected a smile, she was disappointed. Tiberius scowled.

Duaal sighed theatrically. "Prianus? What in the name of God could they want all the way out there?"

"Xen didn't say," Xia told him.

They reached a huge silver column of lifts. The metal was stenciled with a huge, flaking number 4. Duaal bumped his hip against a glowing call button.

Tiberius looked skeptical. "What does this hawk of yours do, exactly? I'm not flying anything illegal or dangerous out to Prianus."

"Xen's a professor of archeogenetics," Xia said. "He's head of the department at Vostra Nor University. I don't think he so much as experimented with any chems when we were in college. Not outside the laboratory, anyway. But he didn't leave any details in the message. If you want to know more, we'll need to fly out to his office on Tynerion."

"Go out there on speculation?" Duaal asked skeptically.

"Tynerion isn't that far away from Axis. We probably would have gone further to pick up anything for Armon. No one can afford to keep anything on Axis. CWAAF keeps too close an eye on this planet."

But that wasn't the detail that Tiberius had latched onto.

"A professor...?" he protested. "The Blue Phoenix is a cargo bird, not some fancy science vessel!"

The lift tube on the right chimed and the light flashed from orange to blue as the doors slid open. A short, stout Lyran business-woman pressed herself against the back wall as they all filed into the lift canister and her bristling tail curled against the back of her legs. Gripper delicately pressed the close button with a huge claw.

"Please stand clear of the doors," instructed a politely sexless computerized voice. "Please stand clear of the doors."

No one spoke as the elevator seal hissed shut again and slipped into smooth motion, falling down deeper into Axis. On Level Five, it stopped and the Lyran woman squeezed out, avoiding the eyes of the strangers who had shared her ride. When she was gone, Duaal jabbed the door controls again.

"I don't know how picky we can be about work," he said. The mage gave Maeve an accusatory look. "Since *she* spent all of her money on that damned bounty, we don't have anything to fall back on. We've got to work, Tiberius."

"Hey, it was her money!" Gripper cried. "Smoke never asked for any of yours!"

"It was a lot of money, and she blew it all on that stupid bounty. So she could kill herself," Duaal said. "Where's all that color now? In the pockets of the Gharib police, just when we could use it!"

"That money bought your salvation on Stray, too," Maeve re-minded Duaal. She narrowed her gray eyes at him. "Your youthful temper and weak spells did little to combat the Nihilists when they came for us!"

"Easy, Maeve," Xia said. "He was terrified of Gavriel. It was very difficult and very brave of him to do anything at all."

"Great. Thanks, Xia," Duaal mumbled, blushing.

"She's just trying to help, Shimmer," Gripper said, always eager to leap to the Ixthian's defense.

"She doesn't know how to help anyone but herself!" Duaal said.

He thought Gripper was talking about Maeve. Xia opened her mouth to correct him, but Tiberius interrupted them all.

"Enough!" The old captain's voice thundered uncomfortably in the closed confines of the elevator. "Maeve's money and what you all did or didn't do on Stray doesn't matter anymore! Since we flew out of here with Kessa and ducked the Axis police, we're criminals on this planet. Damnably petty ones, but still criminals."

"I'd just like to point out that Maeve brought Kessa on board, too," Duaal grumbled.

"What's done is done," Tiberius said.

"The captain's right. There's no money and it's been hard to find work. Times have been a little rough and lean." This was from Xia, who looked at Tiberius with arched antennae. "But we've got a solid lead now. Yes, it's academic work, but Xen says the money is good and we really can't afford to be picky."

Gripper stood behind Xia, fidgeting uncomfortably as the rest argued. He gave his captain a crooked smile.

"Besides, you get to go home," he said. "That's great, right?"

Tiberius' only response was a short, terse grunt. The rest of the long ride down into Axis' lower levels was spent in silence, leaving Maeve with little else to do but think. Seven months had passed since Stray, since stealing the infant Baliend back from Gavriel and his Nihilists. Since facing Princess Titania – *no, she is Xartasia now, the dreamer of death* – under the desert graveyard.

She forgave me for the death of our people. My cousin would be queen of the White Kingdom, if she would but take up the crown. And Xartasia has forgiven me.

Maeve looked down at her hands, at the wrists sticking out from her more or less clean sleeves. The skin was still scarred by battle and chem abuse, but even those marks were beginning to fade.

Was she absolved? Did the gods forgive her for the millions she killed, even accidentally?

Seven months since Logan Coldhand stopped hunting her... The bounty on Maeve was paid – into the hands of the Gharib police, just as Duaal complained – and so the bounty hunter had left. The chase was over and the loss still weighed strangely heavy on Maeve.

But she was tired of being self-absorbed and pathetic, tired of everyone around her paying the price for her indulgence. Maeve clasped her hands in front of her and turned her attention to her companions instead. Her gaze wandered inevitably to the short-ened length of Gripper's mottled left ear. The Arboran noticed her looking and rubbed the shiny scar self-consciously.

The events of the last year seemed to have done nothing to change the unflappable Xia. Sometimes it seemed that her sweet and professionally caring nature was the only thing keeping the Blue Phoenix crew from falling apart entirely.

Next to her, Duaal leaned against the curved wall of the lift, eyeing Maeve balefully through braided locks of bleached hair. Though the surly teenager's clothes remained needlessly expensive and elaborate, he no longer wore the charms and magical symbols – moons and stars and angular knots – that he once did. Back on Stray, Maeve had told him that such things were the tools of only the youngest, least experienced spell-singers and the news had deeply shamed proud Duaal.

Only a child is insulted to be called a child, Maeve thought, but pinched her arm angrily. By the standards of her own race, she was young, too.

Tiberius just looked tired and Maeve's stomach twisted into a tight, guilty knot again. Tiberius scratched his cheek and sighed, lost in his own cranky thoughts. The last of his pewter hair had gone entirely white and he hadn't shaved in days.

The large 9 beside the lift door lit up and the speakers chimed, announcing their arrival. When the doors opened, Maeve followed the rest of the Blue Phoenix crew out into the streets of Level Nine. A gang of young men with shaven heads piled into the vacated lift. Glowing lines of color pulsed beneath their skin. Xia's eyes shone a faint red color, full of disgust. The glowing subdermal implants were almost as disfiguring as cybernetics, at least in the compound eyes of the purist Ixthians. One of the rough-looking males stuck his surgically lengthened tongue out at Xia just before the lift doors hissed shut again.

Tiberius and his mismatched crew walked close together along the dirty road. Vehicles here rode low on poorly maintained null-inertia fields, rumbling past and kicking up clouds of shredded plastic and crumpled mycofoam. Lumapaint tags marked each corner as the territory of one gang or another. The lights shining down from Level Nine's ceiling flickered fitfully and left entire city blocks steeped in darkness.

"You know, considering what we did in Gharib, we should get to land up in the nice fields on Level One," Duaal said. "Even Logan got to put his ship up on the surface!"

"God damn that bounty hunter!" Tiberius growled, but offered nothing more.

"Hey, we'll fix this someday," Gripper said hesitantly. "You know, clear our names."

"As far as Axis Control knows, we're char," Duaal told him. "We tricked them. They're not going to be happy if the Blue Phoenix shows up on their boards."

They stopped in front of a tall black wall that blocked off half the road. Tiberius pressed a button on the bottom of a control box welded to the gate. It buzzed and then a rough voice crackled over the speaker.

"Who is it?"

"It's Captain Myles, Blake. We're ready to get out of here."

"Surely, captain. And by the way, your supplies arrived. They're waiting at your berth."

"They better not be light, Blake," Tiberius said.

"I didn't take any of your stuff, you old coot. If your crates are light, it's not my fault."

The gate lock thunked and Gripper pulled it open. Beyond was a pitted expanse of engine-burned blastphalt that probably used to be a factory before someone leveled it to make room for Blake's illegal landing field. The remains of huge ducts and shafts hung down from the level's ceiling. Long ago, they vented air and waste gasses up to Axis' surface, but now they provided discreet entry and exit for ships small and desperate enough to fly through them.

The Blue Phoenix crouched among a pack of other grounded ships. It was clumsy-looking and covered in bristling sensor spars like a grumpy metal hedgehog. A stack of crates sat behind the Blue Phoenix, just beside the closed loading ramp. Duaal tapped the security code into a keypad. The airlock cycled and hissed, then the ramp lowered and clanked to the ground.

"Maeve, get everything loaded and tied down. Gripper, give her a hand," Tiberius ordered. "Xia, check if anything is missing. Blake's a bastard and a criminal. I wouldn't put it past him to steal from his own mother. Duaal, give him our vector and let him know when we're ready to get out into the black."

"Which is?" Duaal asked. "Where are we going?"

"Tynerion. We'll go take your teacher's work, Xia."

"Great. Hey, captain? Can I fly us out of here?" Duaal asked. The copilot pointed up at the massive, corroded old ducting. "It's going to be a sharp ride."

"Maybe next time," Tiberius said.

He made his way up the ramp and into his ship, patting the wall of the airlock as he passed. Duaal jogged after him.

"That's what you said last time!"

Shaking her head, Xia followed the two human men inside to find the cargo manifest. Gripper pushed a loading jack down the ramp and helped Maeve lift the crates of food, water and filters. When it was full, he activated the null-inertia field and with a light shove, the jack floated up off the uneven ground, as light as a balloon. Gripper guided it back into the ship's cargo bay.

Inside, he turned off the null-inertia field projector and the jack thumped heavily to the Blue Phoenix's fibersteel floor. Gripper pulled an orange net down from hooks on the wall and tossed one end to Maeve. She flew up into the air, caught the corner and dropped it over her side of the stack. As Maeve tied the net down to a row of magclamps on the floor, Gripper leaned against the crates.

"Smoke, are you worried about the Nihilists?" he asked.

"I have been thinking about them since I saw their name on the news," she admitted. "I worry, yes, but I do not know if it is the same as your worry."

"You don't think they're going to... come after us or anything?" Gripper asked.

Maeve shook her head slowly. "No, I do not believe so. The Cult of Nihil will have their own worries. They are far more sought-after criminals than we are, and they have their own goals. Even if he lives, I do not think that Gavriel will concern himself with us."

"Really?"

"Only the gods know for certain."

"Thanks, Smoke," Gripper said. "I guess."

Duaal opened a radio channel to the landing field's tiny control center.

"Blake, this is the Blue Phoenix," he said. "We're ready to take off on surface vector two eighty-eight."

"I hear you, Blue Phoenix," came Blake's rusty-sounding voice. "I'm monitoring Control chatter. We should have a window open for you in about ten minutes."

Duaal propped his feet up on the controls in front of him and inspected his shoes. The leather was getting old. But when would there be money for replacements? Duaal silently cursed Maeve again for every one of her many, many crimes. Finally, he sat back and looked over at Tiberius.

"Are you alright, captain?" Duaal asked. "You've been on edge all day."

Tiberius' joints creaked in audible protest as he dropped into the pilot's chair. "It's nothing for you to worry about, Duaal."

"Can't you just talk to me a little? I'm bored and my head is still curling around the edges."

"Go raid the medbay, then," Tiberius said.

"Come on! Talk to me."

There was a pause before Tiberius answered. "It's all of this."

"All of what?"

"Everything!" Tiberius shouted suddenly, startling Duaal.

The boy jumped and cracked his head hard against the cockpit's low ceiling. He rubbed his scalp and checked for blood.

"Ouch," Duaal groaned.

"I was a cop for forty-one years. I'm not some plucked criminal," Tiberius said. "It shouldn't be like this – squatting on illegal fields, buying our supplies on the sly."

"You only tried to do right," Duaal reminded him.

"And for that, I'm hiding like a rat." Tiberius shook his head. "I don't want to live the rest of my life under a rock."

Duaal searched for something helpful to say, but couldn't think of anything. He sighed and waited for Blake to tell them when it was time to finally fly away.

[2]
SIPHO

"Without laws, there can be no crime. But without laws, we are all victims."

Cedon Barnes was a handsome man. He admired his fine, chiseled jaw and bright blue-green eyes. He really looked nothing at all like a criminal, he thought. Cedon straightened his stylish black tie and checked his pale hair in the darkened window. In the bright Sipho nightlight, the glass threw back a stark silver-and-black reflection of innocent perfection.

He waited on the corner of Malone and Parson Street, just as his client had requested. Cedon leaned against a waist-high iron fence that wrapped around the cafe patio. It was the middle of the night and the chairs all sat upside-down on top of their tables, legs in the air like dogs playing dead. A few other drivers and midnight pedestrians strolled past, but not many. Cedon Barnes waited alone.

The night was clear and cool. Still, if it weren't for the importance of his meeting, Cedon would have been back in his hotel room, in his warm bed and the warmer embrace of the woman he had left there. Both were well outside his price range, but Cedon was about to be a very rich man.

His pay as a floor supervisor in the Narsus shipyards had been comfortable enough, but then an engineer from another team left the new schematics just lying out on his desk. The whole thing, finished and unencrypted. Those plans were worth thirty years' salary, if Cedon could just sell them. So he pulled the memory chip and slipped it into his pocket. Easy as that. Once he got off Kahl, all Cedon needed was a rich enough buyer.

He ran his hand over the top of the patio fence. The metal was spotted with spreading dew, like it had been decorated in delicate glass beads. Cedon flicked the moisture from his finger. It splattered against the window.

The bright core-world stars and multitude of pearlescent blue-white moons filled the Sipho sky and street with radiance that outshone the light of the arched streetlamps. They were more for decoration than anything else. Rain on Sipho was light and never lasted long, more like standing in a shower than a real storm. So there were never enough clouds to blot out the moonslight.

Sipho was really a rather lovely planet, Cedon decided. Maybe he would stay. With the money he was about to make, he could certainly afford it.

A shadow fell across the cobblestone-textured road. His buyer had finally arrived. The other man was a little taller than Cedon and wore a long black coat with the collar turned up as though it was a much colder night. There was nothing remarkable about his face or short blond hair, but there was something in his pale blue eyes that made Cedon's throat clench. He cleared it loudly before calling out.

"Pleasant evening, isn't it?" Cedon asked. When the other man was close enough, he held out one hand. "I'm Cedon Barnes."

His customer kept his own hands thrust deeply into his coat pockets. "Do you have the plans?"

Cedon sighed. He recognized that accent – Prian. Small wonder the man had no manners.

"I've got them," Cedon said. "Do you have my money?"

A curt nod. "Show me the schematics."

Some people had no faith. Cedon reached into his jacket and produced the memory chip with a flourish. It was tiny, only about the size of his smallest fingernail. He held it up, just out of the other man's reach. Starlight flashed on the serial number printed along one side: NSS-NIE-288-37D

"So much precious data on such a tiny thing," Cedon said philo-sophically. "Amazing, really."

But the Prian didn't seem very interested in discussion. He was pulling his hand out of his pocket, probably eager to pay and go play with his new toy. But the hand that came back up held not colorful cenmarks, but a large gray laser pistol. A sudden dread made Cedon's heart skip. He took a hurried step back and flung his hands into the air.

"No... No, wait! Did Narsus send you?" he asked.

"Give me the plans."

Cedon's heart was working again – but at about ten times its normal speed. It slammed against his ribs as though the muscle might break through and run away all on its own. Terrified, Cedon held out the memory chip, but his hands shook so hard that he dropped it. The other man lunged, grabbing for the tumbling card, but it slid through his fingers. He wore a black half-glove over the hand, but his fingers shone dully metallic in the starlight with the same flat gleam as the gun. Cedon's knees turned to water and he staggered back into the patio fence.

"Oh, God! I... I know who you are," he said. "Help! Somebody help me!"

Why were the streets so empty? Surely not everyone could be inside. Why didn't someone save Cedon? Why had he ever agreed to a midnight meeting?

The bounty hunter flicked his gun at the card on the ground. The blue plastic was almost invisible in his dark shadow.

"Pick it up," he ordered.

Cedon pinched the card up from the street. The hunter took the schematics very carefully in his metal hand, inspected them briefly and then dropped the memory chip into his pocket.

"Where are the other copies?" he asked.

"Copies? What copies?" Cedon asked.

"You didn't make any copies of the data?"

"No! Don't shoot me, please!"

An unreadable expression flashed across the hunter's face. He hauled Cedon up by his collar, holstered his laser and snapped a pair of handcuffs around his prisoner's wrists.

"Let's go."

Logan Coldhand shoved Barnes roughly into the waiting arms of two CWAAF soldiers. The middle manager who thought himself a daring thief was still sobbing in terror and very nearly had to be carried away. They vanished through the door, leaving Coldhand alone in the waiting room.

The Sipho government had devoted little time or money to the bounty collection center. The entire building was a white prefabricated cube and every surface had the faintly oily look of janitorial nanites keeping them clean, not unlike those used on nanoblades to maintain the weapons' keen edge.

There were no windows in the building, only a row of monitors that switched between local news and a list of other bounties. Coldhand could have been anywhere in the galaxy, in any one of ten thousand identical collection centers anywhere in the Alliance.

The hunt for Barnes had been... unsatisfying. The man was unbelievably stupid – he had taken a commercial flight from Kahl, booked under his own name. Investigation of Barnes' hotel room on Sipho had yielded only a frightened prostitute and some cheap chems. The self-important little thief really had no copies of his stolen schematics. He was actually selling the original files with no thought about what he might do if he lost them. He threw away his career and his freedom for something he could sell only once. Cedon Barnes was an idiot. An idiot worth a lot of color to Narsus Shipyards, but no less an idiot.

Coldhand waited. There was an indignant yelp from the next room as one of the techs checked and verified Barnes' redprint. The flashing screen on the far wall caught Coldhand's attention: *Cult of Nihil – All members. Wanted for degree one heresies.*

The monitor showed a sallow-skinned man in tattered clothes. Coldhand sat forward. The man on the screen was not Gavriel. This one wore the scarlet of an Emberguard, the Nihilist's most brutal warriors.

Thieves. They took my hand and my heart. My life.

Coldhand pushed the maudlin thought aside and read the text scrolling beside the picture. When the Union of Light banned the Nihilist teachings, the cultists became criminals under Alliance law, subject to all of the associated penalties. The CWA was offering a bounty for any captured Nihilists. Alive only, of course. It was a government bounty, after all.

The price was low. There were only so many cenmarks to go around and the Alliance couldn't pay much for individual cultists. The bounty posting listed an estimated two hundred surviving Nihilists, but Coldhand suspected there were many more than that.

He ignored the rest. It wasn't worth his time. Coldhand had no useful leads. After the destruction of their Gharib cathedral, the Nihilists had probably gone into hiding on Stray. The planet was a long flight from Sipho and Stray was an entire world of desperate people with something to hide. Trying to find the Nihilists there now would be like sifting salt from sand.

Too much work for too little pay.

His leg throbbed dully. Coldhand looked down and found his left hand on his thigh. The illonium fingers had dug hard into the leg of his pants, bruising the flesh beneath. Coldhand forced the cybernetics to release just as a brown-furred Lyran stepped into the waiting room.

"Thank you for waiting," he said. "We've checked over Mister Barnes. According to Narsus instructions, he will be held here for transport. He'll be assigned counsel and tried on Kahl. If you'll just sign here, I can pay out the bounty. It's late and I'm sure you would like to go home, too."

The canine man smiled toothily up at Coldhand, who wordlessly signed his name to the offered datawork. The Lyran tucked the datadex under his arm and held out a single black cenmark chip to Coldhand. The hunter took the plastic square and turned it over. There was a name printed on the front: NARSUS.

The company logo glowed faintly violet at his touch. He flipped it back at the Lyran, who caught the cenmark in his paws.

"Is there a problem?" he asked.

"I don't work for credit. Barnes' bounty was posted in Alliance marks."

"I'm sorry, but this is all that Narsus Shipyards would approve."

"That's your problem," Coldhand said. "Alliance colour only."

The Lyran laid his furry ears back, but left and returned a few minutes later with a stack of colored plastic squares. Much less pleasantly this time, he thrust them into the bounty hunter's hand.

"Alliance cenmarks," he announced.

Coldhand counted the money and nodded curtly.

"We're done here."

The Lyran's ears remained flattened. Coldhand left the canned air of the collection center behind and made his way back out into the warm Sipho night.

[3]
IN TIME

"Wherever there is light, first there was darkness."

- GAVRIEL EUVO, CULT OF NIHIL FOUNDER (230 PA)

Gavriel considered the darkness. The lightless void was perfect. It was deep and distant as the space between stars even as it clung sticky-close as spider webs on his skin. It hid the ugliness of the universe, swallowed nations and worlds into bottomless oblivion. In time, the darkness consumed even suns and stars. Everything.

Gavriel held his hand up before his eyes, but could see nothing. The shadows concealed his thin, brittle skin, spotted by age and too many years under the suns of a dozen worlds. He was stronger now, since Elsa's unwilling sacrifice. His age had not left him, but he wore it now like the robe around his shoulders instead of a weight around his neck.

But even in the darkness, Gavriel could hear his joints creaking, feel the bone-deep ache of long years of life and suffering... if there was any difference between the two. The dark only masked the things that seethed in shadows. It didn't conquer them. That lesson had been hard-won...

He waited in the darkness. The dead girl's blood was warm and sticky on his hands, but cooling rapidly in the night air. The street outside the old mill house flashed with blue lights as the Sunjarrah police searched for him. Gavriel cursed silently to himself. They would tire of the hunt, but not before dawn. Until then, he would have to remain hidden.

The work was too tedious, too time-consuming! Every time someone screamed, the police gave chase and Gavriel had to hide again. Too many such encounters inevitably drove him away, into a new city and then further, onto a new planet.

There were so many billions who needed the gift Gavriel brought, yet he was forced to grant it one at a time. It was too slow! Why did no one ever understand the blessing he gave? The sweet, deep death like falling into a soft bed at the end of a long, hard day?

Gavriel sheathed the nanoknife and scrubbed his hands briskly together. The girl's blood had grown flaky on his palms and sifted to the dusty floor like red snow.

He couldn't hide forever. Eventually, they would find Gavriel and haul him away. The trial would be short and then they would throw him in prison to rot. No one would ever know, ever understand that he was only trying to help. They would think Gavriel Euvo was some common criminal who killed for cheap thrills or perverse pleasures. The very idea made him bristle indignantly.

There had to be a better way.

Gavriel flicked his brittle fingers in an intricate symbol. *"Ka li'ae avael!"*

An ember kindled in the darkness. The spark of light flared and golden-red tongues of fire filled the shadows, illuminating Gavriel's wolfish smile. The flame died away and left nothing behind but the faint scent of smoke. Soon, even that was gone.

There would be nothing left for the police to find this time.

[4]

TYNERION

Tiberius banged his fist on the cargo bay wall. On his other arm, Orphia hissed in irritation. The hawk fluttered over to the stair railing and landed again. Her sharp talons clicked on the metal.

Maeve sat cross-legged on top of the supply crates, stretching her wings. There were few places on the Blue Phoenix with room enough to do so. It felt good and served as a sort of... meditation, Maeve supposed.

Lunch had been less than an hour ago, but her stomach still ached painfully, hollowly. It was the withdrawals. Maeve hadn't taken Vanora White or Pitch or any other chem in almost ten days. And two weeks before that had only been a few swallows of bitter narcohol – just to take the edge off – before she managed to throw the bottle away.

It was still so hard. Maeve woke up each night with cold sweat sticking the sheets to her clammy skin and her mouth full of a vile taste, like something long dead. Her body and soul begged for the release of a needle or drink every day. Did it ever get any easier?

Tiberius called Maeve's name. She shook her head, trying to clear it.

"We need to talk," he shouted down to her. "We'll be landing in a few minutes."

"I am coming."

Maeve stood and then flew up to the catwalk that spanned the top of the cargo hold. She clambered over the railing and followed Tiberius back into the mess. Duaal lounged on one of the patched acceleration couches in the corner, rolling an antique silver coin across his knuckles. The rest of the crew sat gathered around a large table bolted to the floor and looked up as Maeve and Tiberius came in.

"Hi, Smoke. Want to sit?" Gripper asked.

She sat in the chair he offered. Tiberius took the couch opposite Duaal.

"We'll be setting down on Tynerion in about an hour to meet with Xia's friend," the captain said.

"I'll be flying," Duaal announced.

"We should be able to land at the university field," Xia said. "Vostra Nor is one of the smaller colleges here on Tynerion. There shouldn't be much traffic."

"We're not on Axis anymore. No one here should know we're God-damned criminals." Tiberius pointed a thick finger at Maeve. "But we can't take any chances. No making trouble. No getting into trouble if anyone else makes it. We're going to get on and off Tynerion just as quick as we can."

Maeve bristled. "Your species' hatred of my kind is not of *my* making."

"You don't do much to change it, though," Duaal said. "But even if you can behave, I think you should stay on the Phoenix. Gripper, too."

"Huh? What did I do?" Gripper asked.

"You stick out, my friend. Like a giant green monster. Like an alien. You pretty much ground traffic to a halt on Axis."

Xia frowned. Her eyes had gone a thoughtful lavender and she sighed. "Unfortunately, I think Duaal has a point. You do attract a lot of attention on most planets, Gripper, and there are a lot of students and scholars on Tynerion. They'll want to study you."

"You think they might, you know, grab me?" the Arboran asked. He chewed nervously on one of his claws.

"No, but they might make it hard for us to leave," Xia said gently. "Grant money is tight and you never know what some glory-hungry scientist might do."

"Alliance attitudes toward the other races of the galaxy are a disgrace," Maeve spat. "Are Gripper's only options to be caged aboard this ship or to be pinned to a dissection table?"

"Now wait a minute!" Tiberius thumped his fist on the back of the couch. "This is to keep you out of fights and the rest of us out of jail. I don't give two bent pinions about your species."

"You may not," Xia said. "But a lot of other people do. A lot of people who live and work on Tynerion."

"We want to put our best foot forward, captain," Duaal added.

"I guess our best foot is a little smaller than mine," Gripper said. He wiggled his thick, dirty toes. No one manufactured boots large enough for the Arboran to wear. "But do Smoke and I have to hide in our rooms the whole time that we're working for this Xen guy?"

Xia shook her head. "I don't think that's necessary. Once Xen's on the Blue Phoenix, he'll ask a lot of questions, but he won't be able to do much more. Besides, I don't think Xen would be much of a problem. He's a good man. It's everyone else on Tynerion that I'm worried about."

Maeve picked at the edge of the table with her fingernail. It was ridiculous and infuriating, but Duaal and Xia were probably right.

Maeve's all-too-winged presence had made plenty of past deals more difficult, or ruined them entirely.

"I will remain on the Blue Phoenix while we are on Tynerion," she agreed.

"We'll find something fun to do, Smoke." Gripper gave her a friendly elbow that almost knocked the fairy out of her chair. "You can help me with my garden."

"Lucky you," Duaal said with a thin smile.

Maeve sighed.

With only a couple of stomach-churning bumps, Duaal set the Blue Phoenix down on Tynerion. As Xia predicted, there was no trouble landing at Vostra Nor University. Traffic was well-regulated and much lighter than the constant congestion of Axis.

When the ship was on the ground and powered down, Duaal jumped up from his seat and grinned at Tiberius.

"Not bad!" he congratulated himself.

"Looks good. We'll make a pilot of you yet," Tiberius said as he unbuckled his harness. "Now, let's go. I want to settle the job and get underway as soon as possible. This rock makes me nervous."

"Yes, sir."

They met Xia down at the cargo bay airlock. Maeve perched like an oversized bird on the edge of one of Gripper's vegetable planters. The Arboran dangled nearby, instructing her on the care of his garden. Maeve watched Xia, Tiberius and Duaal leave. She didn't look happy. Duaal shrugged to himself. Maeve never looked happy. He ducked through the airlock and followed Xia outside.

It was autumn on this part of Tynerion. The trees that lined the perimeter of the landing field swayed in a crisp breeze. Red, gold and orange leaves covered the black blastphalt and filled the briskly swirling air with a dusty-sweet scent. Duaal took a deep breath and stretched his arms up over his head. Nothing was better than the open sky, inside a ship or out.

"Do you know where we're going?" Tiberius asked Xia.

"Yes. It's not far. Vostra Nor is one of the smaller schools."

The Ixthian smiled. Her steps were bouncy and quick as she led the humans out across the landing field, through an open gate and onto the campus.

Tynerion was one of the first worlds colonized, venaformed and then settled by humans from Axis even before the creation of the Central World Alliance. In those days, it was all so new. There were other stars, other planets and plants, even new species of sentient life.

And from their new colony, humans studied it all. Research centers, observatories and laboratories sprang up all over Tynerion, then libraries and schools. When the Alliance was founded, new students flocked from all across the galactic core to study on Tynerion. Before long, the universities were overcrowded and more schools had to be built. Within a few generations, Tynerion became the center of academia in the galaxy.

If Vostra Nor University was a small college, Duaal had no idea what one of the big ones might be like. White concrete paths wound through lawns and circular rose gardens that separated buildings of myriad sizes and shapes. There were long lines of classrooms and lecture halls like rows of corn. A shiny observatory dome perched high on top of a blue-and-black trimmed building and heliographed blindingly in the light of the white binary suns. In the distance, a slim pyramid of glass and steel rose sharply from a forest-like arboretum.

Xia caught Duaal staring.

"That's the botany department. It's pretty much right in the center of campus. There's a monument out in front to the original Tynerion explorers," she told him, then suddenly laughed. "Every year, someone gets drunk, climbs up the statue and falls off."

"Sounds like fun."

It actually did. Duaal had never given college much thought, but it suddenly seemed like a pity that he would probably never get to go. Tiberius would be his only teacher.

And Gavriel.

A pair of girls bobbed past, balanced on a board suspended by an orange-tinged null-field, talking and giggling to one another. Xia took Duaal and Tiberius across an aromatic herb garden and then past a white stone lecture hall surrounded by a tall colonnade. A carved granite slab in a nearby flowerbed read *Veskin Hall – Physics*. They had to weave and push through a crowd of students, most about Duaal's own age. A Lyran in a tweed suit stood on the roof, holding a leather pounceball over his head.

"Now stand back!" he called out to the students below.

On the other side of a lawn studded with sculptures of twisted metal, Xia pointed to a stately red brick hall covered in a thick net of ivy.

"That's where we're going, Xol Hall," she said. "We used to call it the *Xol Hole*. It's a little cramped inside."

That turned out to be an understatement. They joined the tide of students and professors pouring in through the pillar-flanked entry. Doors lined the long hallway, crowded in between with display cases all full to overflowing with rocks, bits of old cloth in a thousand fading colors, fragments of pottery, shards of metal and vials of dust. The ceiling hung artificially low with sagging maps stapled to the spongy insulation tiles and genetic models hanging from thin, nearly invisible threads.

A kiosk flickered on one corner where the hallway intersected another crowded corridor. Xia stopped beside it and leaned close to make herself heard over the noise.

"Directions to Professor Xen's office," she shouted. The holographic display buzzed and flickered, then showed Xia what she had asked for.

Professor Xen (4)

Office 310

Third floor, fifth door on the left

Office hours: Open

A red line blinked through a wireframe map beside the instructions. Xia glanced down the right-hand hall to the elevators, but the foyer was full of waiting students.

"Come on, the stairs are over here," she said.

By the time they reached the third story, Tiberius was huffing.

"This is ridiculous!" he protested. "I've been climbing mountains – real Prian mountains, not colony-world hills – since before either of you were born!"

"Maybe Prianus isn't the challenge you make it out to be," Duaal suggested.

"Shut it, chickling. I'm just getting old."

Duaal laughed and chased after Xia, who had pulled ahead on her long legs. There were fewer people up here, but even more overfilled glass cases. Xia waved the men over to a closed door, fifth one on the left. A cartoon had been printed out and taped to the window, showing a comically frustrated Hadrian facing off against an exasperated Axial. The two shared a single dialog bubble: *You show me your monkeys!*

Xia laughed. "Pretty good."

Duaal didn't get it and tried to think of some subtle way to ask Xia to explain the joke to him. While he pondered, she knocked on the door.

"It's open. Come on in!" called a voice from inside.

Xia opened the door for Tiberius and Duaal, then followed them into the office. Inside, it was only slightly less crowded than the hallway. A window looked out on the sculpture garden they had passed through on the way in. Monitors filled the other three walls, all displaying maps and news stories, photographs and charts.

Two desks took up most of the office, pushed back to back in the middle of the floor and leaving only a narrow gap around the edge of the room. A slender blonde girl sat at one of the desks. She had large green eyes and a pretty, fine-boned face. She smiled at the three visitors and stood up.

"Good morning! I'm Panna Sul, Professor Xen's assistant." She offered her hand to each of them in turn. "You're probably here to see him, right?"

"Yes," Xia said. "The kiosk said he was in."

"Well, he should be, but Professor Xen is actually downstairs. He's covering Professor Stark's lecture. That should be over in about fifteen minutes. Can I get you anything? Coffee, fizz?"

"No, thank you," Xia declined.

Tiberius and Duaal shook their heads.

"Please grab a seat," Panna said, gesturing to a row of chairs beneath one of the screens. She grimaced down at the computer on her desk. "Are you quite sure I can't get you anything?"

"I'm sure," Xia said.

Panna sighed and sat down. "Back to grading undergrad essays, then. They all quote the exact same lecture. I swear it's the only one they went to."

Xia asked her a little about the college while they waited. Panna was more than happy to talk and answered the Ixthian's questions at length. Duaal stared out the window at the wispy white clouds racing over the campus and a group of students sitting at a table in the quad below. One of them held a large datadex and gestured emphatically with it. The others nodded in agreement with whatever he said and scribbled down their own notes.

Even if he could go to a proper school like this, what would Duaal study? Science? Literature?

Gavriel had raised Duaal from stolen infancy to be a tool for his magic. That was about the only thing Duaal was good at... And he couldn't study magic here.

Duaal pondered if Arcadians went to school for their magic – Maeve talked sometimes about the Ivory Spire, which sounded a bit like a fairy college – when Xen finally arrived. He was Ixthian, like Xia, with smooth silver skin and hair as white as the clouds outside. He was tall for a male of his species, but still stood only as high as Duaal's shoulder. The professor's hair was cut close to his skull and his antennae were the longest Duaal had ever seen. He wore similar clothes to Panna's – dark gray slacks and a collared white shirt rolled up at the sleeves. There was a discarded vest tucked into the back of his belt.

Xia jumped to her feet and hugged him. "Xen!"

"Xia! You came," Xen answered, returning the other Ixthian's embrace. He sounded surprised but pleased. "This must be your captain. Tiberius Myles, isn't it?"

"And our copilot, Duaal Sinnay," Xia said. "I got your message anteday, on Axis. We came straight away."

"I hear you're looking for someone to fly you out to Prianus," Tiberius said.

Professor Xen raised his white eyebrows at the captain. "Your homeworld, to judge by your accent. Yes, that's exactly what I'm hoping to do."

"Why do you need to go out to Prianus?" Duaal asked. "You and your lovely assistant seem to have plenty of work here."

Panna blushed and grinned. Xen sat on the corner of the other desk and flipped open his computer. He touched something on the monitor and then, with a flick of his long forefinger, sent it up to one of the large wall screens. It was a colorful topographical map. Xen pointed to a large patch of dark red in the center.

"Recent tectonic activity out on Prianus has uncovered a new archeological site. It's located up here, in the Kayton Mountains. There's a local dig team up working the site now, but they lack the resources, equipment and personnel to do the job right. So they've requested assistance from Tynerion."

"And you volunteered to go out there?" Tiberius asked, clearly surprised.

"Prianus isn't exactly a popular site. It's remote, hostile and unstable," Xen answered. "No offense intended, Captain Myles."

"None taken. Prianus is a hard world."

"With hard people," the professor said with a bit of a smile. "Now, the Alliance can't actually fund additional archeologists, but is offering a tax benefit to any institution willing to field a team. Vostra Nor owes the Alliance about three years back taxes at this point and could use the break. I've been given admittedly limited funding to hire and supply our part of the dig."

"Do you know what they're studying out there?" Tiberius asked. He squinted at the map, scratching his bearded chin. "Prianus is covered in mountains. I don't know this area."

"The head of the Prian team, Kemmer Andus, has disclosed very few details. I'm not quite sure what we'll find." Xen quirked a small smile. "It's made selecting my people and equipment an interesting challenge."

"How many on your team? And how much equipment?"

"There are five of us in total and about two tons of equipment. Is that going to be a problem?"

"Some of you might need to bunk together," Tiberius answered. "There are only three spare rooms on the Phoenix."

"I'm sure we can deal with being a little cozy," Xen said. "Accommodations on Prianus aren't likely to be plush, either."

"If Vostra Nor is funding you, then why did you call me?" Xia asked. "There are thousands of ships on Tynerion."

"Maybe I just wanted to see you again," Xen said. He gave Xia a charming smile.

She laughed, but wasn't convinced. "You think I can get you a better price."

"You're as discerning as ever, my dear. I always mourned that you didn't remain in research," Xen said. He spread his hands. "Yes.

The board of regents wants to spend less on my venture than they will save on the taxes. I'd like to use most of the color on the dig, not flying out to it. But the starships available on Tynerion charge criminally high fares. And the cargo space for my equipment... Yes, I would like something a little less expensive."

"I appreciate your position, professor, but I'm not getting tax credits out of this," Tiberius said, shaking his head. "My bird needs fuel and my crew needs to eat. What kind of colour can you actually offer?"

Duaal flinched and Xen pressed his shiny lips into a thin line at the bluntness of the question, but Xia watched the exchange with amusement on her face. Had they wasted their time flying to Tynerion? She didn't seem worried about it.

"I can pay four thousand cenmarks for the journey," Xen said. "I can also get you the university discount on any supplies or parts you might need while we're on Tynerion."

"That's twenty percent," Panna supplied.

Duaal scuffed the toe of his boot over the carpet. Four thousand cenmarks was a lot of money, but it was a *long* trip out to Prianus. Fuel alone would eat up more than a quarter of that.

"You can part with a little more than that, Xen," said Xia. She put her elbows on his desk and gave the other Ixthian an arched look. "The regents probably charted out ten thousand for transport. Give us half of that and you still leave another five thousand for yourself."

Xen blinked slowly and curled his long silver antennae. "I have missed you, Xia. Very well, if Captain Myles will agree. Five thousand cenmarks."

"Alright, you've got yourself a ship," Tiberius said. "When do you want to leave, Professor Xen?"

"Panna?" Xen asked.

"Um, Phillip has a lecture at noon," she answered, glancing at her computer. "But I'm sure he would be perfectly happy to hand it over to someone else. We could be ready by seven tomorrow morning. Unless you need more time to buy anything else on Tynerion, Captain Myles?"

"Just basics for the trip," Tiberius said. "We'll need to feed all of you and pick up some extra recyc' scrubbers and air filters."

"I can order those now, if you like," Panna offered. "I think we can get them delivered later this afternoon."

"Let us talk to our mechanic before you order anything," Xia said. She nodded to Panna. "But I can probably get a list to you in about two hours."

"I guess I'll need to finish grading these papers, then," the girl sighed, tapping her computer with one finger.

"You had better. I'm not doing it," Xen said with a smirk. He stood and held out his six-fingered hand to Tiberius, who shook it firmly. "We'll see you tomorrow at seven, captain. I'll transfer your fare this evening, after I speak to the deans."

"About what?" Tiberius asked suspiciously, maybe wondering if Professor Xen would somehow betray the Blue Phoenix to Alliance authorities.

"I simply need to let them know that I'm finally leaving. I'm sure they will be thrilled. I think Charne is tired of my students digging up his quad. Tinkay already has my lesson plan and can take care of my classes for the rest of the semester."

"We'll see you tomorrow, then," Tiberius said.

He gestured for Duaal and Xia to follow him and left the office. They made their way back out of Xol Hall and back toward the Blue Phoenix.

Once outside, Duaal whistled happily. "Finally, some real work! Things are looking a little better."

Xia agreed, but Tiberius only shrugged.

"It's work," he said.

"Aren't you happy to be going home?" Duaal asked. "I would love to see Hyzaar. I haven't been there since I was a baby..."

Tiberius didn't look at Duaal. He stared up into the fluffy white clouds. "Prianus is a long way out."

Duaal wasn't terribly excited to be going back to the cold, craggy planet, either. He had been on Prianus far too long with Gavriel... Still, Duaal could not fathom why Tiberius wasn't grinning like a schoolboy to be going home.

Was that just a saying? Or did schoolboys actually do that?

Duaal studied the Vostra Nor campus. It was full of young men of all the Alliance races, walking and reading in the warm sunlight. An Axial man with burnished auburn hair and a square jaw caught his eye, lounging in the shade of a well-trimmed oak tree. Duaal whistled and Tiberius shot him a warning look.

"Don't attract attention," he reminded the boy.

"I wouldn't mind getting that guy's attention..." Duaal said with a grin.

"You're going to get us arrested."

"I wouldn't mind getting arrested by–"

Tiberius grabbed Duaal by the arm and hauled him back in the direction of the Blue Phoenix.

[5]
PREY

"A man who fears his past fears his future."

- DEVON LIMALLE, SUNJARRI CONSUL (136 PA)

Logan Coldhand stood at the window for a long time, rhythmically drumming his fingers against the reinforced glass. The hotel room was expensive, huge and stylishly furnished. A single long window spanned the entire wall and looked out over the shining, glittering city skyline. Logan's bare feet sank into the deep, soft carpet. Sipho's pale blue dwarf sun was setting, filling the sky with silver fire. All across the sky, stars glittered like bubbles in a glass of wine.

Finally having made his decision, Logan went to the bedroom and dressed quickly. A black shirt over gray pants so dark that they were almost the same color. He considered the Talon-9, wrapped in its holster on the neat, unused bed, and buckled it around his waist.

Coldhand took an elevator down to the garage and climbed into his rented car. It was the fastest model available, procured in case Barnes decided to run. The sleek red car hummed on its null-field and raced out into the street. A freight truck honked thunderously as Coldhand cut them off.

The bounty hunter glanced down at the car's computer. What he was looking for wouldn't be marked there, but it would at least get him to the right part of town. Sipho had a good reputation as a staid, stately planet. It was peaceful, a jewel of the Alliance.

But Coldhand knew better. Every light cast a shadow.

He drove through the bright-lit, holographed commercial district, past restaurants and cafes, and then out through the quiet suburbs. Coldhand came at last to a darkened industrial zone, shut down for the evening. Factories loomed up on all sides, slumbering metal beasts that would wake when the sun rose once more.

But they were heavy sleepers. The shadowed street wasn't silent. When Logan stopped the car and climbed out, he felt deep bass notes reverberating up through the soles of his boots and thumping against his ribs.

Coldhand found a close alleyway that smelled pungently of fuel and melted plastic. At the end stood a tiny concrete shed with a sloped roof and a closed, rusted gate. Coldhand yanked it open on creaking, flaking hinges and ducked inside.

He was at the top of a steep stairwell. The steps were worn and cracked by more than age. Logan had to keep his head down as he descended and water ran in rivulets from the arched ceiling, down the walls to pool at his feet.

Underground, the music was louder and Coldhand could hear a chorus of voices. After a few sharp turns, the stairs opened out into a circular concrete tunnel. Dark, mottled water spots stained the walls and a string of work lights glared along the ceiling, clamped to the support ribbing. The air beat with music, too, echoing and muffled to make out, but already filling the tunnel with a thrumming anticipation.

A huge Dailon lounged against the wall beside the stairwell. It was usually difficult to tell the muscular Dailons apart by gender, but this one wore shiny purple plastihide pants so tight that they left little question as to his masculinity.

He chatted animatedly with a pair of young human women. One of the girls was Mirran and had painted her stripes with dark makeup that matched her dress. She stopped in the middle of her sentence and stared at Coldhand, at the bared illonium below his scarred elbow and the gun on his hip. She whispered something to her friend and the two girls retreated down the tunnel. The Dailon sighed and turned to face Coldhand.

"Thanks for that, *maasquat*," he growled and then crossed huge, tattooed blue arms over his chest. He thrust his chin out toward the Talon. "What's the burner for? You a cop?"

"No," Coldhand said. "Where's a good place?"

The Dailon took in the hunter's stark, utilitarian clothes and his metal hand.

"Try Prey," he suggested. "Might be your kind of place. A Lyran named Vakk owns it. Take a right at the next cross-tunnel and go down two intersections. You can't miss it."

Coldhand followed the Dailon's instructions, heading deeper into the Sipho underground. In the early days of the colony, before the cloud seeding took hold, these aqueducts carried water from the polar icecaps down to the habitable zones of the planet. Now they served a new purpose, arguably just as important to the people of Sipho.

Deeper into the tunnels, the dank, ashy scent of old concrete took on a new life. There was musky sweat and the electric smell of ozone. Coldhand tasted the tang of strong alcohol and the thick sourness of smoke. He could pick out individual strains of music, all loud and thumping and warring with one another for prominence.

Other lights lined the curved aqueduct wall, pirating electricity from the city lines. They were dimmer than the construction lights but far more colorful, bunched together in places like radioactive bouquets. Signs in bright lumapaint and holographics glowed all along the tunnel. These gave way to doors, thrown invitingly open to the sources of the booming, conflicting music.

Strobes alternately silhouetted and flash-froze dancers in pulses of light.

There were other people now, too. Some dressed as modestly as Coldhand, but most wore no more than shreds of clinging, transparent cloth or a thin layer of body paint. It was too hot down here – in every sense – for much more.

Coldhand turned right at a cross-tunnel all hung with tangles of violet light ropes and found himself part of a thick crowd. The curved aqueduct floor forced everyone together, closer to Logan and each other than on the spacious walkways of the city above. The air down here was heavy and humid, pressing in on him from all sides.

Most of the underground Sipho bar and nightclub doors had been cut directly into their gray concrete walls. But the larger ones had smooth circular entrances framed in lights and advertisements, spouts that led into the huge cylindrical cisterns that used to hold the colony's precious water reserves.

Prey, one of them advertised in angular red slashes meant to remind Coldhand of huge claw marks. The hunter separated himself from the throng and paid the ten cenmark cover charge to a black-furred Lyran woman covered in piercings. He went inside.

Prey was packed with people. Mostly other humans, but there were Lyrans and Dailons, as well. A bar ran the length of one curved wall, finished to look like rough-cut basalt and painted in glowing tribal patterns. But it was the dance floor that dominated Prey, full of leaping, writhing bodies. The low, flat ceiling emphasized the claustrophobic crowd of dancers. They were all young and beautiful, dressed and painted up for a long night of pleasures. Some had the look of predators searching out their next conquests. Others enjoyed their role as prey, sought after and fought for.

Perhaps sensing a true predator in their midst, the dancers did their best to get out of Coldhand's way as he crossed the nightclub, but could make little room in the close confines. Logan felt warm, sweat-slicked skin against his. Even this anonymous, uninvited intimacy was… jarring.

He chose a table on the edge of the nightclub and sat. A holographic flame bobbed in the table's center, moving in time with the loud music and twisting occasionally into the stylized shape of a prowling Lyran. The shiny black tabletop lit up at Coldhand's touch and brought up a glowing drink list. He swiped through the menu.

Prey sold a much wider variety than the bars above ground – including narcohol, which was illegal on Sipho. Coldhand skipped over that part of the menu. He wanted something to wake his unresponsive body, not put him to sleep. The next screen's offering came not in shot glasses, but in needles and sealed plastic bags. Frag was at the top, in green letters that arced with animated electricity. No, Coldhand decided. He had tried the popular stimulant a couple of times, but all it ever did was leave a raw, coppery taste in his mouth, like blood.

But none of the other chems sounded any more appealing. He waved his left hand over the display to turn it off, but the sensor beam bounced off the illonium and the confused computer returned a readout of the music throbbing through the club – mostly Lyran hunt metal, full of deep drums beating out an impossibly fast tempo.

A young human woman danced on the edge of the floor, close against her friends. Her lithe body moved sinuously beneath her filmy dress and dark brown hair flared as she spun, then slithered down around her shoulders. The girl licked her red-painted lips and sweat beaded on her smooth skin.

Coldhand's cybernetic fingers scraped over the tabletop. The music drowned out the unpleasant sound and he could barely feel the hard plastic. Even here on a civilized world like Sipho, there had to be at least a few women willing to overlook his cybernetics.

It was only a hand, after all, easily ignored in the dark. If no one was interested, there were always those willing to do it for money. The touch of metal was worth the feel of plastic cenmarks. But none of the girls dancing in Prey seemed worth the effort.

Logan stared at the dancer without seeing her. Twenty percent. That was all he had, all he felt. But twenty percent of nothing was still nothing.

Drugs, drink, sex... They were the end goals for most bounty hunters, but held no interest for Coldhand. The hunt for Barnes had been just as boring as some corporate desk job. At the first sign of an interested buyer, the self-important little thief practically threw himself into the trap.

The underground club suddenly reminded Coldhand of Stray, of the Nihilist catacombs under Gharib. That place was a true monument to death, dug beneath the graveyard of the black cathedral. The bloated dead hung from the crumbling walls and ceiling like grisly cocoons. Prey was only a pale imitation by comparison, the shadow of a hunting hawk while the real thing circled above, far out of reach. For all their funerary black and intricately inked skin, though they were deep underground, these dancers weren't dead. They were alive. So vibrantly and gaudily alive.

It was all so cheap and tacky, but Logan was still jealous. They had no idea how easily it could all be ripped away, replaced by cold machines.

Except that would never happen here. Not in the deep core, where there were Ixthian hospitals in every city, with cloning tanks and redprints for every organ. Prey's patrons thought themselves rebels, sharp-beaked criminals of the Sipho underground. They had no idea how nightmarish, how empty life could become.

Coldhand turned his attention away from the dancers and back to the tabletop display. He closed the menu and music screens, then called up general mainstream access. News of the Nihilists was easy to find. The Union of Light's condemnation of rival religions was public and vocal. Though it wasn't enough to rouse the Central World Alliance Armed Forces to action, the Nihilists' many crimes – assault, abduction and murder – earned each and every one a CWA bounty.

There were some scattered and sporadically investigated stories of new converts told by the frightened families they left behind. Had Gavriel or Xartasia survived the attack on their cathedral? It was possible and Coldhand couldn't imagine many other Nihilists convincing anyone to join in their twisted death worship.

He tapped his identification into a government node and pulled up the bounty information on the Cult of Nihil. The money for capture of the individual members was no more impressive now than it had been the night before, waiting in the blank white-walled collection center. Coldhand read through the rest of the posting. He wasn't the only one who suspected that Gavriel and his guardian angel might still be alive. The CWA Lyceum was offering a much more impressive reward for anyone who could hunt down either Gavriel or Xartasia and bring them to face trial – five thousand cen-marks each.

It was good money. Not enough to retire on, but enough to keep Logan flying for a while.

But that wasn't the point. Barnes had been good money, too.

What would it be like... feel like to face Gavriel's Emberguard again? Logan touched his good hand to his chest, felt the thick knot of scar tissue there, even through his shirt. Did the Nihilists hate Coldhand?

Did he hate them?

If Gavriel had lived – the irony of a Nihilist fighting for his own survival might have made another man laugh aloud – then chances were good that Xartasia had, too. Would Maeve be searching for her cousin?

Coldhand cleared the table terminal and strode purposefully through the tight pack of Prey, back out into the aqueducts. At the stairs leading up, the Dailon bouncer waved and asked if he had enjoyed Prey. But Coldhand stalked past without a word, lost in his own thoughts.

[6]

DIRTY

"Ixthians don't believe that lovers have chemistry. They have bio-chemistry."

— PROFESSOR XEN, VOSTRA NOR UNIVERSITY (229 PA)

Everyone on the Blue Phoenix rose before the sun to get to work. The flight out to Prianus would be almost a month long. There were many preparations to make and precautions to take.

Xia called each member of the crew into her tiny medbay in turn and injected them with tailored immune updates.

"This is especially important for you," she told Gripper as she held the injector to the Arboran's huge arm. "You've never been to Prianus. You wouldn't believe how many diseases they have there."

"Have you been to Prianus?" he asked.

Xia shook her head. "No."

"Did you have to take one of these?" Gripper asked.

He winced as the needles jabbed him and poured a cold stream of chemicals into his blood. The Arboran's skin was too thick for Xia's compressed air injector.

"Me?" Xia said. She shook her head. "No. I should be fine. I have seven times the leukocyte count that you do."

"Why?"

"Good breeding," the Ixthian answered. She wiped the needles clean and replaced the injector on a nearby tray. "A good immune system is one of the top traits we seek in our mates."

"Um, that's not very romantic."

Xia just laughed and sent Gripper to go find Maeve.

Duaal was up in the cockpit, downloading updated astronavigation charts off the university mainstream and mapping out their course. Stars and planets were only a few of the potential dangers between Tynerion and Prianus. At superluminal speeds, a single surprise comet or solar plasma ejection would tear the Blue Phoenix apart and scatter wreckage across half a stellar system.

Tiberius and Gripper had spent the morning getting the Blue Phoenix fueled and tuned up, replacing filters and checking seals. With twice the usual complement of passengers on board, the aged recycling systems would be hard pressed to keep up.

That left the final task to Maeve, who lacked the technical expertise to help with much else. She surveyed the bunkroom and sighed. The spare quarters were closed up and sealed when not in use, which was most of the time – the Blue Phoenix didn't take on many passengers.

Logan Coldhand had been the last one. Her hunter…

Maeve pushed up her sleeves and got to work. She scrubbed the floors and walls, changed light tubes and sheets, and cleaned each room's single small viewport. By the time she was done, her clothes were caked in dust and her short black hair stuck to her neck with sweat. Maeve carried the full dustpan outside the ship to empty it.

No point in running more dirt through the Blue Phoenix's recycling system than she had to.

How in the name of the All-Singer could sealed rooms get so filthy? There was a sharp crash behind her. Maeve turned to find a slender, pretty blonde woman standing with hands pressed to her mouth. She looked like she was going to be sick. There were three men with her. One of them – a serious-looking Dailon with a long black braid – retrieved the suitcase she had dropped.

"God, Panna. Take your meds next time," said a brown and white patched Lyran. He looked at Maeve. "Is this the Blue Phoenix?"

"It is," she answered. "Are you Professor Xen's colleagues?"

"That's us. Gruth Rommik," said the Lyran. He dipped his snout to indicate that this name was his own, then pointed to a short, round human man with freckles and red-orange hair. "This is our geologist, Phillip Arno. The big Dailon there is Enu-Io Crath. And the girl who can't hold onto her luggage is Panna Sul."

"I was surprised," Panna said. "I didn't expect... an Arcadian."

The spoiled coreworlder girl had probably never seen a fairy before, but Maeve made herself smile at the scholars. They really *did* need paying work.

"Where is Professor Xen?" she asked.

"He'll be here soon with the rest of our equipment," Panna answered. "We came early to hand off some of the delicate stuff."

"Then let us hope that you were carrying none of it," Maeve said with an arched eyebrow.

The Lyran, Gruth, laughed and elbowed Panna in the ribs. "The bird-girl's got you there."

Panna recovered and held out her hand. "Ignore the furball. I'm so sorry. May I ask your name?"

"Maeve Cavainna." She took the offered hand briefly and Panna looked uncomfortable. "I am first mate of the Blue Phoenix. Your accommodations are prepared, if you wish to board."

"We should wait for Professor Xen and help him with the equipment," said Enu-Io.

Maeve nodded. Duaal appeared at the airlock and waved.

"Are these our passengers?" he called out.

"Hello again, Mister Sinnay," Panna said.

"Just Duaal. And who are the rest?"

The Hyzaari copilot came down the cargo ramp and exchanged introductions with the archeologists, then winked flirtatiously at Enu-Io. Maeve fished her com – short not for *communications*, but *compound phone/radio* – from her pocket and called Tiberius. There was a metallic clang and some shouting before he answered.

"Myles here. What?"

"Most of our guests have arrived," Maeve reported. "Professor Xen will join them soon, along with the majority of their equipment. Is Gripper finished inside? We could use his help in loading."

"We'll be there in just a minute. Keep your wings on!" Tiberius grumped.

"Yes, captain."

Duaal was deep in conversation with the stout geologist, Phillip, who was familiar with Hyzaar. Panna watched Maeve again, but blushed and turned away when she saw the Arcadian staring back.

At precisely seven o'clock, Professor Xen drove onto the landing field in a flatbed truck piled high with crates and cases. He pulled to a stop behind the Blue Phoenix ramp and called out to Panna.

"Would you supervise the loading?" he asked. "I need to have a word with Captain Myles."

Panna nodded. She climbed up onto the truck bed and began checking over the crates. Gruth, Phillip and Enu-Io went to help. Xen asked where Tiberius was.

"He is in the engine room with Gripper," Maeve answered. "He will arrive shortly."

The Ixthian professor looked at her for a moment with eyes shifting through a spectrum of colors too quickly for Maeve to read, then nodded. A moment later, Tiberius and Xia emerged from the Blue Phoenix. Xen exchanged a handshake with Tiberius and a hug with Xia. They all joined the rest of the team in grunting and straining as they unloaded the truck.

A few of the crates were marked with yellow biocontainment stickers and had to be handled with care, but most were just heavy. Only the large Enu-Io wasn't streaming sweat. Maeve's feathers made Gruth sneeze every time they passed one another. Most of the work was done when Gripper swung down from the upper walkway and landed in the hold.

"Sorry, Claws," he apologized. "That last bolt got stuck. Had to replace it."

Xen stood to one side, alternately talking to Xia and checking over a datadex that Panna held. He caught sight of the Arboran and whistled sharply. Gripper looked at him and colored.

"Hi, I'm Gripper. Professor Xen, right?"

"Amazing," Zen breathed. "What are you, my boy?"

"His species is called Arboran," Xia said.

Xen's eyes flickered again through several colors. "Arboran? As in the *arborus* genox? Trees?"

"Um, yeah. The Lyrans who found me gave it a name in Aver," Gripper said. "Back home, we didn't really have one. We called the forest *Weh-weh*, though. It uh... it means *tree-tree*."

"Amazing," Xen said again. "Simply amazing. How many other secrets are you keeping on this ship, Xia?"

"Gripper's the big one, I think. I'm sure you can understand why we didn't want to drag him across the university to meet with you."

Xen looked Gripper speculatively up and down. "I suppose I do, at that. This will be a fascinating trip."

"It won't be if we can't get this stuff loaded up," Gruth shouted from across the cargo bay. "Why doesn't the big whatever-you-are come help me with this drill? Bring me that NI pallet!"

"Yeah, sure," Gripper said and did as the Lyran asked.

"Absolutely fascinating," Xen murmured.

Tiberius waved Duaal over and hooked his thumb over his shoulder, in the direction of the nose of the ship and the cockpit.

"It looks like we're about done here," Tiberius said. "Go submit our clearance to the control tower."

"Do I have to?" Duaal asked plaintively. He looked around the field and lingered on Enu-Io, who had removed his shirt to keep it clean as he repositioned crates in the Blue Phoenix hold. "The view out here is much nicer."

"Go call it in," Tiberius told him.

"And then take the Phoenix up?"

"And then wait for me."

"Come on! I'm wasted on you, captain," Duaal said, then sighed. "I really am."

He looked around for someone to agree with him. Maeve just shrugged, but Xia put a silver hand on Tiberius' shoulder.

"It's a clear day and should provide a smooth flight," she said. "He could use the practice."

Tiberius considered and finally nodded. "Alright, sure. When you get clearance, you can fly out, Duaal. Just watch out for the morning traffic. These eggheads can't fly straight before they've had their first pot of coffee."

"Yes, sir!" Duaal snapped a silly, over-elaborate salute and ran up toward the cockpit.

"Is he your student?" Enu-Io asked in a deep, quiet voice.

Tiberius grunted, still watching the door through which Duaal had vanished.

"Duaal has been the Blue Phoenix copilot for five years," Xia answered. "He's pretty well qualified, if that's what you're asking."

"He doesn't look much like a pilot," Panna said with a smile. "More like a fashion holo for deep club types. Where's he from?"

Before anyone could answer, the engines howled and the Blue Phoenix lurched under their feet, throwing everyone to the ground.

Maeve flapped her wings hard to keep her balance. Professor Xen arched a white eyebrow at Xia and she smirked back at him.

"You wanted a cheap flight, Xen," she reminded him.

"I better go check on that," Tiberius said. He ran for the stairs.

Dinner the first night out was fresh fare from Tynerion, mostly fruit and vegetables with a dessert of strawberry ice cream that had them all picking seeds out of well-fed grins for hours afterward.

"Sorry," apologized the red-haired Phillip, who had made it. "I forgot to strain the pulp."

"It is still better fare than we are used to," Maeve said.

With the addition of five more bodies, the room that served as the ship's kitchen, lounge and crew dining room all at once was crowded, forcing everyone to sit close together around the table or at the couches. Despite the close quarters, Panna still managed to stay across the mess from Maeve.

Gripper burped happily and then covered his wide mouth. "Oops. Thanks, Strawberry. I haven't had ice cream in months."

"Strawberry?" Phillip asked, afraid that Gripper was making fun of him.

"For the ice cream and because of your hair."

"Oh." The geologist covered his coppery hair with his hands.

Gruth barked a short laugh.

"We never use birth names," Gripper explained quickly. "It's a sort of nickname. I use them for everyone. Smoke and Shimmer. Claws and Little Claws for his hawk. Silver for Xia, because she's so shiny and pretty..."

"That she is," Xen said. He pushed his bowl back and rested his sharp chin in one hand. He peered across the table at Xia. "You're as lovely now as the day you left, my dear. You did cut off your hair, though, and I must confess that I miss it."

"I didn't cut it the first time. Someone else did," Xia told him. She brushed a six-fingered hand over her scalp. "I guess I just got used to it after that. I hadn't really thought about it. Maybe I should let it grow out again."

"I like it short," Gripper said. "It's all fuzzy."

"Fuzzy?" Xia frowned.

"Um, yeah..." Gripper bit his brown-mottled lip and gave her an uncertain smile.

"We have a lot of catching up to do," Xen said. "Why don't you show me the ship, Xia? You have medical facilities, I assume?"

"A small medbay," Xia answered demurely. "There's not much to show, but come on."

She deposited their empty ice cream bowls in the sink and led Xen out of the room. Gripper watched them go with his mouth hanging open.

"Perhaps you should not have said that her hair looked fuzzy," Maeve suggested gently.

Duaal stifled a laugh and Gripper looked mortified.

"But it does!" he groaned. "Like my favorite moss!"

Duaal could contain his mirth no longer and began giggling. Gruth and Phillip laughed, too.

Tiberius didn't seem to get the joke. He stood and cracked his knuckles loudly. "I've got to feed Orphia or she'll have my fingers. Duaal, check our vectors before bed."

"Will do, captain," Duaal said. He wiped a tear from the corner of his eye.

Gripper glared at the mage for a moment, but then stared wistfully out the door as Tiberius departed.

"What do you think they're talking about?" he asked.

Maeve frowned. "Tiberius and Orphia?"

"No. Silver and Shorts."

"Shorts?"

"Professor Xen. Shorts. Because he's so short."

It was easy to make light of Gripper's infatuation with Xia. He was absurdly inept in his courtship. But for all of its comedy, his pain was no less real. Maeve put her hand on top of Gripper's huge one and gave it a small, reassuring squeeze.

"They have a lot to catch up on," Panna said. She stood up and collected the remaining bowls from the table. "They haven't seen each other in years. They used to be quite close."

"Close?" Gripper asked. "Like what kind of close?"

"Well, they were involved, back when they were both students," Panna said.

"Involved?" Gripper's voice was breathless. "Like... dating?"

Panna deposited the dishes beside the sink and leaned on the counter. "And they were pretty serious."

Gripper looked down at Maeve with such a look of youthful, boyish lovesickness that her heart ached, all jokes forgotten. Young love was hard. Maeve thought of her Orthain, of her brother Caith, and his love. She laid her cheek against Gripper's rough brown skin and badly wanted a drink.

There wasn't much to show Xen in the medical bay. It was more of an alcove than a proper room, but even that was an improvement on the Blue Phoenix's original design. The starship was made for short distance travels, not the sort of long hauls that required the presence of a doctor.

"Then your superluminal engines and NI generators must be modifications, too," Xen said.

He leaned in the door, surveying Xia's small domain.

"I believe Tiberius had to install more powerful models," she answered. "They're both a little more than the internal systems can handle. The repairs kept us in port longer than Tiberius likes, so he hired Gripper on to keep the Phoenix flying."

"Is there a lot of call for a medic?"

Xia gestured around the medical bay. "I've used everything in here. I had to update everyone's immunizations this morning. Six months ago, I delivered a baby. And Duaal can singe himself quite badly with some of his fire spells."

"I've been meaning to ask you about that boy. Soon."

"Maeve gets into a lot of fights, too," Xia said. "It used to be worse, when Coldhand was chasing her."

Xen's long antennae twitched.

"Coldhand?" he asked. "Is that a name I should know?"

"I hope not. He's a bounty hunter," Xia answered. She sat down on the corner of the examination table. "He and Maeve spent a year trying to kill each other. At least, that's what it looked like. As it turned out, Maeve had posted her own bounty and was trying to get Coldhand to kill her. He's gone now."

"That sounds rather convoluted," Xen said. "You've landed yourself on a very mysterious little ship and I hope you'll tell me more. I want to know all about that alien, Gripper, and your mage. I've never heard of a human one. He *is* human, isn't he? But later. It's going to be a long flight to Prianus."

Xen sat beside Xia. She smelled his warm, sweet pheromones.

"And most of all, I want to know about you," Xen said. "What happened, Xia?"

"What?"

"We all expected great things from you. You were so dedicated to your studies, more devoted to them than you were to me."

There was no bitterness in Xen's voice and Xia supposed it was a testament to her years away from other Ixthians that it surprised her. Though their genetics had been compatible, their career goals were not. Once the young couple realized that, there was little reason to continue their courtship. But they had remained friends for years after.

"I'm still a doctor," Xia pointed out.

"But after you graduated, you just... vanished. For the longest time, I heard nothing. Then you appear on a tiny, unaffiliated ship as their medic. This was never one of your ambitions, my dear, and I knew your ambitions well. What happened? Where did you go?"

"You heard that I won the grant from the Alliance to open an office on Koji, right?" Xia asked.

"Yes, I heard. I bought a round for everyone at the campus bar when I found out. I sent you a dozen Hyla roses," Xen said. He brushed his fingers over his curling pewter antennae. "I guess you never got them."

"No. I went home before heading out to Koji. I wanted to see my parents and pick up a few things from the Kynfarr laboratories before I flew out to the frontier. My mother lectured me a little. Like you, she always thought I should have stayed in research. But otherwise, everything was fine. Until I left."

Xia laced her fingers in her lap and took a breath before she continued.

"A pirate ship, the Caitiff, intercepted my passenger liner. They took everything of value, killed anyone who resisted and took many others as prizes. I was one of the second group, but I wasn't on the Caitiff long before the captain, Gelden, figured out that I was a lot more valuable as a medic than a sex worker."

"You don't have to tell me anymore," Xen offered.

"No, it's alright," Xia said. She unwove her fingers and wiped her damp palms on the knees of her pale green pants.

"So you were a doctor for the pirates?"

"Not at first," Xia said. "I refused to work for them, but then Gelden brought in some of the other prisoners from my ship. He told me that if I didn't obey, he would kill one of them. I didn't believe him, naturally. Gelden was a petty, spiteful little man. I didn't think he had it in him. I was wrong.

"The next time that the Caitiff landed, I tried to escape. I was terrified and clumsy. Gelden's men caught me easily. When they dragged me back, Captain Gelden shot one of the other captives, a human girl. Right there in front of me. There was nothing I could do for her.

"I didn't push Gelden again. I worked for him for two years. After a while, he even let me carry my own weapon. I still have the pistol he gave me, stolen off one of the ships he attacked."

"But you left, eventually," Xen said softly.

"Gelden stopped the Blue Phoenix. It was carrying some transistors. Gallium-errol, very delicate. He didn't want to risk damaging the cargo by firing on the ship, so he boarded. Tiberius, Maeve and Duaal fought back. Gripper wasn't around back then. Maeve chased the boarding party all the way back to the Caitiff and she found me there, waiting to care for the pirates. Maeve rescued me, if you can believe it, and brought me back to Tiberius. He offered me a job and I took it."

"And here you are." Xen looked around the medbay with a new appreciation in his faceted compound eyes.

"Here I am," Xia said. "Tiberius built all of this for me. It used to be a closet. He had it expanded and bought some equipment so I could do my job."

"Why didn't you go back to Koji?" Xen asked. "They still need doctors in the colonies."

"I'm sure my grant expired a long time ago."

"You could get a new one," Xen suggested.

Xia shrugged. "I don't know. There aren't a lot of grants."

"I could help you secure one."

"Maybe..."

They sat in silence for a few minutes. The bulkheads rumbled as the engines worked, wrapping the Blue Phoenix in a huge null-inertia field and hurling them between the stars, flying faster than light. Voices echoed quietly from the rest of the ship as the crew and passengers went about their evening routines. Xia could just make out Orphia's harsh calls as Tiberius flew her in the hold.

"It's good to see you again, my dear," Xen said at last.

"And you, Xen. It has been a long time."

"I meant what I said earlier. I really do want to hear all about your strange companions. I'm quite curious."

Xia nodded. "I knew you would be. I'll be making breakfast tomorrow. If you want to get up early and lend me a hand, I can tell you some about them."

The other Ixthian stood and took Xia's hands in his smaller ones. He kissed her forehead, between her antennae.

"I look forward to it. Until tomorrow," Xen said.

He left Xia sitting alone in her medical alcove. It was good to see Xen. He seemed much older, more mature than the over-eager young man who had been her lover six years ago. Or was she the one who had changed?

Her relationship with Xen seemed like a lifetime ago, but the memories of the intimacy they had once shared stirred a longing in Xia that she had nearly forgotten.

Life on the Blue Phoenix could be isolating. Xia spent every day with the rest of the crew, but when she wasn't working, her off-duty hours were long and lonely. It would be good to have passengers, especially other scholars, if only for a little while.

Xia shut off the lights in the medbay and headed back toward the mess. She could help with the dishes before bed.

[7]

PIECES

"Every truth is a lie in someone else's eyes."

- ENU-IO CRATH, VARNUM ARCHEOLOGIST (220 PA)

Coldhand spent the next three days in his hotel room, sorting through every available report on the Cult of Nihil and using his E3 status to request more. Where were the Nihilists now? There were speculations and panicked police reports of suspicious strangers in black, but very few actual facts.

It made sense. If there were enough easy leads to track down the Cult of Nihil, local authorities would have found them already. There would be no need to post bounties. The Nihilists had gone into hiding.

Logan sat at the hotel room desk and ran his right hand idly over the smooth wood – actual wood, alternately banded in light and dark brown. It was probably the most expensive thing in the room and Coldhand supposed most of the hotel's guests were there on business. How many contracts had been written and reviewed at this desk? Logan probably wasn't the first to spend more time here than in the bed.

Coldhand pulled up one of the police reports on the monitor. The video of a woman's hysterical testimony was full of low-resolution rude gestures, but the audio was clear enough. Her husband had run off with an Arcadian – "A bird-back slut!" – that she was convinced was a Nihilist. The husband turned up two days later, floating face-down in one of Giadeen's huge violet lakes. Someone had remotely emptied his accounts, using his codes. They found his Arcadian mistress a week after that, dead from a chem overdose.

But despite his widow's loud and adamant accusations, Giadeen police found no evidence of Nihilist involvement. The Arcadian appeared to have been working alone. After rereading the report for any overlooked details, Coldhand found no reason to doubt their conclusion and moved on.

There were other stories of Nihilists appearing throughout the galaxy – some substantiated by other witnesses – but none with any more evidence than the Giadeen case. Coldhand pulled up the four most likely reports side-by-side on his computer display: a pair of self-proclaimed Nihilists giving death sermons on Glaw, an Arcadian looking for converts on Koji, and a series of brutal murders on the Devros moon, Frast.

In most cases, the local authorities had caught the culprit, only to have each one of them kill themselves before questioning. On Frast, another bounty hunter found the Nihilist and cornered him in front of a crowded restaurant. Fifty-eight witnesses confirmed a short, brutal fight between the hunter and a tall human in a dirty red robe.

An Emberguard?

Coldhand swiped a bead of sweat from his forehead before it could drip down into his eye. The other bounty hunter had been no match for his opponent and was still laid up in a Frast hospital, recovering from multiple deep lacerations and a major concussion. Of the Emberguard, there had been no further sign.

Logan checked the clock. It was getting late again.

He sat back in the desk chair, making the leather creak. Each of the incidents was suspiciously public. The first three gave their speeches on street corners, in the middle of parks or even on the steps of Union of Light churches. The Emberguard on Frast had never made the slightest attempt to conceal his crimes, usually killing in plain sight and dropping the discarded bodies in front of busy public centers.

Even back on Stray, when the Nihilists were at their strongest, they never acted so openly. Gavriel gave his sermons, but never let his subordinates so blatantly criminalize themselves. The abduction of Kessa's baby was done quickly and quietly. Gavriel kept his people under careful control.

Coldhand closed down the four reports. They didn't mean that the Nihilists weren't hiding, only that these ones were acting on their own, outside Gavriel's authority and influence, if he was still alive. They still believed in the old bastard's teachings, but without his guidance, they couldn't fly straight.

That didn't mean they were dead ends, though. Coldhand read over the planets again: Glaw, Koji and Frast. He kicked his feet up onto the desk and frowned up at the shadowed ceiling.

The colony of Glaw was being extensively mined. A pulsar only a few systems over swept the planet with frequent radiation bursts and the colonists lived far underground in an expansive network of caves and tunnels. It was an easy place to hide and was a popular smugglers' stop.

The CWA always sought out new planets to venaform, to feed and settle their ever-growing populace. Koji was the most recent to become a full member of the Alliance. Thousands of ships came and went from Koji every day, carrying colonists and the multitude of supplies needed to sustain the young world.

The two planets didn't seem to have much in common. What about Frast, the innermost moon of Devros 2? Much like Hyzaar, oceans covered most of Devros 2's surface and made dry land a rare commodity. Starports were too large to put on such expensive real estate and most ships landed on the nearby moon. Passengers and cargo moved down to the planet on hourly shuttles.

Coldhand closed his eyes. They were sandy and dry from hours of staring at monitors. Fractal patterns in red and green danced in the darkness behind his lids. There was a pattern to all of this, if he could just see it. The hunter pressed his fingers against his closed eyes, making the shimmering shards of color jump and spin.

Had the Cult of Nihil fragmented? Devros, Koji and Glaw were nowhere near each other. Maybe the church simply dissolved, scattering among the stars. One of the first accounts Coldhand had read was a police report from Stray. The Nihilists arrested in Gharib killed themselves shortly after capture, just like those on Koji and Glaw. But when the Stray police stormed the other cathedrals, they found only dusty, empty buildings. The Nihilists were gone.

Coldhand cracked his eyes open again and frowned at the dark hotel room. There had been hundreds of the death-worshipers in Gharib. Half of those escaped the collapsing catacombs, but the Stray police only managed to arrest ninety-three of them.

And that was just one of Gavriel's cathedrals. There must have been thousands of Nihilists. So why could Logan only find four?

The remaining cultists must have gone somewhere. The ones on Glaw, Koji and Frast had to be stragglers, fledges fallen from the nest. But all three worlds were major ports. What if these cultists were part of larger groups, left behind because they arrived late or were troublemakers?

Coldhand brought up images of the four known Nihilists. None of them were Arcadians, but the majority of Gavriel's following on Stray had been made up of fairies. The hopeless and unhomed Arcadians made perfect targets for the cult's escapist preaching. So where were they? Was Gavriel trying to keep the Arcadians close?

Why? To remain in Xartasia's good graces? Did the princess care at all what happened to the broken fragments of her people?

Or maybe Logan was trying to build a nest from a single twig.

It was a possibility. Coldhand had very little information and could have been taking it all in the wrong direction.

A quiet sound distracted the bounty hunter from his thoughts. Only after a minute sitting in stony silence did Logan hear the noise again and realize that it was his stomach gurgling. He hadn't even noticed the empty aching in his gut.

Coldhand pulled up the hotel's internal node and ordered some food at random from the room service menu. It would be expensive, but he had no desire to leave his desk long enough to find something else.

The Cult of Nihil was moving off of Stray, or had already done so. Where could they go that such a large influx of fairies wouldn't attract notice? One of the sparsely populated colony worlds, like Koji? No, the Central World Alliance watched their new colonies closely. They farmed and manufactured important products and foodstuffs for the older worlds.

Axis, maybe? The vast capital city-world was home to ten times more Alliance citizens than any other planet. The appearance of a few hundred or even thousands more would never be noticed. The lower levels of the megatropolis were a mystery even to natives of Vanora and were an easy place to hide. The idea of finding the cult on Axis was a daunting one, but Coldhand didn't think about it for long. He had found Vyron Fethru there, and that was just one man. If the Nihilists were there, Logan could find them.

There were only a few other civilized planets where Gavriel's cult could go and escape the notice of the CWA. Glaw might have been a good choice, full of places to hide away from prying Alliance eyes. Those places were all located underground, however, and unlike even the lowest levels of Axis, Glaw was made up of close tunnels and caves.

It seemed unlikely that even the most lost and depressed Arcadians would be willing to make their homes in a place where they could never fly. And even if they endured the interminable tons of stone burying them away from the sky, someone would eventually notice the Arcadians in a place so alien to them.

Coldhand had almost forgotten about the food he ordered until the door toned softly. He quickly pulled on a shirt and answered. Out in the hall, a human girl held a covered tray and squinted into the darkness. Her freckles stood out starkly against her pale skin in the bright light of the hallway.

"Having a nice night, sir?" she asked.

Coldhand took the tray and tapped the glowing lock. The door slid shut in her face.

Through the uncovered window, red and amber light filtered up from the city. It was beautiful but illuminated little in the shadowed hotel room. Coldhand carried the food back to his desk. His legs were stiff and prickled unpleasantly as blood flowed back into them after sitting for so long.

Dinner turned out to be some sort of white fish on a pillow of brown rice and drenched in a pale wine sauce. Coldhand picked at the unfamiliar meat. Fish was never a common food on mountainous Prianus. There were fish in the fast-flowing rivers, but not enough to ever become a major staple of Prian diet. Even after five years away from his homeworld, Logan still found meals in the rest of the core ridiculously extravagant. How many kinds of food could one man need? Whether it came from fish or cloned algae, it all ended up in the same place and served the same purpose.

Coldhand began eating quickly and returned to his work. It seemed unlikely that Gavriel would choose Axis as his church's new home. While the lower levels of the city might make for excellent – if dangerous – hiding, it was the capital world of the Central World Alliance. Transporting that many wanted criminals onto Axis might be difficult, but far more problematic was the proximity of the CWA

Armed Forces, whose center of operations was located there. A single Lyceum dictum could flood even the dankest, darkest recesses of Axis with CWAAF soldiers.

But Prianus had a much lower population, and with less habitable surface area than the gleaming globe of Axis, it suffered even worse overcrowding. Still, there were Arcadians everywhere. The fairies on Prianus never met with the same hatred that they had on other planets. Despite their long wings, though, the Arcadians who appeared a century ago were no more able to leave Prianus than the native humans. Most of them were still there, living in the same poverty and desperation as the Prians themselves.

Coldhand wasn't finished eating, but the fish no longer looked appetizing. He replaced the cover and pushed the food away to the corner of his desk.

"Miss Carmine, there's a call coming in for you. Miss Carmine?"

Alexa Carmine sat up with a groan. The previous night's dose of Frag left a thick, sweet taste at the back of her throat. She coughed and then gagged, certain that she was about to be sick. Alexa tried to rise, but a lean masculine shape lay draped across her, holding her down.

She picked up the boy's wrist and let go. His arm flopped bonelessly into the tangled sheets. He wouldn't wake for hours yet. Frag always hit males harder. Alexa scratched her head. The young man looked familiar.

"Miss Carmine?"

Another man stood in the doorway of Alexa's small but lavish bedroom. This one was human, too, but older. Much older and much uglier. A cave-in three years back had broken his cheekbone and ripped most of the scalp from that side of his skull. The entire right half of his face was twisted and scarred, crumpled and hairless as a discarded wrapper. For some ridiculous reason, he would never let Alexa send him to her favorite surgeon to repair the damage.

"God, you're enough to give any woman nightmares, Harrell," she groaned.

"Very sorry, Miss Carmine. There's a call waiting for you."

Alexa flopped back into the inviting warmth of her bed and the comatose younger man. Her dark hair fanned out around her head.

"I don't care, Harrell. Take a message. I'll deal with it later," she said, then gave her bedmate a half-hearted prod. "Who in the seven hundred hells is this, anyway?"

"That's your new secretary," Harrell said. "Miss Carmine, you really should take the call. It's Coldhand."

Alexa jerked upright and the color seemed to drain out of the room. She felt suddenly hot and prickly all over, as though she had just taken another shot of Frag.

"How long has he been waiting?" she asked.

Alexa gave her unconscious secretary a hard shove. He groaned and curled into a ball on the corner of the bed. She kicked her way out from under him and wrapped herself in a thick, wine-colored robe.

"A few minutes," Harrell said. He frowned with the left half of his face. "It was very hard to wake you, Miss Carmine. You had too much last night."

She didn't have time to argue with him. Besides, Harrell might have been right. Alexa could remember nothing of the night before. But if she didn't give Logan Coldhand what he wanted, Alexa suspected she would be spending a lot of memorable nights in prison. She ran from the bedroom and into the adjoining office. The stone floor was cold and hard against her bare feet.

Alexa leaned over her desk and told her computer to open the call. Coldhand appeared on the screen, sitting so still in the deep shadows on the other end that Alexa wondered for a moment if it was a photo-mask. The Prian bounty hunter looked just as he the last time he had been on Glaw: short, dark blonde hair framing those glacial pale blue eyes that alternately made Alexa want to run in stark terror or else rip off his clothes.

Right now, she could do neither. Alexa Carmine, the self-made smuggler queen of Glaw, needed to remain a more useful ally than a bounty.

"What do you need, Coldhand?" she asked. Did the quivering in her stomach come through in her voice? "More phenno? It's hard to move goods off Glaw right now. There's a burst covering the whole eastern hemisphere tomorrow."

"No. I need information, Carmine."

"What kind of information?" Alexa asked suspiciously.

If Coldhand was after one of her smugglers, giving him any information would cut into her profits and might make her look unreliable to the other captains. Alexa didn't like it. The answer came after a tense moment, the delay between transmissions from Glaw to wherever the hunter was.

"I'm not interested in your people," Coldhand said, perhaps reading something of Alexa's fears in her voice. "I'm just verifying a theory. Has anyone new come into the Glaw tunnels?"

"A lot of people come and go every day," Alexa answered. "Can you be more specific?"

Another transmission delay. Coldhand seemed to be considering how much to reveal to Alexa. She couldn't blame him. If he ever tipped his hand too far, if he ever revealed some useful vulnerability, it would be a lot safer to remove the hunter than to keep working with him.

"There would be a lot of them, probably upward of a thousand, and many would be Arcadian," he said at last.

Carmine thought about that, drumming her long red nails on her desk.

"I had a large group of passengers come through a few months back. Not in the numbers you're talking about, but two or three hundred. I noted them because almost all of them were bird-backs. I don't like it when anyone makes trouble in my tunnels."

"Came through?" Coldhand asked. "Are they still on Glaw?"

"No," Alexa said. "They left again a few days later on another ship. Nice Narsus thing, custom job. Crewed by more bird-backs," Alexa said. "The whole thing was more than a little strange."

"Tell me." Coldhand's voice was icy and intense, like falling into cold water.

"They had color. Enough for fuel and supplies, but they were going to Prianus. If they had the money, why fly out to that God-forsaken place? Anyone who can leave Prianus never goes back."

Alexa realized what she had just said and fell uncomfortably silent.

"Like me," Coldhand answered a few seconds later. "Did they do anything while they were on Glaw?"

"Do anything? Anything illegal, you mean? No. They were quiet and kept to themselves. They all stayed together in one of my caves and never complained."

When Coldhand received her answer, he didn't seem surprised. He nodded once and cut the transmission without another word. Alexa flopped down into her chair and wiped a sheen of sweat from her forehead. Harrell stood in the door of the office, curiosity on his ugly face.

"What did he want?" Harrell asked.

"If you weren't already listening in, then you're as stupid as you look," Alexa snapped. Unfairly. She sighed and waved a hand. "Go take my secretary home. I'm not in the mood for him anymore."

Harrell inclined his head. "Yes, Miss Carmine."

Coldhand had woken up early, after only a few hours of sleep. When he was done talking to Alexa Carmine, he called the CWAAF router on Axis, requesting similar information. A business-like young private verified the bounty hunter's clearance and promised to get back to him soon. Logan sent a message to the Stray police, too, but it went straight into an automated file collection. He didn't expect any information back from them, but doubted that he needed any.

It was just verification, anyway. Carmine had already confirmed his theory. The Cult of Nihil had gone to Prianus. Three hundred quiet Arcadians with the money to fly out to the edge of CWA space? It had to be the Cult of Nihil. Still, Coldhand was curious where the money came from. The crooked, patchwork cathedral in Gharib didn't exactly conjure images of vast wealth.

There was something else – the Mirran Emberguard who had taken a younger Logan's hand and heart in battle one cold, frozen night... The Nihilists had been on Prianus before. Now they were going back.

It made sense. The Alliance chased Gavriel off Stray, so he was retreating to old and familiar territory.

While Coldhand waited for information from Axis, he ordered the fuel and water he would need to make the flight to Prianus. Twenty days in the cockpit of his Raptor was going to be uncomfortable, but finding a larger ship to make the journey would take too long. It was already hours past dawn and Coldhand wanted no more delays.

It didn't take long to order everything he needed for the flight and even less time to pack up the handful of scattered clothing, datadexes and his Talon-9. Logan held the gun, feeling the weight of it in his mismatched hands. The Talon was huge and heavy. It weighed twice as much as a similar weapon manufactured anywhere else in the galaxy. Prian construction was sturdy, but no one could accuse it of being stylish or sleek.

Deep scratches scarred the length of the Talon's barrel, a long and violent history etched in a primitive script that only he could read. Coldhand traced his fingers over three parallel grooves. They were shallow and rough at the edges. Those were left by Orphia, Tiberius' aging hawk, back in Gharib as Coldhand circled Maeve in the hold of the Blue Phoenix.

Maeve was trying to bait Logan into killing her then, he remembered. She tried to trick him.

She never succeeded, of course, but the attempt was admirable. Maeve poured more effort and passion into death than most people put into life.

Logan turned his Talon-9 over. A single deep line sliced straight and clean along the back end of the refraction barrel, from the sight and down almost to the stock. Unlike the marks left by Orphia's curved talons, this cut was deep and smooth. Maeve had left that scar during their first battle, a single overhead blow from her glass-headed spear. On that first day, the small, skinny Arcadian princess had seemed so sick and strung out on chems... How could she be any kind of challenge? But underestimating Maeve almost cost him another hand.

Logan held the Talon in his illonium hand and flexed the good one. A slender white scar ran down the back of his hand where Maeve's spear had grazed him. Only a cool head and fast reflexes had prevented that glass blade from sheering away everything past his thumb.

Those weren't the only scars Maeve had left. She was a skilled warrior and a wily mark. Not for the first time, Coldhand found himself wondering where she was. Maeve hadn't put out a new bounty on herself yet, Logan knew. He checked frequently. Had she finally tired of trying to taunt death – her Nameless goddess – into taking her and done the deed herself? Or was she still aboard the Blue Phoenix, ignoring orders from her surly old Prian captain?

Coldhand ran his fingers down the length of the barrel again.

There were other fainter marks in the gray metal. Many of them were older than he was, carved there long before the gun passed to a young Logan Centra. It was an heirloom, like all police weapons. Three generations of Prian cops had worn it before him. But even this Talon-9 had been the newest, most powerful laser pistol in the Highwind precinct.

When I graduated, the others insisted I take it, Logan thought. *I was the best shot. I deserved to carry the newest Talon, they said. When I showed Vorus, he grinned and slapped my back so hard I almost fell over. They were all so proud of me.*

Returning to Prianus would be complicated. There were people who remembered him there, who would recognize Logan as a traitor to the Prian police. If any of the other cops knew Logan was back on their homeworld, there would be duels, at least. They might even try to arrest him. He was a thief, after all. Both his gun and ship were the property of the Prian police.

Coldhand dropped the Talon into its holster. There were other considerations, too. Being a criminal on Prianus meant that he wouldn't be able to use the controlled landing fields. There were plenty of other places to set down his Raptor, but not many where it would be safe. Prians would steal anything that wasn't nailed down, camouflaged and protected by force. Securing the Raptor was going to be expensive, considerably narrowing the profit margin on the endeavor. But if the Nihilists proved half as interesting as Maeve had been, then they would be worth it.

On the desk, his computer chirped to let Coldhand know that it had received a file. He went to the desk and opened it. The screen glowed with the blue and green Alliance auroch masthead above a short notice of compliance from the Axis officer on duty.

The attached file was small and Coldhand read through it in a few minutes. Sunlight streamed in through the window behind him and reflected no glare across the polarized monitor, but prickled warmly against the back of his neck.

Police and CWAAF confirmed Coldhand's suspicions, or at least offered no contradictions. The Alliance had picked up a few Nihilist sympathizers on Axis, but further questioning revealed no actual connection to the cult. Gavriel and his madmen were not on Axis.

There was nowhere left to look. It was time for Logan to make the long flight back home.

[8]

RUINS

"It's easy to die for your people, Consul Varrin. But can you kill for them? Harder still, can you live for them?"

- JULIUS FERRO, PRIAN CONSUL (109 PA)

Gavriel stood at the edge of the shattered floor. One of the frequent groundquakes had torn the building open like an oversized paper sack, spilling out everything inside. Concrete and rusting reinforcement bars lay scattered all around. Linoleum curled in discolored strips at the base of cracked and uneven walls. Every window gaped emptily, glass long ago reduced to sharpened shards that gleamed dully among the refuse. Bent and groaning iron beams ran through the walls, the last failing bones in the sagging slab.

Someone lived here once. The building used to be one of the ubiquitous residence blocks, a termite mound of cheap apartments. A framed photograph still clung crookedly to one of the walls and fading silhouettes clustered in the middle of the picture. They posed with comically flailing limbs in a campsite of tall, thin trees and triangular tents. Their faces were all long gone, bleached into ghostly emptiness by the colorless sunlight streaming in through the torn and broken walls.

A cold, biting wind tugged at Gavriel's black robe. The orange setting sun haloed him in celestial fire and turned him into a dark silhouette, an eclipse forced unnaturally into the shape of a man.

The city below was a tiny, crowded thing, pressed uncomfortably close into the valley between steep, rocky mountain spires. The buildings were all ugly and too narrow, each squashed tightly between their neighbors. A million crooked chimneys covered the city in a dirty shroud of gray smoke. Dim car tail lights choked the crowded streets and even from his high vantage point, the honking horns and angry, shouting voices floated up to Gavriel's ears.

Every line of the city was jagged, cut and torn by the unsettled centuries. No one repaired them. There was no money. Even the mountains were broken, settled and then sundered once more.

"Anaa'ma vanii."

At Gavriel's command, a glimmering splinter of glass flung itself off through the wide crack and out into the city. It shone in the sun for a fraction of a second and then vanished into the distance.

Gavriel tucked his arms into his sleeves. He was stronger now, his magic more powerful than ever, but his body was still old – over a century old – and frustratingly frail. Gavriel had no intention of letting an errant chill kill him yet. There was far too much to do.

A soft fluttering behind him made Gavriel turn around. Xartasia stood behind him, perfect and lovely as an angel, even surrounded in ruin. Her white dress and wings seemed untouchable by the grime. Only her long, inky black hair had anything like color. And, of course, her beautiful violet eyes. The Arcadian princess curtsied deeply to Gavriel.

"You wished to see me?" she asked.

Gavriel looked outside again. "I can't believe I'm back here."

Xartasia stepped up beside him and followed his gaze. "Does it not remind you of your own homeworld?"

"Zeos was a paradise compared to this cesspool." He swept his age-spotted hand across the cityscape outside. "*This* is the problem, princess. Do you know what the death rate is on this planet? One in four by age forty. One in three by sixty years. A quarter will die in accidents. A fifth in assorted criminal acts or their ridiculous duels. Almost a third will die of disease."

"They are suffering," Xartasia agreed. "It seems a poetic home for you and your followers, Gavriel."

"I thought so, too, the first time I came to Prianus," he said, shaking his head. The wind changed direction, carrying the sounds of the city away. Suddenly, all Gavriel could hear was the creaking of fir trees and the lonely calls of hunting birds. "There are two kinds of Prians: the desperate and the noble. It's the second that causes me no end of trouble."

Xartasia pursed her lips and said nothing.

"Staying here is going to be difficult," Gavriel said. "But it is only a temporary home, a moment to stop and prepare ourselves before we take to the stars one last time. Even this broken ruin still has something to offer us. How many Arcadians are there on Prianus?"

"We are still receiving numbers," Xartasia answered. "But about two hundred thousand. Surely, one of those will suit our needs."

"Yes. We just need to find them."

[9]
PRIDE

"Love is like nothing else. Without water, it will not wilt. Without food, it will not die. It will languish alone within us, awaiting its chance to bloom. Sounds like a virus to me."

- GRUTH ROMMIK, LYRAN ENGINEER (232 PA)

Xen's team kept largely to themselves during the long twenty-day journey from Tynerion to Prianus. Enu-Io – dubbed *Big Blue* by Gripper – and Phillip were quiet by nature and spent most of their time secluded in their bunks or in the mess, reading through data-dexes.

Gruth prowled the Blue Phoenix with his brown tail curled. If possible, the Lyran engineer was even more unpleasant in space than he had been on the ground. Gruth complained about everything. The Blue Phoenix was too small and the air reeked of chemicals. He was allergic to Maeve's feathers. What did the fairy even do on the ship? Duaal's flying was too rough and Gripper's repairs made the whole Blue Phoenix ring like a bell. Everything that Enu-Io read was juvenile, unproven drivel. Every meal that Phillip prepared tasted like a dry sponge.

Enu-Io endured his colleague's complaints in stoic silence, but Gruth's abuse often drove Phillip nearly to tears. Panna did her best to soothe the Lyran. Gruth made it perfectly and loudly clear that he didn't appreciate her attempts to play psychologist, but Panna stubbornly argued her case each time until Gruth threatened to shove her out an airlock. After each shouting match, he always seemed to feel a little better.

When Panna wasn't busy fighting with Gruth – despite the ever-rising volume of their arguments, she never showed any sign of being particularly upset by them – she avoided Maeve. Every time the Arcadian came into a room, Panna made some excuse to leave. Whenever Maeve could catch Panna's eye, the human paled and hurried off without explanation.

True to his word, Xen spent most of his time indulging his near-endless curiosity about Duaal and Gripper. But rather than speak to the two oddities himself, Xen preferred to question Xia about them. She didn't mind answering, though Duaal chafed at the inattention and Gripper was frantic.

A week out from Tynerion, Xen was still fascinated. When the crew and their passengers gathered for dinner one evening – an artificial construct of time in the endless dark of space – the Ixthian steepled his fingers and looked over them at Xia.

"I don't know what's waiting for us on Prianus, but this trip has already more than paid for itself," he said.

"Maybe for you, professor," Gruth growled. He pointed with his snout across the table at Enu-Io. "I'm getting tired of smelling this one every damned day. Can't he bunk with someone else?"

"If you were Dailon, you would find my scent irresistible," Enu-Io answered smoothly.

"Don't pay attention to Gruth," Panna said with a nod. "He's just grumpy because he's astrophobic."

Gruth laid his ears back flat on his skull and snarled at Panna.

"The only space that frightens me is the empty one inside your skull!" he snarled.

"Get a hold of yourself, Gruth," Xen said. He looked annoyed. "Panna's as intelligent as you are and twice as dedicated a student, but she lacks your mechanical expertise. I need you two to work together."

"It's fine, Professor Xen," Panna said. "We're not that fragile."

Gruth grumbled something under his breath, but his ears pricked back up to their normal elevation. Phillip, who had held his breath through the entire exchange, finally exhaled and continued eating.

Maeve looked over at Duaal, who appeared unperturbed by the argument. Did he not care or was he simply used to fights? Maeve supposed that the exchange had been shorter and more productive than most of the squabbles between herself and the mage.

All of that bile, all of that spite, and what did Maeve accomplish by any of it? She had only wanted to die, but Xartasia laughed at her pain and said that the fall of Arcadia was not her doing.

Maeve rubbed her fingers over the worn, chipped edge of the dinner table. She was condemned either way. Was Maeve the genocidal villain who brought the Devourers to Arcadia? There was no punishment enough for such a monster.

Or was she just a foolish, self-absorbed girl? If so, then she had tormented Duaal and put the rest of the Blue Phoenix crew in terrible danger for nothing. How could she ever make up for that?

She didn't even have the money to make amends to Tiberius for what she had done anymore.

Even as Xartasia forgave Maeve one terrible injustice – if it was even in the older princess' authority to forgive – she found herself entangled in another. The depressing thought made Maeve crave a needle of White to wipe away the pain. But no money meant no chems... Maeve wanted to cleanse herself of the drugs, and being too poor to pay for them certainly helped the process along.

Maeve rubbed her temple hard against a sudden ache in her skull and felt eyes on her. When she raised her attention from the tabletop, Panna looked away.

"Gruth's rudeness aside, this ship has been an endless source of curiosities," Xen said, continuing the prior conversation. "Xia told me about your unique education, Duaal."

The young mage took an interest for the first time all day. He sat up straight in his seat. "Oh, she did?"

"I would be fascinated to see what you can do. How many spells do you know? What exactly can they do?"

"Mostly fire and lightning spells," Duaal told Xen. "Gavriel was an expert killer. That's... most of what we did. I know a few other charms, though. How to inflict pain by stimulating the nerves and a nice little *push* spell."

He demonstrated with a couple of words in Arcadian – *"Anaa'ma vanii!"* – and the still air swirled around him. It ruffled Duaal's hair and set the napkins on the nearby table flying. Panna laughed in delight and applauded while Gruth snarled and snatched at his napkin with his claws.

"Very impressive," Xen said with a grin. "And your teacher used to cast these spells through you, correct? How did he do that?"

"I don't know," Duaal answered. "It was horrible, if that helps."

Xen's shiny silver brow furrowed. "Can you elaborate?"

Duaal shifted uncomfortably on the couch. The attention was apparently not as pleasant as he had hoped. Xia cleared her throat and curled her antennae toward Xen.

"That was all years ago now. Duaal was very young and probably doesn't recall very much," she said.

Xen nodded in understanding and turned his attention toward Gripper. The Arboran stood at the counter beside the cooktop, poking a serving spoon uncertainly at the thick stew. Phillip had almost managed to make it taste as though it was made of meat instead of brown protein paste.

"And an actual alien, a species I've never seen before," Xen said. "Simply amazing."

Gripper looked up, spoon dripping brown protein sludge onto the counter. He dropped it back into the stew and took a couple of large somatoes from the refrigerator. "Yeah, I thought so, too. We had no idea there were people living on other planets either. If I ever get home, I'm not sure anyone will believe all this."

"There's been no discovery like you in centuries," Xen said. "Study of your physiology and genetics would tell us a great deal about your species and your planet."

"Really? It would?" Gripper asked. He sat down next to Maeve. "Like what?"

"An examination of your lungs might reveal differences in your native atmosphere. Obviously, it's close enough to CWA standard that you can breathe. But *how* close? And your bones will be quite telling about the gravity of your homeworld..."

"My bones? You want to look at my bones?" Gripper looked around the room, searching for help.

Xia came to his rescue. She touched Xen's elbow gently. "I don't think that's necessary."

"Thank you!" Gripper said.

"I took several samples when he came on board," Xia told Xen. "I've still got his complete redprint on file."

Xen smiled. "You do? May I take a look?"

"Now?" Gripper objected. "But we're still having dinner!"

"I'm done eating anyway," said Xia.

Xen offered his elbow and she took it. Panna jumped up.

"Mind a little company?" she asked. "I'm curious, too."

Xen beckoned over his shoulder. "Come along, then."

Enu-Io and Gruth looked at each other, then followed Panna as she chased after her teacher, leaving Phillip alone with the Blue Phoenix crew. He noticed everyone looking at him and held up his hands.

"I'm just a geologist," he said. "But I made pudding for dessert. Anyone else want some?"

"She spends all day with Shorts!"

The engine room was almost as large as the mess, but with far less space to move around. It was full of machinery, canisters, pipes, ducting, dials and controls. In the center loomed the bulky engines themselves, massive cylindrical constructs of fibersteel, copper and ceramic. They thrummed loudly, providing a mechanical backbeat to a symphony of grinding, buzzing, clunking and clanking.

A wide workbench filled the remaining space. Pieces of a half-disassembled device lay scattered across the top. It was as long as Maeve's arm and twice as wide, full of circuit boards and alternating green and red wires. Maeve looked around for somewhere to sit, but the room was crowded and Gripper was pacing, so she stood awkwardly in the doorway.

"Xia has not seen Xen in years," Maeve said. She had to shout to make herself heard over the engines. "They were close friends once, and her desire to spend time with him is easy to understand."

"But they were... you know... together," Gripper groaned. He clutched a huge wrench to his chest as he paced. "What if... what if he's trying to get Silver to fall for him again?"

"I doubt that."

"But what if he is?"

Gripper stopped pacing and threw his wrench to the floor. It rang off the fibersteel mesh and made them both wince. Maeve picked at an orange stain on the doorframe for a long moment, trying to figure out what to tell her anguished friend.

"Your challenge remains the same in either case," she answered at last.

Gripper looked down at Maeve. "My challenge?"

"Xia does not know your affections. You must show her," Maeve told him. "Orthain courted me for a year."

"A year?"

"Two hundred and eighty-eight days of gifts and songs, dancing under the pale starlight. And we shared our oathsongs under Aes' bright eye."

"I don't think I can dance," Gripper said unhappily. He looked down at his huge, calloused feet. "I can't sing, either."

"It is the spirit of the thing, the chase. If Xia does not know your heart, then you must show it to her!"

Why hadn't Maeve thought of it before now, every time Gripper watched Xia with his huge, love-struck eyes? The pain of her own losses had blinded her to hope.

The Arboran was nodding as he thought about what Maeve said. He picked his wrench back up and cradled it in his claws.

"You're right, Smoke," Gripper said. "I'm a catch, right? I'm... I don't know... exotic?"

"You are," Maeve agreed. "Xen will find it difficult to compete."

"Yeah. Yeah!"

Gripper grinned and, contrary to his earlier protestations, spun in a pirouette. The mechanic brandished his wrench and turned his attention back to his messy workbench. He grabbed a large datadex and a bent stylus, talking to himself as he got to work, designing... something.

Despite the noise and heat of the engine room, Maeve lingered. She had no other pressing duties right then and it was nice to see Gripper happy. Her friend hadn't been happy since Professor Xen set foot on the Blue Phoenix.

Maeve only wished it was so simple to improve Tiberius' spirits. Nothing had been right with him since Stray. Since Kessa and flying illegally away from Axis.

I did not see it. I was too involved within myself, Maeve thought. Everything always came back to that, it seemed.

When Maeve first brought Kessa to the ship, Tiberius protected her. He was a Prian cop and would have done anything to help Kessa and her baby. But now Kessa and her family were gone, leaving Tiberius alone with his shame.

Superluminal flying was boring, but Tiberius was convinced that it was good practice. At the end of the second long week, Duaal sat at the controls in the Blue Phoenix's cockpit, occasionally checking the instruments. The only change was the numbers ticking slowly by on the taximeter.

Duaal leaned back in the copilot's chair, worn by years of just this kind of practice until no one else could sit in it comfortably. But it wasn't comfortable for Duaal now, either. He closed his eyes and rubbed them uselessly.

It was another headache, the second one this week. The pain was an almost tangible thing – a hard ball of tight, knotted brain matter between Duaal's temples. It pressed at the back of his eyes and made his nose burn acidly, like it was bleeding, but there was no trace of red. The pain was almost enough to make Duaal scream, but it never lasted for long. Just a few seconds – maybe a minute – and then it always vanished.

Thank God. The last thing Duaal wanted was to go shrieking around the Phoenix for everyone to hear.

And the pain was fading even now, leaving as mysteriously as it had come. Duaal supposed he should talk to Xia, but he didn't want her or anyone else to think him weak. He could handle it.

The headaches had started about six months ago, just a week after Gharib. The first time, the pain had been so sudden and so shocking in its intensity that Duaal had screamed. And then kept screaming until his throat was raw. But he had been alone in the Blue Phoenix that night, while everyone else was off visiting Maeve at the hospital. Only Orphia had heard Duaal. She had clawed and screeched behind the door to Tiberius' room for a half hour after it was all over.

Duaal glanced sidelong at the hawk, perched on the back of Tiberius' shredded chair. She glared straight ahead with clouded black eyes, oblivious – or uncaring – of Duaal's suspicion.

"There aren't as many stars in the sky there, but the air up in the mountains is so thin and clear that they glow like fire. They look so close that you swear you could reach up and touch them. I've been to twenty-seven worlds and none of them have a sky quite like Prianus."

Tiberius was talking about his homeworld again. It wasn't the first time Duaal heard about the wonder of the Prian skies. The perfect, endless black. The diamond-glittering stars. Polar auroras like the bridal veils of old heathen gods.

"Some of the highest mountains in the entire galaxy are back on Prianus," Tiberius said. "Mount Vessan is over fifteen miles high. There's so little air up at the top that most atmospheric ships can't make the flight."

Duaal listened, but his eyes kept drifting shut. "Sounds... big."

"The Spiral Falls are in the Oak District, where I used to work. Have I told you about them?" Tiberius asked. He didn't wait for the answer, which was *yes*. "It's the cinder cone of an ancient volcano. One of the glacial melt rivers cuts waterfalls in a spiral all around the mountain."

Duaal's boots thumped to the floorplates as he turned to look at Tiberius.

"If you love the wonders of Prianus so much, why aren't you more excited to go back?" he asked. "You've been raw about it ever since Xia told us about it on Axis."

But a monotone beeping forestalled Tiberius' answer. He sat up and glared at a round yellow light that blinked on one of the control panels. The discolored label read *vpA pressure*.

"Damn!" Tiberius said. "Did Gripper check the carbon filters?"

"Maybe he forgot to," Duaal answered. "He's been working on something for the last few days. I have no idea what."

"Maeve!" Tiberius bellowed.

He stomped out of the cockpit in search of his first mate. Duaal sat alone amidst the controls of the Blue Phoenix, wondering why Tiberius was yelling for Maeve instead of the engineer. Sometimes it was a miracle anything got done on the Blue Phoenix.

Maeve made her way aft, toward the engine room. Panna stood in the fibersteel corridor, looking over Phillip's shoulder and pointing to something on his datadex.

"Is that close enough to cause any problems with the densito-meters?" she asked.

"Not unless there's a groundquake," Phillip told her. "But then, you're going to have a lot more to worry about from rockfalls than instrumentation failures."

"That's reassuring," Panna said with a laugh.

Even in the dim, dingy light of the narrow hallway, her blonde hair shone like polished gold. The girl was irritatingly pretty, with a delicate, heart-shaped face and wide emerald eyes. Panna heard footsteps and turned those green eyes on Maeve's gray ones. The human's jaw clenched and she hurried through the nearest open door. Phillip blinked in surprise, waved shyly and then followed Panna to finish their conversation.

Maeve stood in the suddenly empty passageway for a moment, shaking her head, and then headed down the hall to the engine room.

The Arcadian held her wings out awkwardly behind her to prevent them from dragging along the stained floor or tangling in the bundles of wire hanging from the ceiling. The ship's mechanic sat on a stool at one end of the workbench, perched on the too-small seat like an owl in a treetop. He didn't seem to notice Maeve's entrance or hear her calling his name.

"Gripper?"

He started and jumped up to his feet. "Smoke! There you are. Come look!"

Gripper held out what seemed to be a small computer monitor attached to a metal cone stuffed with a jumble of circuit boards all wired together. Maeve had absolutely no idea what she was looking at, but Gripper appeared quite pleased with himself.

"What is it?" she asked.

"Isn't it obvious?"

"Not at all."

"This here is part of Silver's polytomograph," Gripper told her, pointing to the conical section of the device. He carefully pulled aside some of the wires so that Maeve could see the disk-shaped battery inside. "I've got a smaller power supply in here and a screen up on top."

"I still do not understand."

"It's portable now!" Gripper announced, brandishing his new creation. "I just need to put on backing and a handle on the bottom. Then it's done!"

"Is it a gift for Xia?" Maeve asked. "A token of your affections for her?"

"Of course! Do you think she'll like it?"

"I have no idea," Maeve answered. "But Tiberius requested that I speak to you. Is there time now?"

"Uh, sure. I guess so."

Gripper looked down at the polytomograph in his huge hands. He was eager to get back to work, but Maeve gingerly pushed the partially disassembled electronics aside and sat up on the edge of his workbench.

"Is Claws mad at me?" Gripper asked.

"The captain is often angry," Maeve said. "Tiberius knows that he is a difficult man, so he asked me to speak to you. He claims to have told you to look after the carbon processing."

"I did!"

"There is a system warning on his controls."

Gripper slapped one huge hand against his forehead. "Right! I didn't load the new filters. The transducting is still empty. Great Green, I'm sorry. I can't believe I forgot about that!"

"You have been distracted lately."

"I have not!"

Maeve arched her black brows at him. Gripper sighed.

"Maybe a little. But you have to admit, it's going to be worth it!" With a grin, he held up the polytomograph again. "I'll go load the filters, and then finish the backing. I can give it to Silver tomorrow!"

"I hope she likes it as well as you do," Maeve said.

It wasn't the sort of gift she had in mind to court Xia, but who knew what sorts of things coreworlder women enjoyed?

Xia leaned over Xen's shoulder. Gripper's redprint was displayed on the computer screen, filling the monitor with a densely packed map of code. Xen pointed to one of the sectors. Even after two weeks of looking at the Arboran's genetics, taking advantage of every free moment that he could find, Xen was still just as excited as a first-year student.

"Look at that!" he said.

"At what?" Xia asked, squinting. "That's not an active sector. It's all just spacer code."

Active sectors coded for actual proteins and physical structures, but they made up only part of a genetic strand, and not the largest part. The working sectors were all separated from one another by long segments of dead spacer code, which represented nothing that ever manifested in the organism's growth. Medical doctors had no reason to study the useless junk code, but archeogeneticists did a great deal of their work with it.

"This line here is *right* out of a human redprint," Xen told Xia. He underlined a short string of characters with a silvery finger. "Amazing!"

"That's a pretty small section, Xen. We share more in common with bees than Gripper does with humans. It could be random."

"It could," Xen agreed with a shrug. "But it's worth looking at."

"You spent a year staring at the redprint for the Vanoran wolf. All it told you was what we already knew," Xia said. "Where did you even get that, anyway? Wolves went extinct on Axis two centuries ago."

"The Axials built up an extensive genebank during their expansionist period, when they colonized Cyrus and Tynerion. Most of the bank is still intact on Tynerion." Xen winked at Xia and touched a sly finger to the side of his nose. "And I'll have you know that I won an impressive grant for that analysis."

Xia scoffed. "For a reminder that all wolves in the galaxy are related to the Lyrans? Everyone knows that. They must have been looking for a charity case that semester."

She ruffled Xen's short white hair.

"I'm not a charity case," Xen said primly, but he was smirking. "I am a brilliant archeologist and geneticist. I'm head of my department at a prestigious Tynerion college. In any case, that's not what I wrote about."

"Vostra Nor isn't that prestigious. What *did* you write about?"

"If you hadn't gone off to play pioneer on Koji, I would have asked you to go to the award dinner with me," Xen said. "The dean read the synopsis there. What I proposed was not that the Vanoran wolves were just related to Lyrans and other lupines, but are actually their primary ancestor."

Xia blinked and her eyes whirled orange in disbelief.

"The primary ancestor?" she asked. "You mean... you mean that all other wolf species are *descended* from the Axial breed? How could that be?"

"Axis has a long and complex history," Xen answered. "They've been through five dark ages, Xia. And those are just the ones we know about. It's entirely possible that this is Axis' second or third generation of space travel."

Xia stroked one of Xen's long, delicately arched antennae.

"Alright," she said. "I suppose you are a little brilliant."

"A little." Xen glanced at a clock in the corner of the medbay. "We can pick this up after dinner tonight, my dear, but now I need to lend my brilliance to my students for a few hours. We'll be on Prianus in just four more days and I need them to be ready."

"You don't even know what they've found in those mountains," Xia reminded him.

"All the more reason I need my team ready to handle anything. God only knows what the Prian team has found and how they've treated it."

"It doesn't sound like you have much faith in the locals."

"With all my respect to Captain Myles, I doubt the Prians would have asked for help from Tynerion if they could handle the find on their own. The colleges of Prianus are hardly the highest centers of learning in the galaxy."

Xia raised an eyebrow. "I wouldn't say that too loudly. Prians are a proud race."

"Perhaps. But pride is the enemy of good scholarship," Xen said philosophically.

Xia swatted the back of his head. "You're going to get yourself shot on Prianus talking like that."

"The Prian police are legendary in their stoic attention to duty. I expect to be well protected." Xen stood and stretched. He gave Xia a speculative look. "I know it's been a while since college, my dear.

Medicine was always your love, but you used to have an interest in archeology."

"I catch up on the journals when I have a chance," Xia said with a shrug. Archeology had been a hobby. She always meant to volunteer for a student dig, but medical studies ate up too much of her time. "I'm a little surprised that I missed your thesis, actually."

Xen's eyes darkened. "It was published while you were a pirate prisoner. I can get you a copy, if you like."

"I would enjoy that," Xia answered. "Do you still want to see what that sector of Gripper's redprint looks like? I can sequence it, if you like."

"I'd like that very much, my dear."

"Right over here." Xia gestured Xen over to another counter, this one lined with a number of different imagers. She stopped, frowning. "Wait, what happened to my polytomograph?"

She stared at one of the machines. The side panel was gone and bare wires spilled out onto the countertop like intestines from an evisceration. With an effort, Xia turned the polytomograph up onto its side and peered inside. The case was a heavy box of heusion alloy, but little more. It was empty.

"Does this sort of thing happen often?" Xen asked curiously.

Xia sighed and replaced the polytomograph on the counter. It wobbled. There was something underneath, something that had been wedged behind that machine, but rolled free when she moved the polytomograph. It was a strangely disproportionate screwdriver, with a small, slender head and a huge, claw-scarred handle.

"Does that belong to your mechanic?" Xen asked.

Xia turned away and strode out into the close fibersteel corridor. "Gripper!"

Her furious shout echoed through the Blue Phoenix.

———— • • • ————

"Where's Xia?" Duaal asked later that evening. "I thought she was on dish duty tonight."

Gripper winced. He stood over the sink, scrubbing the dinner dishes. The green fur covering his forearms was dark and matted with water.

"Um... I gave her a present," he sighed.

"Must have been some present."

Duaal laughed and left Gripper alone with the dishes.

The day before the Blue Phoenix was scheduled to land on Prianus, Tiberius called Maeve up to the cockpit again.

"Gripper intended only to–" she began, trying to stave off any argument.

"I need you to go talk to Panna," Tiberius said.

"Why is that?"

"Do you have to question *every* order?" Duaal asked, sitting next to the captain.

"I am not questioning the validity, simply the purpose," Maeve said. She hated the angry tightness in her own voice. She had come ready to avoid a fight, but she found herself drawn into one anyway. Why did Duaal have to attack her at every turn?

And why did she always fight back?

"I want you two – and anyone else Panna thinks necessary – to double-check their equipment," Tiberius told Maeve. "It's been a long flight and they need to make sure nothing's shifted or settled. It's all got to be secure for the landing."

Maeve nodded. Professor Xen was still busy with Xia, much to Gripper's chagrin, and Panna seemed to handle most of the logistical details of the archeologist's mission.

"I will speak with her, if I can," Maeve said.

"If you can?" Tiberius furrowed his lined brow.

"Panna dislikes me. She avoids me as though I might somehow infect her," Maeve said bitterly.

"You're imagining things."

"No. Maeve's right on this one," Duaal said. "Panna hates being in the same room as her."

It stung no less coming from Duaal's mouth. Maeve thrust her hands into the pockets of her patched spacer's pants.

Tiberius frowned. "Do you want me to talk to her?"

"No!" Maeve said it far more sharply than she had intended and flicked her wings in irritation. "I have few enough duties on this ship and I will do them."

After a short search, Maeve found Panna climbing the stairs leading down into the cargo bay. Maeve stood at the top, blocking Panna's way. The pretty human girl stopped mid-step, approaching Maeve no closer.

"Can I help you?" she asked in a flat, breathless voice.

"Tiberius sent me to help you ensure that all of your team's gear is secured. It has been in this hold for some time, unchecked. It would be a pity for your provisions to make most of the journey intact, only to break in tomorrow's landing."

"I... I'm sure it's just fine."

"It is better to check." Maeve tried to sound pleasant. "There is nothing else happening today. We can finish the task quickly."

Panna wouldn't look her in the eye. "Sure. There's a lot of heavy stuff and chemicals. I'll check it myself. You don't need to help. I can call Enu-Io."

Maeve's whole body went hot and prickly with a sudden fury. She spread her wings and fanned her feathers in a white halo. She stomped down the stairs, boots ringing loudly on the fibersteel, and stood face-to-face with Panna. The human was only barely taller than Maeve.

"My wings make me no more foolish or clumsy than you are," she shouted. Panna winced. "Dislike me and my kind all you wish, but you and I have jobs to do! Let us finish them and then I will leave you alone once more to loathe me in solitude."

Panna recoiled as though struck. Her face went pale and her mouth worked for a long moment without managing any words. At last, Panna nodded and climbed unsteadily back down into the Blue Phoenix cargo bay.

Maeve followed her and over the next hour, they checked each of the archeologists' crates. A few had shifted under their orange nets, but Maeve and Panna muscled each one back into position and tightened the straps.

Panna sheepishly pointed out a half-dozen cases of solvents, slides and chemicals. All of the plastic containers were intact, but the pressure fluctuations on the ship had cracked three of the glass ones. Maeve held them delicately while Panna wound the fractured glass in an epoxy-coated tape packed for just such an occasion.

They worked in near silence. Panna spoke only when she had to. Maeve was content with her victory, such as it was, and when they were done working, she left Panna alone in the cargo bay.

[10]

FACES

"The cost of keeping a secret never stops rising."

Gavriel sat on the edge of the collapsed couch and squinted critically at the figure kneeling before him. The man wore a frayed black robe that fluttered like a funeral shroud in the frigid drafts sifting in through the cracked walls.

"Look at me, Arkan," Gavriel commanded.

Arkan raised his face to his master. He was only thirty-four, but looked considerably older. The death of his infant daughter – at his own hands – left lines at his brow and a dark, haunted look in his eyes.

Arkan was from the farm colony of Cyrus. He had broad shoulders and a muscular build, but without the profoundly powerful look of a high-gravity native like those from Hadra and Orsin. The sun had darkened his skin and lightened his hair to a middling blond. Arkan could never pass for an actual Prian, not under scrutiny, but he would attract little attention among them.

"Do you understand what you're looking for?" Gavriel asked.

"Yes, Lord Gavriel," Arkan said. He bowed his head again.

"You will defer to the Arcadians. I'm sending you to support them, not command them. Can you do that?"

A muscle twitched in the farmer's jaw, but he nodded. "I can, Lord Gavriel. If you say I must, then I will do whatever the bird-backs tell me to."

The man's bigotry was annoying, but his loyalty was stronger than his stupidity. Arkan would do his job. Gavriel dismissed him with a wave of his hand.

"Go change your clothes and then join the fairies in the Arcadian quarter," he said. "Be careful and be discreet."

"Yes, Lord Gavriel."

Arkan rose, bowed and then left. A pair of hooded Emberguard flanked the splintered door, as still and silent as statues.

"Your approach is too hesitant, Gavriel."

Xartasia stood primly a short distance away, holding her long wings delicately up off the dirty floor. In blatant defiance of Nihilist tradition, the Arcadian princess wore one of her pristine, expensive white dresses. This one was of pure white wool and trimmed in thick, soft fur. Xartasia's black hair cascaded over her high collar in artfully arranged curls. Surrounded by filth and decay, her beauty was breathtaking.

"You are a man of power now," Xartasia told Gavriel. "What need do you have to hunt from the shadows? The Prians are a fearful people. They fear their world and each other. You are a wolf among sheep. Strike from a position of strength!"

Gavriel scowled at her. "This is your first visit to Prianus, isn't it? But I've been here before, princess. You have no idea what we're facing. You're right, in part. They're afraid of each other, and with good reason. The Prians are a brutal people and will not take kindly to anyone encroaching on their territory. These are not simple Sisterhood thugs, Xartasia. And the criminals here aren't the worst of our problems."

"You still fear the Prian police?"

"I do," Gavriel said. "And if you knew anything about them, you would, too."

"I have little faith in the tenacity of humans," Xartasia answered.

"Is that so?"

The Arcadian princess recoiled slightly at his tone. "There are... strong ones among all species."

"You're every bit as bad as Arkan," Gavriel said. "We all deserve the same death, princess."

"And you believe the Prian police will resist?"

"I've never known people as unyielding and dangerous as the cops of this world. With so much death and pain, this seemed a natural home for us. Prianus was the first world on which I tried to build my cathedrals. But the police hounded me night and day."

The three knelt at Gavriel's feet. Their red robes spilled around them like pools of blood. He touched each of their shoulders in turn.

"The police of Prianus hunt us," Gavriel said. The room rang with the deep, sonorous notes of his voice. "They are dedicated and devoted, men and women of honor and integrity on a world that tests them to their limits. They are fools. They don't understand the futility of their war, fighting against an impossible enemy. Fools, but fearsome fools. I need those equally strong and devoted. You are the best of my flock, the most deadly and the most loyal."

Duaal huddled for warmth beside the ashes of the dying fire. Gavriel kicked the embers, scattering sparks in every direction like tiny, short-lived red stars.

"We are still but embers in the dark, my children," Gavriel said. "If the police have their way, they will snuff out our light! I call upon you, my Emberguard, to protect us until the flame grows strong, bright enough to burn it all away."

The tallest of them was a long-limbed Mirran with hair that hung around his striped shoulders in dirty green tangles. Hallax drew his nanosword and planted the point against the floor.

"Through death and life, Lord Gavriel," he said. "We will serve and kill in your glorious name."

Gavriel made a low, growling sound of frustration. "My Emberguard held them at bay for three years, but in the end, the police came for us. I only narrowly escaped, with a handful of survivors."

He looked up at the two Emberguard beside the door. Hallax and an Arcadian man of surprisingly powerful build met his gaze unwaveringly.

"I've trained a new generation of Emberguard, my lord," Hallax said. His hair had lost some of its verdant luster since Gavriel first discovered him, and there were jagged scars through the brown stripes of his skin. "The police will not drive us off again, I swear it."

The Arcadian nodded, though his eyes were fixed on Xartasia.

"Through death and life," he said in awkward, halting Aver.

Hours later, Xartasia wandered aimlessly through the drafty gray halls of the crumbling apartment slab. Men and women of all races stood, hunched and lay in the shadows, wrapped in black robes like filthy ghosts haunting the ruins that had killed them. They bowed and whispered as Xartasia passed.

So many of the Nihilists were sick. They coughed and shivered, slumped against cracked walls and lying in creaking beds. Those who were not yet ill would be soon. Prianus teemed with a whole array of deadly pathogens and dozens of Nihilists had died in those first months after arriving on Prianus. They found more cold, stiff bodies every morning. If the Nihilists shared anything in common with the Prians, it was their familiarity with death.

Xartasia held her sleeve over her mouth and nose. It would do nothing at all to protect her from disease, but it blocked some of the smell. Even so, it was almost unbearable. There was no running water in the building. Whether quakes had sheered through the pipes or the city authorities had shut them off, Xartasia didn't know, but the result was the same. No showers or baths and no working toilets.

There was no washing away the smells of life and death.

There wasn't power, either. The Nihilists cooked and warmed themselves with open flames. One miserable woman ventured out to steal a battery-powered stove, but Gavriel had dictated that the Nihilists would take no unnecessary risks that might bring down the wrath of the Prian police. The transgressor had been punished, thrown into one of the deep crevices in the cracked foundation of their new home. Every night, Gavriel's Emberguard threw food and a bottle of water down to her.

Punishment in the Cult of Nihil was never death. As far as Xartasia knew, the woman was still down there, sobbing in the dark.

Though most of it had been spent to bring the Cult of Nihil to Prianus, there remained enough money – Xartasia's money – to buy some small necessities, but it was against their code to ease the burden of a painful life. Life was suffering, so the Nihilists suffered. Death remained their only release.

Xartasia climbed a narrow staircase that led out onto the apartments' slanted roof. The sudden glare of sunlight made the Arcadian princess slit her violet eyes nearly shut. She perched on the corner of the crumbling building, wings spread for balance. Icy wind ruffled her well-groomed feathers and streamed her long hair out behind her like a black banner.

The apartment block leaned dangerously out from the steep mountainside, overlooking the city. The entire building clung tenuously to the Kayton Mountains. Another quake might tear through the last bolts and topple the whole thing into the city below. Killing hundreds, Xartasia thought.

Yet the apartments remained. No one tore them down. Nothing was wasted on Prianus. There had been squatters living here before Gavriel and the Nihilists, people that had to be quietly removed.

Gavriel's transgressing stove-thief was not alone in her fetid crevice prison, though she was the only one still alive.

A gang of dirty, gangly teenage boys chased another child down the steep street, perilously close to the racing traffic. One of them caught up to their target and snapped a foot out in a hard, vicious kick. The younger boy tumbled, scraped along the asphalt and then skidded out into the road. A low-slung racer honked and swerved, but not fast enough. The car slammed into the boy, who flew back and smashed into the chipped sidewalk. Blood pooled around his shattered legs. He screamed for a few seconds before finally falling unconscious.

The pursuers and the car's driver paused, staring, and then scattered. Several minutes more passed before someone else pulled over, jumped out of his car and knelt over the dying boy beside the road. He shouted a frantic call into his com, but not until he had taken the injured boy's wallet. He was gone long before an ambulance arrived.

These were the people Gavriel feared will stand against them?

Xartasia turned away from the darkening red stain on the street and looked up into the sky. Birds and larger winged figures wheeled and dove. Arcadians. Over two hundred thousand of them lived on this horror of a planet – and most of those here in this city.

Not for much longer, if only Gavriel would act boldly...

But Xartasia dared not defy him. She needed Gavriel and the Cult of Nihil. She retreated back into the desiccated apartments. The police would arrive soon to investigate the boy's death. It would be wiser to remain hidden.

[11]
FORCES

"It's not the job of the police to convict a man. That's the lawyer's job. We just make sure he gets to the courthouse to face the law."

- HEON CERRO, PRIAN POLICE OFFICER (229 PA)

"In three, two, one... Alright, take us out."

At Tiberius' cue, Duaal pulled gently back on the controls and punched the large square button that dropped the Blue Phoenix out of superluminal flight. The multicolor kaleidoscope of SL lurched and gave way to the star-studded blackness of space. Fewer stars than the luminous skies of the deep core, Duaal noticed, and the blue-gray shape of Prianus loomed between the stars, a gunmetal crescent in the light of the pale primary star.

Prianus. I never wanted to come here again.

"Duaal!" Tiberius shouted.

"What?"

Duaal searched wildly. A huge, roughly oblong white object was hurtling toward the Blue Phoenix, pocked by craters and flashing with bright red and orange warning lights. They were closing on the rocky moon fast.

"Shit! Where did that come from?" Duaal shouted. He jerked back on the control yoke.

"What were you looking at? I told you to watch it! Trinus has an unstable... Damn it! Pull up!" Tiberius jabbed at buttons to regain primary control of the ship, but the moon was hurtling up to meet them too quickly.

"You told me when to drop!" Duaal cried.

"Just pull the hells up!"

The moon's gravity yanked on the Blue Phoenix, jerking it to one side and tugging hard opposite the internal gravnet. Duaal's stomach leapt up into his throat and he couldn't breathe. He shoved and strained against the moon's pull, but could not break free.

"I can't get us out!"

"Turn into the gravity well," Tiberius shouted. He yanked at a red-striped handle in the ceiling. "Turn!"

Duaal stopped pulling and jammed the yoke down. The Blue Phoenix jerked, rolled as it aligned with the gravity, and then finally smoothed out. The Prian moon's jagged surface raced along close beneath. Tiberius took a deep, rasping breath.

"Come up at twenty degrees," said the captain. "Fine. Now bring us up out of the well. Hold your vector. Don't fight the gravity."

Duaal did as Tiberius instructed. It seemed easy enough now. The Blue Phoenix arced gracefully around the moon and toward the dim gray disk of Prianus.

"I... I've got it," Duaal said.

The radio popped suddenly and a voice hissed with static over the channel. "Unidentified ship, this is Prian Orbital Control."

"Call it in again, POC," Tiberius said.

"We read a little trouble over one of the Trinus sensor outposts. Is everyone intact out there?"

Tiberius gave Duaal a pointed look before answering. "This is the Blue Phoenix. Sorry about that. My copilot was a little wobbly on the drop and we came in right over a moon."

"Hear that, Blue Phoenix." The woman on the other end of the connection had the same accent as Tiberius and seemed to recognize his in spite of the poor connection. "Are you on your way home, captain?"

"Not today," Tiberius answered, then had to repeat himself. "Not today. We're inbound to the northern Kayton Mountains. We have some passengers from Tynerion."

"Tynerion? I'd love to hear that story, if there was time. Your closest landing to the north Kaytons is going to be Pine Spire."

"Pine Spire? What's wrong with Pylos?" Tiberius asked.

"Quakes. They're still digging out the landing field there, but Pine Spire will only put you a little further south."

"Hear that, Control," Tiberius grunted. "When can we land? We only need a few hours to unload our passengers and help get their equipment up into the Kaytons."

"It's going to be a while," said the other Prian. "We've got a backlog of intersystem traffic."

"Is it that busy?" Duaal asked.

"No, but with Pylos down, we're flying into problems. Sorry, but they've got priority. I can put you down in Pine Spire in about two hours. Until then, keep a high orbit."

"Wilco, POC," Tiberius said.

He closed the channel and Duaal drew another breath to point out that the captain had, in fact, approved their flight plan, but Maeve appeared in the door. She rubbed a darkening bruise on the angle of her jaw.

"Our passengers are curious if they should prepare for their impending deaths," she said. "Can I tell them that they will not so easily avoid their work?"

"Everything's fine," Duaal answered quickly. "You can tell them that we'll be setting down in about two hours."

"We'll need to be ready for some ground travel to get them to their site," Tiberius said.

Maeve nodded. "I will inform Professor Xen. I suppose it was wise to check over the security of their equipment."

When she left again, Duaal sullenly released the controls and let Tiberius guide the Blue Phoenix down toward Prianus.

The skypads were a network of patched landing platforms all suspended between the sharp mountain crags above the city of Pine Spire. As Tiberius and Duaal set the Blue Phoenix down on one of the platforms, Gripper connected to the local mainstream and put in a call for the rented trucks to wait for them down in the city.

The crew met Xen and his team in the hold. Gruth shook his claw at Duaal for the rough SL drop, but the Lyran was still in a much better mood than he had been the whole trip. Together, they unfastened the cargo nets and loaded everything back onto null-inertia pallets.

Tiberius opened the airlock and lowered the ramp. A bone-chilling wind raced into the ship, carrying a few flecks of ice. Maeve waved to Gripper and Enu-Io as they guided the pallets down the ramp. Tiberius whistled for Orphia, who fluttered to a scarred pad of leather strapped to his shoulder.

Outside, the landing platform vibrated under their feet like a struck drumhead. Gruth looked queasy again.

"How do we get down from this damned thing?" he howled over the wind.

"We just need to get over there," Tiberius said.

He pointed across a trussled bridge to another platform bolted to the stony mountainside. A huge gondola ferried passengers and cargo away from the skypads, swinging and bumping down a cable as thick around as Maeve's waist.

"Why don't you people just use null-field lifts?" Gruth asked.

"Too expensive," Tiberius answered.

There was a long, cold delay as they waited for another group to load up their boxy gondola cart. When the next one arrived, a long-faced overseer hauled the squealing door open and – for a modest fee – helped the Blue Phoenix crew push and pull the equipment inside. The attendant slammed the door shut behind them.

The gondola lurched into motion. Cracked seals around the windows and doors let in gusts of icy wind. Maeve couldn't stop shivering. There was nothing like this frigid cold anywhere in the White Kingdom. She had dressed that morning as best she could for Prianus: two layers of pants, high socks and boots, a long-sleeved thermal shirt with a sweater and a long gray felt coat over *that* – all sliced up the back to make room for her wings. And she was still freezing.

Maeve stared out the gondola window. From high above, they had an impressive view of Pine Spire. Though the view was impressive, the city was not. It was small, even by Arcadian standards, but close-packed and densely populated as a beehive. Streets and gray-black buildings all crammed between sharp mountains and rivers that ran so swift and forceful that they were milky blue-white with trapped air.

At the bottom of the mountain, another rawboned Prian man took their names and told them that their rental trucks had been delayed. They waited on a sort of long porch made of cracked concrete until a caravan pulled up to the curb, cursing and shouting at other drivers. A dark-haired woman signaled them from the lead vehicle and didn't offer to help their customers load the trucks.

Xen handed out printed maps to the Kayton dig site and then the teams scattered, piling into each of the trucks. At his request, Maeve went with Gripper. She was the Arboran's second choice, but Xia wanted to spend these final hours with Xen, before the Blue Phoenix carried them all back into space. As they climbed up into the last truck, the driver winked at Maeve and then stared wide-eyed at Gripper.

"Bloody hells, what is that thing?" he asked Maeve, who struggled to find a comfortable place for her wings.

"An Ixthian experiment," she answered. It wasn't the first time she had used that particular lie. "Grown from an artificial redprint."

The driver whistled sharply. "Ain't never seen anything like it. Musta been one hell of a tube they grew you in, big fella."

"Uh, yeah," Gripper said forlornly.

"That what happened to your face? You get smashed up against the side?"

"Huh? What's wrong with my face?"

"Nothin' at all." The Prian driver fell strategically silent.

They followed the rest of the truck caravan through Pine Spire. Outside, Prians wrapped themselves in long coats, thick hats and scarves tucked into their collars. They squinted across their city streets with fear and suspicion as their birds wheeled through the faded blue sky overhead. Deep violet shadows lay over Pine Spire as Prianus' small white sun struggled to rise up over the needle-like mountains. Gripper, who had never been to Tiberius' homeworld, stared out the windows.

"Look up there! I've never seen mountains like those," Gripper said. He rubbed his shortened ear. "Is there anything at the top? Look at the trees. They stop only halfway up."

"Only one-fifth of Prianus is capable of supporting human life," Maeve told him.

"That's still more than Hyzaar, right?" Gripper asked.

Maeve shrugged. "Perhaps, but Hyzaar is a more temperate and hospitable world."

"No one ever called Prianus the bright spot of the galaxy," their driver agreed. "What brings you–?"

He shouted in alarm as a small, dented airplane dropped out of the sky, roaring down over the busy road. Thick black smoke trailed from one sputtering engine and the battered sides were scored by laser burns.

The airplane swooped to one side and grazed a tall starscraper. The wing tore through windows, spraying the city below in broken glass, then caught on something more substantial. Metal and by-standers shouted as the plane slammed into the side of the building and tumbled down toward the street.

Something metallic glinted in the billowing smoke. A battle-scarred Raptor fighter flew down from the shadow of the moun-tains and fired huge magclamps on thick cables. One of them arced off target, but three more slammed into the side of the falling plane.

The Raptor climbed sharply, yanking the other craft skyward. But under the tension of the clamps and cables, the plane's hull was peeling away like paper. It was never meant to be carried like this and was falling again, tugging the Raptor down with it.

Another pair of police Raptors dropped out of thin clouds and fired smaller, more carefully aimed clamps. These found secure anchors on the exposed frame and tugged the faltering airplane skyward again. As quickly as they had appeared, the three Raptors and their snared prisoner flew away again, vanishing off into the distance.

Maeve didn't realize that she had been holding her breath until she made herself relax and slumped beside Gripper, who was still staring in slack-jawed wonder at the aftermath of the scene. Their driver shook his fist and swore in equal measure at the police and their target.

The delay in traffic cost them another twenty cenmarks in fees, but by late afternoon, the trucks were out of Pine Spire and climbing up into the Kayton Mountains. The jagged spine of granite and green serpentine speared high into the clouds. Steep roads wove up into the clinging cold, through emaciated but tenacious forests of fir and aspen trees.

After a sidelong glance at their driver – who was absorbed by navigating the steep, icy mountain roads – Gripper twisted as much as he could in his seat, turning to face Maeve.

"I didn't get to give Silver the polytomograph," he whispered.

"I heard," Maeve said. The Blue Phoenix was a small ship.

"She came looking for it before I was done." Gripper rubbed his long ear nervously. "I've got to try something else, Smoke. What do you think?"

Maeve considered, chewing her lip as she thought.

"What about flowers?" she asked.

"Yeah, flowers!" Gripper forgot to whisper and brightened visibly. "That's great! Everyone loves sweets."

The Arboran licked his lips, suggesting that he was a perfect example of this universal truth.

"That... is not quite what I meant," Maeve said. "Even if it were, you may have to wait. I do not think that there are many flower sellers in the Prian mountains."

"I guess not..." Gripper looked out the window.

They were up above the trees. Some pale-leaved shrubs pushed tough, ropey roots through the rocks – and in a few places, the road – but little else grew so high in the mountains.

At the edge of the road, the ground dropped away steeply into the distance. Far below was the skirt of firs and pines, dark green and gray. Beyond that was a narrow, jagged valley, full of cluttered, blocky gray shapes. The city of Pylos, larger than Pine Spire but no more attractive.

At least the traffic up here was an improvement. In fact, Maeve had seen no other vehicles for hours. Not on the ground, at least. Like the birds they so loved, the Prians seemed to prefer flying to crawling over the ground. Gripper had his face glued to the window and pointed out another Raptor-styled fighter that flew overhead.

"That looks just like Coldhand's ship," he noted with obvious excitement.

"He stole it from this planet," Maeve said.

The truck driver gave her a strange look, but had to keep most of his attention on the aging, crumbling road.

There were no trees or plants of any kind now, only greenish lichen that covered the stones in dark, frondy blotches. Blue-white glaciers lurked in crevices and ravines like great, pale leopards, beautiful but deadly to the unwary traveler.

The trucks labored through the thinning air. Engines coughed and wheezed, slowing their progress to a crawl. At her driver's request, Maeve radioed up to Xen in the lead vehicle.

"Are we nearing our destination?" she asked.

"We should be there in about half an hour," Xen said. "I think. The signal is a little scattered this high up."

They carefully crossed an arched bridge over a deep crevice. It creaked ominously and swayed in the wind. Maeve looked down over the bridge's edge at the wisps of clouds that raced below and flashed with veins of white as they unleashed spitting flurries of sleet into the distant river.

Finally, the caravan came to a stop in a flat moraine of grainy gabbro. A row of heavily insulated white tent domes hunkered in the middle of the glacier-carved plain, alongside a pair of work-worn trucks and a scratched red and green car. The last of these was stenciled with large block letters: POLICE.

Maeve sat up from her tired, cramped slouch. What were the police doing up here?

When the caravan pulled to a stop and parked in a semicircle, Maeve and Gripper gratefully climbed out of their truck. The fairy slid on a patch of ice and beat her wings for balance, but the air was too thin. She fell to the frozen ground just as Duaal emerged. He took one look at Maeve and burst out laughing. A moment later, he was coughing as he tried to breathe at this high altitude and Maeve couldn't help a tiny smirk.

Xen walked toward the tents and put his hands to his mouth. "Doctor Kemmer Andus? Are you here?"

"First tent on the right!" answered a muffled voice from the indicated dome.

"Panna, will you take care of unloading?" Xen asked.

His assistant nodded. "Sure, professor."

Gripper remained to help Panna, but the rest followed Xen into the first tent on the right. Closer now, Maeve could see that it wasn't the domes that were white, but thick layers of frost that covered them. She touched it and came back with powdery, feathery ice on her gloves. Doctor Kemmer must have been up in these mountains for some time.

There were two human men inside, one dressed in the same sort of long coat and boots Maeve had seen back in Pine Spire. The other wore a long-sleeved uniform in dark blue with a Talon laser pistol on his hip. With the man's short blond hair and narrowed Prian eyes, Maeve felt a jolt of recognition like an electric shock.

Logan...?

But it wasn't Logan Coldhand, of course. This Prian man was older than her hunter and a burn scar along his cheek tugged one corner of his mouth down into a perpetual frown. There was an aged shield-shaped badge pinned to his chest, the brass even more scarred than the cop who wore it.

Either Kemmer Andus kept an incredibly messy house, or else something terrible had happened. The tent was full of overturned tables and datadexes scattered across the floor, many with screens spiderwebbed in cracks or entirely snapped in half.

Kemmer slumped in a folding chair, rubbing his eyes. Though he was probably about the same age as the police officer – somewhere in his late thirties – he wore his age much more handsomely. Kemmer had a square jaw and high cheekbones, roughened by a few days of stubble. His hair was a dark brown turned bronze at the tips by the sun. He looked up at the newcomers.

"Ah, you must be Professor Xen," he said in the increasingly familiar accented Aver. "I hope you brought a lepton microscope."

Xen blinked his colorful eyes. "Yes, I am. And we did."

"Good." Kemmer stood and smoothed his shirt.

"Why? Don't you have an L-scope here?" Xen asked.

"We did. It was stolen earlier this morning – along with some other equipment – while the rest of us were down below," Kemmer said. He went to one wall of the tent. There was a small hole in the insulation and a spray of dried blood around it. Kemmer wiggled one finger in the puncture. "They shot one of my diggers."

Xen paled. He couldn't seem to think of anything to say.

Tiberius sighed. "Don't know what exactly a lick-on microscope is, but it sounds expensive. It would be worth a trip up into these mountains to snare it."

"Yes. This is Captain Cerro," Kemmer said. He gestured to the blue-uniformed police officer. "He's taken my report, but he can't be bothered to stay to protect my dig or my base camp."

Cerro didn't flinch at the archeologist's bitterness. "We'll recover your equipment and bring in the guilty party as soon as we can, sir, but I'm afraid we can't spare the personnel to post a sentry. We have all of Pylos to protect."

"Welcome to Prianus," Kemmer sighed.

Tiberius grinned broadly at the younger cop. He extended his hairy, calloused hand. "Captain Cerro, is it?"

"It is." Cerro took Tiberius' hand firmly.

"Tiberius Myles. I was captain of the Blacktails before I retired."

Cerro smiled with half his mouth. "From the Oaks?"

"Those are my hawks, my fine hawks. I've been off-world for a few years now. How are they doing?"

"I don't get a lot of news all the way from Oak, but I'm sorry to say that the Blacktails got shot down last year. Only three of them survived. Actually, I sent one of my pilots out to shore up the new squadron."

Tiberius nodded heavily. "The hawks will keep flying, through high heaven and hollow hell."

Kemmer had been listening to the exchange with frank interest. "Captain Myles, if I understand this correctly, you used to serve in the Prian police. Right?"

"That's right," Tiberius answered.

"This isn't the first loss we've suffered and this expedition can't take much more," Kemmer said. "Captain, would you be willing to stay on to provide security for my project?"

Professor Xen tore his eyes from the blood on the tent wall.

"Yes," he added quickly. "I would be happy to pay you for your time. Please stay, Captain Myles."

"I don't know..." said Tiberius.

"We could use the work," Duaal told him. "Just fuel and food ate up a lot of Xen's money."

"Duaal's right," Xia said. Her antennae twitched. "And if Doctor Kemmer just lost a digger, I'd be happy to fill in."

"Do you have any experience?" the Prian archeologist asked.

"Only a few classes," Xia admitted with a shake of her head. "I don't have any field experience."

"Xia's a surgeon," Xen told Kemmer. "She's a fast learner and a light touch."

"If it means Captain Myles will stay, then I'll take it," Kemmer said. He ran a hand through his dark hair and looked at Tiberius again. "Well?"

"Maeve?" Tiberius asked.

She thought for a moment, considering the terrain outside. "You said that the crime was committed while you were down below. Where is your site, Doctor Kemmer? It seems that you have two locations to protect."

"That's correct," Kemmer answered. "There's the base camp up here, and then the actual dig site. It's sub-surface, down inside the mountain."

His tone became suddenly guarded. His eyes took on a glacial coldness that Maeve was all too familiar with. The Prians were a hard people, as stony as their homeworld.

"Protecting two fronts will be difficult, but if one of them is underground, it may make the task achievable," Maeve said. She counted off on her fingers. "We have to our benefit three combat-ready members of our crew."

"Three?" Tiberius asked.

"You, Duaal and myself."

Tiberius frowned and cast a sidelong glance at the Hyzaari boy. So did Kemmer, confusion written plainly across his face. Duaal straightened.

"Alright, but I want the two of us to handle most of it," Tiberius told Maeve. His tone brooked no argument. "Duaal, you're backup."

"Then you'll stay?" Xen asked intently.

"For..." Duaal said, hesitating as he twisted one of the golden buttons on his cuff. "For another four thousand cenmarks."

Xen and Kemmer exchanged a look.

"That would exhaust my remaining budget," said the Ixthian. "And then some."

"I have even less of an operating fund than you do," Kemmer snorted. "I can cover five hundred colour, and even that is going to come out of *my* pocket."

"We can pay three thousand cen, then," Xen said.

"That's fine," Tiberius agreed.

"When I've verified his identity, we can coordinate our efforts through Captain Myles," Cerro offered. "Mind if I get your badge number, sir?"

Cerro pulled a small datadex from a side pocket and scribbled down the number that Tiberius gave him.

"I'll call back as soon as we've got anything on your thieves," Cerro said.

The com on his belt buzzed insistently. Captain Cerro excused himself and went outside to take the call.

Kemmer glanced around the tent and put his hands on his hips. "Welcome to the team, Professor Xen. We've got a lot of work to do. Let's get started by bringing in your equipment."

"We're going to have to tell Gripper that we're staying," Duaal said. "No trees and we don't have a coat that fits him. Maeve, I nominate you to break the bad news."

"I hope you are braver if thieves return to this camp," she said.

But as they stepped out into the cold once more, Maeve called out to Gripper.

[12]
PAIN

"One who lies to herself cannot speak the truth."

- ALLONAR CAVAINNA, ARCADIAN MONARCH (5,104 MA)

On any civilized world, it probably would have been called torture. The flight from Sipho to Prianus was weeks long and Coldhand couldn't move during any of it. Not much, at least. Not enough. A combination of vitamins, nutrients and muscle stimulants kept his body from suffering the sort of withering that crippled and even killed early spacefarers.

But Logan's mind wandered. A cocktail of sedatives could have stopped that and were popular among long-range fighter pilots. Coldhand never took them.

He stared out into the scattered rainbows of superluminal flight without seeing them. In the six years since he had become a bounty hunter, Logan had never gone home. He barely thought about Prianus. He wasn't ashamed of his homeworld. He didn't hate it. Prianus was just a planet, like any other.

But now Coldhand found himself... What? Reminiscing...? Or daydreaming? There were memories waiting for him on Prianus.

It was easier, somehow, to think of them as memories instead of people. Jess Ephrya, the woman he was going to marry. His mother, Lynn Centra, who struggled alone to raise her son on a grocery clerk's meager paychip. Arctan Vorus, the old palaestrum master who taught a dirty-faced little boy how to be a man.

He didn't care what they thought of him now, Coldhand reminded himself, of the traitor who turned tail and vanished. It only mattered that they might become problems if they learned that Logan Centra had returned to Prianus.

They were pointless concerns, Coldhand told himself firmly. He ran metal fingers through his hair, lank with sweat from too long in the Raptor. Prianus wasn't the largest world of the Alliance, but even it had billions of citizens. There was no reason to believe that he would encounter anyone... anything that might cause a problem.

Still, he couldn't stop thinking about them. Not for the first time since beginning the journey, Logan found himself clenching his cybernetic hand and tapping his feet restlessly against the Raptor's deckplates.

All of this to hunt down the Nihilists. For a good chase.

For something... exciting.

This had better be worth it.

A warning beep from the navigational computer roused Coldhand from an uneasy half-doze. He had been dreaming... something about searching through a store full of caged birds for a white owl. The owl's sharp, sad gray eyes were the only thing Logan could remember when he sat up, but even those faded quickly. The whole cockpit smelled of recycled sweat.

He was entering the Prian system. Coldhand checked over his astrogation charts. All mapped comets, asteroids and moons were clear of his vector. Coldhand waited until the countdown hit zero, then shut off the superluminal engines. The sounds of the Long Wings pod was sucked away into the emptiness of space, but the down-cycling engines made the Raptor shiver.

Stars and moons leapt into focus outside, floating in the deep black of space. Prianus' far side faced the sun and the planet was a barely-visible crescent, a slender silver thread through the heavens. Satellites blinked in orbit like indecisive miniature stars.

Coldhand steered a wide course around the sensor stations on all three of Prianus' moons. If they picked up his ship, it would end up in a database somewhere and Coldhand wanted no record of his visit. There were blind, hidden routes, used by the smugglers he had hunted in this very ship back when he had two good hands.

Logan pulled into low orbit and then dropped down into the atmosphere at a shallow, oblique angle. Storm clouds streamed past the wings and beaded into streaking droplets along the Raptor's hull. A bolt of bright lightning lit the sky a sudden, blinding white and then the deafening crash of thunder buffeted the fighter. Logan banked with the tugging wind, letting gravity pull him down, and then he was free of the clouds.

He was flying over a dark tarn. The long, flat lake lay high in the mountains, flanked by steep shores covered in coarse white snow. Coldhand checked his instruments. He was closing in on his destination, the city of Blue Oak.

The Raptor crested a spine of sharp, glacier-carved stone. Blue Oak glowed through the heavy rain. The city stretched through the diamond-shaped valley and out into the nearby passes, looking by night like a huge, well-lit nerve cell.

Coldhand circled low over the city, alternately looking out the glassteel canopy and at his instruments. He found a small landing field outside Blue Oak, marked in the stormy night by a single bright yellow spotlight. The hunter called down, requesting clearance. A sleepy-sounding female voice told him to hold his damned vector while she waved another ship to the ground, then brought

Coldhand around and set him down in a gravel-strewn lot. Not an illegal port, exactly, but one of many private, family-owned plots. It was unlikely that their computers were connected to the planetary control stations.

Logan heaved himself out of the Raptor and thumped heavily to the ground. Prian ground. He was actually back on Prianus. Ice-cold rainwater soaked his hair, seeping down the back of his neck.

An adolescent boy – probably the son of the woman he had just spoken to – jogged up to Coldhand, carrying a datadex in a protective sleeve and shielding his face from the driving rain.

"I need to get your signature and fees," he said.

The boy wore a lightly armored vest and a gun tucked into his waistband. Coldhand took the datadex and had to press hard with the stylus to sign through the plastic cover. He signed his assumed name. The boy was looking at the fighter.

"Wow, is that a Raptor?" he asked, picking out the shape under the bulky Long Wings pod fitted over the hull. "Are you a cop?"

Coldhand thrust the datadex back at the boy, the wet plastic slipping in his cybernetic fingers.

"Yes." He didn't explain which question that was an answer to. "How much is parking?"

"Just eight cen a day."

That was three times what Logan had paid six years ago. Unless this little field charged a lot more than their neighbors, inflation was on the rise again. The bounty hunter tossed a white twenty-cenmark chip onto the datadex.

"I'll only be here a day, but I don't carry any smaller colour."

The boy's eyes widened a little. "We can't change this, sir."

The child was lying, but Coldhand shrugged. So was he.

"Fine," Logan said. "Have you got showers? I've been flying a long time."

"Inside there," the boy answered, pointing toward the shadowy shape of a small building squatting beside the spotlight. "Showers, latrines and a terminal connected out to the mainstream if you need to catch up. We can call you a car, if you like, but we don't have any rooms."

Coldhand wasn't tired. "I don't need one. I'll call for anything else myself. Go back to bed."

The boy hurried back the way he had come, eager to get out of the rain. Coldhand locked up his Raptor and splashed through the muddy puddles toward the showers. His legs felt like old rubber. The rain hissed off the slowly circling spotlight and filled the air with steam.

The showers were plain and far from private, but it was the middle of the night. The pilot of the ship grounded just before the Raptor briefly visited the bathrooms, but then left to pursue her own business. After Logan thoroughly scrubbed himself clean in the tepid shower, he dressed in a fresh pair of pants and a thick, long-sleeved shirt.

He went to the offered terminal and pushed the stool away with one bare foot. He had been sitting for weeks. The computer was a small machine, bolted into a thick plastic case on the wall of the little hospitality house. Coldhand made a quick search through the mainstream, but as expected, found nothing helpful. Gavriel was being subtle and quiet. There was nothing in the news but outdated reprints of the wire stories from Axis and Stray.

Where to begin...? In the morning, he would go into Blue Oak to ask around for anything that had not made it onto the mainstream, but Coldhand's hopes were not high. Even if the Nihilists moved right into the middle of the city, chances were low that anyone would even notice. The cultists were sickly, murderous chem addicts, but that described half of Prianus.

There were two types of Prians: the noble and the desperate.

The desperate might not notice a man murdered right on their own doorstep – not unless he had something worth stealing – but the noble might. Watching closely over their cities, the Prian police would have some useful information, even if they didn't know it. They had no particular reason to be looking for the Nihilists on their planet.

But getting information from the police would be tricky. Coldhand had no contacts on the force anymore, no one willing to speak to him. He briefly considered simply calling one of the stations and seeing what he could pry out of the desk officer. His E3 bounty hunter status would be more than enough to get him access to any records he requested, but the moment the police checked his CAID number, they would know who Logan was.

It was a frustratingly circular problem. The very identity that could give him what he needed would get him shot as a traitor.

Coldhand went back to the terminal, brought up a transit node and ordered a taxicab. Maybe he would just get lucky down in Blue Oak.

Not likely... He had flown across the galaxy on a wish. It was never like this when he was hunting Maeve.

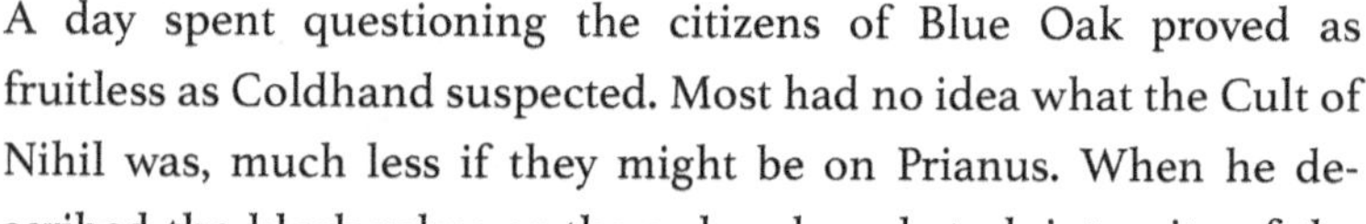

A day spent questioning the citizens of Blue Oak proved as fruitless as Coldhand suspected. Most had no idea what the Cult of Nihil was, much less if they might be on Prianus. When he described the black robes or the red garb and stark intensity of the Emberguard, the Prians simply shook their heads. They knew nothing.

Questioning them instead about an influx of Arcadians, Coldhand received a few shrugs. The fairies were always flying back and forth between cities. They never seemed to stay in one place long enough for the Prians to count them very accurately.

Nothing useful.

Coldhand paid the cab driver and walked back up the hill to the landing field. The rain had given way to a fine sleet that dusted his shoulders in glittering ice. He kept his hands in his pockets. The ice would stick to the illonium of his left hand and make the joints stiff.

He couldn't sort through every single city on Prianus. It would take a lifetime and there was no guarantee that he might happen upon the right people who had seen the right things. He was out of other options.

Logan went into the landing field's little hospitality house and powered up the terminal again. He did another quick search, half hoping to find nothing, but the results came back quickly. Cold-hand had his contact.

Highwind was on the other side of Prianus from Blue Oak, but it took only a few hours to make the flight and land. All too soon, Logan was walking along the cracked roads of his hometown.

I grew up here. I trained here. I served here. I died here.

He stood in front of a large window. The glass was chipped and dotted with taped-over holes. Inside, a group of small boys and girls took turns punching at sand-filled bags hanging from the sagging ceiling. A short, bald man limped between them, tapping shoulders and turning hips, refining their form.

Don't just hit with your arm. Use your whole body. Turn. Make gravity your ally instead of your enemy. Coldhand knew it all by rote. *Don't pull back so far, don't give your opponent any warning of what's coming. Just a handspan. That's all you need.*

Coldhand went inside. The palaestrum students looked up, but their instructor whistled sharply, pulling their attention back.

"Eyes up here, nestlings."

"Send them all home, Vorus," Coldhand said. "I need to talk to you."

Arctan Vorus furrowed his white brows at the hunter. "I'm in the middle of class. You can wait your turn."

"I can't stay in Highwind for long."

"That's your own fault, Logan. You'll wait."

The students looked curious, but knew better than to ask their stern old teacher about things that weren't their business. Coldhand had little choice but to wait, standing on the edge of the patched practice mats.

The years had not been kind to Logan's teacher. Vorus looked much older than the last time Coldhand had seen him. The last wisps of thin white hair around his ears were gone, leaving his scarred scalp bare. The lines at the corners of Vorus' eyes were deeper, too, etched there by decades of hardship.

When their lessons were done, the children made respectful farewells to Vorus and filed past Coldhand, out into the unfriendly Highwind streets.

Vorus beckoned to Logan. "Now, we'll talk."

The bounty hunter strode out onto the mat. It was thin and he could feel the hard concrete of the floor even through the soles of his boots. Lessons in Arctan Vorus' palaestrum were no kinder than those taught out in the back alleys of Prianus. But they taught much, much more. Honor, strength... Coldhand crossed his arms over his chest.

"I didn't plan to come here, Vorus," he said. "But I need some information."

"Is that so?"

"I'm hunting the Cult of Nihil and I believe they're on Prianus."

"Hunting? I had heard that you flew off and became a bounty hunter," Vorus said. "Looks like the gossip was right."

"You're not the first old cop to curl his claws at it. My last good mark had a Prian captain – a retired officer, just like you. He set his hawk on me."

Vorus grunted and scratched his bulging belly, hard and round as a boulder. "And you want me to give you information. You can't go get it from the station, so you think you can get it from me."

"You still play cards with the city captains, don't you?"

"Yes, I do," Vorus said. He looked at Coldhand for a long, heavy moment. "Your mother moved back to New Empyrean after you left. She couldn't bear it here anymore, not without you. Lynn died three years ago of trycho fever."

Coldhand didn't answer.

"Jess got married a little after that. She has a little boy now, eight months old. He's a good kid." Vorus took a step toward the bounty hunter. There was a storm brewing in his eyes. "She named him Logan. After you. Jess always thought you would come home. She never believed the things they said."

Logan's jaw clenched. "I don't care. Tell me about the Nihilists."

"You don't care? Don't you?" Vorus grabbed a handful of the younger man's shirt in a gnarled fist. "You were my best. Thirty years I've taught kids in this palaestrum and I never had one like you. You burned, Logan. There was fire in you!"

Coldhand didn't move, could not rise to Vorus' anger.

"And you were a good teacher," he said. "But that was a long time ago. Do you know about any cultists on Prianus? Large groups of new Arcadians?"

"What makes you think I won't go tell the police that you've come back?" Vorus asked, ignoring Coldhand's question. "There's a whole generation of cops in Highwind who would just love some payback. They trusted you, Logan. You were the best of them!"

"I couldn't stay, Vorus. I had to leave," Coldhand said flatly. "But it doesn't matter anymore. You won't tell the cops I was here. You won't sell me out because you're an honorable man."

"As I tried to teach you to be, for all the good it did!" Vorus was still holding Logan's shirt tightly.

"It wasn't like that."

"What was it like then, little hawk?"

"I didn't forget the things you taught me. That Emberguard cut them out. He cut it all away and they replaced it with metal…"

Logan closed his mouth with an effort. He didn't need to justify himself to his old teacher. So why was he?

"You got hurt, and so you ran away? You never used to be afraid of pain," Vorus snarled.

He shoved Logan back a step and then jabbed stiffened fingers into the bounty hunter's chest, just beneath his breastbone. The breath suddenly whooshed out of Logan's lungs and he folded over nearly double. He pulled swiftly back and straightened to find Vorus standing there, right in front of him, as though he had not retreated at all.

Vorus swung a scarred fist and Logan jerked back, but the old Prian kept coming. Coldhand parried another strike, but it turned him to one side and he didn't see the next flat-handed blow. It connected hard against his neck. Coldhand's blood pulsed hard and his vision went dim for a computerized heartbeat.

"Did that hurt?" Vorus asked.

Logan slid away again. He held up his illonium left hand and curled it into a fist. The high whine of servos was loud in the quiet palaestrum.

"It doesn't hurt," he answered. "Nothing hurts. This metal the doctors gave me only has twenty percent feeling, Vorus. That's it. That's all I get."

The bald old cop came at him again, hands raised in the close guard stance of a Lowland boxer. Logan feinted one way and then dodged the other. But Vorus wasn't so easily fooled. He cut the angle, jabbing and swinging. Logan threw himself back and rolled away across the mat.

Vorus grunted. "Just not as fast on my feet as I used to be, am I? But I make do with what I have. I'm scarred, not dead. Scars are lessons, little hawk. What did you learn from yours?"

Coldhand looked at the palaestrum door. He was faster than his old teacher. He could get away easily enough, but Vorus was his only lead, the only one who might give him information.

He couldn't leave, not yet. Logan had nowhere else to go. He approached Vorus warily.

"Tell me what I need to know and I'll go," he said. "You never have to see me again."

"You're not listening, little hawk. Looks like I'll have to give you a few more scars."

Vorus shuffled forward and launched into a new attack. He had taught Lowland boxing to all of his students, including a younger Logan Centra. Coldhand knocked aside the flurry of punches. He brought his left hand up and slammed it into Vorus' wrist. The old cop grunted and rubbed at his already bruising flesh.

"I'm not here to fight you, Vorus," Coldhand said. "You're not my mark."

"No, I'm your teacher," Vorus spat back. "I taught you how to live with honor. You've forgotten that. Have you forgotten how to fight, too? Stop dancing around and stand fast!"

Vorus pressed a hard, furious assault, but Logan was young and agile. He moved only at the last second to duck or block a punch, staying just out of Vorus' reach and hoping to tire out his teacher. But the old man showed no more signs of tiring than making Logan a cup of tea. He was going to have to end this fight somehow, and quickly.

Logan circled Vorus, turning aside the old man's attacks. Every other step, Vorus' left foot dragged just a little. Long years ago, during his days on the police force, he had jumped onto the rear fender of a fleeing suspect's car and been dragged nearly two blocks before climbing up over the cab, smashing through the window and taking control of the vehicle. He lost a great deal of flesh down his left leg. Without cloned replacements, Vorus had received grafts for the damaged ligaments and tendons, but he still bore a limp that Logan knew very well.

Coldhand aimed a low kick at the weak joint. Vorus crouched down onto his good leg to meet the kick and curled his fingers into claws like a scythe-bird's, then stabbed them hard into the meat of Logan's calf. The hunter's nerves jolted. Before he could recover, Vorus jabbed those viciously hooked fingers into Logan's thigh and then groin. Logan staggered back, jaw locked and limping on his own left leg.

"What's the matter, little hawk? Does that hurt?" Vorus seized Logan's illonium wrist and twisted against the joint. The machine whined loudly in protest as it resisted. "Now this? This doesn't hurt. This is metal, and it doesn't feel. Just twenty percent, right?"

Coldhand pulled, but could get no leverage to pull free.

"This?" Vorus chopped the edge of his hand down on the elbow joint just above the place where Logan's living arm joined the illonium hand. "This is flesh, and it hurts like all the hells."

Logan twisted out of the leverage and planted his elbow in the center of Vorus' chest. He followed with another swift kick to the old man's scarred leg.

"Got two steel pins in there, myself," Vorus said. He lifted his knee with a groan and then jammed it into Logan's inner thigh. "Aches when it rains. Does that make me a barometre?"

Logan willed his shaking legs not to buckle as he closed in more cautiously this time, throwing kicks only to gauge distance and keep his opponent at bay. When Vorus tried to strike at his knees, Logan slid forward and struck out with his metallic fist. Vorus fell to the mat with a loud thump.

The old man rolled to his feet with a grunt. "Low blow, little hawk. Are you angry? I sure hope so. Heart's just a muscle, Logan, or just a computer-driven valve. Forget that poetic shit about them. Your soul isn't hiding behind your ribs. No one can cut it out. A cybernetic heart can't stop you feeling any more than a cybernetic hand can stop that leg from throbbing."

"You're wrong. I don't feel. You don't know what I went through, what happened to me," Coldhand shouted.

The echoes bounced jarringly from the walls of the palaestrum. He advanced on Vorus again.

"I couldn't play my guitar," Coldhand said. "I couldn't feel Jess' hand when she held mine. It's all gone! I can't feel any of it!"

Logan jumped, kicking out in the air and punching even as he landed. Vorus' teeth clenched as Logan's fist found an old dueling wound in the hollow of his shoulder. But through the pain, Vorus' lashed back, instinct honed by years of training.

He jabbed a pressure point in Coldhand's arm and slammed his knee into the bounty hunter's diaphragm, stomping on his booted instep. As Logan pulled back, Vorus seized him by the hair. He held Logan in place as he grabbed the younger man's face in a clawed grip, fingers digging into nerves in his cheek and jaw.

It hurt. Coldhand cried out.

Vorus dropped Logan to the mat and stood over him. There was nothing broken, nothing even really damaged. Every one of Vorus' blows was meant only to cause pain, but Logan curled up on the floor like a newborn.

Vorus turned his head and spat blood onto the mat.

"I don't know anything about your Cult of Nihil, little hawk," he said. "But Arcadians are going missing in Pylos, on the other side of the mountains. But somehow, there's more fairies in Pylos than ever. These new Arcadians are a hard lot, not like the ones we're used to. Might be worth looking into."

Vorus turned and stalked away to his office in the back of the palaestrum. He closed and locked the door behind him.

Logan's heart detected the lowered rate of exertion and reduced his pulse accordingly. The floor mat was rough and lumpy under his right palm and just a vague firm sensation under his left. Logan pushed himself slowly to his feet. The blazing pain was already fading.

He took one last look around the palaestrum, at Vorus' closed door, and then left.

[13]
SHADES

"History doesn't repeat itself. We do. Scholars just love to hear ourselves talk."

- KEMMER ANDUS, PRIAN ARCHEOLOGIST (229 PA)

The two archeology teams spent that first day cataloging and calibrating their instrumentation. Kemmer brought only two generators up into the Kayton Mountains. They were barely enough to power his own systems. But Xen, unsure what sort of situation he was shipping himself and his team into, made certain to bring more than enough batteries and generators. Gruth got to work setting them up and running cables out to the rest of the camp.

That left erecting the Tynerion team's tents to Tiberius and his crew. About an hour before sunset, a dirty Prian man and slightly older woman appeared at the edge of the moraine. They stopped at a safe distance until assured that the newcomers in camp weren't thieves or worse. Tiberius explained their presence and that they were, in fact, there to protect the archeologists. The Prians introduced themselves as Darius and Ava Jaenes, a brother and sister team who worked for Kemmer as diggers.

"You don't have anyone else to help you?" Duaal asked. He seemed more than happy to have an excuse to take a break from setting up camp. "It's just the two of you?"

"We had Dannos to help with the microexplosives," Darius said.

"Until those rats killed him this morning," his sister added.

Maeve flexed one wing and then the other, trying to keep warm. She thought Ava sounded more annoyed than grieving.

"Will your lost companion be replaced?" Maeve asked.

"I doubt it," Darius said. He scrubbed at his dirty cheeks with a sleeve. "Doc Kemmer probably won't bring anyone else up here. We could have used a larger team from day one, but he doesn't trust many people."

"What could he have found up in these rocks that's worth all this?" Tiberius asked.

The captain stood not far away, shouldering a recently assembled table through the open tent door. Gripper squatted on the other side, pounding some pitons into the stony mountainside. Ava and Darius looked at each other.

"We better let Kemmer tell you about it," Ava said. "We should check in with him, anyway. As soon as that's done, we'll be back out to give you a hand."

"Thanks," Duaal said with a wink at the two Prians.

Maeve laboriously flew a radio antenna up out of the glacial valley. The thin, freezing air would barely support her weight, but it was still easier than sending one of the others – even large, strong Gripper – to climb the steep stone.

From above, Maeve could better see the damage done by the groundquakes. The entire glacial bed lay tilted down at a different angle than the rest of the mountainside. Where it had separated from the peak, there was a long, narrow ravine torn deep into the stone. The crevice ran jaggedly along the north edge of the moraine and then turned abruptly east.

A chain ladder was bolted to the edge and dangled down into the ravine. Deeper than that, Maeve could make out only shadows.

Was the base camp safe? The Tynerion geologist, Phillip Arno, had wondered the same and now walked a careful spiral out from the camp. Phillip held a pointed metal walking stick and prodded occasionally at the ground. He scribbled some hasty notes on a datadex, blew some warm breath into his hands, and moved on. His red hair was as bright as a candle flame in the monochrome white and gray of the Prian highlands.

The last thin beams of sunlight played across pale rocks and the dark threads of roads that wove in and around the Kayton Mountains. A thick bank of evening fog and smoke sifted up from distant Pylos, rising like a tide through the forest below and turning tall pine trees into lonely towers. Long-winged birds wheeled and wove between them like lonely ghosts as they returned to their nests for the night.

Maeve perched on the edge of a crumbling granite crag to catch her breath. The view was beautiful, in a cold and harsh sort of way.

But wasn't that the truth of Prianus and its people? Maeve swept a small pebble down the slope with the tip of her wing. It was not Tiberius she thought of, or the Prian archeologists working below. There were stones softer than Logan Coldhand, and blizzards with a warmer touch, but Maeve felt a sudden, heavy pang of loss.

Why did she miss her hunter? Maeve wasn't trying to trick him into killing her anymore... Not that she could even afford his rates anymore. Logan commanded a high price and deserved it all.

She stood and stretched her wings. The muscles were tight and stiff, but no longer burned painfully from the lack of oxygen in her blood. Or else too much carbon dioxide... Xia had given them all a brief lecture on altitude sickness, but Maeve couldn't remember which gas was the source of the problem. The cramping, acidic feeling in her stomach certainly suggested that something was still affecting her body. She would adjust, but it would take more time.

Maeve glided carefully down and back into the archeologists' camp. She shook a few flakes of snow from her wings and short black hair, then ducked into Kemmer's tent to report success at her task. The Prian team leader held up a finger to silence Maeve when she tried to get his attention. He stood opposite Xen and Tiberius at a table covered in bagged and labeled stone fragments. Xia was watching curiously over their shoulders. Kemmer placed a pair of datadexes on the table.

"What the hell are these?" Tiberius asked.

Xen picked one up and began reading over the contents. The Ixthian's eyes whirled a distinctly unhappy reddish color.

"This is a nondisclosure agreement!" he said.

Xia looked at the other datadex. "The terms of this are pretty demanding. No discussion with other sources, on- or off-world. No independently authored files or publications."

"No publishing?" Xen asked. He seemed to have recovered some of his spirit – previously dampened by the harsh realities of Prianus – but now he frowned. "Doctor Kemmer, I'm taking considerable losses on this expedition, including the cost of hiring Captain Myles to provide us some measure of safety. Need I remind you that I am shouldering the greater share of his fee?"

"That's not including the color you're saving by my volunteering to replace Dannos on your dig team," Xia said. She scanned a few more screens on the datadex. "Free of additional charge, I remind you. The consequences outlined here are steep. And you want any breaches prosecuted on Prianus?"

"I know you think I'm being paranoid," Kemmer told them. He didn't look at all apologetic as he rubbed the angle of his jaw. "But I promise you, what I've found is well worth any and all precautions. Even signing your name to the find will be enough to get you all the funding you'll need for life."

"You're asking for a lot of faith and a lot of trust," Xen said. "I still don't know what you have up here."

Tiberius scowled at Kemmer. "None of my hawks and doves will be publishing files, except maybe Xia. But I'm going to be conferring with Captain Cerro on his investigation. We'll need to talk about what's going on up here."

"I have no intentions of interfering with the police efforts, of course," Kemmer told him. "But I expect all of you to be as discreet as possible."

Tiberius shrugged and signed his name to the datadex. "I'll pass it around to the rest of my crew."

Xen twisted a stylus in his silver fingers. "I don't like it."

"I can't take you down to the site until you and your team sign, Professor Xen," Kemmer said. "Believe me, it will be worth the trouble."

The Ixthian archeogeneticist sighed. "Fine, I'll sign. But I want an extra copy of the agreement."

"You can copy one off whenever you like." Kemmer could afford to be generous now. Some of the taut set to his carriage eased.

Xen seemed to have absorbed it. He signed his short name with an angry flourish and then pulled a slim white plastic com from his pocket. It was much shinier and newer than the one Maeve carried.

"Panna? Are you back yet?"

Xen's assistant had spent most of the afternoon in one of the Prian team's two trucks, making the long drive down into Pylos to purchase adapters for their Tynerion-manufactured computers and equipment. There was a hiss of static over the com.

"I'm back in camp, professor," Panna answered. "I'm in our work tent, setting up with Gruth. Do you need me?"

"Yes. Come over here."

A moment later, Panna joined them in Kemmer's tent. She kept her eyes downcast as she passed close to Maeve and smiled brightly at everyone else in the tent, cheerful as ever. Kemmer – who had heard her voice over the coms all day but was only now finally meeting Panna – smiled right back. Xen handed her the datadex.

"Panna, this is a non-disclosure agreement for everyone on our team," he said. "I need you to sign it and take it around to Gruth, Phillip and Enu-Io. When you're done, pull down a copy and start comparing it to the local laws. I want to know what we're up against if I decide to challenge it."

Panna's expression sobered. She looked uncomfortably between Xen and Kemmer.

But the Prian nodded. "It's fine. If it helps Xen feel better, go ahead. I've got copies of pretty much all the Prian judicial codes, if you need them."

"I'll get started on that. Do you want to check over the setup in our tents, Professor Xen?" Panna asked.

"I'll go take a look in a few minutes. First, I want to have a few words with Captain Myles."

"Sure, professor." Panna nodded and retreated.

Xen turned toward Tiberius. "Captain Myles, I may very well have just signed away everything I've invested in this venture. I need to know that you'll do everything you can to protect it. This is very, very important."

"I said that I'd keep you and your site safe," Tiberius answered. "Leave it with us, professor."

That seemed to be enough to reassure the Ixthian scholar. He nodded and left to follow Panna, Xia close behind.

Tiberius stood and cracked his knuckles loudly. "Well, we better get started on all that. Kemmer, it's getting dark and I'd like to post Maeve on watch over your site. Once she signs that agreement, can she do that?"

"Yes," Kemmer said. "Not that there will be anything to see. All the lights have been shut down for the night. I'd like to place her on the surface, on the north face. That's just downhill from the site entrance. I can show your Arcadian the place."

It was hardly the first time someone had talked about Maeve instead of *to* her, but never a Prian before.

"I know the place," Maeve said stiffly. "I have successfully placed and secured your new radio antenna. While carrying out that task, I had a clear view of the ravine to our north."

"That's the spot," Kemmer said. "There's–"

"A ladder. Yes, I saw it." Maeve snatched the datadex away from Tiberius and signed her name. "I will watch over it until dawn."

"I'll cover the base camp. I don't suppose you have any sort of surveillance equipment?" Tiberius asked Kemmer. "Cameras, perimeter lasers?"

The other Prian snorted. "I did. They stole it all this morning."

Tiberius rose and gestured for Maeve to follow. "Come on, dove. Let's get to work."

Maeve threw the nondisclosure agreement onto the table and left to begin her watch.

The night was cold, but uneventful. The sky glittered with stars, but nothing like the close, brilliant pack of stars in the core. No, this sky was deep and dark, like the skies of the White Kingdom. Only one of the moons, Duos, was in the sky and even that was an irregular gray crescent.

Maeve stood vigil on a jutting spar of stone, wrapped in a reflective silver blanket. The crinkling foil was plainly visible, even in the dark, but Maeve supposed that was part of the idea. Perhaps if thieves realized that the site was protected, they would look elsewhere for their profit. Still, Maeve wished she had her spear. She felt again for the strange weight clipped to the waist of her pants. Xia's laser pistol was still there, loaned to her earlier that evening. The weapon felt so... alien.

By the time the sun rose, turning the sky a seashell pink and the clouds into scarves of pale gold cloth, Maeve was feeling the effects of a night without sleep. Her bleary eyes were sticky and her fingers stiff with cold. But her job was nearly done. Maeve yawned and stretched. Her wings ached, but at least the weariness dulled her desire for some Vanora White.

Whatever else could be said for the archeologists, they were not lazy or late sleepers. The Prian team – only three of them in total, including Kemmer – woke first, followed shortly by the Tynerion group. The last to rise were the Blue Phoenix crew. Xia, Duaal and Gripper emerged from the furthest tent, squinting and looking disheveled.

Maeve's com beeped at her. It was Tiberius, calling her back to the camp.

"We'll check in with Kemmer and the professor, then get some sleep," he said.

"I will be there very soon," Maeve answered.

She made the short flight back down into the base camp, where Tiberius and the rest were waiting for her.

"You stayed up all night?" Gripper asked when Maeve landed. "You must be hungry. And frozen!"

"One of the Prians loaned me this," the fairy said, holding up the thermal blanket. She had folded it up around the small heating control wired into one corner. "It is quite effective."

"Prians know how to keep warm," Duaal said. "If they didn't, there wouldn't be anyone left on this hunk of rock."

The Hyzaari, too, seemed to know how to keep warm. He had clothed himself in a more flamboyant version of the standard Prian dress: a long sapphire coat and a multicolored scarf tucked into the collar, with high, polished black boots.

"We should probably have some breakfast and get moving if we want to get down into the dig with everyone else," Xia said.

"I will leave the archeology to those educated in such things," Maeve told her. She stifled another yawn.

Xia grinned like a schoolgirl. Maeve supposed on this expedition, that's exactly what she was. The Ixthian raised an eyebrow.

"If I am to continue my promised work," Maeve said. "I will need sleep."

"I'm with Maeve," Tiberius agreed. His eyes were bloodshot and had purplish circles under them. He stroked Orphia's feathers. The tawny hawk nuzzled his hand and nipped at his fingers. "I'll stay up here. But you three can climb down into Kemmer's secret crack if you want."

Duaal snickered and Xia sighed.

"You two have the curiosity of turnips," she said. "Don't you want to know what's down there? Maeve, Ava seemed to think that you might be particularly interested. Can't I tempt you?"

Maeve looked at Tiberius. Even dull and heavy with fatigue, she *was* curious now… though that might just have been a response to Xia's taunts.

"I will go," Maeve agreed. Gripper cheered.

Xia arched her antennae at Tiberius. "What about you, captain? Can we convince you to go?"

"Hmm. Someone's got to stay to keep an eye on the base camp," Tiberius said.

"Darius and Ava can cover that, if you'd like to come down for a look," Panna offered. She had come over to the Blue Phoenix team and held out a stack of steaming mycofoam trays. "There's some halfway decent coffee in our tent. The cream is powdered, but it's not bad. Here, I've even got a breakfast pack without meat for you, Gripper. We brought them for Enu-Io, but he says he's happy to share."

"Thanks!" The Arboran took the food and shoveled it into his wide mouth.

"Doctor Kemmer wants us to spend the day familiarizing ourselves with the site and take some scans," said Panna. "He seems to think it's going to take a while. That means there's no work for Ava and Darius today. They're going to stay up on the surface."

"Are they armed?"Duaal asked.

"They're Prian," Tiberius answered as though that was all the explanation needed.

"I expect they are. Armed, not Prian. Both, I mean," Panna said, then gave up with a sheepish laugh. "Anyway, they know exactly what kind of threats we're facing up here. Most Prians know at least the basics of handling a weapon."

"Fine," Tiberius said. "I'll go down for a few minutes, just to see what all the fuss is about."

Both archeology teams and their guards from the Blue Phoenix gathered around a glowing orange heat lamp set up in the circled tents. Ava and Darius were in high spirits, all too happy to spend a day in the open air. They sat close and laughed at some private joke.

Gruth's brown and white fur stood out, fluffy and full, and was doing as good a job keeping him warm as any of the blankets and coats the other archeologists wore. Ixthians had tough, reinforced skin that made them resilient pilots, but did nothing for the cold. Xen and Xia were as heavily clothed as the humans and had fleece headbands that they kept pulling up over their shivering antennae. Gripper sat close to Xia, providing a large windbreak.

In odd disregard of Dannos' death just the day before, Kemmer seemed to be in a good mood. When he finished his steaming cup of coffee, the Prian archeologist slapped his knees and stood.

"Are you all ready?" he asked.

The Tynerion team nodded together.

"I'm just going to take a look for some context," Phillip said. "I'll cut out some samples from the bedrock, but I need to spend most of the next few days mapping out the new fault lines. It looks like the same quakes that uncovered your big secret might have destabilized some of the underpinning stone. I brought some reinforcement injectors to put in around your dig."

It was probably the longest speech Maeve had ever heard from the shy geologist. Phillip seemed to realize that and blushed under his freckles.

"No one can publish anything if you all die in a cave-in or rock slide," he said.

The other scholars laughed.

Gripper leaned in close to Phillip. "Hey, Strawberry?"

"Yes?"

"Did you see any... any flowers while you were out poking the rocks yesterday?" Gripper asked in a quiet voice.

Phillip thought for a moment.

"A few," he said at last. "There seems to be some kind of snowdrops on the west slope, where there's the most sun. Why?"

"No reason," Gripper answered quickly. He saw Maeve watching and pointed surreptitiously at Xia and mouthed *flowers*. Maeve hoped that the flowers would work out better than the polytomograph had.

They finished eating and gathered up datadexes, imagers, scanners and lights. Twenty minutes later, everyone had climbed up the slope to wait at the edge of the crevice – the same one Maeve had spent her night guarding. Tiberius whistled at Orphia. She cocked her head at him and then took wing, soaring up into the cloud-streaked sky.

Her long night's guard duty still sat heavy and gummy-feeling in Maeve's joints, but it was hard not to be caught up in the rising excitement. Even Xen seemed to have put aside yesterday's tragedy. Xia fidgeted impatiently nearby. Both Ixthians' eyes shone a bright, pleased aqua. Panna could barely stand still and kept flipping a rectangular recorder over in her hands. Only staid Enu-Io seemed unmoved. Duaal was trying to follow that calm, cool example, but was grinning as he stood beside the muscular Dailon man.

The ravine was long and narrow across the top. Even without her wings, Maeve could almost have leapt across the deep tear in the mountain. But as she followed the others across stones that glittered with frost, the ground felt strangely taut under her boot – hollow, like leather pulled over a drum.

The ravine must have opened up into something wider below, overhung by the moraine above. But when Maeve looked over the jagged edge, the steeply slanting morning sunlight illuminated only swirling blue-gray mist and indigo shadows.

Kemmer unlocked the rolled ladder and lowered the galvanized rungs down on their coated chains.

"The ladder can only take one of you at a time, so call out when you get to the bottom," he said. "Watch your step down there. The ground is wet and frequently freezes over."

Maeve and the others nodded. Then one by one, Xen and his team climbed down into the crevasse. When her turn came, Maeve pulled her wings tightly against her back and climbed carefully down the ladder. As she suspected, it only followed the stone for a short distance and then dangled through empty air as the ravine's wall pulled away. The ladder wriggled unsteadily under her, but the fairy was light and her wings helped her to keep her balance. By the time she felt stone under her feet again, the sky was a barely visible sliver of light high above.

Maeve was the last down the ladder. The archeologists switched on lights and shined them around, illuminating uneven walls of craggy stone and an uneven floor strewn with rocks shattered by the quakes.

"Let's get moving," Kemmer said. His voice echoed eerily off the stone. The Prian archeologist gestured with his flashlight down the ravine. "This way."

Most of the stone surrounding them was mottled granite and pale quartz, but as they followed Kemmer through the zig-zagging angles of the ravine, the stone began to turn dark and glassy. It was obsidian, Philip explained. They were passing through an ancient volcanic flow.

"Wouldn't lava destroy anything down here?" Gripper asked.

"Yes," Phillip said. "Unless it's much newer or much older than the volcano. If it's newer, then it could have been laid down or built over the stone after it cooled. If it's sufficiently older, it might just be deeper than the lava flow."

The rock passage was getting easier to navigate. It wasn't just the sunlight beginning to filter down into the narrow crevice. Someone – probably Ava and Darius – had cleared away the tumbled stones and heaped them against the sides.

Finally, Kemmer guided the newcomers between two huge piles of tailings that nearly choked the ravine. Far above, the broken fringes of the stone blocked out most of the sun, but a little light bounced off the water winding in rivulets down the crevasse wall. Ahead, at the end of the ravine, Maeve could catch only glimpses of flat, geometric shapes, curves and glints of... glass? Metal? It was hard to tell.

But it felt strange. And familiar. The hairs stood up along the back of Maeve's neck. The excitement was gone and she suddenly wished she hadn't come, not climbed down into the belly of Prianus to face Kemmer's secret. The Prian archeologist searched around until he found a generator.

"Watch your eyes," he warned. "I'm going to hit the main lights. Ready?"

Kemmer was far too excited to wait for an answer. He hauled back a lever and the generator buzzed loudly. A perimeter of bright lamps flickered to life, one by one, and filled the fissure with harsh white light.

The single shape that rose from the floor of the ravine was too clean, too deliberate to be anything natural. It was a sort of steep, graceful ziggurat made of seamless white material, about the size of a large house. Wide, deep stairs ran up the center of each face, bordered on each side by intricately carved banisters that stood taller than Maeve.

At the top of the pale ziggurat stood a huge, segmented ring. Each section of the vast circle was crafted from a different material, some with the burnished shine of metal, others with an iridescent moonstone gleam. A faint, wavering light swam over the great ring, flowing like water and moving from one segment to the next with apparent disregard for the joints between them.

Maeve's stomach lurched sickeningly. She knew it at once.

By Anslin Sky-Knight... It is a Waygate. A Waygate on Prianus.

[14]
NEEDS

"If you worry about what a child will become, you're not worrying enough about what they *are*."

- GAVRIEL EUVO, CULT OF NIHIL FOUNDER (227 PA)

"We've found one, Lord Gavriel. He says he was on Illisem."

"Bring him to me, then."

Iboe bowed. She was shivering violently, her patchwork robes utterly inadequate against the cold. But she left and returned a few minutes later with another black-clothed Nihilist. They carried a slumping, white-winged shape between them and dropped it at Gavriel's feet. The Arcadian fell to his knees, panting.

"Did he fight?" Gavriel asked curiously.

"No, my lord. He's very sick."

Iboe was right – the fairy's wings and skin were patchy with blotches of raw-looking pink. There were scabby, scaly streaks on his cheeks and the back of his bowed neck.

Gavriel stood. Even stooped, he loomed over the sick, prostrate fairy.

"Do you know why you're here?"

The Arcadian looked up at Gavriel with blank eyes. His pale hair was shaved away and one of his ears was missing, leaving only a red stump.

"*Ua'li eru Aver*," he answered. He didn't speak Aver.

Gavriel nodded. "*Uma'li eru Arcadi'na.*"

The fairy gave him a wide-eyed look of surprise. The Prians harbored little racism toward the Arcadians, but few bothered to learn their language. The ignorant, back-water hicks never saw the point. Gavriel knew better.

"*Ai muan?*" he asked. *How old are you?*

"*Ima'ae lia.*" *Three hundred and six.*

Gavriel wasn't sure if that was counted in Arcadian years or the longer Alliance CSYs, but it didn't matter. Either way, the fairy was old enough to remember the fall of the White Kingdom.

"*Ai na?*" Gavriel asked. *What is your name?*

"Timaen."

Gavriel reached down and curled his long fingers around the side of Timaen's face. His skin was rough under the old Nihilist's touch. He was feverishly warm in places and clammy cold in others where disease had killed off his blood vessels.

Gavriel sang, softly at first but with growing power and volume. Timaen's brown eyes went glassy and drifted closed, lulled into lassitude. But as Gavriel's song wound through him, Timaen's eyes snapped open again. He pulled back, away from the old Nihilist, and Iboe shoved the Arcadian to his knees once more. Gavriel held Timaen's face in both hands now, staring into his frightened, blood-shot eyes.

Show me. Show me what I need to see.

The Arcadian's mind opened before Gavriel's spell like a knife-shucked oyster. Sounds, smells, images and less identifiable sensations washed over Gavriel. Memories... Snatches of song, the feel of the rising wind beneath his wings, the bitter taste of ashes on the air as Timaen flew as fast as he could away from the Devourers.

Blood everywhere, pounding in his ears, darkness that blotted out the sun. Memories of tragedy a hundred years old.

I flew, Timaen remembered. *And the darkness chased me. It flew without wings and reached for me with hooks and fangs. The molten shadows pierced my shoulder and I fell. I screamed. Death was everywhere, an army of storm clouds that flashed with red fire. I was going to die...*

A flash of glass. A knight! She caught me out of the air and carried me to the ground. She told me to run. So I ran, dragging my wings behind. Useless. Slow... There were screams behind me. Blood on the white stones of the Great City.

I ran.

I ran and I did not look back.

Gavriel's fingers tightened on Timaen, pressing into his broken, ravaged skin.

"Show me what I need to see!"

Black clouds... Shadows that tore, shadows full of teeth...

But Timaen's memories were incomplete. He had seen little and even that was clouded by time and disease. Gavriel pushed the Arcadian to the floor. The other Nihilists backed quickly away.

"Ka li'ae avael!" Gavriel sang.

The fairy on the floor screamed as fire caught in his dry, patchy wings. Gavriel sang it on and the flame spread quickly, as hungry as any Devourer. The fire burned away his clothes, then his body, and Timaen clutched at Gavriel's feet.

"Mercy!" he croaked. So he spoke *some* Aver...

"That is exactly what I'm giving you, Timaen." Gavriel said. "Go in peace."

When the flames finally died, Iboe and her companion dragged the smoking corpse away. Gavriel smiled as he stood alone in the darkened apartment. It was good to finally possess the power – the true power – of a mage. He alone wielded fire and lightning and truth and pain... And he did it without Duaal's help.

"Lord Gavriel! My lord, they're at the doors!"

The Nihilist threw herself at her master's feet and Gavriel kicked her away.

"Who is here, woman?" he asked.

He was in a foul mood and had no patience for her wailing. She raised her hands imploringly.

"The police! They've come for us, my lord. They'll take us away and send us to rot in prison," she cried. The woman's eyes were full of terror. "They'll put us on suicide watch!"

Gavriel curled his hands into impotent fists at his sides. The beads and sigils that covered his elaborate robes flashed in the lamplight.

"Where are my Emberguard?" he asked.

The Nihilist shook her head. Strands of gray hair escaped her hood. "They're at the doors, my lord, but the Prians are coming through."

Gavriel heard angry voices arguing outside. Lasers whined and bullets cracked, but not as many as he expected. The Prian police were trying to take the Nihilists alive to face trial. Hallax leapt through the door and slammed it shut behind him. His green hair was disheveled, his nanosword naked in his hand and shone bright, wet red with blood.

"The Prians are closing in, Lord Gavriel," the Emberguard said. "You must go. If you die here, nothing we've done will mean anything."

The woman was still at Gavriel's feet, weeping and screaming. "Kill me, Lord Gavriel! Send me down into the sweet, endless dark!"

He could do it. Even now, even without the boy. Gavriel still kept the silver-bladed knife tucked in his robes. It was a ritual implement, but it would do as a weapon. He could slit her throat and probably many more before the police could stop him.

But how many wretched souls would live on?

No, he would not give up so easily. Hallax was right. Gavriel had to leave. He had to survive until the end. Gavriel took the Nihilist woman's hand and pulled her to her feet.

"Death will come for you another day," he told her. "Now, you must be brave. Go. Help the others hold the Prians back."

"Are you coming?" she asked in a shaking, frightened voice.

"No, dear one," Gavriel said. "I must go, but I will not forget how you fought for me."

She rose unsteadily and ran back the way she had come, out the door and toward the sounds of fighting. Red and orange flashes lit the hall in staccato bursts as the Prian police closed in. Hallax raised his gleaming sword.

"What of me, my lord?" he asked. "I have killed many Prian cops and can take many more with me into the darkness."

"No," Gavriel told the Mirran. "Come with me. We're not done yet and I will need new Emberguard. You must get us out of here."

"Yes, Lord Gavriel." Hallax shouldered the window open, filling the room with Highwind's fetid air. "This way."

Together, the Nihilists fled.

Now Gavriel stood at the window, high above Pylos. His smile faded. Though it felt good to be strong again, he still had not found the memories he needed. All he had was another dead Arcadian. Another failure. How long did Gavriel have before the Prian police found him again? Wind howled outside the empty window.

[15]
SECRET

"If we learned anything, it's that we still have a lot to learn."

- PHILLIP ARNO, CYRAN GEOLOGIST (232 PA)

Duaal stared up at the Waygate. His head rang with sudden agony, worse than ever. He had to be dreaming or... or something. As suddenly as it had come, the pain was gone. But the Waygate remained, stark and graceful and impossible.

"How can that be here?" Duaal asked.

His voice was shockingly loud in the stunned silence. Everyone winced.

"You recognize it?" Kemmer asked.

"That's a Waygate," Duaal answered. "I heard a lot about them from Gavriel. There were loads of them all across Arcadia."

"As well as on the worlds of the Jinn and within the great Nnyth hive," Maeve said.

The Arcadian's gray eyes were fixed on the Waygate. What could she be thinking?

"But no one's ever seen a Waygate in the core," Kemmer said. He sat on top of the generator powering the floodlights and grinned at the other archeologists. "I'm sure you understand now why I've kept this thing such a secret. The discovery of a Waygate on an Alliance planet is going to change absolutely everything."

Xen was walking dreamily toward the Waygate. "This is absolutely amazing. The foundation is cracked, but the structure has remained completely intact!"

"We've been able to find a few shallow scratches and chips here and there," Kemmer told him. "But no more damage than that. The material is pretty close to indestructible."

"Simply amazing!" Xen said. "How old is this thing? Phillip, how far down the strata are we?"

The geologist shined a flashlight over some of the lighter stripes in the fissure wall. The stone was flattened in places, cracked and blasted away to clear the rock from around the Waygate. Probably microexplosives, Dannos' contribution to the dig before his death.

"I couldn't tell you for sure without some testing," Phillip said. "But I estimate about thirty feet below that old volcanic flow. If the surveys are accurate, then we're about three million years down."

"Three *million* years?" Xia gasped. "Are you serious?"

"It could be even more than that," Phillip said apologetically. "It depends upon how much things have shifted."

"Now, that doesn't necessarily mean that the Waygate itself is that old," Kemmer said. He motioned and they all followed the Prian archeologist to the pyramidal base of the gate. "It could have been placed here at some more recent point. One of the things I've been unable to do is get an accurate age on the structure itself."

"Have you gotten samples?" Gruth asked.

"A few, yes, but the materials are all *very* hard to cut."

The Lyran grunted and examined one of the sculpted stairways. Duaal looked over his twitching pointed ears. From a distance, the uniformly white carvings had been difficult to make out. But closer now, he could see the designs raised in relief from the smooth, milk-white... whatever it was. Stone, maybe? Ceramic?

The decorations were all celestial in theme: intricately rendered stars and planets, nebulae and comets. There was no mistaking the Waygate's purpose – travel between the stars.

"Each Waygate is unique. Their structure and purpose remain the same, but each of them is subtly varied," Maeve said. Slowly, she approached to look at the same part of the banister as Gruth and Duaal. "This one is similar to the Waygate in Kiarra'Na, on Wynerian. I... I went there often."

Kemmer crossed his arms. "Well, what else can you tell me? I've questioned several Arcadians, but they won't tell me a damned thing about the history of the Waygates. How did you build them? Why is there one on Prianus?"

Maeve shot the archeologist an irritated look.

"You are hardly the first to assume that Arcadians are simply unwilling to share our secrets," she snapped. "There are none! We did not craft the Waygates. They existed on our worlds even before Cavain's time, ten thousand years ago. We learned the secrets of their use, but neither we nor any of our cousins – the dryads, nyads or long-dead pyrads – claim to have built them."

Maeve hesitated now. High above, the slithering, multi-colored glow playing over the surface of the segmented Waygate ring flared and swirled, but didn't seem to illuminate the deep ravine at all. Maeve took a step back, away from the Waygate.

"The Arcadians are not the greatest scholars of the Waygates' workings," she said reluctantly. "The intricacies of their operation were taught to us by the Nnyth. The star-wasps know more about the gates than any race we have ever encountered, but even the Nnyth do not claim to have built the Waygates."

"So you don't know what they're made of?" Kemmer asked.

"My brother was an adept of the Ivory Spire, so named in honor of the Nnyth Tower. The Spire was dedicated to the training of those who opened the Waygates. Caith and I spoke often of his education," Maeve said. She nodded to the great blue-white ring.

"Some of the sections of the gate itself are of a kind of glass, much like the glass we used to craft our armor and cities."

"Our refraction tests seem to bear that out, as far as we can tell," Kemmer agreed. "Do you have any of that glass armor? Captain Myles mentioned that you were some kind of knight."

"I... lost my armor shortly after the fall of the White Kingdom," Maeve answered. "I still possess the blade of my spear, though I have not replaced the shaft."

"And that's Arcadian glass? I'd like to examine that."

Kemmer sounded only slightly more respectful now that he wanted something from Maeve. Duaal didn't like her, either, but it wasn't because of her race. Kemmer's unexpected bigotry annoyed Duaal. The Prian had no right to hate Maeve. He didn't even know her enough to hate her for the right reasons.

"Is this Waygate any different than the Arcadian ones?" asked Enu-Io.

"Other than the decorations, not as far as I can tell," Kemmer answered with a shrug. "And it sounds like even those in the White Kingdom varied between sites."

"Then it seems safe enough to assume that this specimen is at least ten thousand years old," Enu-Io said. "If the Arcadians have documented their age at least that far back."

Xen nodded. "Then we can start there. What else do you know about it?"

"Not much yet," Kemmer said. "We've spent the last six weeks just clearing away the bedrock."

Kemmer showed them the eastern face of the Waygate's base. The floor of the crevice was rougher and bore the circular marks of recent cutting. The ashy scent of cold stone filled the ravine. Phillip squatted and inspected the ground at the base of the Waygate, then angled his flashlight up at the fissure wall.

"There are stress fractures all throughout the matrix," said the geologist. "It must have shattered in the quake."

"And that didn't break or crush the Waygate?" Xia asked. "You haven't repaired it at all?"

"No structural damage that we've found so far," Kemmer told her. "Whoever *did* create these gates built them to last."

Xia grinned at Tiberius. "Still want to go to bed?"

"Yes," he grunted. "Sounds like this thing has been down under these mountains for thousands of years. Maybe millions. It'll still be here when I wake up. Maeve, are you coming?"

The fairy stared up at the Waygate for a moment longer, then nodded. "Yes. A Waygate requires able and rested guardians."

"This thing is going to make every one of us rich and famous," Kemmer said. "I don't want anyone stealing it out from under me."

Maeve shot the Prian an odd look. That wasn't what she meant at all. Duaal shuddered. Suddenly, he didn't want to be down here, either. Something about the gleaming light of the Waygate made Duaal feel like there were insects crawling up his spine.

"I think I'll come back up, too," he said. "It's quite a sight. But now comes a lot of dirty, tedious work. I think I'll leave that to the experts."

Duaal followed Tiberius as the old captain traced the ravine back to the ladder. Maeve simply spread her wings and flew away.

Panna stood on the steps of the Waygate. It was... amazing. She had never seen anything like it. Heard about them, read about them, yes... But the truth of the gates was something else entirely. It was monolithic, beautiful. Alien.

The strange alien, Gripper, stood nearby. Even after most of his crewmates left – of them, only Xia remained – he stood still, jaw hanging open. Kemmer cocked his head toward the Waygate.

"Do you want a closer look? I need all of you to be familiar with this thing before we begin," said the Prian archeologist.

Xen grinned. "I thought you'd never ask."

Following close behind the two senior scholars, Panna climbed up the smooth white stairs. They had a polished, perfect finish – like porcelain plates. Even through her thickly cushioned winter boots, every step sent a jolt up Panna's spine. She felt dizzy. Was it the Waygate or just the altitude? Or maybe just her balance failing her. It hadn't been good ever since the surgery.

Or perhaps it was the unnatural spacing of the steps. They were huge and deep, as though meant for much larger creatures than humans – only Gripper could climb them easily. The balustrades were as tall as Panna. They seemed more like walls than guide rails as they closed in around her.

So Panna examined the carvings instead. Designs, really, since she could see no marks from any tools. Had they been poured or cast? Regardless, Panna didn't recognize the arrangement of stars. She made a mental note to see if they corresponded to the constellations anywhere else in the galaxy. Was this the Prian sky or something else altogether?

The star and planet patterns grew fewer and farther between as the archeologists made their way up toward the Waygate ring. Panna wondered if the gate's creators had simply lost interest in the designs, but doubted it. Everything about the Waygate seemed very... deliberate.

The top of the stepped pyramid was the size of a small lecture hall and was just as seamlessly smooth as the rest of the structure. The bottom segments of the ring – one made of a translucent ice-blue substance and the other of what looked like copper fish scales – seemed simply to be submerged in the white floor, as though dipped in cream, and left the gate's inner surface flat and even with the ground.

"How big is it? Do you have measurements?" Gruth asked.

"The interior diameter of the Waygate is one hundred forty-four feet," Kemmer answered. "The ring itself is about eight feet wide and five thick. We estimate that each section weighs an average of nineteen tons. There are sixteen segments."

"How are they held together? Or to the base?" Enu-Io asked. He walked around the bottom of the Waygate.

"That's one of a thousand things we don't know yet," Kemmer said. "We haven't been able to get a sample from the seams to see if there's any mortar. You can't even slide a razor between the pieces."

"Self-tensioned?" Enu-Io asked.

"Nope." Kemmer swept his arm to encompass the whole huge ring. "The angles don't line up. We have no idea why it doesn't just fall apart."

Panna looked up at another piece, made of a glittering black... stone? It was hard to tell. She pulled on a pair of green vorlex gloves and ran her fingers over the joint where it met the next section. It was fitted so closely that Panna couldn't even feel the change of material. Not even a different texture. It all felt slick, almost wet, and... warm?

"What's the temperature?" she asked.

"Ambient," Kemmer answered, then laughed at Panna's shocked expression. "I know the Waygate feels warm, and we have no idea why. But it doesn't register on a thermometer."

"It looks like the portal thing on Arborus," Gripper said.

Xen looked at Xia, then at the alien. "She's told me about your experiences, and that you believe you might have come to the CWA by means of a Waygate, or something similar."

"Yeah." Gripper stood at the base of the ring. He didn't touch it. "It was the same shape, and all in pieces, but that gate wasn't on a pyramid. This one has more sections, too."

"How many more?" Xia asked.

"I'm not sure," Gripper said. He traced one of the shiny, eddying striations in the air with a huge, clawed finger. "This is the same, though. The ones that were put together all had this kind of finish... or whatever the light is."

"They? Then there were more than one?" Kemmer asked. His eyes lit up.

"A whole plaza. And they were a lot smaller than this. About as tall as I am, maybe."

"Built to a personal scale, perhaps," the Prian mused.

"Then I wonder what this one was used for?" Xen asked. "Without a loading ramp or something similar, it couldn't have been used to move cargo."

"Not necessarily," Panna said. The awe hadn't worn off or even faded, but she was full of ideas. "The Waygates were clearly built with much higher technology than we understand yet, but even we use null-fields. There's no reason to believe that they couldn't just fly or push anything they needed right up these stairs. The steps might just be for foot traffic."

"I don't think I'd call it *technology*, exactly," Gruth grumped.

Like every Lyran that Panna had ever met, the man was an elitist when it came to machines.

"Just because you don't understand magic doesn't mean that it isn't technology," Panna reminded him, exasperated. "Waygates can cover more distance in less time than even the best superluminal drives. If we can just understand how these things work, places like Prianus don't have to suffer just because they're far away from the galactic core."

Panna realized she might have gone a little too far and glanced at Kemmer. The Prian looked back with eyebrows raised. She bit her lip.

"Sorry," Panna said.

"No need," Kemmer said. He smiled. "Prianus isn't a pleasant planet. I'm hoping this find will be enough to secure a tenured position at a Tynerion college."

Xen crossed his arms. "That's why you don't want *me* authoring anything about this."

Kemmer was unfazed by the Ixthian's irritation.

"You've already got a Tynerion office and a beautiful assistant," he said. "You'll get plenty of grants off this, Professor Xen, but I need the credit. I don't want to be stuck on Prianus my whole life."

Panna blushed at the part about Xen's *beautiful assistant* and returned her attention to the Waygate. The film of light playing over the surface had taken on a different texture. The layer of pale, multi-hued light moved faster now, curling and swirling like water eddying around rocks.

"What about this?" Panna asked. "This light? Is it some sort of reflection?"

"We haven't been able to determine the source. Like the warmth you feel, it doesn't register on anything," Kemmer said. "No kind of photometrics or chemical composition. And it seems to react to people, too."

"What do you mean?" Xen asked.

"Notice how quickly it's moving now? It slows and fades when no one is around," Kemmer answered. "We've set up cameras to record the changes. This is the most active I've seen it, but there are more people down here than ever before."

"There are a lot of things we don't know about the Waygates," Xia said. Her eyes swirled with colors, not unlike the gate stones. "All things considered, I'm a little surprised you don't have any Arcadians on your team."

"Some Arcadians saw the base camp and came asking for work. I asked them some questions, but they had nothing to tell me," Kemmer said. "I assumed they were keeping secrets, so I sent them on. If your friend Maeve is telling the truth, maybe they just don't know much. Anyway, we don't need their help."

Xen clicked his tongue "The Arcadians know a lot more about them than we do. We should pay them a little respect, if only because we may need their help later."

Kemmer shrugged. Gripper shifted his impressive weight back and forth, from one foot to the other. His bare feet, Panna noticed, and wondered if they were cold. But if Gripper was uncomfortable about anything but the arguments, it didn't show. He was a tough creature. Physically, at least.

"I'm still not hiring Arcadian diggers," Kemmer said, crossing his arms and narrowing his blue eyes at Xen. "They're not suited for this kind of work, anyway. As for Arcadian consultations, we've got Maeve for that now. She seems to know a thing or two about Waygates."

Gripper flinched at that. Panna wondered why, but Xen looked up at the much taller Kemmer and grinned.

"That's all I ask," he said. "We've got a lot of work to do. Let's get started."

Everyone in the ravine relaxed visibly as the tension in the air eased and the curiosity returned. Panna wanted to thank Xen for that, but remained quiet and did as she was told.

[16]

PYLOS

A red light blinked in the Raptor's cockpit. There was no positioning signal from any of the Pylos landing fields. The skypads were out of commission in the wake of some ubiquitous local catastrophe. Coldhand circled over the city once, switching between different frequencies, but picked up only the local police signals. He turned east and flew away from Pylos. He couldn't land in a police field and did not want to linger in a stolen Raptor.

Logan's fighter pierced the heavy, thick gray clouds and then he was soaring over the mountains. The Kayton range was one of the largest on Prianus, rising ever higher each year as the tectonic plates that formed the mountains pushed together and thrust the peaks starward.

The mountain slopes were streaked in pale blue glaciers and deep, dark ravines. The same forces that built the mountains were tearing ever-widening cracks in Prianus' stone skin.

As wrinkled and fragile as an old man. It's like the whole planet is getting too old.

Logan wove between the peaks, searching for a place to land. He flew over a broad, flat stretch of stone, an ice-carved depression more than wide enough to hold the Raptor. But someone else had found it first. A half-dozen domed tents circled up in the center of the moraine, just to the south of another dark crack in the mountain. Even if the campers below were discreet and would be willing to quietly share their campsite, it was too far away from Pylos for Coldhand's purposes.

He skimmed his fighter lower over the slopes until he found a wide lip of stone jutting out from the side of the mountain, only half visible through the surrounding trees. Coldhand cut his engines to minimum and set the Raptor gently down on the outcropping. Between the surrounding forest, the clouds and fog, it was unlikely that anyone would find his ship. It would be a long hike into Pylos, but once within range of mainstream access, he could rent or hire a vehicle.

Coldhand unbuckled his safety harness and then pulled back the Raptor's canopy. Rain and sleet sprayed down into the cockpit, carried on an icy wind. Thunder rumbled in the distance, but the worst of the storm was still far off.

Logan climbed out of the Raptor. His entire body was sore and bruised from Vorus' beating. It wasn't enough to hinder him, but it hurt with every movement – a dozen reminders of how much he could still feel. Logan sealed and locked his ship, then set off down the mountain, toward Pylos.

It was an eight-hour hike through the cold Prian forest. The rain was lighter beneath the trees, at least. They creaked in the wind and birds called from the branches. A pair of soft brown doves watched Coldhand walk under their perch, blinking round black eyes. They huddled together, two fluffy balls of feathers shielding each other against the chill.

The ground was muddy under Coldhand's feet. His toes ached. The feeling was so strange... Why did it hurt? Logan had suffered much worse injuries without difficulty.

Vorus was a master. He knew how to inflict the most pain with the least damage. This was Vorus' fault, not Logan's.

But the excuse sounded hollow, even to him.

The rain turned into hail and then back to rain as Logan made his way down the mountain. Somewhere around noon, he found a narrow road winding through the thinning trees. Logan checked his bearing and followed the road west. An hour passed before any of the vehicles pulled over to offer him a ride. It was a primer-gray truck driven by a pair of tattooed young Prian men. A short exchange and brief display of Coldhand's Talon-9 convinced them to drive on.

Logan kept walking. Passing cars – most moving on wheels and spherical bearings instead of the more expensive null-inertia fields – kicked up sprays of muddy water. The trees and boulders were eventually replaced by apartments and stores, all with the same dull, colorless spray-on finish. But the anti-frosting microbes had long since died and left the gray city covered in a fragile skin of ice.

Why had he lost to Vorus? Logan was younger, faster, and far more ruthless than the old cop. He didn't feel, did not tire. How could Coldhand lose? But winning would have meant hurting his teacher, the man who had saved young Logan Centra from a life as a street thug.

He didn't care, Coldhand told himself. He didn't feel shame. If he felt anything, he would have felt it when he left Highwind, when he left the police. When he left Jess, when he stole his Talon and his Raptor. A good man couldn't live with the things he had done.

There were signs of the recent groundquakes all through Pylos. The streets and sidewalks were broken, some places so wide that the gaps had to be bridged with planks of wood. Some were filled with gravel or rubble from shattered buildings so that the cars could drive over them, but these were temporary measures at best. Vehicles jolted over the cracks and creaked on worn-out shocks.

Logan was going to be in Pylos longer than he had in Highwind. He waved down a striped cab, made sure the driver knew that he was carrying a weapon, and bought a ride to the nearest rental lot.

All of the closed vehicles were already sold out – they were too valuable during the rainy seasons. Even the deposit on a small, fast streetcycle was almost more than Coldhand was willing to pay. They always were on Prianus. Chances were all too high that the drivers would never return their rentals.

Logan cinched his coat tightly closed around him and drove the rest of the way into Pylos. The city was considerably larger than Highwind. It filled and overflowed the valley, crawling up into the mountains like a spreading mold. The gray sky was full of birds, both wild and tamed. The larger winged shapes of Arcadians flew through the driving rain, more than Logan had ever seen in a single city.

It made sense. A hundred years ago, this was where the fairies first appeared on Prianus, by the hundreds of thousands in the mountains above Pylos as they fled the destruction of their home-worlds. Most of the Arcadians had never left the city.

Coldhand pulled to a stop at a traffic signal and leaned against the weight of the bike, steadying it. The muscles in his leg protested sharply and the knee threatened to buckle. He had been trying to feel anything for so long. Shouldn't he be... pleased?

The colored light changed and Coldhand kicked the bike back into motion. He had to swerve around a street-train hauling a long line of trailers that sat low on their null-fields. A truck cut so close to the streetcycle that Logan banged his elbow and scraped the edge of his cybernetics on the driver's door. The illonium peeled a strip of paint from the truck and the impact jarred Logan's already bruised arm. The other driver yelled at him through the closed window, then raised his thumb and smallest finger. *Fly off.*

Coldhand didn't bother returning the gesture. Instead, he eased his weight opposite the dangerously tipping bike. The tires hydroplaned uselessly for a moment before they caught. Rebalanced, Logan drove on through Pylos. Rain splattered against the visor of his helmet and the cold water seeped in through his sleeve, torn where he had hit the truck.

When was the last time Logan had really tried to feel anything? Sex? A chem? Was it the cedrophin on the Temptation?

He had made no more attempts, not since Gharib and Stray. Not since Maeve. Coldhand was so used to being numb that he didn't even try anymore.

Then what am I doing on Prianus? I came here to hunt the Nihilists, didn't I? Because I thought it would be exciting.

But Logan didn't feel excited.

Coldhand rented a room. Not much of a room – just a coffin, as they were commonly called. The tiny, padded cell was just large enough to lie down. Coldhand showered in the common bathroom and traded out his torn shirt for a fresh one. He had only brought a single change of clothes from the Raptor. If he ruined any more, he would have to take time out of his hunt to buy new clothes. It would be a small but annoying waste of time and cenmarks, but Logan couldn't bring himself to care very much.

He climbed up a ladder and slid into his coffin. Logan lay in the darkness, staring at nothing. He was tired, but couldn't sleep. In the sound-sealed box, the only thing he could hear was his own breath sawing away, unaccountably as ragged and frayed as the torn sleeve of his shirt.

Logan held his breath, but that was even worse. The only sound then was the dull thud of his mechanical heart, ticking away the seconds.

Twenty percent.

Zero percent.

Coldhand unlocked the coffin door and climbed back down the rusted rungs into the lobby. The Lyran receptionist watched Coldhand cautiously as he left, safe behind her thick window of reinforced glassteel.

It was the middle of the night and the already low temperatures had plummeted. Still damp from his shower, Coldhand's hair felt like icicles against the back of his neck. A low, thick fog filled the streets and turned the coffin motel into a dim, ghostly apparition. There was very little light and no warmth outside, but Pylos was far from empty.

A flock of sex workers – representing a wide variety of genders – stood on the street corner, all dressed in layered clothes of transparent plastic that showed off their wares but kept the killing cold barely at bay. Their scarred pimp lurked just outside of the lamplight with a dangerous bulge beneath her long navy coat that had nothing to do with the attractive merchandise under his protection.

An Arcadian prostitute blew a kiss to Coldhand and he turned away. If he was going to be awake, then he may as well get some work done. A stray thought nagged at Logan, asking why he bothered at all. If he didn't think that the Nihilist hunt would bring him some kind of excitement, why not leave Prianus? Why not forget this whole thing?

Logan made his way down to the underground parking lot and swung his leg over the plastihide seat of his rental streetcycle and a thin crust of ice crackled under his weight. Coldhand pulled out into the light midnight traffic. He had no idea where he was going.

As the bounty hunter drove through Pylos – ostensibly familiarizing himself with the city – Logan found his thoughts lingering on the Arcadian girl back on the street corner. Her wings and the slim, dancer lines of her body. Her black hair and stormy gray eyes...

Black hair? Gray eyes? That wasn't what he had seen back there.

I'm thinking of Maeve Cavainna.

Logan didn't know why, but knew that he didn't want to. Regrets were bad color, as his mother used to say. They burned a hole in your pocket, but you couldn't buy anything with them.

Regrets? Do I have regrets?

Pylos was no lovelier by night. Logan was a child of Highwind, a town that not even the most affectionate residents would call pleasant. But many of those living in his own hometown had come from Pylos in search of greener pastures.

A century ago, Pylos had been little different than any other Prian city – no better and no worse. But then the Arcadians had appeared. Hundreds, thousands, and then hundreds of thousands of fairies flooded into the city from apparently empty air. Many of them were injured. They filled the Pylos hospitals and then the streets, even the surrounding forest.

The police did their best to keep order, but those early Arcadians were still frightened by the sudden, unprovoked Devourer attacks. None of them spoke Aver and there was simply no place for them. Not enough food, not enough shelter, certainly not enough jobs. There weren't many people on Prianus who hated the fairies, but most of those who did lived in Pylos.

Coldhand would have liked to ask the police about Vorus' information. If Arcadians were going missing, then the Prian police were surely trying to find out how and why. Were the fairies attempting to do anything about their losses? If the ones Logan had met so far were any indication, probably not. They were a hopeless, broken people.

Maeve fought. She was one of the rare ones... but even she was just trying to die.

Coldhand drove through a particularly thick bank of fog – so heavy that it even blotted out the flickering yellow streetlamps – and skidded to a stop. The roads were steep here, where Pylos grew up against the side of the deep mountain valley.

The buildings that lined the dark, empty road were laced with cracks, jagged reminders of Pylos' unstable bedrock. The broken windows were all patched, but quickly and cheaply, with parkboard planks and strips of plastic sheeting nailed into place.

The leaning building across the street from Coldhand was one of many apartment tower-slabs, built cheap and tall to make the best use of minimal ground space. A lone staircase was bolted to the front, but it was crooked and half hanging from the concrete. Logan doubted it would support his weight and probably hadn't been used in years. The slab had to be an Arcadian tenement. What use were stairs to those with wings?

Coldhand couldn't see into any of the boarded-over windows, but suspected the same was not true for those inside. Someone was watching him. He could feel it.

Logan looked up and caught a glimpse of a white-winged shape on the cornice. It stepped back and out of sight. He briefly considered giving chase, but the watchful fairy would be long gone by the time he could climb up there.

What did that Arcadian think of the hunter down below? Just a midnight driver with nothing better to do? Maybe a new chem seller looking to expand his business? A thief casing his next hit? Or something worse, something more dangerous?

Like a Nihilist, hunting down his Arcadian prey?

Even if he could track down that vanished rooftop fairy, Coldhand doubted that he was interested in talking. The Arcadians were closed-mouthed and clannish.

Going door to door and canvassing like a rookie beat cop wasn't going to yield much, Coldhand decided. If he wanted to catch the Cult of Nihil, he would have to think like the predator, not the prey.

[17]
QUESTIONS

"We explore the stars at the cost of ourselves, Doctor Andus. What do we ever find but more planets with few resources to offer? We need to focus here and now, on the constant and present needs of the Prian people."

A week ago, Maeve never would have thought anything could fascinate Xen as much as Gripper did, but the discovery of a Waygate seemed to have banished all thought of the alien. The archeologists spent each day in the mountain ravine, scanning and studying the Waygate. Xen and Panna scoured every surface of the huge artifact, searching for some genetic trace of its creator. They found nothing, but Professor Xen climbed down into the ravine each morning with a wide grin across his angular silver face.

With most of the heaviest excavation done, the Prian diggers, Ava and Darius, spent most of their time running hoses up from the deep mountain ravine to drain the accumulating rainwater and snowmelt. Gruth and Gripper helped the siblings keep the pumps operational, melting and chipping away the ice that had a tendency to build up around the intakes.

Morning and evening meals were usually taken together as they huddled around the cluster of heat lamps, eating from cans and mycofoam boxes. But most of the archeologists remained with the Waygate during the relatively warm daylight hours. Xia alone made the journey back up the ladder to see her friends during their lunch break.

"It's absolutely amazing," she told them for the hundredth time in the past few days.

"Have you been able to figure out how it works?" Duaal asked. He sipped coffee delicately from a plastic cup that steamed in the cold air, even under the brightest noon sun.

"Only what Maeve has been able to tell us," Xia said with a nod toward the groggily blinking Arcadian princess.

Tiberius, who shared responsibility for nighttime watches, was still asleep in his tent. Orphia sat at attention on a perch outside, apparently unaffected by the thin air.

"The Waygates are just a part of the full device," Xia said. "They need an operator, not just to guide the linkup, but to be the center for the entire process."

Maeve was having a hard time making herself listen to the conversation. Her dry eyes felt like peeled grapes and she desperately wanted to lie down. But the whole thing – a Waygate here in the core – filled her with a nervous, disquieted energy. Maeve's daytime sleep was plagued by dreams of the Devourers pouring forth from the Kayton Mountains like a swarm of dark, deadly locusts.

More than anything, Maeve wanted a drink. Enough narcohol to drown her fears and put her to sleep for days… She found herself chewing on her nails again, biting them down to the raw red quicks until they bled.

"What does that mean, exactly?" Duaal looked tired, too, but seemed actually curious. "A center for the process?"

Xia gave him an excited grin. "There's no sort of controls or external interface that we can find. Maeve says that's standard. The operator interacts directly with the Waygate."

"How?" Gripper asked.

"Magic," Xia answered with a waggle of her white eyebrows. She laughed and her breath puffed into small, icy clouds.

"Do not mock such forces," Maeve said suddenly. "The Waygates are powerful and deadly mysteries!"

It was stupid to get so angry – Xia was just making conversation – but the rage burned so hot and so sudden that Maeve couldn't stop herself. She felt sick.

"Sorry," Xia apologized. "I don't mean to make light, but it really is quite mysterious. You've opened a Waygate yourself, Maeve, and even you don't entirely understand how. They operate on memory, right? That's what Kemmer said."

"Their operators opened the Waygates to places that they know. That is how they make the connection," Maeve said. Kemmer's questions had been more uncomfortably detailed, but Maeve still couldn't seem to quiet the nervous fluttering in her stomach. "Only those with keen minds and sharp memories were taught at the Ivory Spire. They visited many places during their training in order to memorize as many locations as possible."

"Kemmer and Xen have been thinking about that–" Xia began.

"If you can only open a gate to a place you can remember, then how did you find the Devourers?" Duaal interrupted. He didn't seem tired anymore, despite sharing daytime guard duties. Tiberius still adamantly refused to let him work at night. "You don't know where they come from."

Maeve combed her fingers through her short black hair. It needed to be washed. There was plenty of water up on the mountain, rain and snowmelt, but little way to heat it. Showers were short and infrequent. Maeve chewed one of her nails again. A bead of blood oozed from the torn skin and she spat it on the rocky ground.

"No, I do not. But I am no Spire adept," Maeve reminded Duaal. "The nuances of the Waygates are far beyond me. I do not know how it happened."

"What about when the Arcadians came into the core, Smoke?" Gripper asked.

Maeve cocked her head at the Arboran and blinked. "What of them? Orthain and I devoted ourselves utterly to the closure of the Tamlin Waygate, to banishing the Devourers from the White Kingdom. The evacuation of our people was not my doing."

"But it was some sort of memory, wasn't it?" Gripper asked, his enthusiasm still rising. "To open the Waygates?"

"I suppose."

"Well, if the Waygates just need memories, I could go home!" Gripper said. When the other three stared blankly, he hurried to explain. "Smoke says that Waygates open to a place you remember, right? Well, I remember Arborus! So I could use the Waygate to get back there!"

Xia's jeweled eyes went wide and whirled a bright blue. "Is that true? Could it be that simple?"

Maeve gave Gripper a sad look. "No, I am afraid not. The song to open a Waygate is not simple and it is the singer who must know the destination. You do not know the spell and if you sang it incorrectly... That is what I did in Tamlin. You know the consequences."

"Can't we just find one of those Spire people?" Gripper asked, crestfallen. "Could they just use magic to copy my memories or something? Like a file?"

"I have heard rumors of such charms, but never known if there was any truth to them," Maeve said, shaking her head. "There are rumors of all things under the sun."

"Maybe you could teach me, Smoke? You know how to use a Waygate..." Gripper said. He looked at Maeve for a moment with huge, liquid brown eyes and then dropped his head. "I... I'm sorry, Smoke. I didn't mean to... I just want to go home."

"So do I," Maeve answered quietly.

She turned away and went back to the tent for some sleep.

The next thief came late on the sixth night, as the excited scholars rested and dreamed of their amazing discovery.

Tiberius heard them coming first and called Maeve with a quiet warning. Over the whistling of the wind, she could just hear a small engine laboring up the barren mountain slope. Something glinted on the darker stripe of the road that wound up toward the mountain peak. A car, maybe? She grabbed the laser pistol in her belt so tightly that her cold joints ached.

Had they come for the Waygate...? The gate was huge, far too large to be stolen. The theft Kemmer feared wasn't quite so literal, but Maeve's raw, jittery nerves would not be so easily soothed.

She leapt from her high post and glided down over the camp, as silent as an owl, but the would-be thieves must have seen her. Arcadian wings were quiet, but large and pale, too easy to see against the dark night. The motor sound slowed and then grew quieter as it retreated back the way it had come.

Maeve landed on the ground next to Tiberius. The old Prian stood in front of an unfolded chair, scratching his bristly chin with one hand. The other was wrapped loosely around the null-inertia pistol holstered under his arm. Orphia perched on the back of his chair, raking the moraine with her piercing avian gaze. Finding nothing of interest, she tucked her beak under her wing and went back to sleep.

"Shall I wake Duaal?" Maeve asked.

"Let him sleep. Those vultures must have seen us and changed their minds," he said.

"Perhaps they will warn others that this place is protected."

"Or he's just going back to town to get some of his buddies."

Tiberius drummed his fingers on his gun.

"There was a time, not so long ago," he said, "that you would've been more than happy to start a fight. I'd have been grabbing you by the feathers to keep you from flying after those thugs."

Maeve wrapped her wings close around her. She was shivering already, her heated blanket left behind on the crag when she flew down into the camp.

"I have no particular argument with those men," she said.

"That wouldn't have mattered much a year ago," Tiberius told her. "You would have picked something just because your talons were a little itchy, or because they might kill you."

Maeve couldn't bring herself to look at Tiberius. "I am sorry for... for all I have done. I brought danger upon you for the sake of my own pain. You have only been kind to me and I repaid you with selfish recklessness."

Tiberius was quiet for a while. Maeve could hear him breathing – a deep, steady rumble like the distant rush and roll of the sea. The stars shone high above, cold and incurious.

"It's not as simple as all that," Tiberius said at last. The words came slowly. "Just back on Axis, you were ready to fight over that stupid goose in the bar. That wasn't very long ago. Something else is eating at you."

Maeve realized she was holding Xia's laser in her hand, clutched so hard that her fingers were going numb. She pressed the safety and thrust the gun back into her belt.

"It has been weeks since my last dose. The desire has faded, but stubbornly refuses to vanish," Maeve said. Her throat was dry and tight. "And... I am frightened to find a Waygate here."

"God above, shouldn't you be dancing?" Tiberius asked. "They found a Waygate!"

"Prianus is only barely part of the core," Maeve snapped, then sighed. "My temper frays. Please forgive me. *Ja'hiraa ilvae!* I cannot seem to help myself."

"What's the problem, then?"

"It was with a Waygate that... that I destroyed my people."

"You didn't do that, dove," Tiberius told Maeve almost gently. "The Devourers killed the fairies. Bringing them was an accident. Hells, even your bat-crack crazy cousin said that!"

Maeve didn't disagree, not really. But she still wasn't sure she entirely agreed, either. Some of the guilt had to be hers. She *had* failed to properly finish the opening spell, after all.

"Perhaps," Maeve said at last. "But even so, the Waygates are dangerous. How long will this one remain in the possession of the Prians before they wish to use it? Until my own people find out and want to return home through it? Until another inexperienced voice tests its power?"

"You think the fairies would leave Prianus?" Tiberius asked her. "We've done no wrong by your people. Do you think the Arcadians want to leave that badly?"

"Not for any hatred between our races, though Kemmer seems to have little love for us. But neither are the Arcadians better off than the Prians born under these skies," Maeve said. She swept a wingtip across the two silvery-blue moons in the sky, streaked in fast-moving clouds. "Your world is a hard one, Tiberius. It is cold and it is brutal. Men like you fight to bring justice to Prianus, but your war is an endless and bloody one."

Tiberius sighed and nodded, conceding Maeve's point. But she wasn't done.

"Even if Prianus were a lush and lavish world, it is not *our* world. I miss my home." Maeve's voice cracked a little and she paused to steady herself. "*Ma'varri essae na!* But only broken glass remains of the White Kingdom. There is nothing to return to."

Maeve felt the weight of a hand on her shoulder. Maeve looked up. Tiberius watched her with a raw pain in his eyes. It amazed the Arcadian to realize that she still thought of Tiberius as *old*, even though she was almost three times his age. But he was so much tougher and stronger. He wore his age like a thick, scarred armor. Tiberius squeezed her shoulder.

"Home is a hard thing, dove," he said. "Coming back can be just as tricky as leaving. Rough as it is, I missed Prianus. I'd be glad to be back here, but bringing Duaal is something else entirely."

"He has been on Prianus before," Maeve pointed out. "He lived here with Gavriel for some time."

"And it was a nightmare!" Tiberius said. His voice shook with sudden anger, but he kept his volume down to avoid waking those sleeping in the tent behind them. "I don't want Gavriel to be the only thing Duaal remembers about Prianus, but what the hells else can I show him? One of Kemmer's men is already dead. It's too dangerous here."

"Duaal might be offended to hear you say so." Maeve smiled a little. "He enjoys danger, as most young men do."

"I'm not going to let anything happen to him," Tiberius said. A shadow passed over the old man's face. "The next time you start talking about getting him out here to chase after some hooligan, I'll break your wing."

Tiberius' affection for Maeve didn't extend to putting Duaal in danger. Her smile was warmer this time.

"Heard and obeyed," Maeve said. "Though it makes covering all hours of guard duty difficult."

"We'll get it done, but leave Duaal out of the heavy stuff."

Maeve nodded. "Then I should return to my post. Call if you need me."

She took wing and flew over the base camp toward her sentry point. When she looked down, the door flap of the Tynerion team's tent trembled like the curtain over a drafty window. Had someone been standing there?

Maeve dropped to the ground and pulled the thick, weighted cloth aside. She reached for her weapon. What if someone had used her conversation with Tiberius as cover to sneak in? But by the dim green nightlight, Maeve counted only the five sleeping shapes of the Tynerion scholars in their ring of heated cots.

Maeve slipped out of the tent again and alerted Tiberius to the potential threat. They quietly searched the base camp, but could find no sign of anything amiss. Finally, Maeve bade a second farewell to Tiberius and returned to her perch.

The rest of the night passed in tense, watchful silence.

To Duaal's surprise, both the Prian and Tynerion team spent the next day up at their base camp. Only Phillip ventured out into the mountains. At Kemmer's suggestion, Ava accompanied him.

"You may know mountains, but she knows Prianus," Kemmer said. "This area is still unstable. She can help you if the quakes start again."

Phillip smiled shyly at the Prian woman and didn't argue. Ava winked at him and went to gather her things. Gripper raised his big brown hand.

"Hey, can I come along?" he asked.

"Um... sure, I guess," Phillip said. "But the view from the peak isn't great, if that's what you want. The ridge there will be between us and Pylos."

"No, nothing like that," Gripper answered. He lowered his voice conspiratorially. "Can you show me where the flowers are?"

The geologist nodded. "Sure."

The three of them left shortly after finishing breakfast. Maeve and Tiberius were catching up on sleep, so Duaal spent most of the day above the camp, watching over the ravine. He squinted down into the big, dark crack and wondered why he couldn't see the glowing Waygate. A moment later, he forgot about the question as a sharp pain lanced behind his right eye. He rubbed his temples and groaned. The headaches were back.

They had gotten worse since landing on this God-forsaken rock. Humans were never meant to be up this high.

Duaal looked up. They were only halfway up the mountain, but even here, the air was thinner than an old man's hair. What was it like at the peak? Tiberius said that even the Prians couldn't live up there.

A keening, lonely cry made him look even higher. The sky was clear and blue today. Not that it did anything for the cold, Duaal noted. The Prian sun was a silver-white disk very, very far away. A dark shape wheeled through the blue, singing out her fierce, shrill homage to the free air. It was Orphia, untethered for the day and enjoying the open sky. How hard was it for the old hawk, Duaal wondered, to live in the close confines of the Blue Phoenix? Hard, he guessed, but not as hard as it would have been to live away from Tiberius. Orphia must have been so happy to have both up here...

But Duaal was *not* happy. He kicked a shard of stone over the edge of the crevasse. It bounced down into the darkness. His head ached. When Darius came to relieve him, Duaal walked gingerly back to camp. He ducked into the largest tent.

"Xia?" Duaal asked.

He tapped the Ixthian medic on the shoulder. She was pouring over some readouts, sitting next to the equally excited Panna. The computer was hooked up to a large white box that hummed loudly. A green graph spiked up and down across the monitor.

Xia looked up. "Duaal. What is it?"

"Do you have any blockers?" he asked her. "My head is killing me, and everyone else if I don't get some meds."

"Sure. Panna, can you handle this?" Xia asked. The girl nodded. "Thanks. I'll be back in a minute."

Xia stood up and motioned for Duaal to follow her. She took him across the camp, back to the Tynerion side. Orphia flew a tight downward spiral and then landed on an upthrust spar of granite.

Her talons scraped on the stone and she regarded Duaal with un-blinking black eyes.

Was she watching over him, too?

"What were you working on in there?" Duaal asked Xia.

"Gruth finally managed to cut a good sample from one of the Waygate segments. It's only a few microns thick, but it's enough to date."

Duaal stopped. "So... how old is that Waygate?"

Xia turned and looked at him. She laughed. "I don't know just yet. We're not done with the analysis."

They kept walking, moving quietly when they passed the tent where Tiberius and Maeve slept. Xia went into one of the smaller tents and rooted through her supplies. She found what she wanted and handed Duaal a bottle of blue pills. He tapped a few out onto his palm, swallowed them and then handed the bottle back.

"Altitude sickness?" Xia asked.

"Maybe," Duaal said grudgingly. "I don't think so. They're worse now, but I've had them for months."

"Why didn't you say anything?"

Duaal shrugged.

"Any dizziness? Nausea?" Xia asked.

"No, nothing like that," he said. "Just headaches. Sometimes a sort of... I don't know. A sound, maybe."

"A ringing or buzzing?"

Duaal shook his head gingerly. "More like... singing, maybe."

The Ixthian medic frowned, brows furrowed. With Duaal's per-mission, she checked his temperature and blood pressure, peeled back his eyelids and shined a light into his pupils. She looked at his fingertips and ears for any sort of discoloration. After a few more questions, Xia sighed.

"You're right, it doesn't look like altitude sickness," she said. "I don't see anything wrong. But if the headaches get worse or any-thing else changes, come tell me."

Duaal agreed and turned to leave the tent, but Xia grabbed his hand and pulled him inside again. Duaal was perfectly happy not to venture back out into the God-awful cold. So he sat down on an inflatable cushion next to the door flap. The plastic floor rustled under his feet.

"Aren't you in a hurry to get back to dating the Waygate?" Duaal asked.

Xia smiled. "I've always had an interest in archeology, but I'm a doctor first. It's my job to take care of you. You've been moody, Duaal. The headaches could be stress-related. How are you doing?"

"I'm fine," Duaal said.

She waited.

"It's nothing."

Xia blinked at him.

"It's just Tiberius," Duaal admitted. But then the frustration came boiling up all at once. He jumped up to his feet. "He won't let me do anything – flying the Phoenix, working security here. Any of it! Why not? How do I show him that I can handle this?"

"You've been sharing guard duties," Xia pointed out.

"Only during the day! At night, he sends me to bed like a child!"

Duaal's vision smeared with angry tears. He swiped them away before Xia could see. She took his hand again and coaxed Duaal down onto the edge of the cot where she sat.

"Tiberius just wants you to be safe," Xia said. "Yes, he can be a little restrictive at times, but it's not out of a lack of trust. It's out of love. You're the only son he's ever known."

"If he loves me that much, doesn't he want me to grow up to be a good man?"

Xia laughed. Duaal gave her a wounded look and the Ixthian squeezed his hand gently in hers.

"You never knew your parents, so I shouldn't laugh," she said. "Of course he does, and you have. But I was one of the youngest of a very large family. I watched my mother and father go through this every time one of my brothers or sisters left home. It was hard for them. It's not rational and it's not fair, but no father really wants to see his offspring grow up. Be patient with Tiberius."

Xia wiped a tear from Duaal's cheek. His face still stung, but he found himself nodding. She stood and pulled the human upright, too.

"How's your head?" she asked.

"Better."

"Let's get something to eat," Xia suggested. "And then let's get back to the main tent. I'm eager to find out what they discovered."

[18]
ANSWERS

"Protecting yourself is the first step in protecting others."

— BRAXAN ARMS ADVERTISEMENT (135 PA)

Logan Coldhand returned to the Arcadian quarter early the next morning. Once the morning fog burned away, the day was bright and clear. In spite of the oppressive chill, the sky was full of winged shapes. Those Arcadians lucky enough to have jobs went to and from work much like any other Prian citizen.

But most of them had nowhere to go. They sat on rooftops and balconies, spreading their wings to warm in the sun. Even on the ground far below, Coldhand heard their songs. They seemed to be prayers and filled the morning with a slow, sad sound.

Logan was familiar with the Arcadian language, but could pick out only a few words here and there, snatches of song carried on the wind. *Erris, Aes* and *Anslin*, the fairy gods. *Alla'si*, which seemed to mean both food and drink. *Wyner'ii* meant dragons, but as far as Logan knew, even the Arcadians didn't actually believe those creatures were more than myth. It seemed instead to be a metaphorical term for all manner of evil.

And then *Lae Marnavae*. The Nameless, the Arcadian goddess of death and destruction.

Logan remembered hearing Maeve's story of the cruel, deceitful goddess. Down in the Nihilists' tunnels, Maeve had said that no one prayed to the Nameless, that it was forbidden by some ancient law. Perhaps by Cavain himself, for all Logan knew. But he heard her name now. Had Maeve been wrong?

Back on the Blue Phoenix, all those months ago, Maeve was so perversely pleased to share her people's mythology. It was a sacred tale of Arcadian creation, of their deaths, and finally of their own capacity to create life.

But the Arcadians didn't make much anymore except trouble. Where were the fabled glass towers of the White Kingdoms? They hadn't built a single one anywhere in the core. There were a few glass weapons – like Maeve's spear – and suits of armor that had come through the Waygates, but none manufactured since they fled from Arcadia. The fairies never even crowned a new monarch for their kingdom...

Coldhand wondered who that would be. Titania, that raven in white? Maeve?

The hunter drove up one street and down the next, exploring the Arcadian quarter. In the case of Pylos, it was something like an actual quarter of the city... Logan had never seen so many of the golden-haired fairies before. They were everywhere, on every side-walk and rooftop, filling every window and alleyway.

Thin lines of smoke rose from crumbling chimneys and holes cut directly into the upper story ceilings. Heat lamps glowed orange and yellow between the boards nailed over windows. But it wasn't enough. Never enough. As Coldhand drove slowly by, he heard the sounds of crying and hoarse, sickly coughing.

Coldhand spent the entire day scanning the Pylos streets with a predator's eye. If he were to hunt these Arcadians, as the Nihilists did, where best to corner them? Like all Prian cities, Pylos was full of crooked roads built around obstacles where there was no money to remove them. The constant groundquakes jostled the city further askew.

Logan slowed as he drove by a shop and postal office half-sunk into a fissure. Even under the midday sun, everything inside was murky and steeped in shadows. After a moment's inspection, Coldhand could make out piles of rubble and refuse choking the hallway beyond, but little else. It would be an easy place to hide. For a human, at least. With their long wings, an Arcadian might find the close confines difficult.

Another part of Maeve's story suddenly came back to Logan. Her people's oldest myth held that the Nameless, made wingless by her creator's angry curse, went on to mother a race of her own. Like her, the Nameless' children were bound to the ground and could only stare longingly up at the heavens.

It was just a myth, of course. Coldhand believed in no gods, not the Arcadian trinity or the old Prian ones or the all-encompassing conglomerate god of the CWA Union of Light. But could that story have some basis in truth?

Logan pulled his streetcycle away from a curb and back out into the road, watching other Prians drive and swerve past. A blonde woman perched on the back of another bike looked not unlike a wingless Arcadian. Much larger, of course... But did humans share some common ancestor with the Arcadians? The Ixthians would know – and if it were true, it would be all over the news.

Coldhand stopped at a shop to buy a cheap dinner of canned petrimeat stew, complete with orange cubes that were supposed to be carrots. The hunter ate mechanically, sitting on the corner and watching the street carefully. Gavriel was not a fool. If he wanted Arcadians, he would send other Arcadians – not humans – to get them. Vorus had said as much. The fairies were going missing, but there were no fewer in the city.

Vorus told Logan so much, even when he only said a little.

An aching, nauseating sensation made his small meal sit uneasily. Coldhand tried to ignore it.

Gavriel was looking for Arcadians. *An* Arcadian, maybe. He was killing or taking them, but there was no drop in the fairy population because Gavriel had brought his own. But if the Nihilists were done here, they would leave... So if they were still in Pylos, that meant that Gavriel was still searching.

Coldhand tossed the stew can into a full trash bin and climbed back onto his bike. There were no easy clues to find, no simple way to identify the Nihilists. He hadn't seen a single black robe all day. The cultists were hiding themselves too well for that. They wouldn't wear the telltale signs of their faith in public.

Logan remembered the smell of the cultists, the twin stinks of infection and decay. Many of them were sick, painfully dying. But so were an unsettling number of the local Arcadians. They were twig-thin creatures with no fat to keep them warm and caught ill easily in the Prian cold. Without the black robes, there was no way to tell the Nihilists and locals apart.

Coldhand's last chance was an old-fashioned stake-out, just like in his police days. He would watch from the shadows and wait for the Nihilists to strike. The work would be tedious and held no promise of success. Logan was only one man. If he was in the wrong place at the wrong time, a hundred Arcadians might be snatched out from under his beak and he might never know. He would need patience and a lot of luck.

It was late in the afternoon. The sun sank early behind the tall Kayton Mountains that surrounded the city and violet shadows stretched across Pylos, frost blooming in the deepest of them. The long twilight would come soon, and then the deep black night. The best time to hunt.

Coldhand found a narrow alley between a pair of buildings that leaned so close their roofs created an uneven but unbroken surface. He parked his streetcycle and then threw a tarpaulin over the shiny metal frame. At a glance, the dark cloth blended into the growing shadows. It wouldn't deter a serious thief, but most should overlook it.

If someone stole the streetcycle, it was going to cost the bounties on five or six Nihilists just to repay the rental yard. This hunt could get expensive... It already was. Coldhand would have to bring in at least fourteen Nihilist bounties to break even.

More if anything went wrong.

Logan buttoned up his black wool coat and stepped out into the street. He looked no different than any other Prian and the Nihilists shouldn't notice him at all. Their attention would be on their prey, the Arcadians.

Over the next days, Coldhand witnessed several crimes against the Arcadians, but none for which the Nihilists appeared responsible. There were thefts, some in the fairies' homes and others at gun- or knife-point out on the street. They had so little... If he hadn't grown up on Prianus himself, Logan might have wondered who could be desperate enough to steal cheap, patched cooking pots and gray bouillon cubes. But there was always someone colder, hungrier and more desperate.

Some of the thieves were Prian humans, but almost as many were other Arcadians. Coldhand was surprised to see any of the fairies taking such an active hand in their own fates. Most of the winged aliens were as passive as water... but not as many as Logan had first thought. He remembered the Arcadian on the rooftop who supervised his first visit.

But there were no abductions or kidnappings on Coldhand's watch.

The hunter stood at the corner of a small theater, long since closed down and flooded with silty mud washed down from the

Kayton Mountains. A flock of buzzards had taken up residence in the rafters and shrilled indignantly at Coldhand's intrusion. They ruffled their striped feathers, but retreated meekly further into the darkened recesses of the rotted ceiling, unwilling to do more than scold the intruder.

The setting sun was only a distant glow behind the mountains. An evening mist rose from the street in colorless tendrils, as though some ethereal, tentacled creature stirred beneath Pylos.

Logan stepped out of the sunken theater. He was watching the warehouse across the street, where several Arcadian families were living in makeshift tents huddled up against the remaining walls. But in the thickening fog, he didn't have a good view. He needed to get closer.

Coldhand waited for a dented truck to drive past, then slipped silently across the road. A supervisor's nest hung crookedly from one corner of the warehouse. It would be an uncomfortable place to spend the night, but Logan had endured far worse. He grabbed the bottom rung of the ladder leading up to the nest. Vorus' bruises were stiff and ached in the cold.

Something passed between Coldhand and the streetlamp. The shadow flickered over him like fog in negative. Logan whirled and whipped his Talon-9 free as an Arcadian man alighted on the sidewalk with his feet and wings splayed in a ready fighter's stance. He didn't wear the gauzy scarves and skirts that seemed to have been their native dress back in the White Kingdom, or even the sorts of stained, disheveled winter clothes that were all most fairies could afford. This one dressed in dark denims and a leather jacket slit up the back over his wings. Most Arcadians – men and women alike – wore their pale hair long, but the fairy facing Coldhand now had cut it short. In the Prian fashion, actually, not unlike Logan himself.

Other shapes landed behind the hunter – two more Arcadians dressed much like the first. Coldhand slid back against the crumbling wall. The fairy in the street advanced cautiously, fists balled and fingers laced through strips of flexible fibersteel that covered his knuckles in metal. Boxer's bracelets, as they were often called.

"You've been perched here for days," the Arcadian said in perfectly clear Aver.

Coldhand kept his gun trained on him, but watched the other two. They were closing, too, but more slowly than the first.

"I saw you a few nights ago outside my flat," said the fairy.

He was close enough that Coldhand could make out details. He was a small man, like the rest of his species, and quite young. Much younger than Maeve, Logan guessed.

"I saw you, too," answered the hunter. "What do you want?"

The young Arcadian stopped at a distance, eyeing the Talon-9 leveled at him. "I was going to ask you that. You've been haunting these streets day and night. What do *you* want?"

"That's my business," Coldhand said.

"Anything you play against mine is *my* business. Ballad's boys keep this block."

The fairy thumped the heel of one hand on his chest proudly. The other two in Coldhand's peripheral vision nodded their agreement with this sentiment. The first Arcadian's weighted words and proud, erect carriage seemed to suggest that he was the Ballad in question. Coldhand glanced skyward, through the fog. How many other Arcadians lurked nearby?

"Go away," Coldhand told them. "I'm not interested in territorial pissing matches. I'm just doing a job and then I'll be gone."

"A job? What kind of job?"

Ballad's Aver was very good. In fact, he spoke it with the Prian inflection, Coldhand realized. There was no trace of an Arcadian accent. Interesting though that was, Coldhand still didn't feel like answering the boy's questions.

But their confrontation was attracting unwanted attention. A bent-backed old Arcadian woman perched on the edge of a crack in the warehouse wall and shouted something down to Ballad that sounded scolding. He shook his head and yelled something back. The old woman sang a sad note and then vanished back inside.

"Vellania worries too much." Ballad had never taken his attention from Coldhand, but now he glared at the hunter. "She wouldn't have to worry if buzzards like you would just go away and leave us alone."

"I don't have time for this," Coldhand said.

He holstered his gun – the kid was annoying, but hardly worth shooting – and headed back toward the street. He would have to find another place to wait and watch.

Ballad didn't get out of the way. The Arcadian spread his wings wide so they blocked the entire alley.

"Hey, I'm not done talking to you!" Ballad said.

"Yes, you are."

Coldhand was much larger and shouldered his way through Ballad's feathers. The fairy boy spun and grabbed his shoulder. The other two Arcadians took to the air and dropped down in front of Logan, but kept their hands in the pockets of their leather jackets. They were cutting off his exit, but let their leader handle the rest.

Ballad grabbed Coldhand and yanked him back hard, intent on answers. The hunter turned into the pull and drove his right hand into a low punch. Ballad twisted to avoid the worst of it, releasing Logan and stumbling back.

The boy sucked down a gasping breath and came at Coldhand again. But not in a light, aerial leap as Logan had come to expect after a year of fighting Maeve. Ballad's stance was solid and low. His feet moved at right angles from each other, always keeping his weight centered and balanced – a Lowland fighter's stance. One of the styles that Vorus taught, one that Logan himself had spent his youth studying.

Ballad was a good fighter, but not as good as Vorus. Coldhand parried aside punches that impacted hard against his forearms – Ballad was using his slight weight to its best advantage – and moved in close to jam the Arcadian's strikes. Ballad had the warm-soft smell of feathers, just like Maeve. It had been months since Logan's last fight with the princess, but he remembered her scent so clearly.

Ballad brought his knee up between them and shoved to create some distance, to make his opponent reach and chase. But Logan had spent most of his boyhood being the smaller combatant. He knew the strategy well. Coldhand brought his cybernetic arm down and let Ballad's own kick slam his knee into the metal. As the boy recovered, Logan landed a solid punch against his ribs, just under his arm.

"That's a sharp hook you've got," Ballad said grudgingly. "Low-land boxer?"

Logan let the boy slide back a pace and nodded.

"You've had training in it, too," he said. "Good training."

Ballad threw out a few light, range-finding fist jabs. Coldhand brought up his illonium hand and parried the harder follow-up. Metal rang on metal as the fairy's fibersteel-striped knuckles hit hard against his cybernetics. Ballad uncurled his fingers and shook them out as he circled Logan, searching for a gap in the hunter's defense.

"How did you learn this?" Logan asked.

"Jocasta Lux had a palaestrum here," Ballad said. "She taught us to fight."

Coldhand remembered Jo. They had spent long years together on the mat, listening to Vorus' lectures on honor. So she had gone on to open her own school...

"She *had* a palaestrum?" Logan asked, pausing but not dropping his guard.

"Miss Lux was killed about a year ago."

"How?"

"A duel," Ballad answered. Both his fists were still up, his boxer's bracelets flashing in the orange lamplight, but he was keeping his distance for the moment. "Someone tried to steal her man and it came down to hawks."

The news was unexpectedly painful. Jocasta had been a good woman. She didn't deserve to die. Something must have shown in Logan's face and Ballad cocked his head curiously.

"You knew her?" he asked.

"Yes," Coldhand said shortly. "Vorus taught us both."

Now Ballad dropped his hands and a smile lit up his youthful face. "Vorus? Arctan Vorus? In Highwind?"

Coldhand nodded slowly. Where was this going? Ballad thrust his hands into his pockets and when he withdrew them again, they were bare. He extended one toward Logan.

"Any student of Arctan Vorus is good with us," Ballad said seriously. "Miss Lux told us he was the best and only trained the best."

Logan stared at the young Arcadian's outthrust hand. Just like that, he offered trust to a strange man? Coldhand couldn't imagine such faith from anyone, much less an Arcadian in a Prian slum. Was it a trick? Logan searched Ballad's face for some sign of deception, but found none. Hesitantly, he took Ballad's offered hand – his left one. The fairy's eye widened a little when he felt cold metal against his palm, then nodded and grinned.

"Cybernetic, right? I thought you were a falconer, but it felt too solid, even for a good glove," Ballad said. He shrugged and gestured for Coldhand to follow. "There's a pub not far from here. It's not good, but it's better than standing out here."

Logan didn't move. "I have work to do tonight."

"Looking for something, right? Well, no one knows Pylos better than we do. We can tell you how to find whatever or whoever it is."

That was an exaggeration, Logan knew, but it was the best lead he had. He followed Ballad and his winged friends down the street.

———— ● ● ● ————

The pub was small and dark and smelled of smoke, but at least it was warm and dry. At a table in one corner, Ballad introduced his companions as An'assi and Kashan.

"My highest and sharpest," he boasted of them. "If you took me down, they would have finished what I started."

If Coldhand's unusual – and obviously assumed – name struck the fairies as odd, they made no comment. They drank their beer and listened quietly as the hunter got down to business.

"I heard that Arcadians are going missing. What do you know about it?" Logan asked.

"Just about that much," Ballad answered with a shrug under his leather jacket. An angry glint in his green eyes undermined the casual gesture. "Almost a hundred are gone. I don't know where. Maybe just flew away. There have been a lot of new fairies. Might have been turf spats."

Coldhand leaned against the table and it wobbled on uneven feet.

"Can you tell me where to find the new fairies?" he asked.

"Sorry, I've got nothing on them," Ballad answered apologetically. He hissed a short Arcadian oath. "They come and go quickly. I don't know where they're going or who they are."

The boy lapsed into silence, but he chewed his lip.

Logan tapped his fingers on the tabletop. "What else?"

"I have some guesses," Ballad said. "One guess, really."

"What is it?"

Was there something eager in Logan's voice? Desperate? Ballad gave him an odd look. He seemed only half Coldhand's age, but appearances were deceiving. Arcadians lived long lives.

"There's this camp up in the mountains," Ballad answered at last. "When we first heard about it, Kashan and I flew up there to ask about work. It's not easy to find a job, see? But no one would talk to us. There was a big crack down into the mountain that had everyone there really interested."

"What was in it?" Logan asked.

"No idea," Ballad said. "There wasn't any work, so we left. I've taken a wing over a few times, in case someone changes their mind, but it's all under guard these days. There's an old human guy and a black-haired woman watching over the whole thing."

"An Arcadian woman? With black hair?"

Ballad nodded and Logan's fingers tightened on his drink. He remembered flying over a camp in the Kayton Mountains. Was that the one?

An old man and a black-haired Arcadian. Gavriel and Xartasia. They were alive and they were here on Prianus. Hiding? Searching? Coldhand intended to find out.

He thanked Ballad curtly and started to rise, but his curiosity finally got the better of him.

"You speak Aver better than most Arcadians. Why?" Coldhand asked.

Ballad exchanged a look with Kashan.

"Most the others insist on using the old tongue. They say Aver's an ugly language," Ballad answered. "But it's about what you say, not how you say it."

"My dad says there's no point in learning," Kashan said, shaking his head. "That we're all dead anyway."

"Not many of the older Arcadians want to live here on Prianus," Ballad told Coldhand. "Or at all. They just sing their songs and wait for something to come along and kill them. Hells, some of them do it themselves."

"But not all of us," Kashan said. "We were born on Prianus. This is our home."

Coldhand had to admit that Ballad certainly talked and fought like a native.

"If you're so intent on being Prian, then why do you stay in the Arcadian quarter?" he asked.

Ballad took a long drink, emptying his beer, and then stared down into the glass as he answered.

"We're not all ready to give up. Sure, it's terrible what happened to the old kingdom, but it wasn't the only star in the sky. We're not dead and it's stupid to act like we are. I keep trying to convince my mother of that, but..."

"But that doesn't mean we don't try," An'assi finished.

"The old ones may have given up on themselves, but we haven't given up on them. We protect them," Ballad said. He finally looked up and his pine-colored eyes were intent. "Morningfire Court might be gone, but that doesn't mean there's no one willing to fight."

"Morningfire Court...?" Logan asked. He had heard the name from Maeve.

"That's where they trained the knights back in the White Kingdom," Ballad said. "When Miss Lux started her palaestrum here, she always told us that you didn't have to wear the glass to be a knight. She offered training to any Arcadian who wanted to learn."

The three young fairies shared a moment of silence for their departed teacher. Logan regarded them with a hard, heavy sensation in his chest.

Vorus would be proud of them. Jocasta taught them well. They were good, strong young men. Strong even for those who couldn't be strong for themselves.

But a painful thought followed close behind. They had lost so much. The White Kingdom and the Morningfire Court. An entire cultural identity. Their teacher, too, and their families.

Logan clenched his metal hand in his lap. Ballad had lost much more than twenty percent, but he found a way to live. Something twisted inside Logan... Shame. It hurt, far more painful than the Emberguard's sword or Vorus' fists.

He turned away and stalked from the bar, ignoring Ballad's startled questions.

[19]
VOICES

"Never carry a sword when a knife will do."

- MALKAIN BRONE, MIRRAN MONARCH (592 MA)

Gavriel stood next to the fire. The flames blazed and twisted like graceful golden dancers. He held his hands out, warming them. The cold had stiffened his joints and his work called for precision. Gavriel rubbed his hands briskly together and felt the sting of blood rushing back into his flesh. He peered through the flames at the Arcadian sitting on the other side.

"Prianus is a world of ice," he said. "The cold of this place seeps into the very souls of those who live here. How long have you been on this planet?"

"For a... a long time," she answered unhelpfully.

Gavriel stepped around the makeshift concrete fire pit and lifted the fairy's chin. Her remaining eye brimmed with tears that dripped down her pale cheek and burned like molten metal across Gavriel's cold skin.

"Your face is so young. Yet even the oldest of my kind are only children in the eyes of yours," Gavriel said. He stroked her cheek.

"The Arcadians are such a wise and lovely race. None know death so intimately as the angels of the White Kingdom. Tell me, do you remember the worlds of Arcadia?"

The fairy sobbed. She wore the tatters of a hooded fleece jacket and pants of similar fabric. At least, that was Gavriel's best guess. At his instruction, the Nihilists who had brought her were less than gentle. Broken white feathers littered the floor.

She didn't look at Gavriel. Instead, she strained weakly against the nails driven through her delicate wrists and into the splintered arms of the chair. Wailing and gasping in pain, she fell back into the bloody ruins of her own wings.

"Please, kill me!" the Arcadian cried.

"Life is so painful, isn't it?" Gavriel said. "And death such a sweet refuge. Once you reach that safety, you will never hurt again."

"Then kill me, I beg."

Her Aver was quite good, but her strength was already waning. The others had lasted much longer. Gavriel sang a few soft words and gestured. A line of blood appeared across her skin, just below her delicate collarbone. The Arcadian screamed. Her cry stretched out, thinning like melting ice and Gavriel slid the spell down across her soft inner arm.

More. Gavriel sang a new song in the fairy's own language.

"Marnavae eru nai'i illithae vernae isha, xellae nai esha arae ilvae imma, shie'i junno kash."

It had been a song taught to take away pain, one popular among the knights and healers of the White Kingdom. But it took so little to turn the spell's purpose to something more useful. Just a few words, just the will... The captive Arcadian's wail rose to a razor shriek of agony as the spell plucked her nerves like harp strings. Gavriel let the last notes of his spell linger and gave himself a moment to savor the satisfaction of the pure, powerful tone.

And then there was silence, ringing in Gavriel's ears. He stroked the fairy's cheek again. Her golden hair was streaked in bright red blood, the mingled colors of sunset. The final bright flare of light before night came.

"I can kill you, dearest one," Gavriel said. "I can deliver you to death, but there are things you must tell me first. Tell me, were you born on Prianus?"

"No..." the fairy rasped. Her answer was a dry whisper, as soft as the woman's feathers as they sifted through the air, down to the stained floor.

"Where were you born?" Gavriel asked.

"Orindell."

That confirmed what Gavriel had heard. She was from the right planet, the first world attacked by the alien Devourers one hundred years ago. Gavriel's heart sped in his fragile old chest.

"Do you remember the Devourers?" he asked intently. "Did you see them? Do you remember them?"

"The skies were full of smoke and the Devourers tore the very ground apart," the fairy said. The memory wounded her almost as much as Gavriel's spells. "I saw demons in the skies. They flew as though on black wings, like the pyrads, and armored themselves in living ash! One of the great shades leapt down and tore my mother away. Erris forgive me, I flew. I fled and left her behind. I did not look back."

"You didn't look back," Gavriel repeated, disappointed and then angry. "Then you didn't see them."

"The shadows were red with blood..." The Arcadian was crying again, but Gavriel hadn't raised his voice. This pain was her own. "I could not look back."

Gavriel trailed a finger down the side of her throat. The fairy's pulse fluttered under his touch, as swift and delicate as the beating wings of a hummingbird. So lovely... and so useless. Still, he wasn't without pity for the girl.

"You have suffered so much, my dear. Such pain and such terror. And such guilt for your own weakness. You have endured enough.

So I release you," Gavriel told her. He closed his eyes and sang once more. *"Anu'aa quai eru oraiva'i na!"*

The captive fairy strained against the nails through her wrists, freeing new streams of hot red blood. She screamed, twitched once more and then finally went still. When Gavriel was finished, he gestured toward one of the robed Nihilists standing silently beside the door.

"Korso, go get Xartasia," he instructed.

"She's busy with Arkan," Korso said. "He really wanted to come to you, but Xartasia told him you were busy."

"And so I was. But no longer. Bring them both here."

"Yes, my lord."

Korso hurried off to do as he was told.

"Surely such news would have reached us by now," Xartasia insisted with a frown.

Arkan gave her a sullen look, but had better sense than to argue with Gavriel's favorite. He sneezed and wiped his reddened nose. The Prian weather didn't agree with him at all.

"I'm sorry, Lady Xartasia, I have no idea why no one's told you," he said. "But I swear it's true. Someone is up in those mountains and one of them is a bird-back."

Xartasia ignored the slur.

"And you believe that this information requires Lord Gavriel's attention?" she asked.

"Yeah, I do."

There was a challenge in Arkan's tone, but not enough. He was clearly still nerving himself up for something more volatile. They stood at one end of the apartment block's littered corridor while a crowd of other Nihilists watched from the doorways and further down the hall.

A Lyran with patchy fur growled at Xartasia. "You don't have to take her shit, Arkan."

"Watch it," said a tall human from a leaning doorway opposite the hall. The Nihilists gathered around him murmured and nodded in agreement. "Lady Xartasia doesn't answer to you!"

"Why the hells isn't she working with the rest of the bird-backs down in the valley?" the Lyran asked with a snarl. "Or are you such a worthless slat that you have to wait up here?"

The princess turned her violet eyes on the Lyran and smiled coldly. He laid his ears back along his skull. Wiry fur bristled down the length of his spine, all the way to his bottlebrushed tail. Xartasia raised a hand and pointed to the rude little dog-man.

"Anu'aa quai eru oraiva'i na," she sang out in a clear, pure voice.

The Lyran's snarl became suddenly shrill. His eyes rolled back and he thumped to the floor. Blood poured from his open mouth. A white-eyed Hadrian woman kicked the Lyran's body once, then dragged him out of the hallway.

"Damn it, Mrell," she sighed. "You lucky furball."

"Arkan! Lady Xartasia!"

Xartasia looked up a nearby stairwell. A shaven-headed man in Nihilist black was calling to her.

"What is it?" she asked.

"Lord Gavriel wants to see you," he said. "Both of you."

Xartasia vaulted into the air, landing high on the stairs. Arkan and Korso huffed their way up the stairs after her.

She lifted the hem of her gown as she made her way down the hall and stopped at the door of Gavriel's latest torture chamber. He had been at his task for some time. Xartasia stepped over a still-wet spatter of gore and several teeth, probably where another Arcadian prisoner had fought back. Whether the blood and teeth belonged to aggressor or victim, she did not know.

Xartasia found Gavriel silhouetted against the flames of a large fire burning right in the middle of the bare concrete floor. A dead

Arcadian girl sat nailed to a wooden chair nearby. Xartasia noted the many cuts and bruises all over her exposed skin. Gavriel had been playing with his new spells.

"She didn't remember enough to be of use," said the age-spotted old Nihilist, his back turned to the door.

Xartasia glided across the room, still eyeing the dead girl. "What did you expect, Gavriel? I warned you that the memories would be difficult to obtain."

Arkan and Korso entered behind her. They bowed and waited for their master's attention, but Gavriel wasn't done with Xartasia. He turned and advanced on her in a few swift strides. He was aged and frail for a human, but his passion and fervor lent a powerful, purposeful weight to his movements.

"There were millions of Arcadians, princess," Gavriel said, his voice rising. "Millions of fairies across five worlds! And not one of you can remember the faces of the Devourers?"

Xartasia thought of the dead Lyran downstairs, Mrell, the way his ears had flattened in obvious anger and could almost imagine hers doing the same. She *had* warned Gavriel... But trading a few snarls and killing a Nihilist was one thing. Challenging the master of their faith was another. Xartasia didn't dare meet Gavriel's anger with her own. She spread her wings and held them low in a gesture of submission.

"As you say, there were millions of my people. The Devourers ravaged the entire White Kingdom in under three months. Three months," Xartasia said, gently emphasizing the words. "There is no force in the Alliance or the rim kingdoms that could ever match such savagery."

"You fought them," Gavriel said.

"And lost terribly. The Devourers killed all of our knights, tore them from the skies with their black smoke. All of those who came close to the monsters are dead. Finding one who remembers more than shades and nightmares will be difficult."

"So you said," Gavriel said, still as ominous as a storm but no longer shouting. "And we came to Prianus to find more Arcadians. We climbed through ice and broken mountains because there are more of your fairies here than anywhere else in the galaxy. But none of them remember any better than you do, princess!"

"We have not yet spoken to all of them," Xartasia answered.

Her eyes were drawn inexorably back to the broken, mutilated body in the chair. She was just a girl. An innocent girl.

Xartasia closed her eyes.

"Princess Titania?"

At the sound of her name, she looked up from her sketch. The likeness was rough – she couldn't seem to get his eyes quite right – but it looked enough like Anthem, her beloved enarri, to make her heart ache in her breast. Titania hadn't brought any images of her lover from the White Kingdom and had to content herself now with these clumsy pictures.

I miss you, my love, *she thought.* Erris All-Singer, please hold my Anthem close and protect his spirit until I join him.

Titania's young handmaiden, Alarra, knelt before her. The overturned crate on which the princess sat was hardly a throne, but Alarra always acted as though it were a majestic seat of her mistress' power. The girl's curly hair was a beautiful gold, even under the flat, colorless daylights of Axis' lower levels. Titania was affectionately jealous of Alarra's lovely hair. The black mane of Cavain's bloodline was a royal mark, but she always thought that it lacked that sunny vibrancy.

Titania had been using a piece of charcoal to draw and now wiped her hands carefully on a scrap of cloth. She touched her fingertip to her own hair. It was lank and greasy. How long since she had been able to wash it?

But Alarra's eyes were wide and frightened.

"They are back!" she said in their own language. "The Sisterhood has returned!"

A tall, powerful-looking human woman came around the corner. She flexed bulging biceps tattooed with gruesome scenes of male debasement.

A sheathed knife hung from her belt, but the two women who flanked her carried naked blades in their hands. They were short and dull, but still better weaponry than the Arcadians had.

The Sisterhood's approach startled the other three fairies — the rest of Titania's tiny court — who had been sleeping on the hard ground nearby. Wanni spread her wings protectively around the other two. Titania stood and faced the humans.

"What you want?" she asked in fumbling Aver.

The Sisters laughed harshly.

"We're here to collect your dues," said their leader.

"But you take money already!" Titania protested.

Her face burned hot with shame that she should be barking at these women in such an ugly language, only half understood. Alarra buried her face against the princess' knee and whimpered in terror.

"It's dangerous around here, bird-back," the gangster said. "Especially for aliens like you. It isn't easy to protect fairies from so many enemies. Unless you want us as enemies, you'd better pay up."

"Have no money!" Titania objected inelegantly.

"No money, hmm? Well, you better find some, little bird queen."

Titania already regretted telling the Sisterhood of her royal lineage, but she had been desperate to stop them from slaughtering her people. It had worked... in part. The Sisters only killed the men now and demanded money not to do the same to the women.

How could Arcadians hope to earn money on Axis? Titania fumed impotently, unable to voice her fury to the gloating Sisters. No one on this metal planet would hire fairies. The coreworlders hated the Arcadians and refused to even let them apply for jobs.

"No money," Titania said, struggling with the alien words. "No jobs!"

"Then you better learn to steal," the tattooed Sister answered. She prodded the princess' shoulder with a thick finger. "From somebody else. If you take anything from us, you're going to find yourself paying a lot more than you can afford. Got it?"

"I... I understand."

When they had finally gone, Alarra looked up from Titania's skirts. The girl's wide eyes shined with frightened tears.

"What can we do?" *she asked.* "The people of Axis defend what is theirs and all of our knights are gone. They put Savel'an in prison when he tried to steal bread for us!"

Wanni stood, bowing her head. She was much older than Alarra, a wise crone with gray-streaked hair who had served Titania's father, the king, as an advisor before the princess was ever born.

"Your handmaiden is right, princess," *Wanni said.* "We are ill-equipped and ill-suited to theft."

Titania hated the Sisterhood, but she hated the Alliance even more for failing the frightened, hungry Arcadians. She had to *pay the Sisters, but what could she do? Wanni was right – Titania would make a miserable thief.*

"We cannot steal or find jobs on Axis, but we have one service we may sell here," *Titania said slowly.*

Wanni's eyes went wide. "Princess, you cannot be suggesting that we sell ourselves to these... these alien men! We know nothing of their appetites!"

Alarra stared at the two older women, understanding creeping across her pretty face.

"Prostitution?" *she gasped.* "But, my lady, you cannot! You are of the blood of Cavain."

"I must protect my people, whatever the cost," *Titania said.*

"Alarra is right," *Wanni told her.* "You cannot taint yourself with an alien's touch, princess."

Titania felt sick. Even weeping over her pictures of Anthem didn't hurt this much. She lifted Alarra's chin in trembling fingers.

"Then I must send you, my sweetest girl. Wanni is too old and the others do not know a word of Aver. You must save us."

"Yes, my lady," *she said.*

Wanni helped Alarra scrub the worst of the dirt from her face and combed her lovely hair into smooth golden waves. Elassu and Ferrona straightened out Alarra's white feathers and offered up the finest of their shabby clothes.

When they were done, Alarra lifted her chin bravely and went out into the Axis streets. Titania watched her young handmaiden go and then dropped her face into her hands, wings shaking with the force of her sobs.

Xartasia opened her eyes and looked up at Gavriel with eyes as hard as amethyst. Alarra was seventy-three years dead, shot in a dirty rental room by an unhappy customer. None of this pain would matter much longer. Xartasia spread her hands.

"There are other cities on Prianus. And there is Axis, as well. We will find one who remembers the Devourers," she said.

It was true. It *had* to be true.

"This task would be much simpler if *you* remembered," Gavriel replied.

"I was protected by knights in glass. They died saving me."

"Speaking of all that... Lord Gavriel, I have something I need to tell you," Arkan said, almost forgotten in the fetid shadows. He stood at the counter of the ruined apartment's kitchen.

"What is it?" Gavriel's tone was clipped and curt. He was just as eager as Xartasia to forge ahead with their plans and annoyed at the delays.

Arkan pointed to Xartasia. "I saw an Arcadian last night. One with black hair, just like her."

"Where?"

"In the mountains west of Pylos. A few of the locals heard that there was some sort of expedition and went up to take a look, to see if there was anything worth some money," Arkan said. "They came back with some nice scientific equipment. The Prians aren't big scholars, so I thought that someone else might be out there on an exploration mission or something. If it was an Alliance group, they might be a little close to us."

Gavriel's eyes were narrowed.

"Yes," he said.

"I had to take off a finger or two and bury the bodies, but the Prians told me where they found the machines," Arkan reported. "So last night, I drove up to have a look around. I couldn't get close to the camp, but I saw a fairy woman flying. The moons were all out and I got a good look at her. She had black hair and was carrying a gun."

"Black hair," Xartasia breathed. "Cavain's mark. Did you see her face?"

"No. Like I said, I couldn't get real close. She heard me coming, I think, and I turned back before she could see me."

"Another Arcadian princess," Gavriel said and stroked his lined cheek. He raised his eyes to Xartasia's. "You always told me that you were the only one to escape the fall of the White Kingdom."

"So I believed, until I met Maeve under the graveyard," Xartasia said.

"The coincidence is too great to ignore. Either another of your family made it out..."

"Or else the interloper is my cousin herself," Xartasia finished. "Her companion in Gharib, the cold-eyed human man, was Prian. Perhaps they have returned to his homeworld."

Gavriel was staring into the dancing fire. "Maeve was a knight, wasn't she? She was there when the Devourers came through the Tamlin Waygate. Maeve cast the very spell that summoned them. No one knows more about it than she does."

"Maeve can give you what you desire. What we need."

"Korso, go get me a map of the city and the mountains," Gavriel instructed.

The bald Nihilist returned a moment later with a map. The plastic was torn and melted in places, but still functional. Gavriel smoothed it across the rotten kitchen counter. A beetle with a red-flecked brown shell squirmed out from the flaking wood and dropped to the floor, crawling off in a wandering line in search of a more peaceful nest.

Gavriel crooked his fingers at Arkan. "Now show me where you found them."

"Yes, Lord Gavriel. There's only one road that goes into that part of the mountains. Some of the bridges are in bad shape, but they're passable," Arkan said. He traced a road along the map and then stopped to sneeze into his sleeve. He sniffled and continued. "The camp is here. I don't know quite how big it is, but there was more than one tent and a couple of trucks parked on this side, here."

Gavriel took the pen Korso offered and circled the location.

"You have done very well," he said. "So very well, Arkan."

His voice flowed like a rich syrup, tempting and sweet. He held his hand out to the younger Nihilist and Arkan sank to his knees. Gavriel placed his palm on Arkan's head.

"Thank you, Lord Gavriel. Thank you," said the farmer. Gratitude shone in his wide eyes. "Danice, I'm so sorry. I just wanted you to be safe..."

Gavriel threw back his head and sang. *"Anu'aa quai eru oraiva'i na!"*

It was the same charm that Xartasia had sung at Mrell. A nerve somewhere in Arkan's brain misfired and a blood vessel burst. His body convulsed, dancing in ghastly contortions as his master's spell did its work. The white of one eye bloomed with red and Arkan fell heavily, a smile on his blood-flecked lips.

Gavriel was smiling, too. He knelt slowly and stroked Arkan's hair back from his face.

"It's good to give gifts to my faithful children again. Korso, take his body to the pit," Gavriel ordered. He straightened and looked at Xartasia. "Now, let's go find your cousin. She and I have much to discuss."

Xartasia's eyes drifted back to the dead girl nailed to her chair. The blood was cooling, drying and turning into a dark crust on her pale skin.

"Yes, Lord Gavriel," Xartasia said.

[20]

CLEAVE

"This can't be right," Kemmer said again.

"There was no reason to doubt the results the first time around," Xen told him. "And we've run them three times now."

"But it's just not possible. I can't publish files like... like this! I'll be laughed off Tynerion!"

Professor Xen crossed his arms over his narrow chest and Duaal swore the man was smirking, but it was hard to tell. His eyes didn't change color at all. Xen might have been too professional for that.

"Well, you wanted first publication rights," he told the Prian, then put his hand on Kemmer's shoulder. "Now you can tell all the worlds that you found a Waygate and that it's eight million years old. That's... what? About seven and a half million years before the earliest recorded civilization?"

Kemmer shrugged Xen off and paced across the tent. It wasn't a very long journey. He stopped at the table where Phillip worked. Panna sat beside the geologist, taking careful notes.

"It's consistent with everything Phillip's found," she said. "Even if the tests on the Waygate aren't accurate, all of the surrounding stone is between seven and ten million years old."

"Could it have been moved?" Duaal asked.

"There's no indication of that," Phillip answered. "The ground has moved, but that Waygate hasn't."

He pointed to something on the monitor of his computer and the others gathered around to look. Duaal squinted at the lines and colors. It was a map of the mountains, but one so complex and detailed that it was indecipherable to Duaal.

"Ava and Darius helped us dig samples from every layer of stone in that ravine," Panna told them. "There's no sign that anyone has ever cut into it."

"But there are some other things," Phillip said. He tapped a key and several parts of the map turned a bright green.

"What are we looking at?" Duaal asked.

Kemmer shot him an irritated look, probably wondering what the young Hyzaari man was even doing there. In truth, Duaal was supposed to be watching over the base camp, but figured he could talk while doing his job. The scholarly discussion was only slightly more entertaining than watching the cluster of tents, but it was still better than sitting in the cold and waiting for the next skull-splitting headache.

Phillip didn't care who was asking questions, though. "I've been making a mineral survey of the area. These highlighted spots are leached granite deposits."

"Half of these mountains are granite. Why am I looking at this?" Kemmer asked.

"Have you looked at the slides I prepared?"

The Prian sighed. "No, I haven't. I've been working on the Waygate."

Phillip replaced the map with an enlarged scan from one of the slides. It was a thin slice of stone and it was full of holes, like lace.

Was it supposed to look like that? Phillip pointed to a close concentration of holes.

"See these? The granite's been leached. Something was taken out. Based on shape, I suspect they were magnetite phenocrysts," Phillip announced, pausing significantly. When no one reacted, his shoulders slumped and he blushed. "It's a form of volcanic iron."

"Iron? No one's ever found iron in these mountains," Kemmer said.

"They wouldn't have," Phillip said. "It was all extracted a long time ago, probably millions of years. The remaining stone isn't very strong or stable."

The geologist brought up the map again and Duaal had a new appreciation for the large green patches – it looked like there used to be a lot of iron on Prianus.

"That's why these mountains are so unstable," Panna explained. "The bedrock is fragile because it's full of these tiny holes. A lot of them are microscopic. You can't even see them. But those quakes just crumble the stone like mycofoam."

"I doubt the Prians had the technology to do something like this eight million years ago," Duaal said. The image of ancient Prians trying to suck iron out of the rocks made him smirk.

"Well, they don't have it now," Phillip said with a shake of his head. "There's no natural or mining process known that can extract iron without breaking the matrix rock."

"But leach-mines have been in use for centuries," Xen argued.

"Sure, but not like this," Phillip told him. "Most leaching is done for water-soluble materials, like salts or bicarbonates. There are some acid techniques used for gold and copper."

"How's this any different?" Xen asked.

"Iron doesn't react the same way as either metal. No one has an acid leach that leaves the iron intact. Even if they did, there would be signs of the mining. Bore-holes, acidification of the water table. That kind of thing. Lastly, you can't leach granite."

"Why not?" Kemmer asked.

"It's just too complex," Phillip said. "Granite's made up of several other kinds of stone all mixed together. There's no one solution that can leach it all without destroying the iron."

Kemmer rubbed his chin.

"So this is... unique?" he asked.

Phillip shrugged. "Actually, it's not. This sort of iron leach is interesting and something of a mystery – we still don't know how it happens – but I've seen it on Tynerion, Hadra, Mir, Cyrus and a hundred other planets. It's very common. We've wondered if it was done by nanites, but the leaches long predate their use, even by the Lyrans. The only thing that's a little odd here is that you've built Pylos on top of it. Usually when survey teams find this kind of bedrock damage, they build somewhere else or fill it in with a more stable material."

Kemmer snorted and then dropped into a nearby chair. Duaal suspected that few Prian cities had the benefit of being planned by civil surveyors.

"If it's that common, then why are you telling me about this?" Kemmer asked.

"A good question," Panna said with a wink that made Kemmer visibly perk up. "And we've got an interesting clue: the Waygate. Some of the pieces contain iron and show no sign of being leeched. We've been able to identify a number of other materials, too. None of the types or concentrations are native to Prianus."

"Well, I could have told you that," Kemmer answered, but playfully this time. He smiled at Panna. "We knew that, didn't we? The Waygates have been found in the White Kingdom and the other rimworld kingdoms. Everything about them suggests interstellar travel and trade."

"But Maeve also told us that no one can claim to have built the Waygates," Panna reminded him. "For all we knew, Prianus might have been the origin of the gates. Maybe this is the first one."

Duaal whistled. Now *that* would be a find.

"That doesn't, however, seem to be the case," Xen said, speaking up for the first time in a while. "I suspect the Waygate was brought to Prianus, not created here."

"Why the hells not?" Kemmer asked. "Why do Ixthians always assume that humans can't manage to pick their nose without guidance from a *superior* species?"

"There are large quantities of metals and minerals in several segments not found anywhere on your planet," Xen said. "It seems rather unlikely that the technology was developed locally."

Kemmer raised his blond brows at the Ixthian archeologist.

"But the iron was removed from the bedrock by some unknown means," he said. "Mined, perhaps, by technology much finer than ours. Surely such intelligent miners probably imported the materials to make their Waygates."

"Yes, but importing that many exotic materials would be expensive and difficult," Xen countered. "This is no prototype or first construct. Whoever built this Waygate knew what they were doing. They had tested and refined the process elsewhere."

"Maybe at another site on Prianus. There could be more Waygates here," Kemmer suggested.

Duaal didn't care about the argument. He snapped his fingers to cut off the bickering older men. "There's still the age of the thing. Are you saying that you think someone *other* than Prians built the Waygate? Eight million years ago?"

Kemmer and Xen gave each other a long look.

"I am," said the Ixthian.

"Who?" Duaal asked.

Panna rested her chin in her hand and frowned. "None of the core or rim races have histories going back that far. Not that we know of, at least. Maybe the Nnyth?"

"But that Waygate doesn't look at all like something the Nnyth would build," Duaal said.

"No, I don't think it is," Panna agreed. "We have a few images of the Nnyth Tower and this doesn't look anything like their architecture. But Maeve did say they know the most about the Waygates..."

"I've theorized many times about a common ancestral homeworld," Xen said. "The Lyrans share genes with wolves and canines on most life-sustaining planets. The human races are closely related enough to interbreed."

"And Ixthians are related to the Nnyth," Panna added.

Xen sighed. "Yes, yes. That, too."

"Wait, is that what the cartoon in your office was about?" Duaal asked, suddenly remembering. "The Axials and Hadrians evolved from similar primates?"

"Exactly," Xen said with a grin. "When the Axials – Vanorans, as they were called then – discovered Hadra, they were astonished to discover their similarities. Each race was convinced that the other was some sort of offshoot of their own species, but each one could prove quite convincingly that they had evolved from their own local primates."

Duaal wasn't sure he understood the difference. Panna saw his confusion.

"It's one thing for a subspecies of human to adapt to a planet," she explained. "The Alliance has settled dozens of worlds and the colonists on each of them began manifesting distinctive traits within six generations. It's another matter entirely for two separate species of ape on two separate planets to evolve into such similar species of human. They evolved from one species to the next, totally independent of one another, and yet resulted in humans so similar that they regularly interbreed."

"The odds are incalculably low for it to have happened once, but it's occurred all over the galaxy," Xen said, nodding. "There are the Arcadians, too. They share a lot of similarities with humans, and the gene breakdown of their wings and bones is almost identical to that of the common pigeon."

"The only way it could have happened was that we *all* came from a small set of common species," Panna said. "Long before we evolved into our modern shapes. That we all had the same basic genes to work from."

"To name the roc in the room, are we saying that this Waygate might have been built by this singular common ancestor?" Kemmer asked. He leaned forward onto the balls of his feet. There was a bright spark of excitement in his eyes. "That Prianus may be the source of the species that spread out into the rest of the galaxy?"

"Or at least that it was visited by the root species long enough to leach-mine the iron from your mountains and build that Waygate," Xen answered, curling his long antennae. "Prianus lacks the genetic diversity to have been the source of *all* life in the galaxy. I suspect we all began much deeper in the core."

"On a world like Ixth?"

Xen smirked. "It's possible."

Kemmer scowled, but couldn't maintain his foul mood for long.

"It'll require considerably more study, of course," he said. "But we *can* prove the Waygate's age. That means that there was not only life in the galaxy eight million years ago, but intelligent life."

"And if we're all descended from the creators of the Waygates – which use magic – it may also mean that humans are more closely related to the fairies than we ever thought," Panna added quietly. "Maybe the Alliance will finally grant them citizenship. They can't keep ignoring their own kin, can they?"

Down in the ravine, Gruth held up his grimy paws in surrender.

"Alright," he said. "I admit it. I'm glad we brought that big ape along. He's not nearly as dumb as I thought. We can't get the null-intertia lifts down here, but he doesn't seem to have much trouble climbing up to the top of the Waygate."

Xia raised an eyebrow, but gave the Lyran a smile.

"I told you so," she said.

Gripper bristled. "Thanks, I guess. Is this what you needed?"

He held out the slender probe. Enu-Io took it and examined the tip with a large, shiny black eye.

"I can't see anything on it," he said.

"I didn't see much in the joist," Gripper answered.

Enu-Io slid the probe into a sterile vorlex bag.

"I'll go put this under the microscope and see what there is to see," said the Dailon. "Maybe we can find out what keeps the gate from falling apart even after millions of years underground. Thank you, Gripper."

"Not a problem, Big Blue," Gripper told him. He turned back to Xia and scratched his short ear self-consciously. "I guess Smoke is still busy? Is that why you asked me to help? She could just fly up to the top of the Waygate."

"She's still on the surface." Xia's eyes went a concerned green. "I don't think she likes being down here. It's a painful reminder of the accident in Tamlin."

"Poor Smoke," Gripper said. "It was a long time ago and it still hurts her so much. I wish she could just forget about all that."

"So do I."

"That's the fairy girl you're talking about, isn't it?" The question came from Ava, who stood nearby with her brother and Gruth.

"Yeah, that's her," Gripper said.

Ava touched her fingertips to her breastbone. "She carries a lot of regret. She should stay on Prianus a while. Here, you learn to let go of that stuff. If you don't, the weight will crush you."

"Um... what does that mean?" Gripper asked.

"Prianus is different from deep core planets," Darius said. "You have to make tough choices here."

"If you let them pile up too heavy, you can't fly," Ava finished for her brother.

"That's enough sniffing each other's asses," Gruth barked. "Back to work! A dig this pristine only comes along once in a lifetime and I'm not going to miss a minute of it."

"Why is it so rare?" Gripper asked as the others hurried back to work. "There are a lot of planets in the CWA. I always assumed that new stuff was discovered every day."

"The Alliance doesn't fund a lot of archeological expeditions," Gruth answered. "The CWA finds things during their expansion surveys, sometimes, but they have to move quickly. The demands for food and resources are just too high. We never get more than a week on site."

"Wow," Gripper said.

"We can take away some scans and a few artifacts, but we don't get to study the actual location very often." Gruth's short whiskers bristled. "In this case, though, I'll be happy to be all done. This planet makes Lyra look like a resort."

Gripper laughed, but he was already distracted as he watched Xia working with the two Prian diggers to take detailed measurements of the Waygate segments. The three of them were working on a thick piece that shone like iridescent gold. The film of lights swam over the Waygate, lazy and slow as the eddies of a pond.

Gruth followed the Arboran's gaze. Now it was his turn to laugh.

"Are you eyeballing that Ixthian lady?" he asked. "Better forget about that. I've never met an Ixthian who dated outside their race. They're picky, even about other bug-eyes. Good genetics and all that. Take Panna – she's got it bad for the professor, but I doubt Xen will ever notice."

"Why doesn't she say anything?" Gripper asked.

"Panna's not a shy girl, but she *is* a bit secretive," Gruth replied with a shrug. He cocked a furry ear at Gripper. "Why don't you?"

"Me? Oh, well... I mean... Why don't I what? I have no idea what you're talking about," Gripper said, trying and failing to sound nonchalant.

Gruth gave him a fanged grin. "You don't...? Well, then I don't know about that bucket of flowers you brought back to camp the other day. Even in this cold, they'll wilt if you don't do something with them soon."

Gripper stared longingly after Xia. She was standing up on her toes, arms stretched over her head as she tried to squeeze calipers between two huge pieces of the Waygate. She was so beautiful...

The whole thing with the polytomograph had gone so wrong. But Gruth was right. About the flowers.

Not the other stuff.

[21]

THE BLOOMING HOUSE

"We learn just as much from our mistakes as we do from our
successes."

- SCALLAN HU, CYRUS CONSUL (10 MA)

That afternoon, Duaal sat on his cot with his head in his hands.
The latest headache was beginning to fade now, but he still felt as
fragile as glass. Normal glass, not the Arcadian stuff. One poke, one
stray thought and he would shatter into a million pieces. He rubbed
his fingers across his forehead. Did he have a fever?

"Duaal?"

He sat up slowly to find Xia standing in the flap of the tent with
dust in her pristinely white hair. She stepped inside and came over
to where Duaal lay.

"Aren't you supposed to be guarding the dig today?" she asked.
"After all that fighting the other day about wanting Tiberius to give
you work..."

"Yes, I do," Duaal said. "I do. I swear I do."

"Why are you in here, then?"

"Tiberius' orders," Duaal said. "He's covering for me now."

"He sent you here? What's wrong? Headaches again?"

Duaal started to nod and then thought better of it.

"Yes," he answered instead.

Xia stripped off her muddy coveralls and checked Duaal again, but could find nothing more than on her first examination.

"It's just about time for dinner. Maybe some food will help," she said, shaking her head.

Duaal was about to agree – the meds that Xia had given him certainly weren't helping very much – when the tent flap flew open again. Gripper ducked inside, carrying a huge bouquet of flowers the same bright blue as the sky. They were damp and wrapped in a sheet of paper from the archeologists' tent. Gripper was smiling hugely, brightly.

"Silver, I..." He trailed off when he saw that Xia wasn't alone. His smile faltered.

Duaal held up his hands. "Go ahead. Don't let me stop you."

Gripper swallowed and nodded. He held the flowers out to Xia. "I... I got these for you, Silver."

Xia blinked and accepted the oversized bouquet. Duaal could just see her antennae over them.

"What are these for?" she asked.

"Oh... you know..." Gripper stammered.

Xia's antennae twitched, but Duaal couldn't see her expression behind the wall of flowers. "Thank you, Gripper. What are they? What species?"

"Species? I... I have no idea. They grow on the west slope."

"I see," Xia said. "This high up, they probably have corrupted redprints. At altitude, solar radiation becomes a real issue. Oh, my... Look at the petal distribution. Is this a cyst?"

Gripper stared at her in horror, then turned on his heels and fled the tent. A frigid wind swirled into the tent as he left, making Duaal shiver until the flap fell closed again and the magnets along the bottom sealed it shut once more.

The mage sat up a little and looked over the flowers at Xia.

"The redprint?" he asked. "Really?"

Xia laid the bouquet on a stool and went looking for something. A vase or a scalpel, Duaal couldn't guess.

"Aren't you curious?" she asked.

"Not even a little bit," Duaal said. "You're missing the point with Gripper, don't you think?"

Xia paused her rummaging and gave Duaal a curious look.

"What?" she asked.

"Gripper likes you and God knows we could all use a little break from this. It's bitter cold and barren up here. I know I sure could use a nice piece of Prian to keep me warm at night..."

"The Prians are stern and demanding people, Duaal," Xia said. "I think you've had enough stern and demanding for one lifetime."

"You mean Gavriel."

"Yes, I mean Gavriel," Xia agreed.

She found a jar and poured some water inside, but had to unwrap the paper before she could make the flowers fit.

"I'm not talking about anything involved," Duaal told her. "Just a little fun. You should think about it, too."

"I'd look somewhere else," Xia said. She smiled at Duaal with smooth silver lips. "Somewhere warmer than Prian glaciers."

Maeve sat on the crag of crumbling granite that she had come to think of as her perch, singing quietly to herself. She could smell dinner cooking. Just petrimeat and rehydrated vegetables, but after a long afternoon alone in the cold, it smelled delicious. She would fly down there soon and eat, but only after a visit to the single vacuum latrine enclosure set off to one side of the base camp.

Three people just weren't enough to keep two sites protected at all times, especially when Duaal was the third guard. Between his debilitating headaches and Tiberius' unwillingness to let him work during the dangerous nights, the mage was almost no help. Ava and Darius provided some relief, but not enough.

Maeve shook herself and realized that she had lost her place in the song again. It was getting harder and harder to stay awake.

A shadow passed over the sun and covered the camp in shadow. There had been a few white lines of clouds early that morning, but had grown thicker over the course of the day until they shaded most of the mountain. Only a couple of patches of sunlight still sparkled off the frost.

If this expedition was going to take much longer, Maeve would have to convince Xen and Kemmer to hire some more protection. Tiberius had received a few calls from Captain Cerro, but nothing to indicate that the mountains had become any safer. The updates seemed only to serve to keep the lines of communication open, in case one party could find a way to better help the other.

Maeve scrubbed at her dry, aching eyes with the heels of her hands. When she opened them again, she found Gripper climbing the rocks beneath her. He clambered up over the edge of the outcropping and plopped down beside Maeve.

She was just about to ask him if he was supposed to relieve her for dinner – it should have been Tiberius' job, but Maeve hadn't seen the old captain all day – then stopped. There were tiny blue petals stuck to Gripper's furry arms.

"Did you give Xia the flowers you collected?" Maeve asked.

Gripper leaned in, almost toppling the much smaller fairy.

"Yeah," he whispered.

"Did she take them?"

"Yeah."

"Then what upsets you so much?" Maeve asked. "Your gift was accepted."

Gripper groaned and then flopped back onto the cold ground. He waved his long arms in the air. They cast no shadows in the dim, diffused light sifting through the thickening gray clouds. Something else soft and pale was gathering in his green fur – it was beginning to snow.

"Silver took the flowers, sure, but then she started talking about their genes!" Gripper said. "She said that there was more radiation up here and stuff..."

Maeve furrowed her brow. Whatever Phillip was cooking still smelled good... But if Gripper climbed all the way up here just to talk, she could put off dinner a little longer.

"Did your gift offend Xia?" Maeve asked.

Gripper groaned. "I don't know, but if... if she can't even look at some flowers without seeing the weird genes, what does she see when she looks at me?"

Maeve had no idea what to say. She was certain that there was nothing wrong with Gripper's genetics, but they *were* alien. Maeve could only imagine the outrage if a coreworlder tried to marry into an Arcadian noble house. Their lineages were cared for and cultivated as painstakingly as the elaborate gardens of the *Sua'ii Na*, the Blooming House. And to the Ixthians, all bloodlines deserved such protection.

"You are worthy of Xia's love," Maeve said at last. "Even if you never win it."

Gripper looked over at her. "Thanks, I guess..."

They sat together in silence for a long time, until the needs of Maeve's body finally forced her to ask the unhappy Arboran to watch over the mountain camp until she could return. He sat up and nodded.

Maeve spread her wings and leapt from the outcropping. It would have felt good to fly a little more, but the Prian wind was like icy needles between her feathers. After a visit to the latrines that helped her mood even more than flying, Maeve landed in the ring of heat lamps. Phillip was alone there, carrying a canister toward one of the glowing tents. He waved when he saw Maeve.

"The weather's turning pretty cold," he said. "Dinner's inside tonight."

Maeve thanked Phillip and then followed the geologist into the large central tent. Most of the equipment had been cleared away and plates set out for dinner. It was a little crowded, but pleasantly warm after a long afternoon out in the elements. Maeve paused in the doorway.

"Where is Tiberius?" she asked.

Phillip set the container down on a table and unscrewed the lid. It was filled with mashed potatoes.

"The captain's outside, watching," Phillip answered.

"Why? He always joins you for meals."

"He says a big storm is coming," Phillip said. "The snow's really going to come down tonight. Good cover for anyone who wants to break into camp."

Maeve shook her head. If the snow was going to be that thick, then Tiberius wouldn't be able to see anyone coming. But the old man was nothing if not stiff-necked and stubborn. She collected a plate of food for herself and another for Tiberius. Panna excused herself from the archeologists' table as Maeve headed for the exit.

"Wait," Panna said.

Maeve waited. What did the girl want?

"Are you going back out there?" Panna asked.

"Yes."

The young archeologist hesitated, twisting the hem of her shirt between nervous fingers. "You've been watching the dig all after-noon. Are you going to be out there all night, too?"

"I am. Duaal is not permitted nighttime watches. Why?" Maeve asked suspiciously.

"Well, I..." It wasn't like composed and personable Panna to falter like this. "I thought that I could help out tonight, if you want."

Maeve's brow furrowed in surprise. "Do your daily duties fail to hold your interest? Why would you volunteer for this?"

Panna blushed.

"I just want to help," she said. "Please."

There was something in the way she asked it, as though Maeve would be doing her a favor by accepting. Maeve looked over at Xen and Kemmer. The archeologists were diagramming something on the tabletop, using biscuit crumbs and gravy to draw it out. Phillip had joined them and was shyly flirting with Ava. On her other side, Darius teased his sister until she punched him hard in the arm.

"We could use your help," Maeve agreed slowly. "Come speak to Tiberius about contributing."

Panna colored again, but a bright smile lit up her pretty face. She carried one of the plates Maeve had prepared and the two women ventured back out into the twilight. The snow swirled through the darkening evening in large, fluffy flakes. There were no stars in the sky, and Maeve could only barely distinguish the dim light of a single lumpy moon.

Tiberius sat in the lee of the Blue Phoenix teams' tent, huddled beneath a heated blanket. Orphia perched on his knee with her feathery head tucked under one silvery fold. Both master and hawk looked up at the women's approach. Tiberius shined a flashlight at Maeve and Panna.

"What are you doing over here, doves?" he asked, gruff but not angry. Simply curious.

"We brought you some dinner," Maeve told him. "You are surely hungry by now."

Panna handed a plate to Tiberius. He flipped out a small stand on the flashlight and set it down on a flat rock. No longer blinded by the light, Maeve could see how tired Tiberius looked. His cheeks were scruffy as ever, but they looked hollow under his bristly beard and there were dark circles under his eyes. When Tiberius took the food, he raised his bushy brows at Panna.

"What are you doing out here?" he asked her.

"She would like to help us tonight," Maeve said. Panna nodded.

"Absolutely not," Tiberius said at once.

"Please, Captain Myles," Panna said. "You and Maeve have been up for a week with hardly any sleep. And Xia told me that you've been on since about noon today."

Maeve had not heard that.

"Is this so?" she asked.

"Yes," Tiberius grunted in answer. "Duaal had another one of his headaches."

"You have been working too long," Maeve said.

"I'm fine, dove."

"You are not," Maeve said as sternly as she could. As first mate of the Blue Phoenix, she had some authority, didn't she? "You are overtaxing yourself. You must accept Panna's help tonight."

Tiberius scowled and turned an alarming shade of red. Maeve was wondering if she should go get Xia when he finally answered.

"Fine. But only for a few hours, Panna," Tiberius said. "I don't want you exhausted at work tomorrow."

Panna nodded. "That's fair, Captain Myles. What about Maeve?"

"I will survive tonight," Maeve said. "But I will be glad to accept your help tomorrow."

Panna's expression was uncertain, but she didn't argue.

"Why don't I come out here at about four?" she asked. "I can get about five hours of sleep before that and be fine tomorrow."

"Alright," Tiberius said. "Go to your tent then. I'll see you again later tonight."

The scarred old Prian pulled his scarf tight around his neck and settled down for dinner. Panna waved nervously at Maeve and then vanished through the swirling snow in the direction of the Tynerion team tents. Maeve bade Tiberius a good night, and then flew through the snow back to her post.

Gripper had turned on the yellow-striped spotlight and sat beneath it, idly inspecting the generator. He had the access panel open and picked at the wiring, muttering to himself. The Arboran started and almost overturned the light as Maeve emerged from the snow.

"There you are! I was getting worried." Gripper gestured to the lamp. "I got it started for you. It's getting pretty frozen out here."

"I am prepared," Maeve said. She shook another heated blanket from her pocket. "You should go to your supper now."

"Do you want me to stay? I could cover you for a few hours."

"I will be fine, Gripper. Besides, it is cold and this will not cover you," Maeve pointed out as she pulled the shiny blanket around her shoulders. "Panna will be assuming a part of my watch tomorrow night."

It was hard to tell in the darkness and falling snow, but Gripper looked surprised. "Panna? Really? I thought she didn't like you."

"So I believed, too," Maeve said. "But I suppose that only makes her offer all the more appreciated."

"Why isn't she helping out now?" Gripper asked. The Arboran's teeth chattered loudly.

"She will be relieving Tiberius tonight, who has been working overlong because of Duaal's headaches," Maeve said. She swept a thin layer of snow from the base of the spotlight and set her meal down. "I have my dinner, Gripper. Return to camp. I will survive the night and I will see you tomorrow."

Her friend offered a few more arguments, but finally climbed back down into the base camp. Maeve cinched the blanket tighter around her. It was just big enough to wrap around her wings if she kept them very close to her back. Folding them so tightly was uncomfortable, but far better than the cold.

Dinner was cold by the time Maeve managed to get at all comfortable. She considered putting the plate up on the spotlight for a few minutes – a trick she had learned after the first few frozen nights – but decided against it. Freeing her arms enough to reposition the light meant unwrapping the blanket and cold food was far better than cold skin.

The storm was picking up, whipping the snow into swirling flurries and every bite of food came with a mouthful of wind-tossed black hair. Maeve spluttered and spat, but was surprised by her own good mood. She was tired and cold, but it was good to be working again, to earn her own keep. And Panna actually wanted to help with the protection of the Waygate and the camp. Surprising.

The Waygate... Maeve finished her dinner and wedged her plate under the lamp to keep it from flying away in the rising wind. She couldn't begin to guess what the Waygate's presence on Prianus might mean for the core. What could it mean for the Arcadians? It had been a hundred years since the fall of the White Kingdom. The Devourers were gone. It was too expensive to take the fairies home by ship, but what if they could simply step through the Pylos Waygate and return to Arcadia?

Perhaps they would no longer be the cast-away refugees hated by the Alliance. No longer homeless. No longer broken...

Broken. Maeve remembered what she had told Tiberius. Even if the Arcadians *could* somehow return home, all of their worlds were in ruin. The dryads and nyads – the species that had served their winged masters since Cavain's time – were gone. The Arcadians were only a tiny fraction of their former numbers. Numbers which, Maeve had to admit, were never vast when compared to the trillions that lived in the CWA.

But it was something, a thin ray of hope where none had existed before. Perhaps Xen and Kemmer's work would serve more than the academics on Tynerion. Did they guess that they might save the Arcadian people? Did they care? Maeve doubted it, but even that couldn't spoil her good mood.

She shook the blanket hard to dislodge the layer of ice forming on it. Snow landed on the plastic, melted in the heat and then refroze when the wind chilled it again.

Maeve squinted. The glow of her single light bounced uselessly off the snow, surrounding her in an unbroken wall of bright white.

It was almost like being in one of the meditation cells of Morning-fire Court. There were few other places on an Arcadian world not open to the wind and sky.

How many hours had Maeve spent in those white rooms, deep in daydreams? How many more spent stealing away with Orthain to tug one another out of their glass armor and feel skin against skin? Or just to find a quiet place to talk to Caith about his studies as he struggled through classes at the Ivory Spire?

Maeve shifted her numb backside on the stone beneath her, making the plastic blanket rustle like leaves in the wind. How long since she had been able to think back to her home with anything like joy?

It seemed like lifetimes.

There was a sound, not unlike the crinkling of Maeve's blanket, but she hadn't moved. Maeve held her breath and listened. She heard the moan of the wind and the slow, low grumble of snow settling on stone. A few distant, muffled bird cries and even further off, the creaking of the trees dancing in the storm. It was probably just one of the tents shifting, noise carried on the erratic wind...

No. Maeve heard the sound again, closer this time. She jumped up and grabbed the handle of the spotlight. Those were footsteps, and from more than one pair of feet. Something moved in the darkness, a blurry silhouette against the blizzard. Maeve cupped a hand to her mouth and called out, but the shadows didn't answer. She reached for Xia's gun, but it was slippery and difficult to hold in her gloved fingers.

"Who is there?" she shouted.

No answer. Maeve finally managed to grab the laser and stood her ground in front of the spotlight. Her stark shadow stretched out across the rocks and ice. She could just make out more shapes. Four of them. They stopped just at the edges of the light.

"You will find nothing worth stealing here," Maeve warned in a loud voice. "Return to Pylos."

The shadows moved again. Maeve spun, but she was blind in the glowing snow. She went for her pocket again, searching for her com, but it was gone. Had she dropped it somewhere? Left it in the latrine? Maeve opened her mouth to scream down the mountain to Tiberius, but a man appeared out of the billowing white and kicked Maeve hard in the stomach. The air whooshed from her lungs and she doubled over, choking and coughing.

Her wings and one arm were still tangled up in the blanket and Maeve couldn't aim the gun fast enough. She yanked on the trigger, but managed only to burn a steaming hole in a growing snowbank. Maeve aimed at the next shadow, but one of them was behind her and leapt at the fairy. She staggered as they hit her. Maeve managed to keep her feet, but the gun fell from her cold hand and vanished into the stormy night.

The nearest attacker grabbed her by the shoulders. She slid out of the reflective blanket and dove after the gun. The man – she could see now that it was a man, a bright-eyed Mirran – grabbed at her again. Even in the harsh, blinding light, Maeve could see that he was dressed from head to toe in bright, bloody red.

An Emberguard? Here?

Maeve pushed against him with her wings, and then lashed out with a kick in the other direction. Her heel connected solidly with the lamp. It wobbled and then fell into the snow, plunging the crag into frozen darkness. Maeve leapt into the air. She was unarmed and outnumbered, but wouldn't be that way for long – if only she could alert the base camp.

A hand closed around her ankle and tugged Maeve back down to the ground. She lashed out with her other foot as she fell. It hit a tall Hadrian in a long Prian coat with seams splitting over his bulk. He stumbled back, releasing Maeve. She drove him back with a jab up under his ribs, a blow learned painfully from Logan Coldhand. It worked as well against the Hadrian as it had against Maeve and he fell back, tripping over the spotlight toppled in the snow.

Maeve spread her wings once more and shouted, but the wind whipped hair into her face and snatched her cry off into the empty mountains. Two more figures – a yellow-furred Lyran and a stout human – lunged at Maeve. They grabbed not for her body, but at her wings. She was trying to fly into the gusting wind and Maeve couldn't pull away fast enough as her assailants snared handfuls of feathers. They yanked Maeve back down to the icy ground.

The Mirran in red was on top of her again. His fingers closed hard around Maeve's throat. Was he trying to kill her? But there was a nanosword at his waist, still not drawn. Maeve reached for it, but the Emberguard twisted to one side and her fingers slipped from the cold metal. The striped man lifted her easily up off the ground. Maeve clawed at the hand around her neck and kicked at his body. The Emberguard grunted in pain, but didn't let go.

The Hadrian had recovered himself. While the other two held her wings, he grabbed Maeve's arms. She snarled and writhed, but held by four larger, stronger opponents, Maeve couldn't get free.

She tried to scream out, but could only wheeze past the Mirran Emberguard's choking grip on her throat. He reached into his robe with his free hand and pulled out a short syringe. It was full of a thick, dark substance. As he leaned close, Maeve recognized the cloying, syrup-sweet smell.

"No!" she shouted.

Maeve thrashed as hard as she could. The Emberguard yanked up her sleeve and stabbed the needle of Vanora White deep into her arm. He thumbed the plunger down. Maeve screamed in fury and a hand clamped down over her mouth. She bit and kicked as hard as she could. The emptied needle went flying and disappeared in the snow, but it was too late. The Vanora White flowed through her veins, stealing away the cold and fear and rage, drowning it all in a thick, viscous lassitude.

Maeve's body went slack in her captors' arms and her thoughts vanished into the bottomless white fog.

[22]

SPOKEN AND BROKEN

"No one can hurt you unless you let them."

- PRIAN SAYING

When the pavement became too uneven to drive, Logan left his rented streetcycle on the shoulder of the road. Let them keep his deposit or charge his account for the loss. He no longer cared.

Logan walked the final distance. Walked, ran... The forest was a blur, patches of dark pine trees and smears of pale snow, more snow than when he arrived. Wind tugged at his hair and clothes. Ice and sleet were as sharp as knives against his skin. There was no blood – whatever the poets said, the cold couldn't literally cut – but it *hurt*.

The hunter clambered over a zig-zagging ridge of granite. The stone crumbled like chalk in his hands. Where was his Raptor? Logan swore that his computerized heart skipped a beat. Had some-one stolen it? It should have been safe this far from Pylos.

Logan inspected the rocky ridge again. Growing drifts of snow obscured the brush and stones, but he was in the wrong part of the mountains. He had just taken a wrong turn somewhere. There were no trails in the Kayton Mountains. It was hardly a vacation spot. Nowhere on Prianus was.

Logan made his way north, toward a tall crag of rock just visible above the treetops. Was that the one? More climbing brought him to the foot of the outcropping, but Logan saw no sign of his ship. Was he going to be stranded on Prianus forever? Alone with his betrayal, his shame, his pain...

A weight in Logan's pocket bumped against his leg and finally reminded the hunter of his com. It was programmed with a homing signal for the Raptor. How could he have forgotten? Logan rubbed at his eyes. They were sticky and dry despite the rain and snow. He had slept some the night before, but not very much. He couldn't remember his dreams, but wasn't sure he wanted to.

Following the Raptor's beacon, Logan corrected his course. He wasn't far off, actually, but it would have been enough to keep him wandering through the mountains for days. An hour's careful navigation finally brought him to the edge of the trees and then up onto the narrow ledge where he had landed the Raptor. Snow softened its stark lines, but couldn't disguise the predatory shape.

A brown owl perched on the fighter's nose and hooted at Logan. He waved the owl off and scraped away the snow until he could unseal the Raptor's canopy. His breath steamed in the cold and when the cockpit was clear, Logan climbed inside.

He could leave. He didn't have to stay. He could just fly away and go back to the core. Just leave Prianus behind.

But he couldn't leave his shame behind so easily. It didn't live on his homeworld, but in his heart. The stupid, maudlin sentiment made Logan smash his fist into the Raptor's controls in frustration and the altimeter cracked. So long trying to feel anything – anything at all – and now that he did, Logan would have cut out his own mechanical heart if he thought that it would stop the bitter, sour shame that gnawed at him.

But Vorus was right. It wasn't that simple.

The camp Ballad told him about wasn't far away, with the old man and the black-haired Arcadian woman. Gavriel and Xartasia. Logan powered up the Raptor, yanked the throttle and roared off into the roiling clouds.

***

"Maeve's gone!"

The shout jerked Duaal suddenly awake. The rest of the camp, too, it seemed. Gripper bolted out the tent flap with such haste that he nearly pulled the whole thing down around the rest of them. Xia sat up in her blankets, raking long fingers through her short hair. She looked across the tent at Duaal.

"Did I hear that correctly?" she asked.

Duaal shrugged and stood up. He pulled on his coat and scarf. "I guess so. Maybe Maeve went off for a fly. Come on."

Xia rose and followed Duaal outside. The camp was muted and indistinct under a thick blanket of snow. Duaal's boots crunched softly through the ice.

Tiberius and most of the archeologists stood in the center of the circled tents. Like Duaal, Xen was bundled up in layers and shivering in the icy wind. By stark contrast, Kemmer hadn't even bothered putting on a shirt.

"What's going on?" the Prian archeologist asked.

Duaal shouldered his way into the chaos and was surprised to see Panna at the middle of it. The tiny blonde woman was dressed head to foot in quilted black. She looked tired and panicked, but Tiberius seemed to have just woken up. He grabbed Panna's narrow shoulders and shook her insistently.

"When?" he shouted. "When did it happen?"

"What's going on here?" Xen asked. He shoved Tiberius away from Panna – or tried to. Tiberius didn't move. "Why are you yelling at my student, Captain Myles?"

"Maeve's not at her post or in any of the tents," Tiberius told him. "She's gone!"

Reluctantly, he let go of Panna.

"I... I tried to call her this morning, just to check in," Panna said. She looked furious, but not at Tiberius. Angry tears shone in her eyes and she shook her head. "I should have called earlier! I should have gone up there sooner!"

"Shit," Kemmer swore. "Is anything missing? Did they get down into the dig?"

"The dig?" Tiberius snarled. "Maeve is gone and you're worried about the *dig*?"

Tiberius looked like he might punch the other Prian, but Duaal seized him by the elbow. The captain resisted for a moment, then let himself be pulled back.

"We don't know," Panna said. "The spotlight up there was tipped over. I don't know. It might be broken. But Captain Myles is right. That's not important right now!"

"Is there anything else up there?" Xia asked.

"I don't know. The snow's covered up everything."

"I need to notify Cerro," Tiberius said. He stomped off through the snow to make the call.

Duaal considered following, but he was feeling more than a bit wobbly in the knees. There was something familiar about this... It was hardly the first time Maeve had run off, though it was the only time in recent memory. No, it was something else. Something Duaal had been dreaming about, maybe, but he couldn't pin it down with any more certainty.

"What do we do now?" Gripper asked in a tight voice. "How do we find Smoke?"

"Maybe she's just off flying," Enu-Io suggested. "Somewhere she can't receive your signal."

"Maeve wouldn't do that, not without telling someone," Panna insisted.

Duaal frowned. "Maybe. You don't know her that well. Maeve's got a long and annoying history of winging off without a word to anyone. More often than not, she brings back trouble."

"It's the trouble I'm worried about," Kemmer said. "If your Arcadian left, then I'm sure we'll find her. But if something's happened to her... Well, it was her job to protect what we've got up here."

"Not to be callous, but Kemmer's right," Xen agreed. He looked at Panna with sympathy. "It might actually tell us something if we can find anything missing or broken. If someone was here, we need to know about it."

"I was watching the camp last night," Panna said. "No one was down here. Xen, we have to find her. We have to–"

Xen gave his student a stern, red-eyed look. "Enough, Panna. I know you're tired and upset, but we have work to do."

Kemmer instructed Ava and Darius to go inventory their equipment. Xen told his team to do the same. Phillip returned to the Tynerion tents to take stock, while Enu-Io and Gruth climbed down into the ravine to make sure that nothing was missing from the Waygate site. Panna grudgingly agreed to help them.

"Um, what about us...?" Gripper asked when the other teams were gone.

"What?" Duaal raised his eyes.

He was still trying to remember his dream and figure out why this felt so familiar. Xia and Gripper watched him, waiting for instructions. Duaal looked back at Tiberius, who was pacing a deep furrow through the snow as he spoke into his radio.

"What should we do, Shimmer?" Gripper asked again.

"I'm not sure," Duaal said, faltering. What *could* they do?

Xen and Kemmer were still nearby, too, not yet following their teams into the tents. Duaal tried not to be distracted by the shirtless Prian archeologist, but it was difficult.

Something flew overhead. Duaal shielded his eyes and looked up into the sky. The snow was falling more gently now, but he still had to squint. The loud, angular shape above was a police Raptor. Was it Captain Cerro? If so, Duaal was impressed by his response time. But then the mage frowned. If it *was* Cerro, why did he have the big, bulky Long Wings pods fitted over his Raptor?

The fighter came in for a steep, hard landing and the canopy snapped open. A man jumped out of the cockpit and ran down the length of one wing, then landed on the ground in a spray of snow. The newcomer wasn't here to talk. His stance was tight, defensive, and his gun was in his hand. Duaal finally recognized him.

"Oh, my God," Duaal shouted. "Captain!"

The old Prian whirled and stared at the man.

"Coldhand!" he snarled.

The bounty hunter skidded to a halt. Ice flecked his hair. There was something new in his pale eyes. They looked just like Maeve's used to. Heavy and haunted, but now a sudden surprise widened them.

Tiberius dropped his com and tore his null-inertia gun from the holster under his arm. He sprinted across the gap between them to stand in front of Duaal, Xia and Gripper. Snow drifted softly down around them. The heavens didn't care about the dangerous tension of the moment.

"Where's Maeve?" Tiberius shouted through the snow. "What did you do with her?"

"You? What are you doing here?" Coldhand asked. He shook his head like a man waking from a strange dream. "An old man and a black-haired Arcadian... You and Maeve."

The archeologists watched with confusion written across both of their faces.

"Who is this man?" Kemmer asked. "Is he a cop?"

But no one was paying attention to him. Gripper squealed in terror and tugged on Xia's shoulder, pulling her back away from danger. Duaal stared at Logan Coldhand. The hunter's pale blue eyes were bloodshot, with dark circles under them and his posture had none of the confidence that Duaal had come to expect. *This man looked like a cornered animal.*

"Where did you take Maeve? How low can you fall, you honorless bastard?" Tiberius snarled. "I'm going to rip your God-damned heart out!"

His words finally seemed to sink in and Coldhand started.

"Maeve... She's not here?" the hunter asked.

"Where is she? What did you do to her?"

Kemmer had to shout to make himself heard over Tiberius and waved his hand at the Raptor. "What are you doing, Myles? He's here to help us!"

"I'm not a cop," Coldhand said sharply.

"He's a bounty hunter," Tiberius agreed.

He waved his gun at Logan and it flashed in the wan sunlight. Coldhand watched as the old cop advanced on him. He didn't recoil, but he looked far from impassive. In fact, Duaal thought Logan looked like he was going to be sick.

"I didn't do anything to Maeve," he told Tiberius. "I didn't take her. I... I haven't seen her since Gharib. What happened?"

"No. No more questions," Tiberius said. "You're a buzzard, Coldhand. I told you back on Stray that if I ever saw you again, I would kill you. We're ending this now."

Duaal wasn't quite sure what he meant by that, but doubted it could be any good for anyone. The last time Tiberius fought the bounty hunter, he got shot. Only Coldhand's haste had saved the old man. If it came down to a duel, Logan would kill Tiberius.

And Duaal actually believed Coldhand. Why would the bounty hunter abduct Maeve and then come back to the camp? He seemed surprised to find Tiberius on the mountain and genuinely unsettled by Maeve's absence.

"Captain, wait," Xia protested. She pulled away from Gripper and stepped in front of Tiberius, waving her hands. "You can't just shoot him. He hasn't done anything!"

"Hasn't done anything?" Tiberius asked. He shoved the Ixthian doctor out of his way with a thick arm. "He's a traitor! He abandoned his own people!"

Coldhand flinched visibly.

"Excuse me, I think we're all overlooking something important," Xen interjected mildly. He looked at Coldhand. "When this man arrived, he said something. You were expecting someone else?"

"Yes."

Xen blinked colorful eyes. He wasn't used to Logan's perfunctory answers and clearly didn't quite know what to make of them. He cleared his throat.

"Well, who?" Xen asked. "Who did you think you would find?"

Coldhand was still watching Tiberius. He dropped the Talon-9 a few degrees, but didn't put the weapon away. He didn't look at Xen when he answered, but his eyes flickered over Duaal.

"Gavriel and Xartasia. I came here hunting the Cult of Nihil."

Gavriel...? The world seemed to tip under Duaal's feet. Gavriel was alive and he was here. Here on Prianus. Why? Was he coming for Duaal?

"The cult of who now?" Xen asked.

"Don't you ever watch the news? Never mind," Xia said. "You've always been more interested in the past than the present. I told you about Gavriel, the madman who trained Duaal. The Cult of Nihil is his church."

"They're here?" Tiberius asked. The gun was still in his hand, but down at his side now.

"Yes," Logan said. "The Nihilists have been abducting Arcadians from Pylos."

"What? Do... do you think they took Smoke?" Gripper asked. "Do you know where she is?"

Kemmer glanced over his shoulder. Panna, Gruth and Enu-Io were still down inspecting the ravine, but Ava, Darius and Phillip had overheard the commotion outside and emerged to investigate.

They all stood back and whispered to each other, though Ava and Darius held the heaviest pieces of equipment that they could find.

"Anything missing?" Kemmer asked.

"Nothing that we can find," Darius shouted. The three seemed reluctant to approach any closer.

Kemmer nodded and returned his attention to Logan. "Nothing's been stolen, it seems. Maybe your cult *did* take her."

Logan's pale eyes narrowed. "When did Maeve go missing?"

The question seemed to remind Tiberius that he was furious with the hunter.

"What the hell do you care, bounty hunter?" he asked. "She's not worth anything to you now!"

Logan's jaw clenched and Duaal wondered what the man was biting back. Did he want to argue with Tiberius? What was stranger – the idea that the ice-hearted bounty hunter might care enough about anything to argue, or that he might stop himself? Duaal waited and wondered what could silence a man like Logan Coldhand. He wanted to know. Xia watched the mage out of the corner of one faceted red eye.

"Wait!" Gripper cried. Hiss concern for his missing friend must have outweighed his terror of the bounty hunter. "Coldhand, can... can you help us find her?"

"We don't need his help!" Tiberius snarled.

"Yes, we really do! The police haven't been able to find the one who murdered Dannos," Gripper said, wringing his hands. "But no one is better at finding Smoke than Coldhand."

"Could you find Maeve, Coldhand?" Xia asked.

The hunter stood silently for a long moment before answering. "Chances are good that Gavriel has Maeve. She's made herself an enemy of the Nihilists and nothing else was taken, you said."

"But why take just Maeve?" Duaal asked. "What about me?"

"What *about* you?" Coldhand said flatly. "What do you mean to Gavriel? Does he even know you're here?"

"I... don't know," Duaal admitted. His face went hot. "I don't think so."

"If Gavriel knew where you were," Xia said, "he would have simply taken you back rather than steal Baliend on Stray. He must not know about you."

Duaal wasn't sure whether he should be relieved or insulted. Shouldn't Gavriel know? Shouldn't he *feel* that his one-time slave was near?

"Coldhand, please help us find Smoke. I... I can pay you. I've got some money," Gripper said. He fished around in his pockets but only came back with a few linty pieces of wire. "Um... I do, really. Just give me a minute."

Coldhand's gaze dropped to the icy ground. What was wrong with him? For the first time, Duaal noticed a dark smear along the hunter's jaw. A shadow? No, a bruise, and a nasty one. It was a few days old, just starting to go yellow around the edges. Who could have done that to Logan Coldhand?

"I don't know where the Nihilists are. I've been searching Pylos for a week and found next to nothing," Coldhand said. He gestured around the camp. "This was the only lead I had."

"But you *can* find Smoke, can't you?" Gripper asked. "You always used to do it before, no matter how hard we tried to shake you!"

"We don't have time or money for any of this," Kemmer interrupted. "I'm sorry for your loss, Captain Myles. Truly, I am, but there's work we need to finish. I don't know this bounty hunter and I'm not sure I care to. If he can't help, then send him on."

"He's our best chance," Duaal said.

"We don't need him!" Tiberius brought his gun back up to Coldhand. "We don't! Even if he finds our dove, what do you think he's going to do then? Kill her? Drag her away? He's a traitor and we can't trust him!"

Coldhand looked between his ship and Tiberius, then holstered his Talon-9.

"If Maeve's been taken by the Nihilists, then we want the same thing – to find them. I'm not taking your money," he told Gripper, "but I'll help you."

"No!" Tiberius shouted. He whistled for Orphia and charged toward Coldhand again.

Duaal grabbed him. "No, captain. Don't! You want to see Maeve again, don't you?"

"I..."

Xia stepped up next to Duaal, between Tiberius and Coldhand. "He's right, captain. Even if you hate Coldhand, you know he's good at what he does. One of the best in the galaxy. Don't let your pride get Maeve killed."

Duaal could hear Tiberius' teeth grinding and a vein throbbed in his forehead. The old man's knuckles were white as he gripped the gun in his hand. Finally, he closed his eyes and let out a long-held breath. The weapon wavered and then fell back to his side.

"You're right," Tiberius said. "By the Skylord's balls, I hate it, but you're right. If those Nihilist bastards have Maeve, we've got to get her back. But when this is over..."

Coldhand nodded his understanding and closed in to a more conversational distance. The bounty hunter was even more tired and haggard than Duaal first supposed, and he could see the faint halos of other bruises above his collar and below his sleeves.

"You were on the com when I landed," Logan said.

"I was calling Captain Cerro," Tiberius admitted. "We've been in contact since we arrived. There was a theft and then a murder the morning we got here. We've been working as security."

"And tech support," Gripper added.

"Do you know where Maeve was before she was taken?" Logan asked.

"Yeah. Up there," the Arboran answered, pointing through the gently swirling snow to an angular crag of icy stone. "Smoke was up there every night."

"Why?" Logan asked.

"She was guarding the ravine."

Coldhand frowned. "The ravine? Why was she watching that instead of this camp?"

"The camp was my job," Duaal told him. "And the captain's. But Maeve had the wings, so she was up there."

The bounty hunter turned away and began wading through the snow, up toward the outcropping.

"Now wait just a God-damn minute," Kemmer said, running to intercept Coldhand. "I don't know you and you haven't signed the nondisclosure agreements. We can't just let you poke around up here! This is a sensitive site."

"If Gavriel's really got Maeve, then we can't just leave her on her own," Duaal said. "You have no idea what he's like."

"I'm not trying to belittle your loss, but I don't think you understand the importance of the..." Kemmer looked at Coldhand. "...Of our discovery."

"I don't care about what you've got up here," Logan said. "I'll do my job and then be gone."

"That's all fine for you to say now, but I don't know anything about you," Kemmer said.

"My name is Logan Coldhand. I'm a bounty hunter. I'm going to find Maeve Cavainna and I don't give two tailfeathers about anything else."

Logan shoved Kemmer out of his way and stalked off through the snow. Xen turned toward the other archeologist with his hands tucked into his sleeves, smirking.

"I don't think that man's going to sign anything," he said.

"Shut up," Kemmer snapped back. "With that lot flying around looking for their lost dove, who's going to be left to protect us?"

Xen stopped smiling. Duaal and the rest of the Blue Phoenix crew ran to catch up with Coldhand.

[23]
REMEMBER

"Any man who can torture another is himself tortured."

- DAILON IDIOM

"What are we looking for up here?" Gripper asked.

"Evidence," Logan and Tiberius said at the same time.

The hunter raked his eyes across the fresh-fallen snow. The climb up to Maeve's sentry point was difficult for anyone without wings or an Arboran's climbing claws. Logan's pants were soaked in snowmelt and stuck heavily to his legs. But the snow the whole way up was uneven, churned up last night by several sets of feet and then imperfectly smoothed over by storm.

So whoever came after Maeve would have had to climb. They couldn't fly.

That didn't help Logan very much... Many of the Nihilists were Arcadian, but there were plenty of others who flocked to Gavriel's tattered banner. That meant vehicles to transport them and then to move Maeve once they caught her. From here to Pylos was too long and too treacherous a journey to make on foot. Assuming they were even in Pylos and not somewhere in the mountains...

Behind him, Duaal, Xia and Gripper shivered and watched, not sure what to do. Only Tiberius was proving himself useful, walking a careful spiral from the top of the stone and probing the snow with his toes. His boot hit something under the ice and the old cop swore, but dropped to creaking knees and felt around.

"It's the lamp we set up," Tiberius grunted. "Knocked over, just like Panna said."

"The wind, maybe?" Xia suggested.

"I doubt it," Tiberius said. "I had to help her drag it up here. The thing is damnably heavy. Too heavy to just blow over."

"Either the Nihilists pushed it over, or else there was a struggle," Logan said. He crouched over the lumpiest patch of snow and carefully brushed aside the top layer. There was blood beneath, frozen hard during the night.

Gripper stopped chewing his huge claws long enough to gasp at the sight. "Do you think that's from Smoke? Did they hurt her?"

"They probably had to," Logan told the fretting Arboran. "They wouldn't have been able to take her easily."

He had never battled anyone like Maeve. She fought hard, with true passion.

Coldhand studied the blood. The red was a puddle, not a spray. Whoever was injured had stood or sat here long enough to create a pool of blood. That wouldn't have been Maeve. She would have been moving... Unless she was incapacitated somehow. Logan felt around in the snow.

Downslope, Tiberius had found something else – Maeve's com. The scuffed and dented device was covered in ice, useless. Tiberius tossed it to Xia. The Ixthian held the com up in the wan sunlight.

"I don't think it's actually broken," Xia said. "These things are supposed to be sealed and good for pressure up to five atmospheres underwater."

"Can I see?" Gripper asked. Xia nodded and held the radio up to him. He took it, scratched his shortened ear and shook his head.

"The top's all dented in. It got dropped, but that happens a lot when Smoke's flying around."

"Maybe that's why she didn't call Panna or the captain," Xia suggested.

"Panna?" Coldhand asked, still rooting around in the snow. All of the fingers on his right hand were going numb.

"She's one of the archeologists," Duaal said. "Xen's assistant. That's her down there."

Logan looked up from his work long enough to see what the mage was pointing at. There was the crack in the mountain that Maeve had been protecting, a crooked and narrow ravine torn into the top of the moraine. Three figures emerged from the dark violet shadows, climbing up a ladder that must have been treacherously icy. Coldhand squinted through tired eyes. There was a furry, long-muzzled Lyran man, and then a muscular blue shape with black hair. Dailon, though he couldn't tell gender from this distance.

The last out onto the surface was smaller. Slender, with golden hair spilling out from under her hat. That had to be Panna. Logan watched her closely. There was something odd about her move-ments, how she balanced as she ran to catch up with the others.

Something sharp jabbed into Logan's still-questing fingers. He felt more carefully through the snow and discovered a hypodermic needle. Tiberius and the rest closed in around the hunter as he shook it free of the clinging frost.

"What's that?" Gripper asked.

Coldhand worked the rubber plunger until he coaxed a tiny bead of black from the needle's tip, then pulled the glove off his right hand with his teeth. The black stuff felt sticky as he rubbed it between his fingers. He sniffed. It smelled sweet, poisonously sweet.

"Vanora White," Logan announced.

"I *knew* Maeve was using again," Duaal said.

Again? That meant that she had stopped and Logan wondered why. Were the chems no longer enough? Or maybe she didn't need them anymore. Even in the face of death, Maeve was still more alive than Logan ever was. Just like Ballad. Just like Vorus.

"Come on, Shimmer, you know she's been clean!" Gripper said, confirming Logan's private thoughts.

"Oh really? Then what is that needle doing up here?" Duaal asked.

"I don't know, but I know Smoke," Gripper said. "She's been off this stuff for months!"

Logan rubbed the Vanora White between his fingers again. The substance was thinner than it should have been, and slightly grainy against his skin. He inspected the needle. It was bigger than any Logan had ever bought for himself, and was marked along the side with close-packed measurement lines.

Most chems came packaged in unmarked needles, all filled and premeasured by the dealer. They were meant to be discarded and untraceable after use. But this needle was probably from a hospital or clinic, stolen for drug use. It could be refilled, and wear around the edges of the plastic suggested that it had.

You can't just throw things away on Prianus.

Logan pocketed the used needle and stood. Tiberius watched him, fury all across his lined, reddened face.

"Well?" he asked impatiently.

The bounty hunter wasn't accustomed to sharing his thoughts with anyone else. He hesitated before answering. "Has Maeve been in Pylos since you arrived?"

"We drove through the city on our way up here, but not since then," Xia answered.

"What the hells does that have to do with anything?" Tiberius asked with an accusatory jab of one finger. "You think she ran off on her own now? She wouldn't do that!"

"No, I don't think she would. Maeve always wanted to keep you safely out of our battles," Logan said. He remembered her panic the last time they fought as she tried to convince Tiberius to go away.

"But unless Maeve made a trip down into the city, I doubt that this White is hers."

"How's that?" Tiberius asked.

"It's a local blend," Logan said. "Much cheaper than what you get on Axis, and weaker. It needs a much larger dose to do its job. That's why the needle is so big."

"Then what's it doing up here?" Tiberius asked.

He was a good man, but not very imaginative, Logan decided.

"I think the Nihilists used it to drug Maeve." The hunter held out his metal hand and drew an imaginary line from the crag to the road far below. "If they had to take her to a vehicle down there, they would have had to move her right past your camp. They needed her quiet and still, not struggling. We should check the road."

"See? I *told* you it wasn't hers!" Gripper said.

He elbowed Duaal, making the mage stagger in the snow. Duaal didn't look convinced, but he shrugged and dropped the matter.

"What now, then?" he asked, directing his question to Logan.

"We check out the road," Tiberius answered before the bounty hunter could. "Just like the God-damn traitor says."

The darkness was so complete that Maeve couldn't tell if her eyes were open or shut. Wherever she was, the air reeked acidly of mold and rot. Her wings were tied tightly by rough, scratchy rope and her hands were bound behind her, too. Bands of metal hung cold and heavy around her wrists.

Handcuffs? Maeve gave them an experimental tug and heard the brittle-hard clatter of a chain, confirming her suspicion.

Where was she? Maeve sat with her back to a post of some sort. Her wings and wrists were tied uncomfortably around it, the nub of a rivet digging into the sensitive skin between her wings. A support beam?

The musty air wasn't moving very much. Maeve must have been indoors. She reached out with one foot, but numb toes through boots felt little. Rubble and something softer – cloth, maybe – was scattered across the floor. Maeve thought for a moment and swallowed against the thick, too-sweet taste in the back of her throat, then hummed a short, high note and listened. There weren't many echoes, and even those were close and sharp. The room was small.

So Maeve wasn't being held prisoner in some empty warehouse. The cloth under her left heel could be clothes or curtains. Was she in a store? A house?

Maeve sagged back into the support beam. It was hard to hold herself upright. The last of the Vanora White was still working its way through her blood. Maeve's stomach knotted up like the rope binding her wings.

Even when she strove to live her life cleanly, she couldn't escape these poisons.

Maeve couldn't afford to waste time on self-pity and recrimination, but she wasn't sure what else to do. She pulled weakly against her bonds and sucked in a pained breath at the result. The ropes and handcuffs were tight. Maeve felt around again with her feet for something sharp. Maybe she could pick the lock on the cuffs or cut through the ropes...

Maybe. She needed more information. Maeve wedged one foot under the other and wriggled it free from her boot. The cold raised bumps on her skin. Maeve didn't want to feel around in the darkness with bare toes – she couldn't stop imagining terrible things in the blackness, monsters more accustomed to their blindness than she – but the fairy made her foot move slowly out again.

The floor was gritty and dirty. There were some larger lumps, some hard and some that crumbled at Maeve's cringing touch. She felt the same yielding softness as before, but could make out more of the details now. Thick cloth, heavily textured... Upholstery? Dust clung to Maeve's clammy skin, but she could find nothing useful.

"Sa vaeli'i!" she groaned.

Maeve didn't want to give up, but she had no other ideas. She knew only a few battlefield spells and none of them included fire or anything else useful against handcuffs.

She tried to swallow and coughed instead. Maeve needed water, something to wash away the stale-sweet taste in her mouth and wet her swollen throat. She felt as dry and wrung out as an old sponge.

The deep, dark shadows crept with phantom lights in dizzying, geometric patterns. Was that a voice? Maeve could make no sense of the faint whispers. The muffled voices might have been someone talking on the far side of the wall or the indistinct musings of her own rising fear.

The Mirran in red. The Cult of Nihil took me. Why?

Maeve didn't care who might hear her now. If it was her captors, then what did it matter? Anyone else was a potential ally. Even on Prianus, no one would just leave a half-drugged woman tied and alone in the dark. Would they?

"Help!" Maeve cried. Her voice was rough and much softer than she hoped. "Please, help me!"

There was no answer and Maeve slumped back into the metal beam. It hurt, but she didn't care. Only the gods knew where she was. She remembered the cracked and failing city of Pylos, entire buildings toppled in the huge quake fissure. Swallowed up, as the archaeologists told her, by the unstable leach-mined stone. Maeve might be buried alive under Pylos.

Alive for now, at least.

Pylos. The Waygate... A memory surged suddenly to the fore, of the last hours of the White Kingdom, as Maeve and Orthain battled and crept back toward the Tamlin Waygate. Sneaking and hiding, for the most part. It took a dozen of even the best knights to kill a single huge, smoke-shrouded Devourer with their spears. But for all the horror and all the bloody carnage, there wasn't a single body left behind. No chance to hide among the dead.

So Maeve and Orthain had concealed themselves behind the shattered stump of a glass tower. Not long ago, the transparent glass would have offered no concealment, but after weeks of fighting the Devourers, it was streaked, opaque and broken. Even fire couldn't damage Arcadian glass, but the slightest brush of the Devourer's smoky armor seemed to leech something from the glass, leaving it milky and brittle.

Duaal and Xia said that the Kayton mountain iron – and several other elemental metals, Phillip told them later – were extracted by no known mining techniques. What if that same magic or technology was used in the destruction of the White Kingdom? Arcadian glass was full of carbon, like coreworld diamonds, Maeve knew. What if the Devourers had removed it?

It didn't matter to her current problem, Maeve thought, but she couldn't stop the shiver crawling up her spine. What else might it mean? That the Devourers had visited more planets than those of the White Kingdom? But Phillip said that the iron was mined long, long ago...

Had the Devourers been on Prianus?

Before Maeve could ponder the horrible question further, light flooded the room. Instinctively, she tried to throw her arm across her face against the shining needles of radiance, but succeeded only in wrenching her shoulder. Maeve blinked until the hot tears faded a little and looked up.

A door stood open and the light that had seemed so blinding at first was actually little more than a dim green-gray glow. It cast shallow illumination across Maeve's prison – a small, single-room apartment with one collapsed wall that vomited dirt and crumbling rock out across the floor.

A lone figure stepped into the doorway, silhouetted against the rectangular slab of light. Maeve strained forward again, oblivious now to the pain of her restraints. She recognized her visitor at once.

"Xartasia!" Maeve rasped.

The older princess closed the door behind her, momentarily sinking the apartment once more into utter darkness. But then Xartasia sang a few short words and a faint, sourceless golden light filled the room.

Xartasia looked just as she had on Stray, dressed all in immaculate and pristine white. Cavain's raven-black hair spilled smoothly down across her shoulders and between her long wings. She was beautiful, regal as befit a queen... If she would only lead her people. Xartasia lifted the hem of her dress and picked her way across the filth to where her cousin was bound.

"What are you doing in this place?" Maeve asked in a dry whisper. "How did you survive the fall of the Gharib cathedral?"

"My magic has grown strong, little cousin, and Gavriel's convictions stronger still. I could not let him die just yet. There is work yet to be done," Xartasia said. Her violet eyes shone brightly. "You are surprisingly alert, considering the dose of Vanora White that Hallax gave you."

"I have used these chems for a century to blunt the pain of my deeds," Maeve answered. "I am accustomed to them. What do you want of me? Do you wish vengeance for the cathedral's fall? For the death of the White Kingdom?"

Xartasia shook her head slowly, sadly. "No, Maeve. I have told you that you are not to blame for the death of our people. I doubt that you are the first to sing the Waygate songs improperly, not in a history as long as ours. The Devourers are to blame for the carnage, Maeve. They answered the Waygate's call and came to our worlds."

Maeve wasn't sure what she meant.

"The Waygate's... call?" she asked.

Xartasia ignored her question. "As to Gharib, I cannot afford to linger in anger. You did what you believed best, as I did. We can ask for nothing more. What needed to be done was done."

Maeve remembered tiny blue Baliend under the Nihilist graveyard, crying for his mother.

"Did you… kill another child, then?" Maeve asked.

Xartasia flicked her hand in a small, dismissive circle. "Not a child, but a woman. Elsa. She knew you. Her mind was so much like that of a child that it served our purposes. Now Gavriel's magic is stronger than it has ever been."

Xartasia flexed her pale wings. Her glowing light charm flared, making Maeve's eyes water, and then dimmed once more. When she could see again, Maeve found her cousin's black brows knit in apparent worry. Maeve didn't trust herself to speak.

"Gavriel is driven by deep passions, little cousin," Xartasia said, but she wasn't just making idle conversation with her prisoner. "You have not been brought to answer for some obscure matter of honor or vengeance. Gavriel desires something from you and he will have it. Do not fight him."

"What could he want from me but revenge?" Maeve asked.

She wanted to keep her voice strong, but Gavriel frightened her more than she could ever admit.

"None living know the Devourers as you do," Xartasia said. "You were there when they came through the Tamlin gate. You fought them and banished them from Arcadia when you closed the gate."

"What is that to your master?"

Xartasia pressed her full red lips together into a thin, unhappy line. Was she angry at the interruption, or that Maeve had called Gavriel her master?

"He wants what you have seen," she said. "Gavriel wants your memories of the Devourers and he will tear them from your mind if he must."

Maeve's mouth went as dry as dust. "Why?"

"Gavriel will summon them, Maeve," Xartasia answered. "Using your memories, Gavriel will bring the Devourers back once more to destroy all life in this galaxy."

[24]

BLACK AND WHITE

"Dying for your beliefs shows only that you believe in death."

"Everything is there," Panna reported, exasperated. "What do you think they're going to do? Steal the Waygate?"

Kemmer tempered his irritation with the flirtatious smile that he liked using with Panna. She barely resisted rolling her eyes. What did he think would happen? That his arrogant attempts at charm were going to seduce her one night?

He wouldn't even try if he really knew Panna...

"Even if they can't steal the Waygate, it doesn't mean that they couldn't steal the *discovery*, my dear," Kemmer said, tapping a stylus on the datadex in front of him for emphasis. "A few scans and photos and we'd be falling out. So far, we've managed to keep everything nice and quiet."

"So quiet the police don't even know what's going on up here!" Panna answered in a rising voice. "Doctor Kemmer, if they knew the magnitude of your discovery, surely they would send someone up to help protect the Waygate!"

"Panna, please," Xen said. He put a long-fingered hand on her shoulder. "I know you're upset, but–"

"But what?" Panna turned on her teacher. "But we were discreet. We hired Captain Myles and his friends. And now Maeve Cavainna is gone!"

"For which we're all sorry, but the world turns on," Kemmer said.

Xen frowned at Panna, but she wasn't done.

"She has enemies! Enemies like the Cult of Nihil. Do you know anything about them?" Panna asked, shaking a fist in the air. Her nails were biting into her palms. "Well, I do!"

"What do you know about that?"

The voice came from behind her. Panna was so caught up in her anger that she failed to notice that Tiberius Myles and his crew had returned. She spun to find the red-faced old Prian stepping through the flap of the tent. Duaal and Xia followed their captain inside, and another Prian man that Panna didn't immediately recognize. He was young, with handsome – if tired and drawn – features and sharp, predatory eyes.

Panna's gaze dropped to his hands, one of cold-reddened flesh and the other all made of scarred illonium. Panna stared. She knew him... or of him, at least. Logan Coldhand. He stopped in the tent door and looked at Panna with narrowed blue eyes. Behind him, Gripper poked his head through, noting the fullness of the tent with a small frown.

"I... I read about what happened on Stray," Panna told Tiberius. "I was curious."

"Really?" Duaal asked, surprised. "That was pretty small news to the rest of the galaxy."

Coldhand looked at the mage, then back to Panna. An icy shiver crawled up her spine. She took a step back, away from the bounty hunter, but not fast enough. Coldhand was on Panna in a second, moving as quick as a lightning strike. He grabbed her by the arm, hooked her feet out from under her with one ankle and dropped Panna to the ground. She felt his gun pressed against the back of her head and whimpered.

"What the hells do you think you're doing?" Kemmer shouted. "Release her this instant!"

Tiberius didn't waste time with words. He tore his own gun free and leveled it at Coldhand. The bounty hunter looked up at him through damp blond hair.

"Put that away, Myles," Coldhand said.

"Let the girl go," Tiberius told him.

Panna was too terrified to breathe. Her pulse pounded through her body, beating like a drum in her ears. The pressure of the laser against her skull eased, but only a little.

"She's not a girl," Coldhand said. "Not a human one, at least."

"Don't!"

It wasn't Panna who had protested, but Xen. The Ixthian lunged at Coldhand, but Tiberius stepped into his way.

"One at a God-damn time," Tiberius said in a low, angry voice. "You'll get your piece in right time, Professor Xen. Now, what the hells do you mean *not human*, Coldhand?"

Panna pressed her face against the floor of the tent. Everything smelled like plastic. Could she die just by wishing to? A sob choked her and hot tears spilled out onto the ground.

"This girl is Arcadian," Coldhand said.

There was a moment of stunned silence. Professor Xen was the first to break it.

"I know," he said. "Now will you please let her go?"

The Talon-9 was cold against Panna's skin.

"The Nihilists use a lot of Arcadians," Coldhand said. "They've been using them to abduct other fairies. Is she one of theirs?"

"No," Xen answered. "She's not. Let her up."

And then the gun was gone. Coldhand stood up, reholstering his weapon. Tiberius studied the bounty hunter for a moment and finally did the same. Panna remained still in the cooling puddle of her tears. She wanted to die.

"Panna?" Xen was offering his hand.

He knew. But how...? Panna reluctantly let the archeogeneticist help her to her feet. She sniffled and wiped her cheeks on the back of her sleeve. It was hard to meet the eyes around the tent. How long until Gruth, Phillip and Enu-Io found out?

"She *looks* human," Kemmer said. He stood well away from Xen and Panna, she could not help noticing. "She can't really be a bird-back, can she?"

"She had her wings removed and ears reshaped," Coldhand told them. "But she is definitely Arcadian."

Duaal squinted at her speculatively. "I can see it now, I guess, in the face and build. But how did you know, Logan?"

Panna sniffled and looked up at Coldhand.

"It was a good job, the best my parents could afford," she said.

The bounty hunter nodded. "But it's there in the way you walk, in your balance. You were meant to fly."

Was that sorrow in Coldhand's voice?

"You're Prian," Panna said. "You people love birds. But you have no idea what it's like to grow up like one, like an animal. Nobody believes Arcadians are worth anything. We're not allowed to go to Alliance colleges and I wanted..."

Panna's voice failed her.

"I guess you don't see Arcadians on Tynerion," Tiberius said. He scratched his chin. "That was your problem with Maeve, wasn't it? You were afraid she would notice that you were one of her own."

"Yes," Panna admitted. Her vision swam with a fresh flood of tears. "I didn't want to disrespect a princess, but... but I didn't know what else to do."

There was a gust of cold air as Gripper finally pushed his way through the flap of the tent. "That's why you were dropping stuff that first day! Smoke told me about it. She was really mad."

Panna flinched. She had never meant to insult the princess. She never expected…

"I was just so shocked," Panna said. "My mother always told me none of the royal family escaped the White Kingdom. And then I saw her on the news, after the encounter on Stray."

Xia looked at Xen with orange disbelief in her eyes.

"You… you knew about this?" she asked.

"Does it matter, Xia?" Xen's fingers tightened on Panna's shoulder. She looked up at him. "She's a good student, one of the best I've ever had. What does her species matter?"

"*What does her species matter?*" Xia repeated, aghast. "You can't be serious, Xen! She lied about her race!"

Panna stood up to her full height – which wasn't impressive in a tent full of humans, Ixthians and the looming Arboran outside – and glared at Xia.

"What choice did I have?" she asked. "I was born in the core. On a farm on Cyrus! But because I had wings, I couldn't become an Alliance citizen."

"It's not about your wings, Panna," Xia started to say, but Panna was too furious to listen.

"What is it, then?" she challenged. "Even Gripper got to take the test and become a proper citizen! But Arcadians are still considered refugees. It's been a hundred years! My parents are little more than slaves on Cyrus. They cried when I told them I wanted the surgery, but they understood. I wanted to go to college. I wanted a better life!"

"You had some doctor cut off your wings just to go to school?" Tiberius asked, shaking his head. "I don't understand you, dove."

"You wouldn't," Panna answered as calmly as she could. "You're Prian. You'd probably give just about anything to have wings."

Coldhand was listening very closely. He didn't nod, but Panna thought she saw understanding there in his eyes. The hunter had lost a part of himself, too, an important part. It wounded him still.

Panna looked back at Xen. He had kept her secret. An Ixthian ignoring her species... Panna realized she was blushing.

"All of this is why you're so upset about Smoke now," Gripper said, speaking up shyly but insistently. He wanted Maeve back, too. "She's not just some lady. She's your princess."

"Yes..." Panna admitted. She turned toward Xen again. "Please, professor. Let me help look for her."

"Of course," he said with a sigh. "Since it looks like I can't keep the secret of your genetics anymore."

Everyone in the tent had almost forgotten about Kemmer until the Prian archeologist threw his hands in the air.

"Sure!" he shouted. "First we lose what remains of our security force and now you're letting this... whatever-she-is fly off? Oh right, she can't fly because she cut off her wings!"

"Shut up, Kemmer," Xen snapped.

Panna smiled gratefully at her teacher, then looked between Tiberius and Coldhand.

"So... what do we do now?" she asked.

"I want to go down into Pylos to see Cerro," Tiberius said. "We need to trade some information on what happened to Maeve. He's under the impression that it was the same men who grabbed the equipment and killed Dannos."

"But it's not," Duaal protested. "Logan pretty well told us it was the Nihilists who took her."

Tiberius nodded. "But Cerro doesn't know that the cult is on Prianus. We need to tell him they're here, and they're dangerous."

"The information isn't going to help anyone very much if we can't find the cult," Coldhand said. "If the police have anything on them, call me."

The bounty hunter turned toward the exit, making Gripper – who was standing just inside the tent door – slink awkwardly out of his way. But Tiberius whistled at the bounty hunter and Coldhand stopped with his cybernetic hand clenching the weighted flap.

"What?" he asked.

"Where do you think you're going?"

The hunter took an empty hypodermic needle from his pocket.

"They used this to drug Maeve," Coldhand said. "Vanora White. A local mix. Gavriel didn't bring this from the core."

The core. If only she weren't so badly shaken, Panna would have laughed. The Prians still barely considered themselves a part of the Central World Alliance.

"That means a Nihilist either bought or stole it," Coldhand said. "There are lots of dealers in Pylos, but one of them should be able to point me – us – toward the cult. I'm going to track that dealer down."

"Want a hand?" Duaal asked.

"No," Tiberius interrupted. "We don't need to talk to the dealers. We can go to the Pylos police."

"I can't talk to the police," Coldhand said flatly.

"I can. They'll have more information than the dealers."

Coldhand considered for a moment.

"It would help," he answered slowly.

"Let's go, then!" Duaal said, heading for the tent exit.

"Not you," Tiberius said sharply. "You stay here."

"What?" the mage protested. "Not a chance!"

"You're sick, Duaal," Tiberius growled. "Xia doesn't know what's causing your headaches. You should stay here and rest."

"I've been feeling better! Let me work on this, captain."

Tiberius thought for a moment, then sighed. "Alright. But stick close to Xia and you come back to camp the moment you feel ill."

Xia spared one last questioning glance at Xen, then looked at Duaal. "I'll come keep an eye on him, captain."

After another argument with Kemmer over using his trucks, Tiberius and the rest left the tent. But Panna was the last one out. She lingered, watching Xen. She couldn't leave just yet. Kemmer studiously ignored her.

"What is it, Panna?" Xen asked, furrowing his white brows.

"You... knew about me?"

"I'm Ixthian," he said simply. "Of course I knew."

"And you don't care?"

"Why should I?" Xen asked. His eyes darkened a shade. "Panna, I don't know your reasons and they're none of my business. I'm your teacher and you've earned your right to be here."

"What about Gruth and the rest?" Panna asked.

"I'll talk to them. They're not going to say anything, either."

"But... you're Ixthian," Panna protested, echoing back his own words. "Xia's right. I lied about my race! Doesn't that bother you?"

Xen's eyes went a dark blue and the pain on his face tugged at Panna's heart.

"I once wanted something forbidden by my race, too." He gave a small, self-mocking laugh. "No, that's melodramatic. Not forbidden, but I let go of something I wanted because it was the Ixthian thing to do. When you came to my office and I realized what you were, I didn't want you to let go, too. Now, go find your princess. I'll be here when you get back."

Panna didn't trust herself to speak. She ducked her head and hurried from the tent.

Xartasia left Maeve alone with the horror of Gavriel's intentions. Summoning the Devourers, bringing that nightmare back into the worlds?

"Give him what he wants," Xartasia had urged one final time. There was sadness in her voice, but also a sweet kind of hope. "Be at peace, cousin. Soon, none of this will matter."

Maeve could only scream questions and obscenities as Xartasia pulled the door shut behind her and sealed the rotting room in darkness once more. If there was anyone else outside, they didn't answer Maeve's cries.

Eventually, her voice faded to a rasp. The deep chill silenced her voice, but could not quiet her thoughts. Was Gavriel mad? Yes, to be sure, but what man could possibly be mad enough to go seeking the Devourers? And Xartasia wanted to help him kill trillions? Maeve couldn't imagine such despair.

Even in her worst moments, she only ever wanted to kill herself.

But the thought offered no comfort or vindication now. It didn't make Maeve any better than Xartasia. It only meant that she was less likely to ever understand the Nihilists. How could *anyone* hate life so much?

Hours passed in the utter blackness. Even the glass-sharp edge of Maeve's terror dulled as her body's needs made themselves uncomfortably known. Her muscles cramped and her bladder was achingly full. In cruel irony, she was thirsty, too. The aftereffects of Vanora White made her head throb.

Maeve closed her eyes and tried to sleep. Everything hurt. The darkness behind Maeve's lids was the same as the inky black of her prison and offered no relief.

[25]
THE HEART

"The pure heart cannot be tainted by any art."

- TITANIA CAVAINNA, ARCADIAN MONARCH (233 PA)

The gray and white of the high mountains gave way to deep brown and green forest, then back to gritty, colorless gray as the trucks made their way down into Pylos. Logan drove the smaller of the two vehicles, leading the larger into the city. Against Tiberius' bellowed arguments, Duaal rode with Logan. Xia sat behind them, as silent as snowfall.

Clearly, Duaal felt no such urge. He stared alternately between the dilapidated city of Pylos and the almost equally worn bounty hunter.

"God, look at this place," Duaal said, shaking his head. "And you spent the last week here?"

"Yes," Logan answered.

"Pylos isn't the biggest city on Prianus, or even very important," Duaal said. "It must have taken some real work to find a lead. I'm impressed that you found your way here at all."

Then the boy was easily impressed.

"Someone told me to come here," Logan said.

"Who? Another cop?"

Logan shrugged. Why did Duaal care? Logan just wanted to find the Nihilists, find Maeve and finish his work on Prianus. But Duaal was watching him again, waiting for the hunter to answer.

"Do you really think the Cult of Nihil is here? It certainly seems like... like Gavriel's style," Duaal said when it became clear Logan wouldn't offer up any information. Duaal gave the other man a sly, sidelong look. "I was here with him before, you see. I know more about him than anyone else in the galaxy."

"Including Xartasia?" Logan asked.

Duaal paused. "Maybe not her."

Logan checked the gauges and readouts glowing on the dashboard. Kemmer's truck was in rough shape and probably wouldn't survive many more drives down the mountain. Logan had seen only a little of the archeologist's camp, but the trucks seemed to match everything else there. Kemmer was working as hard and as fast as he could, running through equipment and people if he had to in order to finish the job.

Why was Kemmer in such a hurry? In spite of what he had said, Logan found himself curious about what Kemmer had found in the Kayton Mountains.

"I spent my entire life with Gavriel. Even if Xartasia knows more about him, you'd have to torture her to get it out," Duaal was saying. Did the kid ever shut up? He smiled winsomely. "Of course, you can interrogate me, if you like..."

"What's down in the ravine that Maeve was guarding?" Logan interrupted.

Xia leapt in before Duaal could answer.

"We really can't talk about that," she said. "Kemmer had us all sign non-disclosure forms when we first came on the job. Unless you think it's going to help find Maeve, of course. Do you think it's relevant?"

"Come on, Xia," Duaal said. "You don't really take that seriously, do you? What's Kemmer going to do?"

"What is it?" Logan asked again.

Xia began to protest, but Duaal held up one hand and paused dramatically.

"A Waygate," he said at last.

"An Arcadian Waygate?" Logan asked.

"In a manner of speaking. The Waygates aren't actually an Arcadian invention, apparently," Duaal told him. "They predate even the White Kingdom. What the fairies know about the Waygates, they learned from the Nnyth. Until now, we thought that the Waygates existed only on the galactic rim. The implications are staggering."

"What implications are those?" Logan asked.

"Well..." Duaal faltered. "That there might have been trade or contact between the core and rim long before anyone thought?"

"The problem with trade is convenience, not technology," Logan said. "Alliance ships can fly out to the rim worlds. It's just not worth the fuel and time."

"But that Waygate Kemmer found is at least three million years old!" Duaal sounded a little desperate.

"Seven to nine million," Xia corrected.

Logan considered that. "There weren't humans on Prianus that long ago."

"No, there weren't," Xia said.

"Then someone else built it."

"That's the idea," Duaal agreed. "What do you think? Aliens on Prianus, before humans evolved here?"

"I think that it won't help me find Maeve," Logan said.

"The Cult of Nihil," Xia said. She was correcting *him* now. "You came a long way to find them. Why? Is the money that good?"

Logan didn't want to talk about that. The bounty money was *not* that good. Was it exciting, as he had hoped back on Sipho?

No. But Maeve was here.

But the Nihilists had taken her.

Duaal was staring at Logan... again. He seemed to be thinking of something else to say when his com chirped.

"Yes?" Duaal answered.

"We're a few blocks from the police station," Tiberius said. "Tell Coldhand to turn right at the next intersection."

"I know where we're going," Logan said.

Duaal repeated that into the com.

"Then he also knows he can't go into the station," Tiberius said.

Duaal looked at Logan. "Yeah. Look, captain, maybe Logan and I should start... um, asking around..."

"Canvassing," Logan supplied. "No. We need information first."

Traffic was getting thicker as they made their way along Pylos' cracked and bumpy roads. Logan yanked the wheel hard to one side as a small red car swerved in front of them. The driver waved a rude gesture out the window.

"What the hells was that...?" Tiberius asked. Logan saw him in the second truck, glaring furiously through the windshield. "Does that buzzard even know how to drive?"

Duaal's face darkened a shade as he hurried to answer. "Uh, it's nothing, captain. Everything's fine. We'll see you soon."

Xia's eyes whirled an angry, worried red, but then she seemed to think better of admonishing Logan. Duaal was simply grinning at him. Did the boy think that a moment's inattention made Logan as reckless a pilot as he was?

Did it?

Coldhand was losing his edge. He could feel – *feel* – it slipping away. The bounty hunter was distracted by thoughts of Vorus and Maeve. Would finding his lost Arcadian make Tiberius Myles think any better of Logan?

I don't care.

I don't.

How long since Xartasia left? It felt like days, but Maeve couldn't trust her own sense of time. She was finally getting hungry.

But the hunger was a dull ache compared to the fire of agony in her hands and wings. Maeve shifted her weight, trying to ease the pain. Who would have thought that simply sitting still could hurt so much?

Maeve cursed herself for a fool – she had thought it so unpleasant up on her sentry crag, exposed and cold. Now, she would have given anything to be back up on those rocks, with her silver blanket and the bright spotlight melting the ice until water dripped down onto her wings.

There was no water here, no light and no blanket, but plenty of cold and moldering dust. Every time Maeve sneezed, it banged the back of her head against the metal post. Not hard enough to cause any sort of injury, but it hurt.

Everything hurt, Maeve reminded herself firmly. Complaining about it would change nothing.

The door opened again, making Maeve squint into the light outside. She didn't recognize the silhouette standing in the doorway as either Xartasia or her master. The relief was short-lived, however, when the tall shape stepped inside. Through watering eyes, Maeve could make out a red robe.

The Emberguard surveyed the room. It was the same one who had taken her from the mountain – Xartasia had called him *Hallax* – a long-limbed Mirran with dark stripes across his olive skin.

The Mirrans had evolved their unique and beautiful markings as prey animals on their homeworld, to help them evade and hide from a thousands species of sharp-eyed predators. But there was nothing at all prey-like about Hallax. His dark eyes were narrowed and fixed on Maeve. She was reminded for a moment of Logan Coldhand.

The Emberguard's look was appraising. Hallax was measuring Maeve up, but not for a fight, as Logan would have. For slaughter. This man would run his nanosword through Maeve's heart at his master's word. But not yet, it seemed.

Hallax stepped aside and two more Nihilists – dressed in ordinary black robes – heaved a huge chair through the door and set it in front of Maeve.

"What are you doing?" she asked. Maeve wasn't pleased by the sharp, frightened note in her rough voice. "Leave me alone!"

"I will," said a voice. "After you give me what I need."

It was Gavriel, just as Xartasia had warned. The Nihilist leader looked taller than he had on Stray... No, Maeve realized. He simply stood straighter, no longer bowed by what was, for a human, vast age. But his clothes were much as Maeve remembered, long and dusty black robes like those of a wandering desert priest.

Gavriel seated himself and waved off the two Nihilists who had brought the chair. One of them set a lantern at Gavriel's feet, then they bowed and retreated. Hallax remained at the door, watching Maeve in silence. Gavriel's hands rested against the arms of his chair like huge, age-spotted spiders.

"Good afternoon, Princess Maeve," Gavriel said. "There is something I need from you. When you have given it to me, I will release you."

"Release me from life, you mean," Maeve answered as bravely as she could. Her handcuffs rattled against the beam as she trembled.

"Of course," Gavriel said, utterly unruffled. "But by the end, you will long for death as much as I do. Perhaps you already do."

"You will get nothing from me! Xartasia has warned me of your purpose!" Maeve hissed.

"Did she?" Gavriel asked. He frowned. "Xartasia didn't mention that you had spoken. Interesting."

Maeve had little love for her traitorous cousin, but didn't like to think that she had gotten Xartasia into trouble with the old Nihilist.

He was a dangerous enemy and Maeve closed her mouth resolutely. Gavriel watched her for a moment.

"The Waygates can open a portal to any place that the operator remembers," he said at last, a reasonable tone belying his madness. "I will make the long journey to Tamlin and with your memories, I will open the Waygate there and summon the Devourers again."

The *Tamlin* Waygate? Then that meant Gavriel knew nothing of the one just above Pylos. Silently, Maeve thanked Kemmer for his ridiculous paranoia.

Gavriel must have sensed she was thinking of something else and sat forward in his chair. The lamplight etched every deep line in his face, every wrinkle as black and sharp as an obsidian blade. He caught her chin in his withered fingers.

"Listen to me," Gavriel said. "You and the rest of your kind have known such pain, such loss. And why should the Arcadians suffer alone? Your false gods offer no solace and no justice for the fate of the White Kingdom. But we can ensure that all the worlds of the Alliance suffer as much as you have."

"It does not matter if I agree," Maeve told him. "My memories are shameful, but they are my own. They cannot be shared."

Gavriel stood up so suddenly that Maeve recoiled, striking her head once again on the support behind her. She forgot all about her hunger and thirst. The old human held out a clenched fist toward Maeve.

"I *will* have what I want from you," Gavriel told her. "I am strong now, princess. There are no secrets beyond my grasp. No spells, no songs. You will give up the memories I need!"

There could be no such spell. Rumors, yes, but... Gavriel smiled at Maeve and for a moment, she wondered if he was going to laugh at her.

"Your imagination is so limited, princess," Gavriel said. His thin white hair seemed to glow in the lamplight. "You have no idea the secrets that Xartasia has taught me."

"You… cannot take memories," Maeve repeated stubbornly. "It is simply not possible."

Gavriel opened his clenched hand and then extended it toward his prisoner, palm facing up as though waiting to accept a gift. He closed his eyes and began to sing.

"S'aivarii kivva skie zha'anae estu hae'sva…"

The sound seeped in through Maeve's ears and into her skull. The words were slow, dripping cold like icicles. Freezing, trying to freeze Maeve's scurrying thoughts in place, to hold them still and examine them.

"Vai'a min daekhin ja'hirae vae m'saa…"

Creeping cold so intense that the frozen Prian air was summer-hot by comparison. Maeve ground her teeth and refused to remember. Not them, not the Devourers. But cold, yes. Cold and deadly.

Logan Coldhand.

Maeve closed her eyes and remembered the bounty hunter. The glacial blue of his eyes, the rigid set of his jaw. There was youth there, but hardened too soon. And nobility deeply scarred by loss. Maeve felt Gavriel's presence in her mind, forced to see only what she did. He stopped singing and his long, withered fingers clenched into fists.

"I remember that man myself," Gavriel said. "He destroyed the graveyard. He stole you and the Dailon baby away. I remember him very well. Now show me the Tamlin Waygate, princess. Show me the Devourers pouring through and killing all before them."

"I will show you nothing," Maeve told him.

"Show me! I know that you long for destruction and death. Give me the means."

"No!"

Gavriel nodded. "Xartasia warned me that you would be stubborn, princess."

He gestured back to Hallax. The striped Emberguard stepped into the pale circle of lamplight, knelt down and slapped Maeve hard across the mouth. Her head rocked back, smacked into the beam and then rebounded. Maeve fell forward, jerked to a sudden stop by her bound wrists and wings. She tasted blood in her mouth and spat red at Gavriel's feet.

"You think that will frighten me into giving you the memories?" Maeve asked. "I do not fear you."

"No, I think that it's going to take much more," Gavriel said with a thin smile.

He took a knife from beneath his robe. The blade was Arcadian glass and glittered in the lamplight like diamond. Gavriel held it out, balanced across his palm.

"Do you remember this, princess?" he asked.

"No," Maeve answered. Her voice shook. "It is just a knife. I have seen many."

"But how many have you *felt*? This one has tasted your blood before, twisting inside of you under the Gharib graveyard. I almost killed you with this knife, princess, and would have if Xartasia had not begged for your life."

Maeve remembered very well. She felt the scar every day when she got dressed, a jagged line of shiny white just above her navel. Even the surgical nanites couldn't entirely erase that mark.

"You remember, princess," Gavriel said. "But you will remember this more."

He handed the glass knife to Hallax, who accepted it with a bow. He was going to torture her...

Maeve struggled uselessly against the ropes and handcuffs. Her stomach crept up into her throat and she couldn't breathe, but that wouldn't matter very much before long. The Emberguard knelt beside her. He grabbed a handful of her short black hair and jerked her head back.

"*Alu'ma eru!*" she cried. *Do not do this!*

"*Ja'merruna,*" Gavriel answered. *I must.*

He sang again as Maeve began to scream.

North Pylos Police Station Three was a large concrete building with its name stamped in huge, plain letters on the side. The walls were patchy gray-on-gray with painted-over graffiti.

Kemmer's trucks were parked side by side in a gravel-strewn lot nearby. Duaal reluctantly followed Tiberius, Xia and Panna inside, casting one final glance back at the parking lot where Logan Cold-hand and Gripper waited.

They passed through the sliding metal door into... chaos. Duaal didn't know what he expected of a Prian police station, but this was not it. He was just inside the door, in a narrow concrete hallway, but it was full of people. Men and women jostled each other, pushed this way and that by hard-eyed cops. Many of them shouted threats, insults or even struggled to escape their arresting officers.

Tiberius threw a thick arm across Duaal's chest and jerked him to a stop as a man dressed in leather and chains crashed through a closed door. The man jumped to his feet, waving a squared length of wood that used to be the leg of a chair. People ducked and scattered, all shouting and swearing.

A young Prian woman wearing a blue uniform and a patch over one eye charged through the broken door and slammed her truncheon into the man's midsection. When he doubled over, wheezing, she twisted the chair leg out of his hand and shoved him up against the wall.

"Need a hand?" Tiberius asked.

"No, I've got this," the cop said cheerfully.

She took a pair of worn handcuffs off her thick leather belt and snapped them around the man's wrists. An only slightly older man came running down the hall and she pushed her prisoner into his waiting arms.

"Put this guy in holding five," she instructed, shouting to make herself heard over the noise.

"It's full," the other cop told her.

"Six?"

"Full. There's some cells left in suicide watch."

"Good enough. But move him out as soon as possible. We might need the paddeds for a real suicide." She adjusted her eyepatch and turned to face Tiberius. "Can I help you, sir?"

"Tiberius Myles. I need to talk to Captain Cerro."

"Can you tell me what about?" she asked. "Does he know you're here?"

"I've got a missing dove and I need some help tracking down a chem dealer," Tiberius told her. "I called Cerro a few hours ago. He should be expecting me."

"Sure. He's on the second story. Take the stairs at the end of the hall. His office is labeled. You carrying any weapons?" the police-woman asked.

Tiberius nodded.

"You'll have to leave them up front," she said, pointing down the crowded hall to a barely visible desk. "You'll need to be searched before you can head up."

"That's fine," Tiberius answered. "I was a cop once, too. I know the routine."

The woman with the eyepatch whistled, clearly impressed that Tiberius had survived to such an age. It probably didn't happen often. She waved a farewell to Tiberius, but her gaze lingered on Duaal. She may have winked at him, but with only the single eye, it was impossible to tell. Duaal winked back, just in case.

"Is it always like this?" Panna asked. She had to lean close and repeat her question.

"Pylos is a little worse than most," Tiberius said. "But more or less, yes."

"That's why Gavriel thought Prianus would be a good place to start up his stupid church," Duaal told Panna. "The people here are desperate."

They shouldered their way through the crowd and up to the chest-high concrete desk. Xia stepped around a grim-faced Prian officer dragging a frothy-mouthed Lyran down the hall toward a set of wide doors labeled HOLDING.

"Those cells are full!" Tiberius called after them.

The cop glanced up over his shoulder, briefly conferred with a nearby officer, and then waved his thanks to Tiberius. The slavering Lyran suggested that this was a sign from on high to let him go, but the policeman said nothing and cuffed him to one of the steel rings embedded in the concrete wall.

"Why didn't Gavriel stay here?" Panna asked. She took in the scene with wide eyes.

"Because there are plenty like that guy," Duaal said, pointing at the Lyran. "But there are people like Tiberius and Officer Eyepatch, too. The first outnumber the second, but the Prian police are just as fanatical as the Nihilists. Gavriel hates them."

"But if Coldhand's right, then he's returned to Prianus," Xia said. "Why would he do that, if it was so much trouble before?"

"I'm not sure," Duaal confessed.

Tiberius had made his way to the front desk, signed them all in and had the desk officer call up to Captain Cerro's office. When prompted, Duaal handed over the glass dagger he had bought on Stray. A cop missing all of her hair and one ear took the knife, patted them down thoroughly, then ran a sensor wand of some kind over each of the little party. When she was done, she jerked her thumb over her shoulder and told them to go upstairs.

It was quieter up on the second story. As far as Duaal could tell, this part of the station seemed to be dedicated to storing desks and cops. There were men and women in blue working on paper and datadexes or conferring at chalkboards covered in timelines, lists and printouts. Some looked up at the civilians as they emerged from the stairwell, but not recognizing them as anyone pertinent to their cases, returned to work.

Tiberius seemed to know exactly where he was going. He led Duaal, Xia and Panna through a maze of desks with sagging tops. They matched the patched uniforms of cops sitting behind them – old and shabby, but quite capable of performing their jobs.

They stopped at an open door with Cerro's name painted on it. The Prian police captain stood inside, rubbing his closed eyes as he listened to someone on his com. The frown tugging at his lips didn't seem to be a result of the burn scar on his cheek.

"I... Yes. Arrange it," he said. "Then put together a task force to go back in. We need to know what's happening up there."

Cerro listened for a moment longer, then turned off his com. He looked up at Tiberius and offered his hand.

"Captain Myles," he greeted the older cop. "You said that there were things you needed to tell me. I don't suppose one of them is that you've found Cavainna?"

"No," Tiberius said. "But we know who has her."

Cerro's frown deepened. "You don't sound like that's good news. What's wrong?"

"Have you heard of the Cult of Nihil?"

The police captain thought for a moment, then shook his head. "Sorry, no. I don't think so. I take it they're a problem?"

"You have no idea just how bad a problem," Duaal said with a shudder.

"The Nihilists are exactly what they sound like," Tiberius said. "Cultists who worship death. Maeve made some trouble for them back on Stray, about seven or eight months ago. And now they've grabbed her."

"Are you sure about that?" Cerro asked. "We're a long way from Stray, Captain Myles."

"They're here!" Duaal insisted. "They've been on Prianus before, in Highwind."

"Easy there, kid. I'm not saying that I don't believe you. Just that Prianus is a long way from Stray," Cerro said. "And Pylos is a long way from Highwind. Do you think this cult came here expressly to kidnap Maeve Cavainna?"

"I doubt it," Tiberius answered. "Cold– we were tipped off about the Nihilists. They've been here for some time, I think, working on something else."

Cerro thumbed through a leaning stack of folders on his desk and then pulled out one that was overflowing with printouts and photographs.

"We've had a rash of missing Arcadians, Captain Myles, from all over Pylos," Cerro said. "Do you think your dove's disappearance might be related?"

"Logan asked about that, too," Duaal answered.

"Yes and no," Tiberius said. "There's bad blood between Maeve and the Nihilist leaders. I think there was a personal motive, but maybe they took her for the same reason as the other Arcadians. What happened to them?"

"We don't know yet. But we haven't found bodies," Cerro added quickly.

"Do you know where they're being taken?" Xia asked.

"No," Cerro said. "There are over three million people living in Pylos, with only four police precincts to cover them. I'd like to say we've combed the entire city... but unfortunately, we're not even close. How certain are you that the Nihilists took your dove?"

"It's a long God-damned way up into the mountains to get her, and Maeve's a fighter," Tiberius said. "She's got her enemies, but only the Cult of Nihil is here and hates Maeve enough to go to the trouble."

Cerro nodded. "Alright. We're going to need a lot more than that before we present anything to the court, but it's a place to start and better than nothing."

"There's more," Duaal said, excited to think that they might be able to help the Prian police close in on Gavriel. "We've got some evidence from the scene."

Tiberius nodded and then pulled the syringe from a pocket of his coat, wrapped in an archeological specimen bag.

"We found it in the same place Maeve was taken," Tiberius said.

"We think they used it to drug her," Xia added. "The blood on the needle is a match for Maeve's."

"You checked it?" Cerro asked, obviously a little surprised.

"I'm a doctor. I have Maeve's full redprint on file."

"We think the White's a local blend," Duaal said. "Do you know where it's from?"

"No, afraid not. You'll want to talk to narcotics about that," Cerro told them. "Let me give them a call and see if anyone is free to come down here."

Duaal was pleased that Cerro was willing to listen to them and to help the Blue Phoenix crew find their lost first mate. The young mage actually hoped that Maeve was safe. She wasn't the kind of woman he ever would have chosen to fly with, but she truly seemed to be trying to clean up her life. Duaal still didn't think he really liked Maeve, but it was growing harder to hate her.

Cerro had just closed his com and told Tiberius that one of the station's chem experts would be able to take a look at the needle in about two or three or seven hours. Panna's face turned a dark red and the girl looked like she was about to start screaming at Cerro. Xia saw the storm brewing and put a slender silver hand on Panna's shoulder.

"They're doing the best they can," Xia said gently.

"But... shouldn't Princess Maeve be a major priority?" Panna asked.

"Princess?" Cerro asked, his lined brow furrowing deeply.

Duaal was taking a breath to explain when a blazing pain shot from one of his temples to the other. He screamed and grabbed his head. The sharp, red-hot sensation was like a needle being pushed through his skull, shoving invasively inward. Duaal closed his eyes and pressed his hands against the lids as hard as he could.

Everything was dark. Deep black, but not the clean darkness of the void, of the space between stars. No, this was... different. Dirty. Dusty. Wrong. Something as fragile as ancient cobwebs that crackled dryly with every movement.

There were shapes in the darkness. People? Yes, they were people. A man with a red cowl and striped skin, a Mirran who looked distantly familiar. There was a woman, an Arcadian. Her skin was striped, too, but in blood. The Mirran jerked her head up by a handful of lank black hair.

"Maeve...?" Duaal asked.

His ears buzzed and then rang as though deafened. The darkness rose up around him, over Maeve and the Mirran in red, swallowing them. Swallowing Duaal.

[26]

IN DREAMS

"Life without mystery is boring, but I think I'm about due for some boredom."

Logan watched the station doors long after Tiberius and the rest had gone inside. The scruffy old captain could walk right in and ask whatever he wanted. The police might not be able to give it, but Tiberius could ask. They would welcome him. But Logan sat alone outside, waiting.

Almost alone. Gripper sat over in the other truck, staring out the window at him. Tiberius had insisted on taking Duaal along and was just as adamant that the Arboran remain behind.

"To avoid complications," he had said.

Now Gripper regarded Logan with the terror of a stonemouse staring at an owl. The huge alien was Maeve's closest friend, wasn't he? It was hard to imagine the fierce Arcadian woman befriending someone as frightened and shy as Gripper. But then, it had been so long since Logan could call anyone a friend that maybe he was missing the point.

Gripper gestured at him, then again. He wanted Logan to slide the window down. The bounty hunter did so and cold, wet air blew into the truck's cab.

"What?" he asked.

"Never mind," Gripper said quickly. "It... it's not important."

He fumbled for the window controls, but Logan reached across the gap between the two vehicles and closed his cybernetic hand over the glass. It tried to rise and ground against the illonium.

"Um..." Gripper said, voice thin and squeaking with terror.

Logan wasn't sure what he was doing. His every exhaled breath steamed, a plumed white countdown ticking away Maeve's time as he thought.

"You said that Maeve stopped using White," he said at last.

"Yeah..." Gripper answered hesitantly.

Logan went quiet again. Why did it matter? It didn't. He withdrew his hand, but Gripper left the window open. Slushy snow fluttered down into both vehicles, but the Arboran didn't seem at all bothered by the weather.

"What made her stop?" Logan asked.

"I don't know. Not because I haven't asked," Gripper told him. "I have, and it's not like she doesn't answer."

"What does that mean?" Logan asked suspiciously.

"Don't kill me!"

"I'm not going to kill you. Just... tell me what you mean."

"I don't even think Smoke knows why... but she's been different ever since Stray. So much happened to her. All of the stuff with the Nihilists, then getting stabbed and helping deliver Baliend. And... and you, too."

"She was relieved that I was gone," Logan said.

His jaw clenched. It made sense.

"No, that's not it," Gripper said. "She misses you, I think."

Logan didn't have much time to consider that. The doors of the police station banged open, held by blue-uniformed police officers.

Xia and Panna hurried out, in close and concerned conversation. Tiberius ran behind them, carrying Duaal in his arms. The Hyzaari boy was limp, unmoving. Gripper jumped and banged his head on the ceiling of the truck.

"What happened?" he asked.

Xia yanked open the back of the nearest truck and helped him lift Duaal into the vehicle. The police officers followed, but Panna waved them away.

"We'll take care of him," she assured them. "Please, just let us handle this."

They looked uncertain and told Panna to call them if anything changed. When the police were gone again, Logan climbed out of the driver's seat and went to the other truck, where Duaal was laid out. Xia had covered the Hyzaari boy with her coat and was peeling his eyelids open.

"What happened to him?" Logan asked.

"He just collapsed," Panna said.

"The altitude, maybe?" Gripper asked. "Hyzaar's all ocean and islands."

"No. Duaal hasn't lived on Hyzaar since he was a baby," Tiberius answered. "And Gavriel kept him here on Prianus for several years."

"I've checked for everything I can think of," Xia said. Her expression was frustrated, but her eyes were a frightened red. "Aside from the headaches he's been having for the last few months, he's the perfect specimen of a healthy human in his prime."

"Wow, thanks for noticing," Duaal said. He groaned as he sat up slowly, rubbing his head and squinting. "That's sweet."

"Easy," Tiberius told him. "How do you feel?"

"Sick."

"Does your head still hurt?" Xia asked.

"No, not really." Duaal wrapped his arms around his knees and took a few deep breaths. "But there were some... hallucinations this time. I don't know. I saw things. I saw Maeve."

Xia rubbed Duaal's back gently. "It's only natural. You're worried about her."

"I guess..." he said uncertainly. "There was a human I remember, too. One of Gavriel's old Emberguard, Hallax. I think he was torturing Maeve."

"Do you think that really could be happening?" Gripper asked. "Is Gavriel torturing her?"

"Yes," Logan answered flatly. "Did you get any information on the White?"

"Duaal went down before we learned anything," Tiberius said.

"See? I said I should have stayed out here," Duaal announced. "I could have had a *much* nicer time."

Panna pointed back to the police station. "We should go back in and wait for that narcotics cop that Cerro called."

"I'm getting tired of waiting," Logan said. "If Maeve is still alive, then it's only because Gavriel isn't done with her."

"You're talking about torture again," Gripper whimpered.

Logan closed his eyes. His battles against Maeve had been often brutal and bloody, but not torture. But now...

They're hurting Maeve.

Logan punched the side of the truck hard enough to make the vehicle rock on its shocks. The impact left a dent in the metal.

"Ease up, Coldhand," Tiberius growled.

"It was just a stupid... dream, I guess," Duaal stammered.

He reached out as though to comfort the bounty hunter, but Xia pulled the young mage back.

"You take it easy, too," she said. "You're clearly not well."

"I'm fine!" Duaal protested. "I know what I'm doing!"

"Shut up!" Gripper shouted. Everyone stopped to stare at the Arboran. Gripper's big, brutish face was full of fear and despair. He pulled on his long ears. "None of this is helping Smoke!"

"He's right," Panna agreed. "We need to talk to that cop and find out where the White came from."

"And if they don't know?" Xia asked.

"They *will* find out, but it will take time. At least a few hours, but probably more," Logan said. He hesitated, then shook his head. "There's an Arcadian boy, Ballad. He and his gang tried to chase me off when I was hunting the Nihilists in their territory. They're protective of the other fairies."

"Do you think they might recognize that needle if someone is trying to sell the White nearby?" Gripper asked.

"Maybe," Logan said. "If the Nihilists have been working in the Arcadian district, they may have bought the White there. I'm going to find out."

Tiberius nodded curtly. "Call as soon as you have anything."

Duaal pulled himself to his feet. "I'll go with you, Logan."

"No." Tiberius said it gently, but firmly. He took Duaal's arm. "You just passed out. I want you back up at base camp and I want Xia keeping an eye on you."

"I want to help, captain!" Duaal protested.

"I know. But you're sick enough to be hallucinating," Tiberius said. "Go back to the base camp, Duaal. Rest. I'm not losing you to get Maeve back."

Tiberius and Duaal held each other's gaze for a moment, then the boy sighed. "Fine."

"I'll go with Coldhand, though," Gripper said. "I don't know if I can help, but I want to try."

Tiberius nodded. "Then Panna and I will stay here to talk to the narcotics department. Pick us up when we're done, Gripper."

"Come on, Duaal. I'll drive," Xia said. "Besides, you and I need to talk."

She helped Duaal into one of the trucks and they drove away, back toward the long violet shadows of the Kayton Mountains. Tiberius and Panna made their way back to the Pylos police station, leaving Gripper chewing nervously at his claws.

"What were you going to ask me earlier?" Logan asked.

"I uh... I just wanted to tell you thanks for helping us look for Smoke," Gripper stammered, barely audible through his mouthful of claws.

"I'm only here to find the Nihilists," Logan reminded him.

"Yeah, I guess."

Logan paused. "You can thank me when we've found her."

"She's unconscious. I'm sorry, Lord Gavriel."

Hallax wiped the knife on his sleeve and stood. Maeve Cavainna slumped against the steel support. Gavriel sat still.

"What do you wish of me, my master?" Hallax asked.

Gavriel flicked his fingers toward the door. "Find Xartasia and bring her here."

Hallax bowed so low that his tangled green hair almost swept the floor, then vanished through the doorway. About ten minutes later, Xartasia entered and curtsied, though not nearly as deeply as Hallax.

"You summoned me, Lord Gavriel?" Xartasia asked. "What do you desire?"

As she straightened once more, the Arcadian princess saw her bloodied cousin and faltered.

"Maeve told me that you came to see her," Gavriel said.

Xartasia's violet eyes flicked back and forth between Maeve and Gavriel.

"Yes. I warned her," she said.

"About what?" Gavriel asked.

"That it was unwise to fight you."

"You like her."

"She is of my blood," Xartasia said carefully. "Maeve is stronger than those who wear your black robes."

"No one is strong enough to withstand all of life's torments," Gavriel said.

Xartasia looked down at the blood spattering the floor. "Did she give you her memories of the Tamlin Waygate?"

"Not yet," Gavriel said. "She's being stubborn. Every time Hallax cuts her, she just remembers that Prian man, Coldhand."

"You will not break Maeve with pain," Xartasia told him. "She has spent decades trying to drown her losses in battle."

"You underestimate what I can do to her," Gavriel said. "Before I am done, Logan Coldhand will be her savior, not her hunter."

"I do not doubt the pain you can inflict," Xartasia said. "But this is not the way."

Gavriel stroked his cheek. The skin was as thin and dry as paper folded too many times. Maybe Xartasia was actually right. Hours of torture had done nothing to coax Maeve's memories. She stubbornly shielded them with thoughts of the bounty hunter. He was a source of both pain and a strange sort of pleasure.

Perhaps if Hallax could have plied the full extent of his trade... But Gavriel could risk no damage to Maeve's brain. If Xartasia was correct, pain would win him nothing and opening up too much of Maeve's flesh might kill the fairy. She would do Gavriel no good in a grave.

And Maeve Cavainna didn't deserve death. Not yet.

"What do you suggest, then?" Gavriel asked.

"I am not certain yet," Xartasia answered.

Gavriel stood and stepped over a puddle of feathers and cold, sticky blood. Xartasia followed in obedient silence. Out in the hallway, Gavriel called to one of the clustered Nihilists.

"Wake her," he instructed, pointing over his shoulder to where Maeve sat. "She gets no sleep and no food until she gives me what I need. But if she dies under your care, you will be thrown down into the pit."

"Yes, Lord Gavriel."

Logan parked outside the Arcadian district. The hunter thrust a handful of colored cenmark chips into the hand of a man leaning against an abandoned storefront and told him to watch the truck. The Talon-9 seemed to convince the man that Logan was a police officer and Gripper's hulking presence helped assure his frightened but sincere honesty.

It took them several hours and bribes to find Ballad. An old fairy woman didn't seem to understand Aver very well, but Logan's broken Arcadian was good enough to send them up a rusty, rickety stairwell. Neither of the Arcadians at the top were Ballad, but one of them knew of him.

"You can usually find him or one of his boys at the house on Ovidius," a one-winged girl told them.

The house on Ovidius was a leaning building covered in graffiti. A young Arcadian met them at the door, dressed from head to foot in black leather but wearing a bright green scarf around his neck. Logan recognized him as Kashan, one of Ballad's friends. Kashan's gaze lingered on Gripper for a long moment before he returned his attention to Coldhand.

"I didn't think we would see you again," he said.

"I need to talk to Ballad," Logan told Kashan shortly.

The fairy gestured at Gripper with the tip of one wing. "What about him?"

"You don't need to worry about him. He's a coward," said Logan.

"Hey!" Gripper protested.

Logan looked up. "You are."

"But you don't have to tell them!"

"What is he?" Kashan asked.

"He's an alien, hawk," Logan said. "I don't know what kind, and I don't care. Now, I need to talk to Ballad."

"Fine."

Kashan nodded and stepped back to let them inside. The house was full of Arcadians, most of them gathered around a small stove. They looked up as Logan and Gripper passed, but seemed content to let Kashan deal with the strangers.

Ballad stood over a table in a back room. A rough, hand-drawn map lay stretched across the tabletop, weighed down at the corners by empty bottles and chunks of concrete.

"A'ma saevanii," Kashan said.

Logan had no idea what that meant, but it got Ballad's attention. He waved several other leather-jacketed Arcadians out of the room. Kashan remained, lingering in the doorway behind them.

"Did you find what you were looking for?" Ballad asked.

"No," Logan said. "I need more information."

Ballad frowned. "It didn't seem to help you very much last time. What makes you think I can do better now?"

"This is closer to home," Logan said. "I'm looking for someone who deals in chems."

"I thought you were looking for a cult."

"Does anyone sell Vanora White around here?" Logan asked.

"A lot of chem dealers come through this part of the city," Ballad told him almost apologetically. "I don't know exactly what they were selling. We don't usually take the people we find out drinking. You were an exception."

"You've got to know something!" Gripper said. "Coldhand said you take care of the Arcadians here."

"We do." Ballad's voice took on a hard edge. He frowned across the table at his guests. "And when we find chem dealers, that means breaking their beaks, not taking inventory for them! Some probably sold Vanora White, but I can't tell you any more than that."

"That's all you've got?" Logan asked.

"Please..." Gripper said. He held his hands out imploringly to Ballad. "We're trying to find my friend. She's an Arcadian, too. Isn't there something else you can do?"

Ballad slapped his hand down on the table, making the empty bottles jump. "Look, if I could stop my own people from going missing, I would! But I don't know what's happening to them, either!"

Logan's stomach twisted into a knot. They were getting nowhere and swiftly running out of places to look. He hoped that Panna and Tiberius were having better luck.

A police lab technician pulled a magnifying glass over the tray and the springs in the metal arm creaked. She turned the needle over in gloved hands.

"I don't have much for you, I'm afraid," she said. "The manufacturer's mark is a counterfeit, but that's not uncommon."

It was crowded in the laboratory. Tiberius was downstairs with Cerro, nervously awaiting an update from Xia on Duaal's status.

Panna looked over the lab tech's shoulder. "Anything else? What about fingerprints?"

"None. It was wiped down, probably prior to sale. There were a couple of fibers. Red and synthetic. Whoever used the needle was wearing gloves."

"No prints," Panna said. "Anything else? Can you tell us where it was sold?"

The tech shook her head. "Sorry, no. It's a local mix, but I can't narrow it down much more than that."

"Why not?" Panna asked. "Can't you do a molecular breakdown and analysis? There must be some kind of pollutants that can pinpoint where this stuff was originally manufactured!"

"Look, you're talking about detecting particles in one part per hundred thousand," said the technician. "And trying to find those in a trace sample of less than a drop. We just don't have that kind of equipment."

"Can you tell us anything at all?" Panna asked.

Frowning, the Prian woman shook her head.

"I'm sorry," Panna said with a sigh. "I don't... I don't mean to be rude. This was used to drug a woman in an abduction. We're trying to find her."

The tech looked up. Her eyes were hard, just like Tiberius and Kemmer's. It was easy to imagine that the people on Prianus were carved out of the same stone as their mountains.

"Even if I could tell you where this was made, I don't know that it would help. This stuff gets distributed all across the county. You can find it in any alleyway in Pylos," the technician told Panna. "I'm afraid this needle isn't going to help you find your friend."

Cerro came in with a folder and two cups of coffee. He pushed one of the chipped mugs across the desk and Tiberius took it gratefully. The heat soothed some of the pain in his old joints and Tiberius gulped down a few mouthfuls of the dark, acidic coffee. It tasted pretty much as bad as he remembered. Good coffee beans needed a warm place to grow and there weren't many of those on Prianus.

"Did you find anything?" Tiberius asked.

Cerro handed him the folder. "Nothing recent. There's some mention of the Church of Nihil, but even the latest information is over six years old. I'm not doubting you, Captain Myles, but if the Nihilists are in Pylos, then they're being careful and quiet."

Tiberius put the coffee aside. It didn't mix well with the worry. He opened the folder.

"But you've got something," Tiberius said.

"I think I might," Cerro answered. "There were reports of the Nihilists from Highwind. A Mirran that they called *the Emberguard* was selling some poisoned chems. When the cops cornered him, this mad hawk killed one and maimed the other. The survivor vanished not long after he got out of the hospital."

Tiberius looked at the photograph clipped to the report and was suddenly glad he had stopped drinking the coffee – he would have spit it all over the page. The man in the photograph was a few years younger and still wore his blue police uniform, but Tiberius recognized Logan Coldhand.

How could this bright-eyed young cop be the same man who had hunted Maeve for the last year, as cold and merciless as a wild falcon? Or the same haunted-looking man who landed at Kemmer's base camp only that morning?

Tiberius read over the report's first page. It detailed Coldhand's injuries... Not just the hand, but the man's heart, too. Logan Centra had nearly died on the operating table four times during surgery.

"They think that this Lieutenant Centra might have joined the Nihilists," Cerro told Tiberius. "Precinct officers talked to his dove. She swore that Centra was a good man and would never go over to the other side, but admitted that he had been different, a changed man since his wounding."

Tiberius sighed. "Is this your lead?"

"Yes. What's wrong, Captain Myles?"

"I know this man. He's a bastard, but he's no Nihilist."

Cerro frowned. "Are you sure?"

"Yes. I'm sure," Tiberius said.

"Then we're right back in the nest. We're out of places to look."

A sharp slap jerked Maeve back into wakefulness. Another robed Nihilist – neither Hallax nor his master – crouched in the lamplight and held a cup to her lips.

"Drink," he told her.

Maeve spat half-frozen water back into the Nihilist's face. The man jumped away.

"I will accept nothing from you!" she rasped.

The coarse whisper was as loud as Maeve could make her voice after hours of screaming.

"Please," said the Nihilist. "You can't die yet."

Maeve turned her face away. Every part of her body thrummed with pain. The multitude of cuts were no longer bleeding freely, but one of her ankles was swelling impressively and darkening with bruises. Was something broken? The joint was full of liquid agony and her stifled heartbeat hammered in her ears.

She adjusted her wrists in the handcuffs. The skin was raw and sticky-hot with blood. Her fingers brushed each other and Maeve wheezed a soft cry of agony. How long until her fingernails would grow back? She was useless in this state.

Maeve began singing the anesthetic charm Orthain had taught her as a squire, the same one she had used to ease Kessa's labor. The Nihilist yelped and slapped her again.

"No!" he said. "No spells."

She considered trying again, but the Nihilist grabbed a piece of cloth from her pants, cut away by Hallax as he worked, and stuffed it into Maeve's mouth. She tried to spit it out, but he tied the gag in place with another bit of cloth.

"If you're not going to drink, then I guess I don't need to leave your mouth uncovered," said the Nihilist.

He sat on the edge of Gavriel's empty chair and put his chin in his hands, watching Maeve. Every time her eyelids began to close, the Nihilist guard kicked her wounded ankle. Maeve groaned into her gag.

"No sleeping," he told her.

Maeve blinked her sticky eyes. How long until Gavriel returned, until he was prying at her memories with his songs? Until Hallax was back with the glass knife? Maeve renewed her struggles and the Nihilist guard brought his heel down on her ankle.

"None of that, either," he said.

[27]

THROUGH ICE

"Love is a reason to live. Lust is a reason to kill."

Xia drove in silence so long that Duaal began wondering if she had forgotten that she wanted to talk. Through the dense, loud pack of Pylos traffic, the white-haired Ixthian woman remained quiet. Just driving, focused on her task.

Duaal leaned against the window and pressed his cheek to the cold glass. His skin had the sweaty, brittle feel of a fever. He had felt that way since waking up in the back of the truck.

It all felt familiar... sort of. Headaches were pretty normal for spacefarers. Every planet in the galaxy had different air pressure and atmospheric mix, full of pollens from different plants and the fur, feathers and dander of different animals. A million variations that could be hard on a body.

But now the hallucination and the fever... This was much more like the early days with Gavriel, when Duaal had been just a little boy, living in a half-remembered haze of pain and strange dreams and endless singing. Always singing.

A woman singing, Duaal suddenly remembered. Gavriel's voice, yes, but a female voice, too. Singing to him... *At* him.

Xia finally took the truck up out of Pylos and back into the high mountains. Tall pine trees loomed up from the misty afternoon like ragged black spears. A few white swirls of snow eddied through the thinning forest as the road wound its way up toward the base camp.

Duaal pressed his forehead against the window. The fever-heat was fading. So were the memories, replaced now by other thoughts and a more pleasant warmth.

"We should make sure Logan comes back up to Kemmer's camp tonight," Duaal said. "In case something changes. It would be pretty silly for him to stay in Pylos while we're working together. Wasting that color on a hotel–"

"Damn it, Duaal!" Xia shouted suddenly, slamming one of her hands down on the steering wheel. "What is wrong with you?"

"What?" Duaal asked.

"Why Coldhand? *You can interrogate me?* That's what you told him, Duaal! What were you thinking?"

"I was only flirting a little," he said defensively. "What's wrong with that?"

"Why him? Why are you after that man?" Xia asked.

"You just don't like his cybernetics."

"Of course I don't like them," Xia said, waving one six-fingered hand dismissively. "But that's beside the point, Duaal. Coldhand is dangerous! He's a bounty hunter and a killer. He's bad for you!"

"You don't know that," Duaal answered quickly.

"Yes, I do. I've been watching you do this for years. Remember that man on Hadra? You came back with two sprained wrists."

Duaal remembered him – a huge, handsome pounceball player. But then Coldhand had found Maeve again and forced them off-planet before Duaal could make a second date.

"And that Lyran woman on Axis?" Xia asked.

"Lyrans have claws. Was that her fault?"

"She didn't have to use them, Duaal!" Xia protested. "Coldhand might not have claws, but he's even worse. We're working out of a camp full of intelligent young men and women, but you insist on Coldhand?"

Duaal shrugged and looked out the window again. They were crossing an icy bridge and would be back at the base camp soon.

"I'm just not interested in any of the others," Duaal said. "So?"

Xia sighed. "Why not, Duaal? I thought you liked Enu-Io."

"And I thought you were about to jump back into Xen's arms," Duaal answered sharply. "But you managed to surprise everyone. Look, Enu-Io is fine, but he's just…"

Duaal trailed off with a shrug.

"Smart? Gentle and caring?" Xia asked bitterly.

Duaal wasn't sure what to say. Snow and stone streaked past the window. After an uncomfortably long silence, the base camp finally came into view. Xia pulled the truck to a stop and got out to answer questions from Kemmer and Phillip about their progress.

"Where is everyone else?" she asked Kemmer suspiciously. Her eyes went dark.

"What exactly are you suggesting?" Kemmer asked.

"Nothing," Xia said. "I just want to know where the others are. Are they alright?"

"They're fine," Phillip answered.

The geologist pointed up the slope of the moraine.

"Doctor Kemmer told us to take most of the gear down into the ravine," Phillip said. "We should be pretty much moved down there by tonight."

"So we only have to protect one location," Xia finished, nodding at Kemmer. "That was a good idea."

The Prian archeologist offered no answer, instead turning and walking away through the snow toward the ravine. Phillip had more questions about what was happening down in Pylos, but Duaal was getting cold.

He went back to the Blue Phoenix tent, turned on the heater and flopped down on his cot. Duaal had thrown his arm across his face and didn't see Xia come inside. But he heard her footsteps on the tent's plastic floor and then felt her sit at the corner of his bed. The mage removed his arm reluctantly.

"What do you want?" he asked.

Xia's eyes were a soft, concerned pink. She looked down at her hands, fingers laced in her lap.

"I just wanted to apologize for yelling at you," she said.

Duaal didn't want to think about the argument. "It's fine."

"No," Xia told him. She was still staring at her hands. "It's something I've been considering for some time now, but I didn't say it well. I'm surprised how upset I was."

"What do you care who I sleep with?" Duaal asked. "It's none of your business."

"I know, but I... I worry about you," Xia said.

"Why?"

"You always seem to hurt yourself. You like dangerous lovers... You're always picking fights with Tiberius and Maeve."

"Wait, I thought you said those fights were the captain's fault!" Duaal challenged, feeling suddenly betrayed. He sat up and glared at Xia. "You said that he was being overprotective!"

Xia looked up. "And that's true. He is, but you always make it worse! It's as if you *need* him to be angry with you, or that you *want* Coldhand to hurt you."

"It's not like that..." Duaal protested.

"Isn't it?" Xia uncurled her silvery hands and put one of them on the young human's knee.

"No, it's not," Duaal said stubbornly.

"Oh? What about Gavriel?"

The heater was doing its job, filling the tent with warmth, but Duaal's blood went cold and he began to shiver.

"What about him?" he asked through clenched teeth.

Xia hesitated, reaching for the words. "He was terrible to you, but his abuses were the only attention you had for many years."

"So?"

"So... maybe you're looking for that again," Xia said. "By trying to make Tiberius angry with you, by seeking out lovers like Coldhand."

Duaal didn't like it, but had to admit that the idea made some sense. He dropped his gaze. "Fine. What does it matter? Just leave me to it, Xia."

"No. I'm not just going to stand aside and watch you get hurt over and over again," Xia said. She moved closer, planting a hand on either side of his hips. Her burnished lips were very close, Duaal realized. Her eyes changed to a dark violet. "I want you to have something better than that. I want to give you something better."

Duaal had rarely seen an Ixthian's eyes turn that deep, lustful color.

"But I'm human," he said. "Don't you care about that? You were so angry with Xen about Panna..."

"I... don't know anymore," Xia murmured. "Maybe Xen is right. Maybe he's not. But I do know that you deserve someone who won't hurt you, Duaal."

It shouldn't have sounded strange, he thought, but it did. Exotic, a promise of something brand new. Duaal let Xia pull him into her arms and press her cool silver lips against his.

Xia's lovemaking was everything she promised it would be. Her touch was gentle and tender. She denied Duaal nothing and when they finally collapsed sweating into the blankets, the tent had fallen into twilight dimness. Xia touched her fingers to Duaal's forehead and smiled.

"How do you feel?" she asked.

"Good," Duaal answered with a blush.

"No headaches or hallucinations?"

"None. I do feel a little hot, though."

"So you are," Xia said. She kissed Duaal, then cocked her head. "Do you hear that?"

Duaal listened. There was the sound of ice crunching beneath tires from outside.

"They're back," he said.

Even if she had any food, Maeve would have traded it in a heartbeat just to close her eyes for a few minutes. The single lamp burned blindingly in the darkness and the light seemed to stab right through her eyes like blazing needles, but she couldn't stop herself from looking. Another Nihilist watched over Maeve, ready to hit or scream at her if she did more than blink. If he would only leave for a minute, or fall asleep himself, then she could close her eyes...

Maeve's head drooped. The new Nihilist laughed and hefted a broken towel rod. With an effort, Maeve looked up again, but not in time to keep the cultist from jabbing the end of the metal pole into her stomach. Maeve coughed. With her good foot, she kicked an impotent spray of dust up at him.

"You stay awake, bird-back," he said. "Lord Gavriel doesn't want you missing any of the fun."

"Your master will have nothing from me," Maeve spat.

The black-robed man laughed again.

With Gripper's help – the big Arboran was even stronger than the muscular Enu-Io – the archeologists broke down the last tents and moved their whole camp down into the ravine. Only the trucks and Logan's Raptor remained up on the surface of the snow-covered mountain.

"Is it safe down here?" Tiberius asked.

He carried a sleeping bag over one shoulder and looked around. The two Prian diggers had cleared away more of the rubble to make room along the slanting fissure floor.

"I spent most of the day helping Phil to shore up the walls," Ava said from ahead.

"Unless we get hit by another groundquake, we should be safe enough," Darius said. The sibling pair held the last rolled-up tent suspended between them.

Logan followed at the back of the line. Kemmer Andus had only reluctantly agreed to allow the bounty hunter down into the ravine. Logan walked carefully behind Panna and watched her blonde hair rippling across her shoulders, the shoulders that should have had wings stretching out behind them. Funneled by the sheer walls of stone, the wind howled overhead.

Duaal said there was a Waygate down here, just like those in the White Kingdom. But in the tight confines of the crevice, Logan had a hard time imagining it.

The jagged ground suddenly gave way to something much more broad and even. Logan found himself in a widening section of the ravine, painstakingly dug open into something resembling a cavern and ringed all around by spotlights. They steamed and sizzled as snow filtered slowly down from the distant sky.

Most of the domed white tents had already been set up all along one side of the cavern, where the overhang protected them from most of the weather. Enu-Io and Gripper took the last tent from the Prian diggers and set about erecting it at the end of the line.

The Lyran mechanic, Gruth, followed a short red-haired human around the perimeter of the underground camp. Gruth took notes on a datadex as the human man poked a tapered pole against the stone walls.

The flap of the largest tent was still open and the tables inside were arranged into two parallel lines, all covered in computers and equipment that Logan didn't recognize. Some of it had the bulky, old-fashioned look of Prian gear, but more of it was trim, sleek and modern. That must have come with the Tynerion team.

And towering over it all was the Waygate. Logan had seen a few pictures, copies of those few images brought back from the original Alliance explorers who had discovered Arcadia decades before its destruction by the Devourers. But a few schoolbook prints were no match for the real thing.

The Waygate was huge. A vast segmented stone ring – wide enough to fly the Raptor through the middle – sat at the peak of a stepped pyramid so tall that Logan had to crane his neck to see the top. The circular gate glowed with a strange luminescence that swirled like clouds in a storm.

"Amazing, isn't it?" Panna asked.

Logan didn't answer her. What had it been like for Maeve here, standing before the Waygate? Had she been awed at the sight of the great monument? Or devastated by this enormous and beautiful reminder of her lost home? Or was it a way back, perhaps, if there was a home to return to?

Maeve had used a Waygate to accidentally summon the Devourers, Logan thought. Was it painful to find another Waygate here on Prianus? Frightening? Logan had a hard time imagining Maeve being frightened by much. She had faced even her own death with fierce grace. But what of the Nihilists who had caught her? Was she afraid of them?

Logan turned away. Beautiful and impressive though it was, the Waygate wouldn't help him find Maeve.

Everyone gathered together in the largest tent to share their information and some dinner. Logan sat at the end of one table while the archeologists eyed him warily – which suited the bounty hunter just fine – but Panna had insisted on sitting across from Logan and grilling him for anything about Maeve.

"I haven't found anything yet," he told her again.

"But you've found Princess Cavainna before!" Panna said. "You must have some idea where to find her."

Logan shoved his plate away. The food that Phillip had prepared smelled good, but he wasn't hungry.

"No."

Gripper also sat nearby. The Arboran hadn't touched his food, either. Instead, he stared across the tent to where Duaal and Xia ate. The two sat very close together and smiled a little too often. Panna looked between Logan and Gripper, then shoved their untouched plates back toward them.

"Eat," she told them. "Neither one of you are doing Maeve any good just sitting here moping."

"I'm not moping," Logan said coldly.

Gripper looked down at Panna as though he had forgotten she was there. "What?"

"Eat your dinner, Gripper," Panna said. "Phillip cooked."

"Oh. Alright." Gripper slowly began spooning stewed kale and carrots into his mouth. "You seem to know a lot about Smoke and Coldhand."

"I read about Princess Cavainna after what happened on Stray. Her relationship to Coldhand came up during the trial. That's how I knew who he was – who you were – this morning. Has it really been less than a day?" Panna shook her head in wonder.

"Why do you care about Maeve?" Logan asked. "You cut off your wings and turned away from your own race."

"You left Prianus," Xen pointed out from further down the table. "That doesn't mean you don't care about it."

The rest of the tent had gone very quiet. Duaal whispered something into Xia's ear that Logan couldn't hear and Tiberius frowned. Logan waited for him to answer Xen, probably calling Coldhand a traitor at least twice before he was done. But Tiberius said nothing. Orphia preened on a nearby perch, ignoring everyone.

"I love my people," Panna said. Her voice was quiet, but clearly audible through the tent. "Believe it or not, that's actually why I had my wings removed and my ears clipped."

"I don't understand," Enu-Io said. "Please explain."

Panna swallowed and looked across the faces all turned her way. "I was born after the fall of Arcadia, but that doesn't mean I don't know anything about it. I grew up on stories of the old world. And I loved them. Well, most of them."

Logan clenched his cybernetic left hand. He couldn't imagine where Panna might be going with this story that would make any sense. How could anyone volunteer to have a part of themselves cut off and thrown away like trash?

"All the stories we have left are sad ones," Panna went on. "The beauty and grace of the White Kingdom is being lost every day as the Arcadians give in to their despair. It's like the fall all over again, but slow... so we don't miss a moment of it.

"I wanted to study my own history and people, so I decided to go to college on Tynerion and study anthropology. But Arcadians can't become Alliance citizens, so they can't go to CWA colleges. I had to look human. I thought I kept my secret so well."

Panna gave Xen a sheepish smile.

"You should have known better, my dear," said the Ixthian.

"I can't believe I never smelled the difference," Gruth said. "My mother would be ashamed."

"I never noticed, either, and the Dailon sense of smell is almost as good as yours. Our assumptions blinded us," Enu-Io said, then grinned, white teeth flashing behind dark blue lips. "Or whatever the word for blind is when we can't smell things."

Ava and Phillip – who hadn't paid much attention to the conversation so far – laughed at this and then returned to stealing bites of each other's fried potatoes. Kemmer sat sullenly off to one side of the tent, reading a datadex. Xia and Duaal went back to whispering to each other.

What were they doing? Eating dinner and trading stories while the Cult of Nihil had Maeve. And they had no more leads, no way to find her...

Logan abruptly stood and left the tent. The spotlights were still on outside, illuminating the wet stone walls of the ravine. Logan could feel the tons of rock pressing in all around him, pinning him helplessly in place.

He didn't want to feel this. He didn't want to feel anything at all.

I can still leave. I should.

There were drifts of white snow against the sides of the ravine, but none inside the relatively warm circle of lamps. The Waygate was too high and large to benefit much, but the occasional pale flakes could find no purchase on the smooth material and slid away. Logan heard heavy footsteps behind him.

"What do you want, Gripper?" he asked.

The Arboran stopped not far away, ducking his head sheepishly. "I just had to get out of there."

"Duaal and Xia?"

"Yeah. I've never seen them like that."

"They're tugging tails," Logan said.

Gripper flinched, then sighed. "I guess so. I didn't want to stay and watch them make kissy faces at each other."

"Fine."

"What are *you* doing out here?" Gripper asked. His shadow was long and loomed up over Logan. "Are you thinking about how to get Smoke back?"

Logan didn't look at him. "You still call her that?"

"I was trying to come up with a new name, just before they took her. She's not like she used to be, Coldhand. She actually tries to be happy, I think."

"Tries?"

Gripper stood next to Logan. Neither one looked at the other, eyes fixed instead on the towering shape of the Waygate. The great ring of flowing light seemed to stare back at them.

"I don't think she knows how," Gripper said. "She... Maeve isn't trying to die anymore, but she doesn't really know how to live. She's just sort of... drifting."

Logan understood. He was lost, too, ever since he came back to Prianus – first pushed by Vorus and by the Cult of Nihil, then by Ballad and now by his search for Maeve. Now he was pulled underground, into the shadow of an alien Waygate, while he wondered what to do next.

As the night wore on, Kemmer asked Darius to turn off most of the spotlights. No need to waste power when the archeologists weren't working. But their new camp remained warmer than the mountaintop and more or less dry – as long as Gruth and Gripper kept the pumps operational.

Hoping for a little bit of privacy, Duaal dragged his cot outside the tent and into a secluded rocky alcove. Xen had asked to speak to Xia, but she came looking for Duaal a little while later. He threw back the covers and gave the Ixthian an inviting wink.

"What did the professor want?" he asked.

Xia shrugged out of her clothes and slid into bed beside Duaal. Her silvery skin was smooth against him.

"He wanted me to take a look at Panna," Xia said.

"Why? Is there something wrong with her?" Duaal asked, propping himself up on one elbow.

"Other than being worried about Maeve? No. But Xen cares a lot about that girl. He wanted to know if the surgery she had was done properly."

"Was it?"

"Her surgeon did pretty good work. There are some scars, but they're not bad. And it looks like the operation was done some time ago," Xia reported. "That girl's older than she looks. Younger than Maeve, but older than me."

"You're just old enough to know what you're doing," Duaal told Xia with a grin. He grabbed her around the waist and pulled her close. Her short white hair tickled his cheek.

"Everyone is old to a man as young as you are," she said with a small laugh. "Did you see where Coldhand went?"

"Nope." Duaal shook his head. "Should I have?"

Xia's smile was all shining silver lips and white teeth. "No."

Duaal nuzzled the side of her neck. "I hope we can find Maeve tomorrow."

"So do I," Xia said softly.

They lay together in the darkness and didn't sleep.

"Tomorrow will go hard for you, my cousin. Unless you give Gavriel what he wants."

Maeve jerked and opened her eyes. Had she been sleeping? The pain returned, racing like fire all through her body.

Xartasia stood in the doorway of Maeve's makeshift prison. The other princess was dressed as though to attend her father's court, in flowing white and gold that flashed like sunlight, even in the wan radiance of the old lantern.

Maeve searched wildly around, but they were alone. For now, though there were indistinct voices in the hallway outside. The rest of the Nihilists weren't far away.

"You let me sleep?" Maeve asked. Her mouth was as dry as dust.

"For a little while, my cousin," Xartasia said. "I am sorry I could allow you no more. But if you are too well rested, Gavriel will see it."

Xartasia stepped into the room and then closed the crooked door. Her expression was sad as she took in Maeve's injuries and the dried blood streaking her skin.

"I do not understand you," Maeve whispered. Whatever sleep Xartasia had allowed her wasn't nearly enough. Her entire world was a haze of muffled pain. "You warn and pity me, but you will not help me! Why?"

"I do not wish to be cruel, but this must happen."

"Why?" Maeve asked. "You have power in this church. Order my freedom and it will be done!"

"No," Xartasia said. She shook her head sadly, making her thick black hair sway. "Please, Maeve. Stop fighting Gavriel. It will only hurt you and will come to nothing. You must give him the memories, the key to the Devourers. Do it for me, if you must. I would not see you suffer."

"Then free me!"

"No. I love you, cousin. I love our people. It is for that love that I stand with Gavriel."

Xartasia splayed her fingers over the back of the chair where the old Nihilist had sat, watching his Emberguard torture Maeve.

"I am not a good woman," Maeve said. She sagged against the flaking steel post and her wings ached in protest. "But even I have no stomach for Gavriel's plan. I will fight him to my final breath."

"Gavriel failed to get what he wanted by drawing your blood. I warned him. You are stronger than Gavriel believes anyone can be." Xartasia smiled self-depreciatingly. "Stronger than he believes I am. But tomorrow, he will break through even your memories of Logan Coldhand. Gavriel knows now what made you weak even to your hunter."

"What?" Maeve asked.

She sat up, ignoring the agony in her ankle and wings. The pain seemed suddenly unimportant. Xartasia shook her head.

"I cannot prepare you, Maeve. I beg you this last time to give in. But if you will not relent to Gavriel, I must ensure that he succeeds."

"Cousin!" Maeve cried. "What will he do?"

The angelic princess gave her a long, sad look.

"Have faith, Maeve. This is for the best."

[28]

BLOOD AFIRE

"It is not for the sake of God that we serve life, but for the sake of
life that we serve God."

- REVEREND BRAHM D'MAIR, THE UNION OF LIGHT (180 PA)

Panna woke early after a night of restless sleep and crept quietly
from the Tynerion team's tent. No need to wake anyone else just yet.

Outside, she was surprised to find that she was not the first to
rise. The old Prian captain, Tiberius, sat on a slab of granite jutting
up from the ravine floor. His hawk flew in lazy circles around the
Waygate. Snow drifted and eddied around the softly glimmering
ring but did not stick. Tiberius looked up at Panna as she made her
way through the camp.

"Good morning," he greeted her.

Tiberius didn't look like he had slept at all. His white-shot gray
beard had gone from unkempt to shaggy. He looked down at something he held in his lap. As she came closer, Panna could see that it
was a glass blade. Not a knife – it had no handle, just a few splinters
jutting from the bottom.

"Good morning. Is that a spearhead?" she asked. "An Arcadian one?"

Tiberius nodded without looking up. "It belongs to Maeve. It broke off the shaft back on Stray, when she was stealing Baliend back from Gavriel."

"May I see it?" Panna was hesitant to ask, but she couldn't help her curiosity. "I've never actually seen Arcadian glass. My parents talked about it, of course, but they didn't bring any with them from the old world."

Tiberius seemed about to refuse, but then handed the blade to Panna. She accepted it carefully. The Arcadian glass was heavier than she expected. It was cold and perfectly smooth, much like the Waygate material. The spear was at least a century old – probably more – but the edge remained razor-sharp.

"Why hasn't it been repaired?" Panna asked. "Doesn't Princess Maeve need it?"

"Maeve hasn't actually been in a single fight since Stray, if you can believe that," Tiberius said.

He raised one big hand, whistling sharply. Orphia keened, then circled back and settled onto her master's shoulder.

"These spears were only carried by knights of the White Kingdom. It shouldn't just be... ignored," Panna said. She examined the bottom of the blade. There were a couple of colorful fibers stuck to the glass inside. "There would have been tourney ribbons here. Are those gone, too?"

"Yes," Tiberius said. He stroked Orphia's feathers. "You know a lot about Arcadia, dove."

Panna sat down beside Tiberius, balancing the glass spear blade in her hands. "For most of my people, history is an open wound. But I'm an anthropologist. I don't look at the White Kingdom with the kind of romance that they do."

"You seem fond enough of fairy things," Tiberius said, arching a bushy eyebrow. "Even without your own wings."

"Don't misunderstand me. I love my people, and our culture," Panna told him. "There were many beautiful things in the White Kingdom. Can you imagine what an entire city made of this glass would have looked like, Captain Myles? There's nothing like it in the core, not even on Axis. But I didn't grow up in the White Kingdom. I was born here, in the Alliance. I feel a little differently about some things than the older Arcadians do."

Tiberius frowned. "Go on."

"The other fairy species, for example," Panna said.

It felt good to finally discuss some of her ideas. Concealing her heritage usually meant hiding her interest in the White Kingdom.

"What about them?" Tiberius asked.

"Dryads and nyads were more or less second-class citizens in the White Kingdom," Panna said. "The race we call Arcadians used to be aerads, until Cavain conquered the White Kingdom. He gave them a new name, one to differentiate them from the fairies that they ruled over.

"And then there's the war itself. It's the subject of the entire Lay of Cavain, probably the most well-known piece of Arcadian lore. Most people focus on the etiquette it describes, but do you know what else it discusses? The pyrads, the fire fairies. There used to be four races of fairies, but Cavain wiped out the pyrads because they wouldn't dissolve their own nation to join his."

Tiberius' frown deepened. "I never heard about that."

"I would be surprised if you had," Panna said. "That was all ten thousand years ago. We live longer than humans, but that's a long time even by our standards. The exclusively Arcadian monarchy wasn't cruel and the Arcadian knights kept everyone safe. It wasn't the worst empire in the galaxy. But what the older fairies won't tell you is that it wasn't perfect, either."

Panna turned the spear blade over and caught her reflection on the polished surface. Round ears, no wings... It seemed hypocritical to talk about her people's own history when she looked human.

"I think that's part of why we're still such a ruined culture, even a hundred years after the fall," Panna said. "Without the pyrads to raise hell, everything in the White Kingdom was so peaceful. And then the Devourers come out of nowhere and the survivors ran away. We don't know how to fight, really. Not anymore."

"Maeve always seemed to have plenty of fight in her," Tiberius objected.

"The princess is a strong woman," Panna said with a wry smile. "Some say that there's pyrad blood in the House of Cavain. They're the only black-haired Arcadians, you know."

"That would mean Cavain went to war with his own kind," said Tiberius.

"Yes," Panna agreed. "But it would also mean that there's still a bit of the fire fairy blood left, and that Princess Maeve has it. Maybe that's why she still fights."

"An interesting idea. Total birdshit, of course, but interesting." Tiberius closed his blue eyes. "I'm not a damned Ixthian. I don't believe for a minute that our genes dictate who we are. Our Maeve is strong because she's got fire in her soul, not her blood."

"Well, she's not the only one," Panna said. "The Cavainnas may be fierce, but there were other knights in the White Kingdom. They fought and died to defend their people. There are still strong Arcadians out there..."

Panna trailed off. She hoped that – by blood or spirit – Maeve was strong enough to withstand whatever the Cult of Nihil did to her. Panna held the glass blade out to Tiberius. He looked at it, still stroking Orphia's feathers.

"Do you know how to fix that?" he asked.

"I think so. I've got some experience restoring artifacts. This isn't exactly the same, but if I can figure out the length, the rest shouldn't be too hard. Do you know what kind of wood the original shaft was made of?"

"No idea."

Panna could probably examine the splinters left in the base of the blade and figure it out herself. If the wood originated in the White Kingdom, she would have to find the closest replacement... Panna closed her eyes and sucked in a breath. What good was fixing Maeve's spear if she could never give it back to the princess?

Still, it was something to do. Panna looked up at the huge, shimmering Waygate. And she didn't want to work anywhere near *that* thing today.

Xartasia refused to answer any further questions, but she waited with Maeve until dawn. She had given Maeve all the sleep that she would allow. Xartasia was gentler than her black-robed friends, but her soft wing-tip prods kept Maeve awake until Gavriel returned. The withered Nihilist barely glanced at Xartasia as he sat down.

"Go," he said. "Hallax and I will keep our guest company now."

Xartasia bowed, then departed without a word. Maeve's empty stomach twisted as Hallax stepped into the room. She clenched her teeth and fought the urge to shrink back from the Nihilists. She would not be weak before them. She would *not*... And there was nowhere to go, anyway.

"You will not torture the memories from me," Maeve told them as defiantly as she could manage.

"No, princess," Gavriel agreed. "And I can't risk your accidental death. When you finally die, it will only be with my blessing."

Gavriel gestured over to Hallax, who knelt and pulled back one of the fairy's tattered, blood-stained sleeves.

"There is no pain you can inflict which will break me," Maeve said. She hoped that was true.

Gavriel smiled. "Your cousin said that you were strong and she was right."

"Then... then what are you doing?" Maeve asked.

"Listening to Xartasia," Gavriel said. "She told me about your strength, but also about your weakness. I shouldn't have been angry with her for speaking to you, apparently."

Maeve didn't understand. Even with their sudden and terrible association, Maeve knew next to nothing about her cousin and suspected Xartasia knew little more about her. What could Xartasia have told Gavriel that could be of any use?

"You may actually enjoy this, Maeve," the old Nihilist said. "I understand that you have a certain fondness for chemicals. Vanora White, in particular. How convenient, since we happened to have procured some from the original tenants of this building."

Hallax held a loaded syringe in one hand and now Maeve *did* flinch. She kicked out at him, ignoring the pain in her swollen ankle and lacerated body, but couldn't reach the Emberguard. He jabbed the needle deep into Maeve's arm and pushed down the plunger.

Logan sat on the wing of his Raptor, holding the foil wrapper of his breakfast in his good hand. His neck and shoulders were stiff from a night of sleeping in the fighter.

Both the Prian and Tynerion archeological teams had extended tentative invitations to stay in the base camp, but Logan had no intention of trying to sleep in the long shadow of the Waygate. The scientists said over and over that it was an amazing discovery. That it would change everything. But every time Logan looked up at it, all he could think about was Maeve.

The snow had finally stopped falling and the sky was a uniform clear, bright blue. The thin air was still cold and smelled of ice. Wind tugged at Logan's hair and clothes.

This wasn't about the Nihilists anymore. This was about finding Maeve, about getting her back from Gavriel. And if she was dead...

Logan's cybernetic fingers screeched across the Raptor's fibersteel wing. He let the thought go no further.

One of Kemmer's trucks wheezed up the mountain and stopped on the edge of the moraine. Panna climbed out and pulled a long, straight branch from the back. It wobbled and plopped down into the frozen snow. She looked up at Coldhand, seemed to consider asking for help, then thought better of it and wrestled the branch up the slope alone.

What was she doing? The wingless Arcadian was almost as frustrated by their dead-end investigation into Maeve's disappearance as Logan. He jumped out of the Raptor and caught up to Panna as she tried to figure out how to get her branch down the ladder and into the ravine.

"Climb down," he said. "I'll hand it down to you."

Panna looked up at Logan, surprised and nervous as though he might tackle her again.

"I could just drop it," she said.

"The branch is too long. It'll break."

Panna nodded slowly and began climbing down the ladder. She stopped halfway and waited until Logan handed her the branch. She lowered the tip, then carefully dropped the other end. Logan climbed down after her.

"I'm taking this back to camp," Panna told the bounty hunter.

That was obvious, but Logan let the comment go unremarked. He simply nodded and helped Panna carry the branch down the ravine. When they pushed it the rest of the distance into the Way-gate chamber, Logan helped Panna maneuver the bough between the tents and then lift it up onto one of the tables.

"Thank you," she said.

Logan was curious what she was up to, but Panna didn't seem interested in talking as she began cutting stray twigs away from the branch. Logan lingered until it became clear that he could offer no further help and then wandered away.

He walked a slow circle around the base of the Waygate. The diggers had more or less evened out the floor of the crevasse, but it was still rough in places, icy in others. The Waygate shone with that ethereal glow, like lights shining through the water. Was that what it looked like just before the Devourers poured through and destroyed Maeve's life, her whole world?

The Waygate's radiance pulsed brightly and then darkened as though in answer to Logan's unspoken question. A second later, the gate brightened again. Had he imagined it? Kemmer and Xen stood in the arch of the great ring, talking about something. They didn't seem to have noticed any change.

By the time Logan finished his seventeenth circuit, it was mid-morning. Tiberius and the rest of the Blue Phoenix crew had gathered around Panna's table. In the circle of warm floodlights, Duaal hadn't bothered to put on a shirt. Xia stood behind him with her arms around his waist and her fingers splayed against his dark skin. When Gripper saw Logan, he waved the bounty hunter over.

"We don't need his help," Tiberius said. The old man looked exhausted.

"No one's done much to help at all, actually," Panna pointed out, gesturing with a small hand plane.

She had finished stripping bark off her branch and was now painstakingly straightening the piece of wood. A glass blade sat on the table's edge. Logan recognized it. He had faced that spear too many times to forget the long, thin angle of glittering glass.

"So, what do we do next?" Duaal asked.

"Maybe we could ask around Pylos," Gripper suggested. "Someone must have seen Maeve or the Nihilists."

"Pylos is too big for that," Duaal said. "We wouldn't even know where to begin."

"You just hate Maeve and want her to stay lost!" Gripper cried, waving his long arms.

"Stop it, Gripper," Xia said. "That's not fair."

The Arboran's shoulders slumped, but his expression remained furious. "Isn't it? You never liked Maeve, Shimmer! You never liked anyone until... until now! Until Silver!"

They were arguing... again. They were angry at the Nihilists and afraid for Maeve. Each of her friends thought they had the most at stake. That they were in the greatest pain.

Logan whistled sharply and every face around the table turned toward him. As long as they thought that the bounty hunter didn't care, then they would all assume that he was being objective, even reasonable.

"Arguing won't get us any closer to Maeve," Logan said.

Tiberius gave him a look that might have been frustrated or grateful.

"With the camp relocated down here, our job is much simpler," the old Prian said.

"Thanks for that, at least," Duaal agreed.

"That means we can focus on finding the princess, if we can just figure out where to start looking," Panna said. She measured the freshly peeled stick against the spearhead and marked the width on the wood with a pencil.

"You're saying *the princess* like she's the only one," Duaal said.

Panna looked up from the spear, confusion on her face. "She's the only surviving member of the royal family, isn't she?"

"Almost," Duaal told her. "There's another princess. Xartasia."

"Her name was Titania," Logan said. "She is the king's daughter and Maeve's cousin."

"Titania...?" Duaal asked. Now he looked confused, too. "Wait, I know that name."

"You probably heard it from Maeve," Xia said.

"No, that's not it." Duaal shook his head, unable for the moment to dredge up the memory.

"I've heard of Xartasia, when I was reading about what happened in Gharib," Panna said. She glanced at the looming Waygate.

It shimmered like the inside of a shiny shell. "I assumed that it was some kind of mistake. Xartasia's not a name. It's more like an oath or insult."

Logan remembered Maeve talking about that. He nodded. "It means *the dream of death*."

"Emphasis on dream," Panna said. The anthropologist was in her element now. "There are eleven words for dream in Arcadian, with several nuanced meanings. *Il'atasia* means the sort of dreams you have when you're asleep, but can also refer to something that isn't real, like an illusion or hallucination."

"She certainly seems plenty real," Duaal answered. He leaned on Panna's worktable. "I know my Arcadian pretty well, but I've never heard... *il'atasia*, you said?"

"I'm not at all surprised. Based on what Xia told us on the flight here, Gavriel taught you Arcadian, right?"

"Right."

"Well, you were learning spells," Panna said. "Words for making very real changes. I doubt you ever had any reason to learn that kind of vocabulary. Gavriel had to teach you the basics because that was the language of the charms he was learning from his own Arcadian teacher."

Duaal stood up suddenly straight, eyes wide.

"That's where I know the name Titania! She was the one who taught Gavriel magic," he said. Xia touched his shoulder, but Duaal shook his head. "I'm fine. I should have recognized her back on Stray. I must have been blind!"

"You were only a child when Gavriel took you," Xia pointed out. "It's a wonder you remember anything at all."

"I remember her singing. Hours and hours of singing," Duaal said. "And then... headaches. Like I keep having now. Do you think it's connected?"

"Maybe it's the magic. Have you been using any?" Xia asked.

"Not really," Duaal answered with a wink. "Except the magic between the sheets."

"Magic shouldn't cause any side effects like that, anyway," Panna said. "I've studied magic, but I can't do it myself. Actually, I've been working on a theory about magic. What do you know about quantum uncertainty theory?"

No one said anything. Logan wondered what Panna was getting at. It seemed like an overlong explanation of Duaal's familiarity with the Arcadian language.

Some of his impatience might have been a little... unfair. In the year he spent hunting Maeve, Logan had learned a bit of Arcadian. Enough to understand the names she called him. It was strangely intimate, somehow, a secret between hunter and prey. A secret that Duaal knew much more about, it seemed.

Panna scribbled something onto a datadex and then turned it face-down on the table. "Quantum uncertainty goes something like this: observation influences the outcome. Particles moving without an observer act differently than those being watched."

"So?" Tiberius asked.

"So, it's been theorized that directed observation can influence physical matter. Did anyone see what I drew on that datadex?"

"Kind of," Gripper said. "It looked like a duck, I think."

Panna winked and turned the datadex over and showed them a scribble on the screen. If Logan tilted his head a little, it did look like a very ugly, long-legged duck.

"You all see a duck, don't you?" Panna asked. Everyone nodded. "It was just a scribble. But because Gripper said that he saw a duck, you all did. Now, imagine if this were a little more literal, if your observation could *actually* turn it into a duck. That's how magic works."

"Wow," Gripper said. "Really?"

"Yeah. Now, it only works on a very small scale. It's *quantum* uncertainty, after all."

"That's true," Duaal said. "Lightning and fire and that painkiller charm Maeve likes so much all work on a tiny scale. Molecules and cells. The effects build, but at their heart, they're all very small."

"We have to use microscopes and optics to see anything that small and finely calibrated lasers to make molecular changes," Xia argued. "As far as I know, the Arcadians don't have that sort of technology. How can they observe anything so small?"

"That's where the Arcadian charm-songs come in," Panna said, snapping her fingers at the Ixthian. "Those songs are basic descriptions of what they want to happen, like telling a story. When you listen to a story, you can visualize what's going on. That's what the Arcadian songs are for and that's why Duaal had to learn the language. So he could understand the stories."

"That's why Maeve still sings those songs, even after telling me how pointless the symbols are," Duaal said. "Those are just focal points, but the song actually directs the spell."

"The spell songs are memorized and used to imagine a specific effect, like lightning or anesthetic," Logan said. He repeated Panna's explanation as best he could and she nodded. "But why couldn't Gavriel do it alone? Why did he need Duaal?"

"I haven't been working on that theory as long," Panna said. "But I do have a guess. It's important that the mage *truly* believes that just singing a song will change anything. It's easy for Arcadians of the old world. They grew up surrounded by magic. But not in the core worlds. Out here, only a child has that kind of faith and imagination."

"I felt his... his thoughts inside me," Duaal said with a shudder. This time, he accepted Xia's reassuring touch. "He didn't have to tell me what to do. It was like I was just a part of him."

Across the Waygate cavern, Xen and Phillip were deep in discussion about the Waygate's impact on the stability of the inner mountain. Ava and Phillip sprayed canned foam into cracks in the granite walls, filling the fissure with a sharp chemical smell.

Just how long could they afford to wait? How long could Maeve survive? They were only wasting time, trying to fill the hours until something changed. But nothing was going to change, Logan knew. The only thing that would find Maeve now was perseverance, unceasing vigilance and chance.

Logan turned away, intent on climbing back up to the surface, to his Raptor. Maybe he could see something from the air. It was the same fighter as those flown by the police. Maybe the sight of the Raptor in a search pattern would spur the Nihilists to some sort of visible action... It would probably rouse the interest of the Pylos police, as well, but Logan didn't care anymore.

"Where are you going, Coldhand?" Gripper asked.

"Back to Pylos."

The Arboran trotted after Logan. Duaal and Xia shared a glance and then the medic raised her hand.

"Wait, Coldhand. Do you actually have somewhere to go?" she asked in a carefully neutral tone. "No one seemed to have any ideas a few minutes ago."

Logan didn't answer. His plan sounded thin, even to him. But the helpless frustration was eating him alive and left the hunter a bundle of raw, twitching nerves. The archeologists watched him, too, curious in spite of themselves.

"Coldhand!" Tiberius called to him now, full of authority accustomed to obedience. "If you know something, you better damned well tell us!"

Logan turned back, mismatched fists clenched.

"No, I don't know anything else," he said too loudly. His voice echoed through the ravine. "I don't have any plan. But I'm going back out there. I can't do this anymore. I want this done, Tiberius. I don't care how, but I need to find Maeve."

Logan felt hot and cold at the same time, flashes of fever and chill. He had to end this, somehow, even if it meant roaming the Pylos streets, screaming for the Nihilists until they came for him.

"Can I help…?" Gripper asked. "Please? I… I don't want to just sit here and wait, either."

"You won't fit in the Raptor," Logan answered curtly.

"Your Raptor?" Tiberius asked, narrowing his eyes. "What are you thinking, Coldhand?"

"I'm going to look for her."

"In your fighter?" Duaal pulled himself away from Xia. "No, you can't do that!"

"Why not?"

"That's a police Raptor," Duaal said. "You can't go flying that after Gavriel. He'll see you. He's afraid of the Prian police. He had a lot of trouble with them when we were here before."

"I know."

"You lost that to an Emberguard," Tiberius said, pointing to his illonium left hand. "Captain Cerro showed me the file. He thought you might have gone over to Gavriel."

Logan looked down at his fist. "Is that what they think?"

"Is what you actually did any better?" Tiberius asked him. "The police closing in was what chased Gavriel off Prianus last time. You go in now, without thinking, and you'll send him running. He'll kill our dove or take her off the planet. Either way, we'll never see her again. You stay here until we have something to move on."

Logan closed his eyes. Tiberius was right.

The Vanora White oozed through Maeve's veins, cool and smooth and heavy as quicksilver. She floated to the top on a cloud of bright light. There were shadows, she remembered faintly. Something that was looking for her. Or something that belonged to her…

But that was so far away, so easy to forget.

Maeve stretched her wings, but they were tangled in the clouds. It tickled and she giggled as the sparkling white twined around her.

The softness clutched at her heart, slowing it beat by beat. And it whispered to her.

Remember the Devourers, Maeve. Remember them.

She didn't want to think about that. It hurt and she was tired of pain. It was so much more peaceful here in the White. And warm. It was nice not to be cold. She couldn't remember why she had ever stopped taking the chem.

Show me the Tamlin Waygate, said the light. *Show me your spell. Show me the Devourers.*

"No," Maeve whimpered.

Even through the deep haze of drugs, Maeve shied away from the painful memory. She just wanted to sleep, but the white sky wouldn't leave her alone. It clung as close and sweet and light as cloud-candy.

Show me, Maeve.

[29]
INTO DEEP

"There is a coward inside even the bravest man. This is no insult.
All men know in their hearts that life is an endeavor of pain, ever
to be feared."

- GAVRIEL EUVO, CULT OF NIHIL FOUNDER (229 PA)

"What's wrong with him?" Duaal asked under his breath.

He cocked his head toward Coldhand. The bounty hunter stood
with his back to the rest of the camp, Gripper waiting wordlessly at
his side.

Xia frowned and shrugged her narrow shoulders. "I don't know.
Something's happened to Coldhand. He's usually so collected. But
now he's losing it. And those bruises..."

It had been only one day since Xia gave Duaal very good, very
sweet reasons to stop paying attention to the bounty hunter, but he
had forgotten all about the marks of violence. Now, Duaal remembered the dark bruise along Coldhand's jaw.

"He hasn't been able to do very much," Panna said, even more
quietly. "After all I've read, I guess I expected... I don't know."

"It's not his fault. We haven't done any better."

This was from Tiberius. Xia, Duaal and Panna looked at him in surprise. The old Prian seemed to realize his own words too late and set his lined, scruffy face in a deep scowl. It was good that Coldhand probably couldn't hear them. He would be just as flustered as Tiberius.

Prians were so proud. Duaal leaned against the edge of Panna's table. That was a little hypocritical, he supposed. He was at least as proud as either Tiberius or Logan, Duaal could admit to himself.

Pain flared behind his eyes, white-hot needles of agony that sent him crashing to the ground and grabbing fistfuls of his hair. He was dimly aware of voices calling his name, but he couldn't answer. A giant's hand had clamped itself around Duaal's mind, around his entire being and shook him. Hard. The world spun wildly, and then the alien force flung him out into a blinding-bright void.

Duaal struggled to call out to Xia and Tiberius, but couldn't make his mouth work. Where was his mouth? His whole body was gone.

But he wasn't without form. He felt arms and legs, lungs that could not quite draw breath deep enough. Duaal's back ached. His fingers were as stiff and brittle as twigs, yet he burned. Fire raged unchecked through him, filling him with a poisonous but vital flame.

He was sitting, leaning forward eagerly in a chair that creaked every time he shifted his weight. He sang the old, dark Arcadian songs, the blasphemous spells that Xartasia had taught him with a sad smile on her pretty lips.

Him, not me, Duaal remembered with an effort that would have ground his teeth, if he only knew where they were. This isn't me!

...Then what is this? Another hallucination?

Duaal's eyes opened, but not by any effort or will of his own. Maeve was sprawled in the rubble at his feet again, but this time, the expression on her dirty face wasn't agony. She slumped in her bonds against a metal beam that was dark and scaly with rust. Maeve sang softly to herself as she rocked her head from side to side. Her voice was thick, as though on the verge of turning into another laugh... or a scream.

Duaal's other voice rose, drowning Maeve's. As he sang, Duaal found that he could see into the fairy's misty daydreams. There was ice and clouds, all running like wet paint as she pulled her thoughts away. The song spiraled away across Maeve's erratically fluttering thoughts.

"But that is a secret. An opal in a stone crown," she murmured, almost inaudibly. "The gate must sleep. Sleep. I just want to sleep... Please..."

Maeve sobbed quietly and there was a hazy, smoky image of a Waygate there in her thoughts, surrounded by dark shapes that flickered between tall, sharp mountains and soaring, sparkling glass towers. Indistinct winged shapes soared between the diamond spires like dandelion puffs. That had to be Tamlin, the Arcadian city.

Duaal felt himself leaning close again, weaving his charm urgently as he searched through Maeve's memory. His spell opened the princess' mind like files on a datadex. Duaal's heart caught in his chest.

"Sleep," Maeve sang again, sternly this time.

The image of Tamlin and the great Waygate faded back into blank whiteness. Duaal's eyes – the eyes that were not his own – turned to the Mirran in red who crouched in the shadows of the tumbled rocks and dirt from the broken wall.

"We're getting closer. Can you give her more White yet, Hallax? I'm eager to have this done and send her to the pit."

Duaal knew that voice. Gavriel! He wanted to close his eyes, but he was a prisoner in his old master's body.

This wasn't real. This couldn't be real! It was just a dream, some kind of hallucination. Duaal was mixing memories and fears... Hallax grabbed a handful of Maeve's black hair and examined her glazed eyes.

"Not yet," he said. "She needs another hour or two, Lord Gavriel, or it could kill her."

Duaal felt his head tilt in a short nod. "Fine. Go get Xartasia. I need her to help Maeve... focus."

Hallax rose and bowed deeply, then vanished from the room. Gavriel steepled his fingers and peered through them at Maeve. The fairy's head wobbled on her neck and she could not seem to meet Gavriel's gaze.

"We are so close now, sweet princess," Gavriel said softly. "You crafted your own weaknesses, and now you have broken yourself. You will give me the Devourers."

The Devourers? Duaal couldn't recoil from Gavriel's fantasies of blood and death: Axis in ashes, proud Prian hearts torn from their bodies, gray Zeos consumed in bright and terrible fire. Duaal strained without direction, struggling to wake himself from the nightmare.

Duaal opened his eyes and tried not to throw up. He was on the ground, with his head pillowed in Xia's lap. There was dirt all over his pants. Duaal groaned.

Everyone gathered around, worry and curiosity on their faces. Ava started to say something to Kemmer, who put his fingers to his lips in an uncharacteristic display of sensitivity to Duaal's aching skull.

"Back off, everyone," Tiberius said.

"Is he alright?" Phillip asked. "What happened, Duaal?"

"We'll let you know when we figure it out," Xia said. "Thank you for the concern."

"Back to work, everyone," Xen called out. He clapped his hands together. "Come on!"

Grumbling, the archeologists scattered and turned back toward the Waygate. Panna looked to Xen, who glanced down at the half-assembled spear on the table and twitched his antennae, but said nothing. He followed the rest of the team back to work.

"Does it hurt?" Tiberius asked.

"Yeah." Duaal sat up slowly, rubbing his head. "I had another one of those hallucinations. I saw Gavriel and Maeve."

"What the hells is wrong with him, Xia?" Tiberius asked in a tight voice.

"I don't know," she answered. She clenched her silver hands in frustration. "I've run every test, every scan I can think of. There are no tumors, no bleeding, no pressure and no imbalances. There's nothing wrong!"

"It could be Prianus," Coldhand said. He had gone so quiet that Duaal almost forgot that the bounty hunter was there. "There are things in the air found nowhere else in the core."

"Environmental regulations on Prianus aren't as strict as other Alliance planets," Tiberius admitted. "But no. This started before we came here."

"But it *did* get worse on Prianus," Xia pointed out. "Maybe some toxin or pollutant is aggravating the problem."

"Wait, there is one common element to his headaches," Panna said. She perched on the corner of the worktable. "Gavriel. Duaal, you said before that you haven't had headaches like this since you were with him, right?"

Duaal nodded. "You have another theory, don't you?"

"Let's hear it, then," Tiberius said.

Panna thought for a moment before she answered. "There's another theory of quantum physics that I've been studying in relation to Arcadian magic. It's called quantum entanglement."

"Another science lecture? My head hurts plenty already," Duaal grumbled. Still, he was curious.

"Then I'll keep it short," Panna promised. "Quantum entanglement says that two particles can be linked, connected even across vast interstellar distances. If one particle changes its spin, the other one will, too. Now, this is just a guess, but I think that's what was done to your brain, Duaal."

"How? And why?" Xia asked.

"I think that's how Gavriel used Duaal for his magic. It wouldn't be enough just to tell him what to say. The *exact* thoughts and memories are too important to the magic. So Xartasia quantum-linked your brains, like networking two computers. I can't imagine how complex that must have been." Panna held up her hands. "There's no way to check, though. It's just a theory."

Coldhand gave Duaal a piercing look. "You said you saw Gavriel and Maeve."

"Sort of," Duaal told him hesitantly and shuddered. "I didn't actually see Gavriel. I heard him and felt him, but it was like I was inside of him."

"If your mind was entangled... networked... with Gavriel's," the hunter said, "the link may still be intact."

Panna snapped her fingers and jumped down from the table.

"You said that these headaches started not long after Stray, after Gavriel took that baby," she said excitedly. "That was to restore the magic he lost with you, right? Even though you took Baliend back, he must have succeeded."

"So he's out there casting spells again?" Tiberius asked. His jaw clenched. "Why's it hurting Duaal?"

"Parts of their brains are still quantum-linked, the parts responsible for spell casting," Panna said. "The connection is likely only sparked when Gavriel uses that part of his mind. He must be using more magic now."

"For what?" Xia asked.

"Hurting Maeve." Coldhand's tone was icy and intense. "These aren't hallucinations. He's actually seeing Maeve through Gavriel's eyes."

"I think so," Panna said, surprised. "Yes. Yes, if I'm right."

The bounty hunter turned his pale blue eyes on Duaal.

"Tell us exactly what you saw. Every detail."

Xartasia stood on the roof. The city of Pylos was quiet under a soft blanket of white snow. Or so it seemed from this height. Pillars of smoke rose from chimneys and filled the air with their murky haze. The princess wrinkled her nose as the wind changed and carried the smell of burning to her.

There were sounds on the cold wind, too. Rough voices and the grinding of vehicle engines... But Xartasia couldn't hear Maeve. The knowledge of what must be happening below weighed heavily on the princess. She didn't want the girl to suffer, but Maeve was far too strong and stubborn to give in easily.

So I betrayed my cousin. I told Gavriel of her past with these core-world drugs, her weakness to them.

It wasn't truly betrayal, Xartasia reminded herself. Even Maeve's strength had its limits. Pain and deprivation would have broken her eventually. All Xartasia had done was speed the process along and save Maeve from days of torment.

Xartasia lifted her chin and inhaled deeply, chilly air scraping her throat. They were close now. Soon, none of this would matter. The wind whipped her long hair out like spilled ink. An equally dark shadow fell across her. Xartasia smelled old blood and sour-sweet Vanora White.

"Lord Gavriel has summoned you," Hallax said.

Xartasia nodded without looking at him, but the Mirran didn't leave.

"Now," Hallax told her. "He wants you to help him with Maeve."

Xartasia still didn't look up. She studied the long, scree-strewn slope below and ice-cowled Pylos beyond that.

"He wishes more of me?" Xartasia murmured to herself. "When I have given him my own cousin and the means to ruin her? What more must I give?"

Titania stood in the filth and flickering shadows of Axis' lower levels. She was tired of metal under her feet. She missed the feel of grass and soil, but Titania had gone down as far as she could through the megatropolis of the Alliance's capital and still found only older, darker and more deso-late levels. Here, only one in four lights glowed. Even then, the yellow-green illumination was fitful.

Gavriel stood on an overturned crate with his hands raised. He was dressed all in black, in something that looked like it had once been a suit, but which was now so soiled and torn and rumpled that it hung from his body in rags.

The human man might have looked respectable once. Perhaps even had been respectable. Not unlike Titania herself, she supposed.

She had heard Gavriel's name and even his voice several times in Axis' lower levels. A few Arcadians gathered around him, listening raptly as he praised death, an end to all pain. Dirty wings and dirty faces all turned up as they basked in his promise. Titania waited, watching and listening. He gave them something, a hope that Titania alone couldn't.

I need him.

Gavriel finished his speech and climbed down from the dais of trash. Titania stepped out from the shadowed doorway. There were some humans following Gavriel, too. They eyed the princess suspiciously as she approached, but the Arcadians caught sight of Titania's black hair and fell to their knees. Gavriel smiled welcomingly.

"Good evening, sister," he greeted Titania.

"I am Xartasia," she answered. "I am a daughter of Cavain. You have offered kindness to my people."

"The Arcadians are a tormented race," Gavriel said, glancing around at the genuflecting fairies, taking in their reactions and then returning his attention to the princess. "I offer them what I can."

"You must have greater designs than this," Xartasia said, warming to her subject. She gestured around the filthy walls of Axis' lower levels. "Greater ambitions than these. I hear your words, that you desire to spread your faith and your... gift."

"I do." The hunger, the passion in Gavriel's voice was unmistakable.

"I can help you. I can teach you magic, secrets unknown to the core-world races," Xartasia said. All around her, the Arcadians gasped. She held up her hand, quieting them. "But I am of the House of Cavain. There is etiquette to be observed. You are a leader among your people, but I am a monarch of mine."

"Go on," Gavriel said slowly. He was a younger man then, and not so secure in his power.

"With my magic, you will wield lightning and fire and command the very bodies of those who gather to you," Xartasia told him. "Or those who

would stand against you. But first, you must pay your homages to the line of Cavain. For one Arcadian year – two hundred eighty-eight days – you must show me favor."

"Favor?"

"You will need to serve me, as I am due," Xartasia said. *"There are places I must go, things that I need to see. You will do these things for me, and then I will teach you."*

Gavriel narrowed his eyes at Xartasia. "That's a high price."

"Yes," she agreed. *"But I have secrets that no other Arcadian or Jinn or Nnyth know. I will make you the most powerful man in the galaxy. Only give me my year of service."*

"I'll think about it," Gavriel said.

He hadn't needed to think about it long. But that year of service was decades over. Xartasia had what she wanted, had learned what she needed to. Now... now Gavriel required things and she had to give them.

"Lord Gavriel will tell you what he wants," Hallax said. "And you'll do it."

Xartasia finally turned to face the Emberguard.

"Very well. Take me to him."

High up in the Kayton Mountains, the Waygate's glow rippled and churned.

Panna examined the map of Pylos, downloaded with considerable difficulty from the city mainstream and displayed on a datadex. She leaned over it with a stylus in her trembling fingers. Logan paced beside the table.

"Uh, the dirt in the room doesn't narrow it down very much," Panna said. "There are all sorts of buildings in Pylos that have collapsed walls. The entire city is built in a valley between tectonically unstable mountains!"

"We might be able to compile a list of dangerous and unstable buildings from the police," Xia suggested. "But there will be a lot of them. What else did you see, Duaal?"

The young mage chewed a fingernail as he thought. "There was a counter on the right wall, with a hole like there used to be a sink. I think it was an apartment."

All eyes went back to the map. It was several years out of date, according to the file's timestamp, and took no account of the recent quakes.

"But there are millions of people living in Pylos," Gripper said. "Look at all the houses!"

"It was dark and full of dirt," Duaal pointed out. "I don't think anyone is living there anymore, except for the Nihilists."

"For how long, if you had to guess?" Xia asked. She tapped the datadex. Districts, neighborhoods and buildings were marked out in different colors, with residential areas shaded in with blue. "If the apartment has been unlivable for a while, it might be in one of these condemned sections. How long do you think it's been since that place was habitable?"

"Years," Duaal answered promptly. "The entire place was rotten and falling apart."

"Then we're looking at one of these areas." Tiberius pointed to five different grayed-out areas, and then frowned. "Probably. The apartments might have been condemned more recently, or just not inspected yet. It can take years for someone to get out there and write up a demolition order."

"And in the meantime, no one's preventing people from living there?" Panna asked. "That's dangerous!"

"Welcome to Prianus," Logan told her. "Did you see anything else, Duaal? What color was the dirt coming in through that wall? Brown might indicate something closer to the center of the Pylos valley. Gray could have washed down from the mountains. It has more stone and less organic matter."

Duaal thought, but then he shook his head. "I couldn't see the color. There wasn't enough light."

"Any fixtures? Architecture that might suggest the building's age?" Logan asked.

"It was all pretty basic, and ugly. There's a post in the middle of the room that Maeve's handcuffed to," Duaal said. Then his green eyes widened. "Wait, the post was metal! Steel, I think. It was corroded. Does that help?"

"It might," Tiberius said. "Steel is expensive."

"Especially around here," Logan added. He paused in his pacing and drummed his metal fingers on the edge of the table. "There aren't any useful mines in the Kayton Mountains. You're not going to find a lot of steel used in apartments. And a post in the middle of a room?"

Tiberius arched his bushy gray eyebrows. "It's probably a converted warehouse or something like that."

Gripper looked down at the map.

"This doesn't use any of the standard notations!" he complained bitterly. "I... I think this red tag means that the buildings were repurposed."

"How many are there?" Xia asked.

Gripper's lips moved as he counted, then whistled. "Um... five hundred seventy-two."

Tiberius grunted. "We've got to narrow that down."

"You said it was turned from something else into apartments," Duaal said. He looked over Gripper's arm at the map. "Look, there are notes on some of these about the sort of conversion the builders made. This one isn't what we want – it was a housing block that got turned into a... What is this?"

"A falconry," Logan answered. "So we can focus our search on those buildings converted into apartments."

"That's about half," Gripper said after he checked the numbers. "Still more than two hundred places."

"If Gavriel's trying to be quiet about his presence here – and we have every indication that he is – he would use one of those condemned buildings," Xia said thoughtfully. "He can't move into an occupied one without someone noticing. These ruins might have some vagrants, but that's less likely to get serious attention."

Gripper nodded and shifted his weight from one big foot to the other as he studied the datadex. "That brings us down to about eighty. Most of them are in this block, along the river."

They all looked at Duaal. He pursed his lips. "No, I didn't hear or see any water. Everything was in bad shape, but it was dry."

"Not near the river, then. How many does that leave us?" Panna asked Gripper.

"Fifty-nine buildings."

"Gavriel said something about a pit," Duaal said. He sounded uncertain. "There was an image in his mind, just for a second."

"Did you see enough to help us?" Tiberius asked.

"Maybe...? It's a huge fissure in the ground," the Hyzaari mage said. He gestured to the mountain crevasse all around them. "A lot like this, I guess, but smaller. Gavriel throws problems down there. But I got the impression that it was downstairs."

"So?" Gripper asked. "Lots of buildings have basements."

"But there's dirt coming in through the broken wall on another level – a higher one – where Maeve's being held," Logan said. "That means the whole building is either built on a slope or that it's fallen against one."

"That's got to put our dove somewhere along the valley's edge," Tiberius said, loud and excited. "How many buildings?"

"Um... looking." Gripper's hands shook as he traced the lines of the map. "Fourteen."

"Most of those are along the northwestern edge of the valley," Panna said. "We can find her in that, can't we?"

"Yes." Logan checked his Talon. The charge was at about half. "Gripper, you're with me. Pull off a copy of that map and let's go."

"Yeah," Gripper said. He slotted some memory chips from his pocket into the computer and copied the map.

"Once we find out exactly where they're holding Maeve, we'll call Cerro," Tiberius said. This close to finding Maeve, he no longer argued with the bounty hunter over authority. Tiberius whistled. Orphia, who had been circling high over the ravine, spiraled down to her master. "We're going to need his help. Xia, we need you, too. Our dove is injured."

Duaal and Panna waited. When it became clear that Tiberius was giving no further instructions, Panna cleared her throat.

"I'm coming, too," she said.

"I could use the extra pair of hands," Xia agreed.

Panna nodded and ran back to the Tynerion tent to collect her things. When she returned, Panna began collecting the pieces of Maeve's spear from the table.

"I can finish this on the way," she said. "She'll want it, I think."

"What about me?" Duaal asked.

Tiberius stopped in the act of handing the spear shaft to Panna. "We're going up against Gavriel and his cult, little hawk. I want you to stay here."

Duaal's face fell, but he nodded. "Fine."

Tiberius held up his hand. "No, Duaal. I *want* you to stay, but we need you to go."

"You do?"

Tiberius nodded slowly. Even Logan could see the reluctance in the old Prian's face.

"We need to be quick about this and can't spend a lot of time flapping around where the Nihilists might see us," Tiberius said. "You're the only one who can recognize the right place on sight."

"I... I'm going along?" Duaal asked, mouth agape and eyes wide. He shook his head as though shaking off a dream. "You actually need me?"

Tiberius nodded.

Kemmer was working nearby and looked up from his microscope. "Now wait a damned minute! You can't leave us alone up here again! The northwest side of the valley, right? That's where you think this Cult of Nihil is?"

"That's the idea," Tiberius answered in a tone that invited no argument. "And we're getting Maeve back from them."

Kemmer didn't care if he had an invitation or not.

"That's just down the mountain from here, Captain Myles," he said. "You can't just leave when we're that close to people that you yourself have said are dangerous! They took Maeve from her post, just up there. They know we're here!"

"But they don't care," Logan pointed out.

"You don't know that, bounty hunter!" Kemmer snapped. "You drop out of the sky uninvited and think that you know anything about what's going on here? I don't know who you are and I don't care! But I *do* have an agreement with Captain Myles."

Now Tiberius frowned. Orphia hopped down from his shoulder and chewed on the corner of the table.

"What are you getting at, Kemmer?" Tiberius said.

"You gave me your word that you would protect our dig, Captain Myles. You took payment and you promised to keep the Waygate safe."

"I did," Tiberius said. He closed his eyes and whistled softly at Orphia. The old hawk stopped nibbling and sidled up his arm to perch on his shoulder again. Tiberius opened his eyes again. "Yes, I did promise that."

"Kemmer, this is about a lot more than just getting Maeve back," Duaal protested. "I know what Gavriel is trying to get from her. He wants Maeve's memories of Tamlin and the Devourers."

"What? Why?" Panna asked.

"To... to summon them," Duaal said. "He wants the Devourers to wipe out all life in the galaxy."

Tiberius looked at Kemmer, then at the mage.

"You have to find the place, Duaal," he said. "Find it and call Cerro. We're not going to let Gavriel hurt Maeve anymore and we're sure as hells not letting him get to the Devourers. Got it?"

"Got it, captain," Duaal said.

Tiberius nodded. "I'll stay here. I told Kemmer that I'd keep his damned Waygate safe, and I will. You go get Maeve back and stop Gavriel."

Logan had never seen Duaal smile so hugely.

"Let's get moving, then!" the mage said.

They made their way through the camp and then up the long ladder, out to the moraine. Rain sliced through the blanket of snow and ran in tiny, frigid rivers down the slope. Duaal pointed up to the Raptor.

"Are you going to bring that?" he asked.

Logan had considered the same question on the climb up. "No. Tiberius is right. We don't want the Nihilists to know we're coming and they're going to notice a fighter buzzing their area."

"Just the trucks, then."

Logan hurried down to the trucks and yanked open the nearest door. His blood ran hot and somehow itchy through his veins. He was impatient to be off, to find Maeve. To see her again at last...

Duaal, Xia and Panna climbed into the other truck, but Gripper sat next to Logan, datadex in hand. The two traded a look and then Logan twisted the keychip in the ignition.

[30]
THE WAYGATES

"Being brave only means that you don't tell anyone how scared you are."

- PHILLIP ARNO, CYRAN GEOLOGIST (233 PA)

Maeve sang to herself. The air in this place was stale and smelled of dirt. She wanted to fly, but her wings wouldn't work. Maeve was sure that she knew why, but the memory kept slipping out of reach, like grasping at waves on the beach. No matter how she chased them, her own thoughts slid away again.

But the song was constant. No, Maeve realized sluggishly. It rose and fell and washed cold across the dirty floor. The voice wasn't hers, and neither was the song.

Gavriel, Maeve remembered painstakingly. He wanted something from her.

He was singing a spell. Maeve shook her head, trying to clear away the thick white fog. There was something important that she was supposed to do. Or not do...

Yes, that was it. Maeve couldn't give Gavriel the memories he wanted. With a groan and tremendous heave, Maeve lurched and pulled against her handcuffs again. Her wings ached and a razor sting raced up her arms. It was agony, but the pain helped clear Maeve's mind.

Gavriel stopped singing and a long striped arm reached from the shadows to push Maeve back into the steel beam. Hallax was gentle – careful not to bash her skull and its valuable contents against the pitted metal – but firm. He peeled open an alcohol-soaked pad with his teeth and scrubbed a section of Maeve's arm free of blood and grime.

"She's resistant to this stuff," said the Emberguard. He sounded almost cheerful.

"Is she ready for more?" Gavriel asked.

He sat back in his dusty, brittle old armchair, staring at Maeve. Hallax pressed two fingers up under Maeve's jaw and then peered into her eyes.

"Yes, Lord Gavriel," he said.

"Give it to her, then."

"No!" Maeve protested as loudly as she could, but her voice was no more than a phlegmy whisper.

She *had* to fight, but Hallax slid another needle into her arm. Maeve writhed, but another pair of hands emerged from the darkness, gloved in soft doeskin.

"Please, do not struggle, cousin," Xartasia said. "No more. You have shown your bravery."

Gavriel gave the older princess a stern look. "As we agreed."

Xartasia met his eye and her sharp jaw set. "You have given her enough White to drown any resistance."

"Clearly, we have not," Gavriel countered. "She hasn't given up the memories."

A soft sigh sang through the warm, empty blankness. Distantly, Maeve felt her cousin's slender fingers tighten on her arm. *Traitor, traitor,* Maeve reminded herself, but the Vanora White was taking hold again.

The dark, dirty room dissolved into clouds of pure white. Maeve floated through them and the Nihilists' voice echoed as though they stood inside a crystal cathedral.

"You owe this to our people," Xartasia said. "To me. You destroyed the White Kingdom, Maeve. You killed them all. My father, my mother and brothers. My *enarri*, my Anthem...!"

"No," Maeve whispered. The gently glittering alabaster dancing all around her stilled and began to fall away into a bottomless abyss of shadow. "No! You... you said it was not my fault. That it was the Devourers...!"

"The fault *is* yours, little cousin," Xartasia said mournfully. "Our worlds are dead for your sin. The last of our people die in disease and famine. This is of your doing."

Xartasia's fingers were ice-cold claws as they curled into Maeve's flesh. Blood welled up around the wounds and ran down her skin, molten and burning. Rivers of blood... Not Maeve's blood, but the blood of the millions upon millions that she had killed. The dryads and nyads, all dead...!

Blood filled the room, rising up around Maeve's legs and then her chest, up to her shoulders. She screamed in helpless horror as the flood of sticky red clung around her throat. Maeve twisted and shrieked, but she couldn't move and the rivers of blood would not stop.

"There is only one release for your pain," Gavriel said.

Maeve stared up. A point of light burned above her, a single star in the midst of this terrible night. She moaned and blood filled her mouth.

"Only death will stop this, Maeve," the star told her. "The pain will cease. No more pain, no more guilt."

The sky – *No, I am inside a room! There is no sky!* – wasn't simply dark. There was something else out there. Something reaching for Maeve... Smoke? No, great black clouds of dust and ash, just like the Devourers' deadly, ethereal forms.

Squeezing her eyes shut wouldn't banish the visions of deadly red and black. The star was still singing. "When it's done, Maeve, you will have peace. You will sleep without nightmares of the Devourers. I can save you."

"No," crooned the darkness, full of a deep, cold sadness. "I will never let you go. You took everything from us."

"I... I was forgiven," Maeve whispered. Blood poured down her throat, drowning her.

"Destroyer. Killer!" hissed the shadows. "You will never be forgiven! You will *never* forget. Remember, Maeve. Remember what you have done!"

The devouring darkness was right. As blood closed over Maeve's head, she knew it was right. She wasn't forgiven... Never forgiven. And she remembered why.

Maeve stood atop the great ziggurat. The gentle glow of the Waygate reflected in her glass armor.

It was early in the morning and the sun, Aes, still lay heavy and golden on the horizon. The city of Tamlin shone like a great jeweled crown all around the Waygate. Glass towers climbed up into rose-colored dawn and white-winged Arcadians flew between the delicate spires on the morning breeze. A knight at the Waygate wasn't a strange sight and they paid Maeve no mind.

Gavriel sang. His voice pressed painfully into Maeve's memory. His invasive magic pierced any lingering vestige of the Vanora White's languor. Maeve screamed. She tried to stop, to tear her thoughts back from Tamlin, from the Waygate and the Devourers, but Gavriel's smooth voice and Xartasia's grasp on her arm pinned her there. The charm echoed in the close room.

Maeve took a deep breath, remembering the spell she had heard Caith sing a thousand times. This week, the gate was supposed to be open to Emassu, a city on Jinthalin. Maeve cradled her spear loosely in one glass-gauntleted hand and raised the other toward the Waygate.

The sheen of light paused, swirled and pulsed as though in recognition. Maeve smiled. This would be easy.

Better to die than let Gavriel succeed. Maeve slammed her head back as hard as she could, intent on cracking her own skull against the metal post. Could she do it? It had worked for the Lyran Emberguard on the Blue Phoenix... But she was weak, slow. She managed to slam her head once into the support, but dashing one's own brains out was much harder than the Lyran had made it look. Her ears rang and then Xartasia's hand was there, cradling the back of her head. The princess kissed Maeve's salt-sweaty temple and held her fast.

"You will die," Xartasia promised. "But not yet."

Gavriel stood, hands outstretched like one of the Union saints, singing as Maeve's memories haunted her.

"Allunu s'uelim wain'li mae shassa eth am'avain," Maeve sang in a clear voice. *"Kennu varii lae ellu'da eira sessar. Qu'ii laess lai jaisha dii aes'ii soshin kae!"*

No, that didn't sound right. Maeve hesitated.

"Laennan..." she faltered. *"Laennal emanuu shodav ain'no latam. Aetrix sumanni eleo ma'an... ana va'an... Tii'dai! Alluna s'aelim Emassu!"*

That couldn't have been how the spell was supposed to end. It was too short... For a moment, nothing happened. And then the Waygate blazed. The great ring swam with a warning light, strobing red and orange. Maeve stared. Something was horribly wrong.

The whole smooth white pyramid under her feet began to ring like a huge bell. A voice boomed out from the Waygate, resonating with deep authority, but Maeve couldn't understand the language. She clapped her hands over her ears and leapt back from the bellowing Waygate.

The interior of the gate flashed. Through the portal, Maeve saw only blackness. The Waygate rang again. Something shifted in the black void on the other side of the ring of light. Maeve spread her wings. She had to find help!

And then darkness poured through the Tamlin Waygate.

Gavriel's voice finally faded and his cold presence pulled back from her thoughts. Maeve sagged against her bonds, beyond exhausted. Even her heart beat slow and weak, too tired to sustain her body. Xartasia gently released Maeve and let the younger fairy collapse bonelessly, held only by her bound limbs.

"You have claimed the memories?" Xartasia asked in a shaking voice. "Can you now open the Tamlin Waygate as she did?"

"Yes." Gavriel drew a deep breath, and then another. "Yes, the memories are mine. I can feel the weight of the armor, feel Aes' warmth on my face. The horror at what I have done, what I unleashed on my home! I can do it again!"

Kemmer Andus sat on the top step of the Waygate. He finished his lunch in a few large, hurried bites as he reviewed the newest scans by Xen and his team. They should have been the same, identical to those taken just after Ava and Darius finished their work removing eons of debris, but the Waygate seemed to be in a perpetual state of flux: minor variation in the surface temperature, refraction and density.

Kemmer sighed and rubbed his eyes. There was no way the scholarly community was going to believe any of this. The arrogant bastards would simply accuse Kemmer of more shoddy Prian work.

He could always lie, Kemmer realized. The pretty Arcadian girl, Panna, had certainly done it. It would be much easier to rid himself of the low-brow Prian accent than it must have been for Panna to cut off her wings.

But he didn't want to, not really. Kemmer looked up at the Waygate, pulsing with light like a great, glowing heartbeat. Even he could not escape that ridiculous, stiff-necked Prian pride. The Pylos Waygate was a *Prian* treasure, and if the Tynerion scholars couldn't accept that, then they could fly the hells off.

In the camp down below, Xen and the rest of his team read and argued over the same results as Kemmer. Gruth was quite sure that the problem was mechanical and checked over the sensors for the third time that morning. Tall, quiet Enu-Io wasn't so sure. So he and Xen were working on a theory, something involving extra dimensions in the Waygate's construction, subject to forces that did not register on their instruments. Phillip was a geologist and had very little to contribute except to tell Xen that if the Waygate was drawing on a power source, there was no sign of it anywhere in the mountain.

Ava and Darius took no part in the ponderings of the Tynerion team. They sat together under one of the tarpaulins strung between the tents, playing cards. The rest were gone, including the bounty hunter who stubbornly refused to sign one of Kemmer's nondisclosure agreements.

The archeologist couldn't help being irritated. Maeve's abduction was undermining absolutely everything, stealing away personnel and resources that were supposed to be dedicated to the study and protection of the Pylos Waygate. Kemmer was not totally insensitive to the problem, but it didn't change the importance of his discovery. This was so much bigger than one woman.

If Kemmer could present this amazing find to the right people, in the right light, the Waygate could change the world. Prianus would finally become a real force in Alliance politics. It was an elevation in status that Kemmer himself would appreciate from his comfortable new office on Tynerion. Maybe somewhere on Axis. Someplace warm...

An angry shout suddenly interrupted his daydreams. Tiberius Myles – the sole remaining member of their security force – stood sentry at the edge of the camp and held a battered com to his ear. Phillip and Enu-Io rushed to Tiberius.

"Has something happened?" the big Dailon asked.

Tiberius lowered the radio and drew a deep breath.

"That was Duaal," he said. "Gavriel's got the memories from Maeve. He doesn't need her anymore. We're almost out of time."

● ● ●

When Maeve could see again, she found unshed tears in Xartasia's wide violet eyes.

"You have all you need now, old friend," her cousin told Gavriel. "Now it remains only to go to the Tamlin Waygate and see this thing done. A long journey, but only a moment when held beside the effort of years already–"

"Quiet," Gavriel snapped. He was staring at Maeve, his thoughts still intertwined with hers.

"No," Maeve said.

The old Nihilist sang a low word that filled the small apartment. "There's something else in her thoughts."

The Waygate. The Tamlin Waygate, the Pylos Waygate...

No, she couldn't tell...! Maeve tried to push Gavriel's thoughts away, so hard that sweat poured down her skin. But she could no more expel him than she could grasp a dream.

Clasped in ice, deep in a graveyard embrace. Ice and stone, a wound into the very mountain that seethed with violet shadows. A white ziggurat rose from the heart of secrets and the great ring glowed with slumbering power. A Waygate, here on Prianus! Even after these weeks of work, it still seemed so impossible.

No, it is a secret! I swore to keep it...!

Blood sang in Gavriel's ears and his heart beat like a drum in his brittle old ribs as he sang. A song of triumph. A grin spread across his face.

"What is it?" Xartasia asked. Her wings rustled restlessly, whispering without words.

"There's a Waygate on Prianus!" he said, laughing. "Here, in the mountains. That's why she was in Pylos."

Xartasia's violet eyes gleamed with fervor. "The All-Singer himself watches over us."

"We don't have to fly out to the White Kingdom. We can summon the Devourers right here, right into the core!" Gavriel shouted exultantly. He raised his arms as though to embrace the unseen Pylos Waygate. "Prianus will be the first to fall! I will summon the Devourers onto my enemies' very doorstep and deliver them unto death. The Prians are suffering. I will end that today!"

Xartasia looked down at Maeve. "She has given you so much. Will you finally release her?"

"Maeve will die," Gavriel agreed. His hands fell to his sides, fists tightly clenched. "But for her insolence, she will die slowly. Hallax, break her wings and then throw her into the pit. Come, Xartasia. We have plans to make."

"Titania, no! Do not do this," Maeve pleaded. There was blood on her lips. It was sticky and tasted like the sea. "Please, cousin! You cannot truly wish to bring back the Devourers!"

"It must be done," Xartasia said.

She laid one final kiss on Maeve's cheek as Gavriel strode from the room. She followed, gliding behind him like a sad, silent ghost.

When they were gone, Hallax turned back toward Maeve. The Emberguard rested a striped hand on the hilt of his nanosword.

"To think that you held the key to so much death and that you kept it to yourself," Hallax said. "You're a selfish woman."

"I would have killed myself before giving up the memories had I only been allowed!" Maeve answered with weary rage. "Your lord is a coward, Emberguard! He torments a bound and drugged woman. He would not face me!"

Hallax answered with a deep, grating laugh. He walked around behind her and Maeve heard the distinctively hard hiss of a blade sliding free.

"You want to question Lord Gavriel's honor?" the Emberguard asked. "Honor is an illusion, little bird-back. Just like all the rest."

Hallax tugged sharply on Maeve's arms and then began sawing through the ropes that bound her aching wings. When the last one fell free, Maeve sagged. Every nerve in her back screamed in agony as the tortured muscle and bone suddenly had to support their own weight again.

"Release me," Maeve said through clenched teeth. "Soon your master will unleash the Devourers upon us all. I will be dead before long. Let me go from here. Let me die under open sky!"

Maeve thought that sounded reasonable, at least enough to give the brain-diseased Nihilist pause, but Hallax laughed unpleasantly again and did not answer. He unlocked the handcuffs and they clattered to the floor.

"Get up," he instructed.

Every part of her hurt. Maeve's head seemed to float over her shoulders like a bubble and felt just as fragile. But she had to do something... Gavriel knew about the Pylos Waygate and how to use it to summon the Devourers!

Maeve tried to stand. Her legs were weak and wobbled beneath her. Swollen joints and weakened muscles crumpled under her, dumping the Arcadian unceremoniously back down to the dirty floor. Maeve struggled to her hands and knees. The cuffs had worn away most of the skin around her wrists and they were braceleted in wet blood, as black as ink in the dim lamplight. Hallax prodded at her with one foot.

"Get up, little bird-back," he ordered. "I don't want to carry you. Maybe you'll have a last chance to face death with dignity. Walk."

"You know nothing of Arcadians," Maeve rasped as she climbed slowly, agonizingly upright. "There is no dignity in walking. Let me fly."

"There's nowhere to fly. We're going down."

Her bruised ankle held. Maeve leaned against the steel girder that had been her prison for the last two days. What now? She was weak, far too weak to fight the lanky Mirran Emberguard.

Did Hallax have a gun, some kind of weapon Maeve could steal before he noticed? Only the nanosword, still gleaming in his hand. Maeve could barely control her mistreated body enough to remain upright. There was no way she could wrest the blade away from Hallax. Not like this.

He grabbed Maeve by one wing and roughly propelled her out the door. She stumbled into a slanted, twisting hallway. Pale light filtered in through cracks in the concrete walls and Maeve squinted through watering eyes. Hallax pushed her along the hall.

The corridor was narrow and the uneven floor had buckled in places. Some long-gone designer had tried to disguise the ugly gray walls and painted them over in more cheerful blues and greens, but the concrete glistened with moisture and the paint hung in peeling tatters like diseased skin.

Word must have spread through the Cult of Nihil. A hundred people robed in black stared from splintered doorways and gaps in the broken walls. Some remained silent as Hallax pushed Maeve past, but many of them whispered and pointed. A few even cheered hoarsely, thanking Maeve for what she had unwillingly given. She couldn't meet their eyes. The Nihilists kept a respectful distance – if not from Maeve, then from the Emberguard who escorted her.

Hallax guided Maeve's agonizing progress down to a collapsing stairwell. The going was rough and steep. By the time she had staggered down two flights of warped steps, he had to carry Maeve.

He dragged her by one wrist and a wing into the jagged ruins of a parking lot. Cracked and snapped supports jutted up from the asphalt like great broken teeth. Maeve tried to catch her breath and gagged. The air was thick with a terrible, rancid smell: old blood and rotting flesh and worse.

The pit.

A deep crack tore into the building's foundation like the mouth of some huge monster. Weak, pitiful moans echoed up from the depth, carried by the fetid wind.

Hallax dragged Maeve toward the pit. A choking animal panic rose in her throat. She didn't want to die here, buried far away from the sky and wind. Maeve screamed and dug her heels into the crumbling asphalt.

"No!" she cried.

Hallax was losing patience. He shoved the fairy to her knees and grabbed one wing in preparation to break it, as Gavriel had instructed. After everything, Maeve was about to be thrown down into a hole like a piece of trash. She had served her purpose. No, Gavriel's purpose. Even now, he made ready to unleash the Devourers on a population hundreds of times larger than that of the White Kingdom.

Maeve had fought so long and so hard to die. She spent a year coaxing Logan Coldhand closer and closer. But she had lived. If Maeve's hunter couldn't kill her, how could she let the Nihilists do it now?

She wouldn't make it so easy.

Hallax's foot came down to snap her wing like a dry leaf. With an effort that brought tears to her eyes, Maeve heaved her tortured body forward. Not into a fall, but a controlled roll. It *had* to work on the first try. She wouldn't have another chance.

Pulled off balance by the sudden absence of a fairy under him, Hallax pitched backward. Maeve jumped up to feet that felt like torn sacks of shattered glass. For a heart-stuttering moment, Maeve couldn't remember the spell. Her mind was muddy with pain and chems. Hallax recovered his balance and drew his sword from its well-worn sheath.

"Alon'ii va imanno ishae'na laeling! Vasha imannui eru chen rowshae dae!" Maeve sang.

Her raw voice wasn't beautiful, but it was enough to get the job done. Hallax jerked to a stop as the sudden flare in his optic nerve blinded him. It wouldn't last long and the rangy Mirran was already snapping his sword out, searching for her.

Maeve spun. What could she do now? There was no way she could overpower Hallax. Not like this, not without her spear…

There was only one place to hide down here. Maeve spread her shaking wings. The feathers were matted with blood and grit, but enough of them remained. Cold, stiff muscles protested painfully as Maeve managed to push herself into the air. One wingtip scraped along the ceiling, and then she dove into the pit. If she was going down there, she would do it under her own power, for her own purposes.

Dark gray stone and dirt raced by, all streaked in wetness that didn't bear close inspection. The crevice was wide but irregular. Maeve curled her wings close to her body and tumbled into the darkness. The light was vanishing quickly above. A little further…

Just before the pit narrowed too much, Maeve spread her wings and frigid air pushed against her feathers. They trembled and sweat streamed across her shoulders with the strain, but Maeve slowed and grabbed onto a pipe jutting from the pit's wall. There was something slick under her fingers and Maeve slipped.

She was too tired, too frightened to scream as she fell down into the stinking blackness… And then her left foot came down jarringly hard on a crag of concrete. Maeve pressed her body against the wall of the pit and held her breath, waiting.

The crack was a barely visible line above, just a ragged streak of shadow only slightly brighter than the deep darkness all around Maeve. For a moment, she couldn't help thinking about Kemmer's ravine, and cursed herself. It was just such thoughts of the Pylos Waygate that had made so much trouble…!

Here, now. Maeve made herself focus. Had her deception been enough? Hallax could surely see again. Did he realize where she had gone? Would he think to look for her in the pit?

Maeve waited. Her left leg held most of her weight and began to cramp, but Maeve didn't dare move. No light appeared at the mouth of the pit. Neither did the Emberguard's shadow.

Maeve listened, but could hear nothing more than creaking stone and steel. She was unexpectedly glad that she had not eaten in two days, or she would have been sick. She could *taste* the stench of sickness and decay in the pit. Maeve closed her eyes and made herself count heartbeats, one hundred of them until she could risk the climb out of her hiding spot.

Maeve lost count and started again five times. She only made it to forty-seven of the last count, but she *had* to move. Clinging to the side of the pit, her fingers were trembling and threatened to fail. If she let go now, there wasn't enough room to spread her wings and she would fall.

But Maeve had to reach Gavriel and stop him somehow, before he could summon the Devourers. Sweating, swearing and weeping with the effort, she began to climb.

It would all be over soon. Gavriel barely felt the ground beneath his feet. He walked on high, a savior who could finally deliver sweet, swift death to the worlds.

My Jaissa, my Sarru... The suffering will be over soon, my beloved girls. We will all join you in oblivion.

The Nihilists had heard Maeve's cries and their master's song. They lined the broken halls, clustered in bowed doorways, all shivering in their black robes. The close, cold air stank of disease and blood and waste – the cloying scents of life.

These last months on Prianus had liberated so many... Only one hundred or so remained, those few strong enough to survive the cold. Another hundred Arcadian Nihilists were still in Pylos and awaited only Gavriel's command to return home.

Two hundred of over six thousand who had sworn themselves to the Church of Nihil on Stray. Thousands lost to him because of Maeve Cavainna and Logan Coldhand... Gavriel hadn't forgotten.

Maeve deserved her fate and he gave Xartasia a sidelong glance. The lovely princess' gaze remained downcast, her black eyelashes brushing her cheeks and sparkling with diamond tears.

"Your cousin invited her own end," he reminded Xartasia firmly. "It could have been far worse, in fact."

The Arcadian brought her lilac eyes up to meet Gavriel's. They burned with such obvious rage that several of the Nihilists actually drew back. In her flowing white gown and ivory wings, she was a bright angel reigning over the dirty Nihilists.

"Maeve is a child of the House of Cavain," Xartasia said. "I have aided you against her only for the sake of relieving my *own* people's suffering!"

Gavriel towered over the tiny Xartasia. The Nihilists leaned in again, holding their breath. The icy air was dangerously still. They watched in captivated silence.

"Cavain's was a mighty house, princess," Gavriel told her. "But perhaps you forget who is master of *this* house."

"Have you forgotten why you are master of anything more than a prison cell, human?" Xartasia asked. "I taught you the very magics by which you command these creatures' respect!"

"They follow me because I speak the truth, Xartasia. Because I will free them! My magic is a means, not an end." Gavriel raised one age-spotted hand. The Nihilists shouted, screamed and howled. "For me and for us all!"

"Save us!" wailed a scarred woman.

"Free us!"

"Destroy us!"

Xartasia's alabaster cheeks went bright red. "Without my songs, none of this would be! I have walked beside you on this journey and given you gifts unknown to any human."

"For which you have my gratitude," Gavriel said. "But not my servility."

The princess held his gaze for a long moment and then reluctantly dropped her eyes. "Yes, Lord Gavriel."

He smiled and placed a knobby hand on Xartasia's shoulder.

"Do not lose heart. We are so close to the ultimate end," Gavriel said. He raised his voice. "There is a Waygate here, in the Kayton Mountains! We go at once to call forth the Devourers, to scour life from the galaxy!"

The Nihilists cheered and screamed out their master's praise so loudly that for a long moment, Gavriel did not realize that one of them was pushing his way through the crowded hall. It was Hallax, tall and defiant of his prey heritage as he shouldered past the lesser Nihilists.

Gavriel frowned. The striped Emberguard was furious. Gavriel beckoned him forward and the tall Mirran dropped to one knee.

"Lord Gavriel," Hallax said. His voice and his long body rippled with barely restrained rage and violence. "My Lord Gavriel, I have lost Maeve."

"Lost?" Gavriel asked.

"She blinded me with a spell, my lord, and then she was gone."

"Maeve will seek more than just escape," Xartasia said, shaking her head. "She surely comes in search of you."

"Then she's still here," Gavriel said. "But we won't be. Not for much longer."

"We should go at once," Xartasia agreed. "If Maeve contacts her captain, the Prian police will be upon us before we can reach the Waygate."

Gavriel nodded and then turned back to Hallax, who bowed his head. The dark green tangles of his hair lay sweaty against the back of his striped neck.

"Find Maeve," Gavriel commanded. "As much as she deserves it, we can no longer afford to give her a lingering death. Kill the fairy at once."

"Yes, Lord Gavriel."

"When it is done, my friend," he told the Emberguard, "you are free. You may kill yourself. You have waited a long time."

Hallax kissed Gavriel's withered hand and then drew his greasy-looking nanosword.

"Thank you, my lord," he said. "It will be done! For your glory and the death of all."

[31]

HEART AND HAND

"Anyone in search of revenge tears their own wounds bloody in the hunt."

- DUCHIAN LEMANNE, LI MARRAINE AUTHOR (34 PA)

"Stop!" Gripper shouted. "Stop here!"

Logan slammed on the brakes. It was raining down in the valley and the truck skidded across the wet road. A dented hauler honked and thundered past in the opposite direction as Logan bumped his borrowed vehicle up over a slushy snowbank. There was no appreciable shoulder along the road, so Logan parked on the steep downhill slope.

The second truck slid to a stop right behind him, but the rain poured down so heavily that Logan could barely make out Duaal turning in the passenger seat to confer with Xia and Panna.

On the road, the swift-moving traffic didn't slow. Logan squinted at the far side. Built close against the steep, stony sides of the valley was a cluster of stark, ugly storage slabs. They were tall, unadorned rectangles of concrete with only a few sealed windows staring out over Pylos like the eyes of dead giants. Several of the buildings had cracked badly across the base and barely hung to the mountainside, leaning threateningly over the narrow road below.

"It's got to be one of these," Gripper said. He pressed his ogreish face to the window. "Look!"

He was pointing to one of the cracked foundations. A twisted, broken piece of metal jutted out from the cracked and stained concrete. The snapped-off support was covered in rust that looked a lot like congealed blood. Logan's heart skipped a beat. Was this it? Was Maeve in there?

Gripper's com beeped. The Arboran jumped and fumbled it out of his pocket.

"It's Duaal," the mage said in an unhappy voice. "We're running out of time. Maeve gave Gavriel everything. She didn't want to, but it's done."

"Do you know which building she's in?" Logan asked.

"It's hard as hells to see out there."

"Do you know?"

"I think so," Duaal said. "Everything inside is slanted... or leaning, like it's on a hill."

The concrete slab at the end of the row leaned so far out from the mountain that a single quake might very well shake it free and send the whole tower crashing down into Pylos. The small square windows were broken and dark.

"That's the one," Logan said. He checked his Talon-9 again and grabbed the door's handle.

"What are you doing?" Gripper asked, eyes wide.

"I'm going to get Maeve."

In the other truck, Duaal and Xia started.

Panna grabbed the com. "Wait, you can't go in there all alone! We're supposed to call Captain Cerro!"

"How long will it take him to get here?" Logan asked. He opened the door. Wind howled and rain splattered across the dashboard. "How long do you think Maeve's got?"

"But..." Gripper whimpered.

"Call Cerro," Logan said. "We'll still need the police to deal with the Nihilists. Tell them to come in cold."

Logan closed the truck door before anyone could argue further. Maybe Panna was right, but he could wait no longer. Not now. Not this close to finding Maeve.

The rain was cold and heavy. It matted the hunter's hair against his face and streamed down the back of his neck. Logan shivered. He hurried across the crumbling road, between honking cars and swerving streetcycles. On the other side, Logan darted up the short rampway to the loading doors, but they were all welded tightly shut and covered under layers of mud and paint.

Logan circled around and – after a few minutes of searching – found a still-functional door obscured by an overturned trash bin. The frozen mud was full of footprints and scraped tracks where the bin had been pushed into position. The bounty hunter shouldered it aside and slipped into the darkness beyond.

Maeve's arms and back ached from the climb, but when she finally heaved herself up over the edge of the pit and into the garage, she was alone. Now what?

She sucked down a few rancid, burning breaths, then climbed to her feet and staggered back to the stairs. Maeve heard footsteps and froze, listening. They were too heavy and too fast to belong to Gavriel – it had to be another Nihilist. Hallax? Maeve didn't want to risk an encounter until she could find Gavriel. She couldn't let him escape with his stolen memories.

When the footsteps retreated, leaving the narrow stairwell and heading off down some other hallway, Maeve spurred herself on. She climbed back up the stairs as quietly as she could on her numb, frozen toes.

Hallax had taken her down at least five stories from the apartment that had been her prison. There were many floors above that, Maeve suspected. There had to be more than three hundred of the rotting little apartments in this building. Where in all of that was Gavriel?

Maeve crept up the stairs. On the next floor, she stopped beside an open door. The hallway was full of trash, but empty of Nihilists. Maeve listened. Rain drummed against windows and wind howled across the crumbling edifice. A brilliant flash of lightning suddenly flooded the hall, making colorful sparkles dance before Maeve's eyes. The crack of thunder shook the entire building. But she could hear no voices or any other sounds of life. Leaning on the railing, Maeve climbed up to the next level, only to find it just as empty as the one below.

She made her way along the hall and peered into dark, empty doorways. There were signs of habitation: blankets heaped in the corners or across sagging beds, a few empty cans or foil food packages, candles and lanterns – mostly extinguished but only recently. They were still hot. There were at least five floors more to search, but Maeve didn't think she would find anyone.

The Nihilists were gone.

Logan kicked down another door. The rotten wood splintered and flew apart, scattering across another dark, empty room. Where was the Cult of Nihil? Was this the wrong building? But the narrow halls and cramped apartments reeked of illness and infection that reminded Logan instantly of the Gharib catacombs. But where were the Nihilists?

Where was Maeve?

Logan shined a flashlight around the room, found nothing else of interest and then turned back out into the hall. The next door was in better condition than most of the others, probably replaced within the last few months. Logan turned the handle and shoved it open. The thick oak plank creaked on damp hinges.

The draft that blew out at Logan was full of a familiar scent, one that didn't belong to the sickly, dying Nihilists. This was the smell of blood and feathers, sweat and Vanora White. Maeve... Or some other drugged and struggling Arcadian, Logan supposed. His throat was tight as he stepped through the door and moved his flashlight across the rubble-strewn floor.

No, this *had* to be the place. The room was exactly as Duaal had described it: a small apartment with an aged steel beam running right through the center. The only piece of furniture was an ancient armchair, upholstered in faded scarlet. The floor was covered with dried blood and feathers, all mixed in with stone and mud from the broken wall.

There was something coiled in the muck, tangled around something shiny. A needle – just like the one Logan had found in the snow on the mountain – and a bloodstained tangle of rope. A pair of handcuffs lay in the rubble nearby. Just as Duaal had told them... Maeve had been here.

Then where was she now? Logan lifted the needle in his cybernetic hand. Gripper said that Maeve was off the stuff. But Gavriel gave her chems, forced them on her... It was like a rape and the thought seared through Logan, far more painful than any of Vorus' blows. He crushed the needle and threw it to the ground.

"You're not one of the flock," said a voice from behind him.

Logan went cold. He *knew* that voice. The Emberguard stood in the doorway, a glistening nanosword in his hand. The Mirran that Duaal had called Hallax was thinner than Logan remembered, and his green hair had grown longer – but his mad eyes were the same as the night the Emberguard had run Logan Centra right through the heart and killed his partner.

"You're the one from Gharib," Hallax said.

"We met long before that," Logan answered. "Where is Maeve?"

"I don't know yet, but I will find and kill her, as Lord Gavriel has decreed." Hallax raised his nanosword – was it the same one he had used years ago to kill Logan? – and squinted at the bounty hunter, studying him. "Long before?"

Logan didn't answer. He moved the flashlight to his left hand, gripping it tight enough to dimple the metal casing. Hallax watched him closely and nodded minutely. Whipcord muscles rippled beneath his striped olive skin.

"Ah, yes... I remember you now, Prian," Hallax said slowly. The sword moved in a lazy arc, like a hunting cat's tail swishing this way and that. "You wore a lawman's uniform then. I gifted your partner with death and put my sword through your heart. I left you to die and now you want to do the same to me. You want revenge."

"I just want to find Maeve," Logan said. It was the truth.

"Maeve Cavainna belongs to Lord Gavriel and deep in her own grave." The Emberguard stepped back, settling his long body into an easy fighting stance. The nanosword's point rose toward Logan. "But first, I should finish my apparently shoddy work on you."

Hallax lunged in with an expert fencer's thrust. Logan was still too close to the thick steel post and slammed his shoulder into the pitted metal as he turned aside. The nanosword sliced a neat silver line into the metal.

Logan's feet slid through the blood and loose dirt, searching for purchase. He planted one boot against the rusted steel girder and grabbed for his Talon-9, but Hallax jumped at Logan and tackled the smaller man to the filthy floor. They tumbled, each trying to bring his weapon to bear.

Hallax sliced shallow wounds into Logan's arm as he pushed the nanosword up, seeking out the hunter's throat. Logan tried to wrest his Talon free of the hip holster again, but he was on top of it. The flashlight was smaller, shorter, and easier to swing in close confines. Logan cracked it across Hallax's cheek.

As the taller man reeled, Logan dropped the flashlight, rolled onto his back and finally drew his gun. His first shot was wild, but at such close range, couldn't help but hit. The laser whined and Hallax snarled in pain as smoke rose from his burned hip.

Logan adjusted his aim, but the Emberguard snapped a kick into his wrist that sent the second shot high, slicing upward. The unstable ceiling groaned and buckled. Aging concrete rained down on them, forcing Logan to roll to one side, away from his enemy. Hallax leapt up and bolted for the door. The hem of his tattered red cloak whipped around the frame just ahead of Logan's aim.

The bounty hunter kept his Talon-9 aimed at the doorway as he climbed carefully back to his feet. If he charged blindly back out into the hall, Hallax would be on him in a second. He needed to see where he was going. Logan targeted the side of the door where the Mirran had fled and held down the trigger. The sustained beam did its work as well here as it had under the cathedral in Gharib. The laser seared through the wall, tumbling the cracked concrete down into a pile of gray rubble and exposing the hallway.

Hallax hadn't gone far. If he ran, Logan could easily have shot him in the back, but the Mirran knew it, too. Instead, the Emberguard charged right at the Prian, closing the distance between them with the same graceful, loping strides that Logan remembered from six years ago and wearing the same mad grin.

Hallax's nanoblade flashed in a deadly, decapitating arc. Logan slammed the blade to one side with the Talon's long barrel. Straining, he leaned against the gun and hoped that the lenses inside hadn't cracked. Police equipment was tough, and that wasn't just Prian pride. The Talons had to be rugged weapons to survive generations of demanding use. But was that tough enough?

The sword slid off Logan's gun and the Emberguard spun away. The cloudy windows leaked rain into the hall and muddy water sprayed out from under his boots. He stepped through, sweeping past and whirling behind Logan.

The hunter turned to face Hallax again, but slipped on the wet floor. Hallax's lips peeled back from his teeth in a maniac grin and he leapt at the Prian with his nanosword extended, point leveled right at Logan's heart.

Not this time. Logan stepped into the thrust and grabbed the nanosword in his cybernetic hand, the hand Hallax had given him. The blade slid in his grip, throwing sparks as steel ground against illonium. Logan yanked the blade aside and brought up his laser.

Hallax's grin faltered and then fell as Logan pulled the trigger. The lenses weren't cracked. Red light flared and seared a smoking hole straight through the Emberguard's chest.

◆　◆　◆

The Nihilists were all gone. Maeve had to tell someone what had happened. She needed to find a radio, a com... something to call Tiberius and the Pylos police. They had to know about Gavriel...!

The apartment windows were nailed or sealed shut, those that had ever opened at all. A few laminated glass panes were broken, but none large enough for even the small fairy to squeeze through. Maeve didn't have time to search every single room.

She would have to go back downstairs or all the way up to the roof. Maeve flexed her wings experimentally. They ached terribly. She could fly, but for how long in the driving rain outside? Not long and not far, but surely far enough to find some help...

Her skin was alternately sweaty-hot and clammy-cold. Maeve ran unsteadily back to the stairs and began climbing again, making for the roof. She stared up into the shadows. How much further did she have to go? If only there was room to fly...

A loud clang resonated from far above, followed by the sharp whine of laserfire. Someone was fighting up there. Who could still be here in the abandoned building? Maybe the police had already found this place. Or maybe it was Tiberius and Gripper, her friends miraculously come to rescue her.

Maeve sprinted up the stairs as fast as her wounded legs could carry her. She jumped over the last steps, stumbled and caught herself against a crooked wall. She was running *toward* a battle, Maeve realized. It was too dark to see very much, but she searched the floor until she felt something hard and sharp – a shard of broken glass a little longer than her hand. She hastily tore a rag of cloth free from her already shredded pants and wrapped it around the glass. It was hardly an Arcadian dagger, but it would serve.

There was another ringing impact and more laserfire. Maeve pulled open the door and stepped out into the shadowed hall. She couldn't see anyone... They had to be in one of the rooms or down another hallway. Maeve crept along the corridor as silently as she could, searching the shadows with every step. There was a loud metallic sound, a final shriek of laser, and then a fatal, heavy thud.

Maeve broke into a run.

Logan stood over Hallax. The Emberguard was finally dead, the man who had taken his hand and his heart. His life. But there was no satisfaction in that. Revenge had won him nothing. It couldn't return what Logan had lost.

Vorus was right. He had done this to himself. Logan ruined his own life.

But there wasn't time to ponder his failure. Footsteps echoed from around the corner, light but irregular. Another Nihilist? Logan pressed himself back into an empty doorway, Talon-9 held ready.

Lightning flashed through the shattered windows, the cracked walls and turned the puddles across the floor into mirrored quicksilver. A small, winged shadow crept out into the hallway, holding a glass dagger low.

Logan leapt from the shadows and grabbed the Arcadian. He jammed his gun against her stomach, but she squirmed like a snake in his grasp. The tip of her blade sliced through his shirt and drew a line of blood. It was hot and slick on his skin. Outside, rain poured from the gray sky.

"Where–?" Logan began.

The lightning blazed again and the fairy in his arms had black hair and eyes the same color as the stormy sky. Those eyes widened as she stared up at the bounty hunter. *Her* hunter...

Maeve.

She dropped the curving shard of glass to the floor and it shattered against the concrete. Maeve stood up on her toes, feathered wings held out as though she intended to take flight, and twined her fingers through the human's soaking wet blond hair. Maeve pressed her lips to Logan's and kissed him.

[32]
CALLING

"Even the shortest life lived in the pursuit of duty has not been
lived in vain."

- MARUS HERADONE, PRIAN POLICE OFFICER (193 PA)

A peal of thunder rocked the truck and Panna shifted uncomfortably
in her seat. She should have gone in there with Coldhand. But she
was frightened of whatever was inside. Panna had read every account
of Maeve's encounter with the cult on Stray. There weren't very many
stories, just enough to convince Panna that Gavriel and his followers
were dangerous. But that knowledge was thin armor against her guilt.

Something outside brought Panna's attention up from her unpleasant reflection. The truck was parked on the muddy slope beside the road, with a view over the Pylos valley. A flock of white-
winged shapes flew out from the dingy Arcadian quarter. There had
to be a hundred fairies. They rose up together, wheeled toward the
mountains and then vanished into the swirling gray clouds.

"What's that?" Panna asked.

Xia looked out the side window. "What's what?"

"The Arcadians," Panna said. "There's a crowd of them flying up into the hills."

"Maybe their quarter is flooding in this rain," Xia suggested.

"That doesn't matter right now." Duaal shook his com in frustration. "Damn it, get me off hold! I need to talk to Cerro!"

"There's a call coming in for you, captain," Felsus shouted. The young officer limped over on his cybernetic foot and leaned into the door of his superior's office. "Duaal Sinnay. He says he works for Tiberius Myles."

Cerro picked up a com handset.

"I'm here," he said. "What's on the wind, Duaal?"

He heard the slap of rain against glass wherever Duaal was, and then a peal of thunder. A second later, the sound boomed through the police station, making everything on Cerro's desk rattle and the channel hiss with static.

"Say again, Duaal," Cerro said into the com. "I can't hear you."

"We found the Cult of Nihil!"

Cerro's grip tightened on the handset. "Are you sure?"

"Yes. We're outside a converted storage slab. 2808 Tristail Road. Do you know it?"

It was on the map taped to the back wall of Cerro's office, outside the third district and on the northern corner of the second.

"I see it. Does anyone inside know you're there?" Cerro asked.

Duaal hesitated on the other end of the line. Cerro grabbed his coat from the back of his chair and swept out of his office, whistling to Felsus.

"Collect everyone off the roster and get them down to the cars," Cerro ordered. Thunder made the station shudder again. "I want Talons and hawks, but keep them clipped for now. We don't have confirmation yet and we're not shooting a bunch of civilians. Duaal, are you still there?"

"I'm here," the boy said. "The Nihilists might know we're here. Coldhand went in after Maeve."

"Who? Can you recall your hawk?"

"I don't think so," Duaal said. "He's inside. Even if I can get him to pick up, I don't... I don't think he's listening."

Cerro grimaced and it tugged painfully at his scarred cheek. It was pointless to waste time wishing for things he couldn't have. No one could change what had already happened. Seven other cops gathered around Felsus as he hastily updated them on the Nihilist situation.

"I'll put in the call to Station Two," Cerro told Duaal. "Where is Captain Myles now?"

"He's still up at the dig site. Kemmer made him stay."

"That's the job he agreed to do," Cerro said. "Hold tight, Duaal. We'll be there in ten."

"Logan said to come in... cold?"

"He did?" Cerro asked.

"He used to be a cop, too. What does it mean?"

"It means a quick and quiet landing. Sensitive situation," Cerro said. "Alright, we will."

Felsus held up a clipboard and limped over to his boss. "We've got thirty officers on call tonight. How many should I bring in?"

"All of them," Cerro answered grimly. "If half of what Tiberius says about these people is true, we're going to need them. And get on the wire with Station Two."

"Yes, sir!"

Maeve had no idea how long she stood there with her arms around Logan Coldhand and her lips against his.

This couldn't possibly be real. There was no way that Logan was here on Prianus. Here where Gavriel had her tortured. Logan tasted like rainwater and he stood as still as a statue in her arms... but not stopping her, not pushing her away. Returning her kiss.

My hunter. My hunter is here!

He *was* real. There was a man lying on the floor nearby, in the thin beam of a flashlight. It was Hallax, with a smoking hole burned through his chest. The wall of her one-time cell was gone and the hallway was scored all along its length by laser burns and nanosword slices. Hallax's iridescent blade lay in a muddy puddle.

"What are you doing here?" Maeve asked at last.

Logan didn't immediately answer her. By necessity, the question had ended their kiss, but Maeve hadn't removed her arms. Logan stared down at her with unreadable ice-blue eyes.

"I had to find you," he told her. "You're hurt. We have to go. Xia is outside. She can take care of you."

Maeve blinked. "You came with... with Xia?"

"I had to find you," Logan said again. It seemed very important to him. "I was looking for the Nihilists in Pylos and I found them in the mountains. But you were gone."

The mountains... The Waygate!

"We must find Gavriel!" Maeve said.

"Hallax was the only one here. The whole building is empty," said the hunter. He shook his head and then stepped back, detangling himself from Maeve. "Duaal's calling the police, but there's no one here."

"Gavriel is going to the Waygate!" Maeve told him. "He knows of the Devourers and of the Pylos Waygate."

Logan scooped up his fallen flashlight. "That makes sense. Why fly all the way to Arcadia when they've got a Waygate right here? How long ago did they leave?"

"I... I do not know," Maeve admitted. "I was in the pit. I did not realize that they had left at all until I climbed out."

Rage rippled across the bounty hunter's face and his eyes raked over her, taking in her injuries, her torn and bloody clothes. Logan shoved the Talon back into its holster and grabbed a battered com from his pocket. He checked the display and shook his head.

"No access," he said. "We have to get outside."

They ran back down the stairs together, Maeve leaning heavily on Logan. When they finally emerged from the slab, she slitted her eyes nearly shut. Even the diffused light sifting through the roiling storm clouds was blinding after so long in the dark.

When Maeve could see again, she found a pair of battered old trucks parked on the far side of the busy mountain street. A wide-eyed Gripper scrambled out of one car and dashed across the road. Before she could say a word, he was there, enfolding Maeve in a huge, wet hug. Gripper picked her up and spun the wounded fairy in an overjoyed circle.

"Maeve! You're alive!" he cried. "We were so worried about you!"

She was shocked to hear her given name from Gripper's mouth, but far more pleased to see her friend. Maeve hugged him as tightly as she could while rain poured down on them, soaking her ruined clothes and slicking her hair against the back of her neck.

"It is good to see you again," Maeve gasped. "I did not think that I would ever leave that place…"

Duaal, Xia and Panna emerged from the second truck, quickly crossed the street and the Ixthian shooed Gripper back.

"Maeve's injured. Let me have a look," she said. "How long ago was your last dose of White? Do you know how much it was?"

"A few hours, I think. I do not know the precise dose. Where is Tiberius?" Maeve asked. "But there is no time!"

Duaal looked up at Logan, who remained at Maeve's side as Xia began a cursory examination of her wounds.

"What happened in there?" Duaal asked. "What's going on?"

"There's no one inside," Logan said. "The Cult of Nihil is gone. They're on their way to the Waygate."

A big green van with patched tires pulled over and stopped next to the leaning storage slab. Another parked down the road. Maeve saw several others making their way quickly out of the valley, swerving around other slower vehicles. Police officers poured out of each one, forming up surprisingly quietly in the shadow of another leaning apartment slab.

When they saw Duaal and the others gathered on the rampway, they moved as one to close the distance. Maeve recognized Captain Cerro in the lead. He wore a pauldron and there was a dark brown falcon with its talons sunk deep into the leather. Cerro crouched down. His often-mended blue uniform was dark with rain.

"Princess Cavainna," he said, dipping his head at Maeve. "Glad to see you're alive. What's going on here?"

"There's no one left inside," Logan reported almost automatically. "There was one Emberguard left behind, but everyone else has moved out."

Cerro looked at the bounty hunter, frowning.

"I know your face," he said contemplatively. "Who are you?"

"He's a... a friend," Gripper told Cerro quickly.

The police captain's scarred jaw worked for a moment, but then he nodded. He gestured to another officer. "Take a team and sweep inside. Eyes only. We'll collect evidence later."

The other Prian nodded and hurried off, calling out her own orders. Cerro returned his attention to Maeve and her friends. He thrust his jaw out at the apartment slab overhead.

"You said the Nihilists are gone. Are you sure?" he asked.

"Yes. And we need to reach the Waygate before they do," Maeve said. She winced as Xia squeezed gently up the length of her right wing. "We must fly now!"

"What?" Cerro asked, shaking his head. "What Waygate?"

Duaal's dark face went the color of wet ash. "But... but Tiberius is up there!"

"You mean Doc Kemmer's dig," Cerro said.

The officer he had sent in to check the building came back out, holding up a closed fist to her captain, waved it once and raised one finger. Cerro nodded.

"No one alive inside. One dead," he reported.

Maeve glanced sidelong at Logan. He met her eyes for only a second, then dropped his gaze as though ashamed. Or something else... But there was no time to wonder. Cerro was shouting to his teams, getting them loaded back up into their van.

"We're gone in three!" he called out. "North Tristail to Verigorn and up into the mountains. Follow the lead and keep up! I want weapons and birds ready to fly. Move!"

"What about us?" Duaal asked. "I've got to call Tiberius!"

"Do that," Cerro said, nodding. "Then go back to the station and wait there."

"What?" Duaal cried. "Not a chance! We're going with you."

"You're civilians. You stay in Pylos."

Maeve pushed Xia out of her way and then straightened with a groan. "Duaal is right, Captain Cerro. We would not leave Tiberius to fight on his own."

"You're in no shape to fight at all," Xia pointed out.

"I will survive or I will not," Maeve said. "If Gavriel reaches the Waygate, none of us have long to live!"

"No," Cerro repeated firmly.

Logan looked at Maeve again, then to the police captain.

"There is unanswered blood between us and the Cult of Nihil," the bounty hunter said. "Honor calls us to face them."

His words had a measured, oddly ritual sound. Cerro ran the tip of one finger down the deep scar across his cheek as he considered. Finally, he sighed.

"If you're coming, you come with us," he said. "But you follow orders!"

Xia looked at Maeve. "I'll give you some blockers on the way. They'll help some."

"Thank you, Xia," she answered sincerely.

Logan hesitantly offered Maeve his right hand and helped her limp toward the truck. Duaal shook as he called Tiberius while Xia and Gripper turned back to their vehicles. Cerro whistled sharply to them.

"You're going with us," he reminded them. "We're going to need to move fast to have any hope of catching up with these Nihilists. Felsus, make some room. Alert all officers of our new destination and tell them that we're going in hot."

"Wait!"

Maeve looked over to Panna, who had called out. The blonde woman ran back through the rain and reached into the back of one of the trucks. When she returned, she carried a spear with a long glass blade.

Maeve stared. "My... my spear!"

"If you're flying after the Cult of Nihil," Panna said, holding out the weapon, "I thought you may want this... Your Highness."

Maeve took the spear and inspected the new shaft. It was expert – if unfinished – work. The blade was lashed in place with strands of red thread. Maeve stared.

"Why would you do this?" she asked.

"I..." Panna couldn't seem to find the words.

"She's Arcadian," Logan said.

The world spun wildly around Maeve. She opened and closed her mouth silently, unable to find the words. Yes, she could see it now, in Panna's cheekbones and slight frame. An Arcadian. A wingless Arcadian! Finally, Maeve took one of Panna's cold, wet hands and touched it lightly against her chest.

"Thank you for the repair and return of my spear," she said at last. "We must fly to work, but if we survive the day, I would like to know how all of this came to be."

"Yes, Highness," Panna answered.

[33]

FLY

"God wears the face of your enemy. Whatever the outcome, you will know death. Pay your respects."

- HEON CERRO, PRIAN POLICE OFFICER (224 PA)

Tiberius was on the radio again. He finished the call and turned the com over in his hands. A simple, everyday little item that seemed to age Tiberius a full decade as he tucked it back into his pocket. The older Prian caught Kemmer's eye.

"What is it?" Kemmer asked suspiciously.

Tiberius paused, gathering his thoughts. He leaned against a cracked piece of stone where Orphia perched and scratched the old hawk above her eyes. After a long moment, Tiberius straightened and cupped his hands around his mouth.

"Archeologists!" he bellowed.

Kemmer sighed. "Archeologists? Really? What's going on?"

Tiberius remained stubbornly silent until Xen collected his whole team and Ava brought Darius over. They gathered in a tight knot beneath one of the rocky overhangs. Rainwater dripped from above, collected in the ravine and was piped up to the surface to spill away down the mountainside. Just hours ago, Gruth had complained loudly that he could really, really use Gripper's help. Under pressure, Kemmer supposed that it was easy to forget the other mechanic was an alien.

When you need help, Kemmer thought, *you can't be too picky about where you get it.*

Kemmer looked down at Xen, standing at the head of his small team. The Waygate loomed over them all, streaming rainwater and pulsing with cold light.

"That was Duaal," Tiberius said. "The Cult of Nihil is on their way here."

"What? The same hawks who took your friend? Why?" Kemmer pointed accusingly at Tiberius. "And you wanted to leave us alone!"

"Then it's a good thing I stayed here," Tiberius said. He seemed unruffled by Kemmer's irritation. Was it because he was truly that implacable? Or because he had other, much more terrible things to worry about? "Gavriel's coming for the Waygate. He's going to use it to summon the Devourers."

"The Waygate?" Kemmer asked. He looked up at it. "*My* Waygate? Over my dead God-damned body!"

"Wait, we don't even know if the Waygate still functions," Xen objected.

"What are Devourers?" Gruth asked.

"You're supposed to be an archeologist," Tiberius said.

"I'm an engineer!"

"The Devourers are nasty bastards who wiped out the White Kingdom a century ago," Tiberius told them. "Now Gavriel wants to bring them to the core to kill everyone."

Darius and Ava both looked grim, their rough Prian faces set in heavy, serious lines. Ava took Phillip's hand and held it tightly. The others just seemed frightened.

"You can't be serious!" Phillip said. His voice shook so much that Kemmer could barely understand the words.

"I am," Tiberius answered. "Gavriel and his people will kill you before they summon the Devourers. They think they're doing you a favor. We need to get you out of here."

Gruth skinned his lips back from long teeth and growled low in his throat. Xen put a restraining hand on the Lyran's furry shoulder and shook his head.

"How much time do we have before they get here?" the Ixthian asked.

"What? No! We can't abandon the site!" Kemmer shouted.

He reached back under one of the worktables and pulled a pack out by the worn leather strap. Kemmer rummaged around until he found what he was looking for. He came up with a compact null-inertia gun and thrust it into his belt. Xen's eyes flashed red at the sight of it.

"What do you think you're doing? We can't fight, Kemmer! I'm not asking my people to die for this!" he said. The Ixthian turned to his team. "Take only what you need. We're leaving!"

"We can't take the road. Duaal and Coldhand have the trucks," Tiberius told them loudly to make himself heard as the archeologists scattered to grab their gear. "And Gavriel is probably coming that way. There will be Arcadians flying in, too."

"We can go west," Phillip said. "There are some other cracks and tunnels opened up by the quakes. We can hide there until... until this is over."

"How far away are these tunnels?" Enu-Io asked.

"About half a mile," Phillip answered.

"We only need to hide you for a while," Tiberius said. "Duaal, Maeve and thirty cops are going to be here soon. We just need to get you out."

Kemmer noticed the old man's choice of words.

"What about you?" he asked.

Tiberius was not looking at the archeologist as he answered. He petted Orphia and stared up at the jagged mouth of the ravine.

"I'm staying here," Tiberius said. "I can't just let the cult take the Waygate. The damage they could do is too great. Besides, I have something to settle with Gavriel."

"You're badly outnumbered," Enu-Io told him, returning with a duffle bag over his wide blue shoulders. "How will you fight?"

"Coldhand's Raptor is up on the mountain." Tiberius suddenly laughed. "I'll show that bastard bounty hunter what *real* flying looks like. Gruth, I'll need your help. Those Raptors are sealed with print locks."

"You want me to break in?" Gruth asked, hefting his tool cases. "Sure, I can manage that."

Kemmer lifted his chin and squared his shoulders. "Well, I'm not leaving either, Captain Myles. I'm not leaving my Waygate to those... whoever they are."

"Don't be an idiot!" Xen said. He grabbed Kemmer's arm. The Ixthian archeologist's fingers were trembling and tight. "This is still your discovery! When we present it on Tynerion, you'll have plenty of funding for anything you need and we can come back. But a posthumous award won't do you any good!"

"No." Kemmer pulled away from the Ixthian. "It's not just about who gets credit, Xen. This Waygate is Prian. It belongs to us, not a bunch of off-world rats. If they want to destroy the Alliance, they can damned well do it from somewhere else."

Xen stared with eyes flashing through an entire spectrum of colors. "We're scholars, not warriors!"

Maybe on Tynerion, Xen and his students could afford to think like that. They didn't have to be fighters. On Prianus, Kemmer had no choice. Not learning to fire a gun or call a hawk – or at least to hide behind someone who could – meant not surviving to adulthood. Kemmer shook his head and rested his hand on the gun in his belt.

"You'll never understand," he told Xen.

"Neither do you, Doctor Kemmer," Tiberius said.

"What?" Kemmer asked.

"You hired me and mine to protect this place," Tiberius grunted. "I'm not working with some amateur. You're leaving, too."

Kemmer went hot with fury. "What? Not a chance! I'm staying right here with the Waygate!"

"No. You're not." Tiberius' voice was quieter now, and somehow much more terrible. He wasn't arguing, simply stating an unshakable truth. "We're outnumbered at least twenty to one. Even if every one of you stood to fight, it wouldn't matter. So you're hiding. All of you."

Kemmer could summon up no more arguments. Tiberius called Orphia to his shoulder and whistled to the archeologists.

"Now, if we're all done squabbling, it's time to go. We don't have much time," he said. "Everybody stick close and move fast. We're going up to the surface. Gruth, you get me into the Raptor and then everyone follow Phillip out. Got it?"

Everyone nodded – some more grudging than others – but they dashed through the icy ravine and toward the ladder.

The scream of sirens made Duaal's swollen-feeling head throb even more, but it was hard to care. Tiberius was up there in the Kayton Mountains, all alone against Gavriel and Xartasia and their whole crazy cult! Almost alone... But how much good would the archeologists be against the Nihilist?

Not much, Duaal guessed.

The Prian police cavalcade flashed with red and green lights. Through small windows in the side of the van, Duaal watched rain-soaked gray Pylos streak past.

Cerro sat between two other cops on a dented steel bench on the other side of the van. He looked at Duaal as the driver swerved around a cylindrical fuel hauler.

"We'll be there soon," Cerro said. It might have been meant as reassurance, but his voice was as serious as ever. "There's nothing to win by worrying."

Duaal nodded mutely and raked his hands through his hair. On one side, Xia was hurriedly patching Maeve's wounds, borrowing heavily from the police supplies to stitch and bandage her many cuts. Logan Coldhand watched Xia work, his expression stony. In the bounty hunter's eyes, Duaal doubted that trying to wipe out all life in the galaxy was Gavriel's greatest crime.

At least Panna and Gripper looked just as terrified as Duaal felt. The two sat on his other flank, staring at the floor. What were they going to do? Panna carried no weapons of her own and Gripper knew nothing of battle.

Duaal wondered if he was any better. Could he actually help? After all of his years of begging and complaining about being left out of danger, Duaal was just scared.

Gavriel was up there. Ice flowed through Duaal's veins, and his knees felt like sacks of water. His heart seemed at once to be racing so fast that it was about to tear itself apart and to have stopped beating altogether. Duaal's fingertips were numb and his stomach was full of acid fire.

But Tiberius was up there, too – the rough but kind old man who had taken care of Duaal, even when the stupid boy didn't want him to.

"Can't we go any faster?" Duaal asked. His voice cracked.

Cerro shook his head.

"Do you hear anything?"

"Yeah, I hear you. Shut up!"

"That's enough, both of you," Tiberius told Gruth and Kemmer. "I hear something, but I think it's still far away. Let's move."

He led them up the ladder, out of the ravine and into the rain. Kemmer shielded his eyes with one arm and stared down the slope. Rain seeped through the snow and raised a thick gray fog that shrouded the moraine in gloom. The ground shuddered under Kemmer's feet and a loud rumble rolled through the air, too long to be thunder. Something big was coming.

"Gruth, we've got to get that fighter open," Tiberius said.

"Right," the Lyran growled.

They charged off toward the grounded Raptor. Kemmer hurried to follow, but something swooped out of the low-hanging clouds. It had long wings and a cheap gun gripped tightly in hands red with oozing sores. The gun cracked loudly and echoed off the mountain. Kemmer dove into the snow and Gruth howled in pain. Blood sprayed from a gaping hole in the Lyran's thigh and he sprawled on the icy ground.

"Tiberius!" Enu-Io shouted.

The rumbling was closer now, deep and loud and mechanical. A long metal shape roared up onto the mountaintop and screeched to a stop. It was a truck, a huge one for hauling large cargo. Or a lot of smaller things...

The Nihilists had arrived.

Tiberius' expression became grim as he turned toward the huge truck. Steel doors in the back slammed open and Nihilists all in black poured out, filling the foggy moraine with deadly silhouettes. Arcadians dropped out of the churning gray sky all around them. There were hundreds of Gavriel's people, surrounding them and closing in. There was no way out.

"They're too close! Get down!" Tiberius shouted.

Kemmer jumped back and yanked the gun from his belt. "Back to the Waygate!"

Xen stared around the throng of Nihilists, eyes wide and dull red with terror. Kemmer grabbed the Ixthian and dragged him back toward the ladder.

"Gruth! Gruth, are you still with me?" Tiberius said, shaking the Lyran. "You have to get out of the open!"

Gruth bared his sharp teeth and snarled. "I can't do anything on this leg!"

He was right. The ground all around was crimson and Kemmer could make out the white splinters of bone jutting up from Gruth's matted fur. Another shot cracked nearby and threw snow up in a frozen spray. Tiberius nodded once and ran toward the angular hulk of Coldhand's Raptor, dragging the Lyran along and leaving blood-spotted furrows in the ice.

"Get underneath," Tiberius said. "The ship will cover you some, at least against those guns. And get that canopy unsealed!"

Gruth laid his ears back. "Not likely."

"Do it!"

Before the mechanic could protest or argue, Tiberius freed a bigger null-inertia pistol than Kemmer's from under his coat.

Downslope, the archeologists scrambled toward safety. Enu-Io took Phillip's hand and swung him over the edge of the ravine, but then the tall Dailon sprawled face-down in the snow, a black laser burn sliced deep across his broad back. Darius shouted in fury and yanked a knife from his boot. He flung it at the nearest Nihilist, a one-eyed Hadrian who reeled back, clawing at the blade in his throat.

"Darius!" Ava cried. "Come on!"

He dove toward the ladder as another one of Gavriel's Nihilists snatched the knife from his companion's neck and hurled it back. The blade flipped once and then buried itself deep into the meat of Darius' arm. The Prian clenched his teeth and hauled himself laboriously down after his sister.

Tiberius ran back to the ravine's edge and waved to Kemmer.

"You wanted to stand with your Waygate?" he said. "I hope you meant it. Get down there!"

"What the hells do you think you're going to do up here alone?" Kemmer asked.

"Get out of here and let me do my job!" Tiberius shouted.

Kemmer nodded and jumped over Enu-Io's body, then climbed down the ladder as fast as his trembling limbs would carry him. As soon as he reached the bottom, Tiberius heaved the ladder free and threw it down, narrowly avoiding hitting Kemmer at the bottom of the crevasse.

"Get moving!" Tiberius' voice was barely audible and sounded very far away.

Kemmer turned and ran for the Waygate.

[34]

FATHERS

"The heart that loves will never fail. Even when shattered by loss, it beats ever on."

- TITANIA CAVAINNA, ARCADIAN MONARCH (230 PA)

Gavriel stepped down from the hauler's cab. The blood of its former owner was still spattered across the dashboard as Nihilists surged out onto the mountainside. Black robes stood out against the gray sky, a tide of shadows rising up to swallow all life. Gavriel's heart swelled to see his flock filling the ground and sky.

But a single stone held back the tide... A barrel-chested Prian man stood at the edge of the crevasse. He was considerably younger than Gavriel, but still an old man. His shoulders were squared as he fired into the nearest Nihilists. Thirteen of Gavriel's people were already down, lying in the red-spattered snow, including Pharra, one of his Emberguard. With Hallax gone, only four remained...

A screeching hawk swooped out of the swirling fog, clawing and ripping at Nihilists as they tried to charge at her master. The man whistled and the bird arrowed out. The little beast's wickedly hooked talons shone red. A young Arcadian man was flying toward the ravine and screamed in pain as the hawk tore through the delicate membrane of his wing. The fairy landed in a jumble of wet robes and feathers.

"Gavriel!" the Prian shouted over the howling gale.

Xartasia stepped lightly down from the truck and stood beside Gavriel. "Pay him no mind. There is work to be done."

"Face me, Gavriel!" The challenge echoed across the mountain. "You are mine!"

Against Xartasia's soft-spoken protests, Gavriel strode up the slope. His followers parted before him, pulling back to make way. Gavriel stopped at a distance from the shouting Prian and held up an age-scarred hand. The hawk wheeled and came to rest on the other man's shoulder.

"Who are you, Prian?" Gavriel asked. Thunder punctuated the question. "Why do you challenge me?"

"My name is Tiberius Myles, captain of the Blue Phoenix! I will have your blood for what you've done, Gavriel!"

"What I've done?" Gavriel asked. "I will deliver your world from pain! I will open the way for death–"

"Shut up!" Tiberius snarled at him. "I'm not talking about that. The Pylos police are on their way to stop you. But you'll answer to me for what you've done to *mine*!"

"You are Maeve's captain," Gavriel said slowly. "Are you angry that I killed her? She is free now, Captain Myles."

"Maeve chose her own life, the good and the bad. No, I'm going to burn you down for what you did to Duaal!" There were tears in Tiberius' fierce blue eyes. He held his gun pointed right at Gavriel. "Duaal Sinnay! Do you remember him?"

Now Gavriel frowned, a seething suspicion growing inside him.

"Yes, I remember," he said.

"He was only a boy!" Tiberius shouted. Even his hawk glared coldly at Gavriel. "A child! You used Duaal. You hurt him!"

"And what does the boy mean to you?"

"Everything! I found him on the Phoenix! I took him away from Prianus! But he's never forgotten what you did! He's still suffering... Because of you!" Tiberius' face was red with fury and the tears fell, joining the rain beaded in his white beard. "If I can kill you, maybe he'll finally have some peace!"

Gavriel's fury rose to meet Tiberius'.

"*You* took the boy?" he asked. "It took me over a decade to replace the power I lost with him!"

"You'll face me for what you did to my boy! Duel me!" Tiberius roared.

"I answer your challenge!"

Xartasia fanned her wings in irritation. "Lord Gavriel, we do not have time for such distractions!"

"Take the flock to the Waygate and await me," Gavriel told her. "For what this man has done, what he's cost me, I will send him into darkness myself!"

"Gavriel..."

"Go!" the ancient Nihilist commanded. He shouted out to the Nihilists. "Follow her!"

Xartasia pursed her lips and sang a single high note. She turned away and swept off into the mist. The rest of the Church of Nihil streamed past the old men and toward the ravine.

"Where are we going?" Xen gasped as Kemmer caught up.

"Where *can* we go, you little idiot? Unless you can climb that–" Kemmer pointed to the sheer wall of wet gray stone. "–we're stuck down here!"

Loud thuds and screams for blood chased the retreating archeologists down the canyon. With the ladder gone, the Nihilists were lowering ropes and cables – probably salvaged from their hauler – over the ravine's edge.

They were climbing down fast, with no regard for injury as the sick and less athletic of their numbers slipped or even fell. Darius struggled to keep up with the other and leaned against the wall of the crevice. Every time he reached out to steady himself, Darius grunted. Blood streamed from his wounded arm and Ava scrambled back to help her brother. He pushed her away.

"Just keep moving!" he told her breathlessly. "Those bastards are right behind us!"

As if in answer, shouts and darkly exultant songs echoed across the mountain. The Arcadian Nihilists had no need for ladders or ropes and they wheeled, diving down into the ravine on angelic white wings. A bullet whizzed down the crevasse and cracked into the wall, flinging pieces of rock in every direction. Chips of stone struck Kemmer in the cheek, stinging and cutting a pair of red lines into his skin.

The cultists were closing in quickly and another shot rang out. They didn't have long.

"Get to the Waygate!" Kemmer instructed.

"Doc!" Phillip shouted.

Ava and Xen had made it to their camp and were struggling to pull a worktable up against the side of the Waygate, into some sort of barricade. Phillip darted out from around one of the overturned tables and grabbed Kemmer. They dove back behind cover just as the Nihilists opened fire again. Guns popped and the bullets drove deep dents into the upended tabletops. A laser bored a suddenly molten hole in the steel and seared down the length of Ava's leg. She grabbed the wound and hot blood spurted from between her fingers.

"Ava!" Phillip shouted.

Darius and Xen hunkered behind another one of the tables. Kemmer steadied his arms on the edge of his own makeshift barricade and emptied his pistol into the oncoming Nihilists. They were close together as they charged down the ravine and Kemmer's shots tore through five of them, but there were a dozen more to replace each one.

The Arcadians circled his Waygate like oversized white vultures, beating their wings hard and fast to remain aloft in the wind-swept rain. In the presence of the quickly growing crowd, the light of the Waygate rippled faster and brighter, like an iridescent ocean. The whole thing seemed almost alive. Alive and excited.

"Take the Waygate!"

The order rang through the ravine and Kemmer peered carefully around the edge of the barrier. A woman perched on a thin spar of rain-slicked stone above the Waygate arch. It was another Arcadian. For a moment, Kemmer thought it was Maeve. It wasn't her, he realized, but this fairy looked very much like Tiberius' first mate. She was older – as best Kemmer could guess – and wore her raven-black hair long. Unlike the dirty, diseased Nihilists pouring into the ravine, this Arcadian was gowned all in perfectly clean, flowing white. She raised her hand.

"Take the Waygate!" she sang out once more. "For Lord Gavriel and the end of all! Take it!"

The cult surged forward, guns blazing. Their bullets and lasers sizzled in the rain as they chopped and tore at the archeologists' flimsy barrier. Xen jumped to his feet, screaming for them to run.

"Up to the Waygate!" Kemmer shouted. "Get onto the stairs! It won't help us much against those bird-backs, but we can defend them against the rest!"

Ava leaned on Phillip, blood streaming down her leg, and the two of them ran to the huge white steps of the Waygate. Darius, Xen and Kemmer bolted after them.

The ravine was full of lead and red laserfire and chaos. Ava just couldn't move fast enough. A pack of cultists dashed across the wet ground and then swarmed over her and Phillip. Ava shoved the geologist aside just as a tailless Lyran leapt at her, foam streaking his muzzle. The Nihilist sank long fangs into Ava's throat and tore.

Blood fountained up into the air, liquid rubies in the light of the Waygate.

"Ava!" Phillip screamed.

"Move!" Darius shouted. He grabbed Phillip and hauled him up the steps of the Waygate.

"Let go of me!"

"Ava wouldn't want you to die for her, you dumb slat!" Darius grunted. "Come on!"

A bright laser blast lanced through Xen's stomach. He swayed and pressed shaking silver hands to the wound. Kemmer caught his elbow and struggled, trying to drag the other archeologist up. The clean white of the ziggurat was growing slick with blood and rain... but the lasers and the bullets seemed to simply slide off without leaving a mark. Kemmer yanked Xen's arm.

"Move, you arrogant bastard!" Kemmer grunted. "Get up!"

But Xen wouldn't move and the color was fading from his compound eyes. "I can't. Tell Xia–"

Kemmer never found out what Xen wanted him to tell her. The Nihilists were at the foot of the stair and the air was full of fairies. One of the bird-back bastards swooped low and stabbed a spear into Xen's chest, terribly and finally silencing the Ixthian. Kemmer made a futile grab at the Arcadian, but he was already out of reach. Swearing, the archeologist clambered up the oversized stairs, toward the Waygate.

Darius and Phillip had pressed their backs up against the huge shimmering ring. It protected them from the Nihilists climbing the steps, but offered no defense against the Arcadians circling overhead, shouting and singing. Phillip was doubled over, clutching a wound in his stomach. His freckles stood out against his pale skin.

Darius sported several fresh red wounds. His shirt clung to his skin, wet with blood and rain. The digger had grabbed a one-armed Arcadian and run him through with his own spear. It was a knife lashed to a broom handle, really, but the weapon had done its job.

Kemmer threw himself down against the Waygate beside Darius as the other Prian kicked the impaled fairy cultist off the top of the pyramid.

"I had no idea you were so useful," Kemmer gasped.

"You never asked," Darius said. His voice was tight with pain. "You just assumed I didn't know how to do anything but dig. We're not going to win this, doc."

There was nothing to say. After all Kemmer had done to try to protect the Waygate, he was going to lose it. And to a bunch of... of uneducated aliens!

Darius fended off a Dailon cultist with his appropriated spear, but a cluster of Arcadians dove out of the sky and snatched Phillip. The geologist screamed as they yanked him off his feet, up into the air. Darius shouted and hurled his spear at the Nihilist holding Phillip's arms. The clumsily-made weapon fell well short of its intended target and clattered down the steps of the Waygate. The Arcadians flew higher.

"Phil!" Darius shouted.

If the freckled geologist gave any answer, it was whipped away by the wind. The Arcadians abruptly parted, releasing Phillip. He shrieked and plunged to the rocky ravine floor. There was a horrid crunch and Phillip was still.

Darius swore and charged down the stairs toward the broken body.

"No!" Kemmer shouted. "Darius, hold your damned ground!"

The Cult of Nihil was waiting for him. A human in red and a tarnished-looking Ixthian grabbed Darius, dragging him down to the rain-slicked steps. He shouted and wrenched his uninjured arm free. Darius balled his fist and slammed it into the Ixthian's nose, but before he could stand up, the human stomped down on his knee. The Ixthian pulled a snub-nosed gun from her wet black robe and shot Darius twice in the stomach. The digger groaned, pressing his hands against his bleeding guts as he died.

Hundreds of the moaning, crying, singing and howling Nihilists surged all around the Waygate, closing in on Kemmer. The woman in white watched imperiously from on high.

Another Arcadian dropped on top of Kemmer and he dove out of the way. The fairy couldn't correct his course in time and crashed into the Waygate. He tumbled down the stairs and into the other Nihilists. Kemmer ran after him and landed badly on one ankle. Something inside popped agonizingly, but he didn't slow.

Kemmer snatched up a fallen gun and swung it around at the regal Arcadian woman. He fired, but she was far away and the laser only bored a steaming hole into cracked stone.

Robed cultists leapt at Kemmer. They had guns, too, and bullets slammed him in the chest like hammer blows. A laser burned down Kemmer's side, exposing the bone of his hip and filling the air with the sharp, acrid scent of burnt flesh. Kemmer's legs could no longer support him and he fell. The gun spun away across the slick white stairs.

The black-haired Arcadian spread her wings and glided down to stand before Kemmer, looking at him with startling violet eyes. He struggled to rise, but he couldn't lift his heavy, limp limbs out of the spreading puddle of steaming blood. Icy rain splashed his face, every drop as heavy as lead. The fairy reached into one white sleeve and drew a slender glass dagger. It gleamed like ice.

"You discovered this Waygate," she told him in a musical voice. "By doing so, you have saved me a great deal of work and for that, I thank you."

With an effort that brought tears to his eyes, Kemmer grabbed for the fairy's knife. She smiled – perhaps pleased at his tenacity – and pushed Kemmer's hands back down to the blood-streaked Waygate stairs, then drew the glass knife across his throat. As his life drained away, the last thing Kemmer Andus saw was his Waygate glowing with cold auroral light.

Gavriel faced Tiberius across the field of ice and mist. To judge by the screams and gunshots echoing up from the ravine, Xartasia was leading the Nihilists successfully to the Waygate. All that remained was to deal with this... thief.

Gavriel raised his arms. Wind billowed his ancient robes and raked across his sallow skin.

"Where is the boy?" he asked.

Tiberius stood as steady and unmovable as a mountain. "Duaal. His name is Duaal. He's not your tool and he's not a boy. Duaal's a fine man – in spite of you!"

"In spite of me?" Gavriel asked. "I gave that boy the only taste of power that he will ever know."

"You hurt him! You used him!"

Gavriel flexed long, spidery fingers. The knuckles cracked like snapping twigs. "And what have you done for the boy? What kind of life have you given him? Even you speak of his pain. If you truly cared for the boy, you would kill him and save him the torment of life. When I have called forth the Devourers, I will finish what you lack the strength to do."

Tiberius' face went suddenly as white as the snow. "You'll never hurt Duaal again!"

"That is no longer your concern, Captain Myles," Gavriel said. He laced his creaking fingers together and then brandished them. *"Ka li'ae avael baelenox!"*

"Fly!" Tiberius shouted to his hawk at the same time.

A burning line of flame sizzled through the rain as the hook-beaked bird streaked toward Gavriel. Tiberius lunged to the side and fired, but the bullet cracked off into the low gray clouds over Gavriel's shoulder.

With a short song and a flick of Gavriel's wrist, another red-gold lance of fire lit up the storm. It seared into Tiberius' ribs, burning a smoking hole through cloth and flesh. The old Prian's jaw clenched and he brought up his gun to bear on Gavriel.

"*Na illya ma'naari su!*" the old mage sang.

Summoned lightning arced and snapped across Tiberius' gun. The old Prian's fingers spasmed and the weapon fell steaming into the snow. Gavriel smiled and raised his hands again, but a dark shape shot from the sky.

It was that damned hawk, screeching and diving with her talons extended. Gavriel flung his arms across his face as the hawk clawed at him. Pain exploded in his left eye and the world filled with wet red agony. Gavriel grabbed the bird and flung her away. Her talons gleamed with blood and clutched rags of torn skin.

Gavriel shouted another lightning spell and filled the foggy air with harsh blue-white light. But the hawk was gone, vanished once more into the dark storm clouds. Gavriel turned back to Tiberius.

The Prian lay sprawled in the blood-dappled snow. His breath came quick and shallow. Sky blue eyes stared accusingly up into the heavens, unyieldingly hard. Gavriel stood over the dying man.

"You were brave, Tiberius Myles," he said. "But the darkness is coming. Soon, the boy will join you in death."

Gavriel stepped over Tiberius and then strode to the edge of the ravine. Nihilists were busily reattaching the ladder to steel pegs in the stone. Those who had not climbed down into the narrow crack gasped, pointing to his wounded face and useless left eye.

"Lord Gavriel, are you alright?" one of them asked.

Gavriel waved the man off. The pain blazed, yes, but he had endured worse and there was too much to do.

"It will not matter for long," he said. "When night falls tonight, it falls across the entire galaxy!"

Behind him, the old hawk landed beside Tiberius. She hopped closer to her fallen master through the snow and nuzzled his shoulder, keening pitifully.

[35]

SYMBOLS

"Claws out in sixty!" Captain Cerro shouted.

The close confines of the van suddenly became even closer as the other cops prepared, freeing weapons and unhooding birds.

Maeve inspected herself. There was still blood crusted unpleasantly at the shorn edges of her ruined clothes, but Xia's drugs had done their job admirably. She would be able to fight.

Xia sprayed an astringent-smelling adhesive onto the fairy's broken foot and then dabbed it with powder from a small canister. The glue flared with chemical heat and set into a stiff, surprisingly resilient shell.

"Take it easy on that," Xia warned. "This cast is good enough for light protection, but I don't know how it's going to hold up under any stress."

"It will serve," Maeve said. "Thank you."

"You're medicated, but just because you don't feel pain doesn't mean the injuries are gone," Xia reminded her while she worked.

"Gavriel and his butcher did a whole lot of damage. And there's the Vanora White to consider, too. I don't know how much of it is still in your bloodstream. I would have liked to give you dylominol for the pain. It's safer when there are other chems in your system. But with this many injuries, I had to give you isophelle. If you start getting sleepy, Maeve, you need to tell me."

"We have worse concerns than medicine," Maeve answered in a tight voice.

Her mistake in Tamlin had not only destroyed Arcadia, but unless they could stop the Nihilists, would now kill trillions more. The Alliance never welcomed the refugee Arcadians, but Maeve had no desire to see another civilization wiped out.

And Maeve didn't want to die. Not anymore, not here in the gray cold, at the fangs and black blades of the Devourers. She wanted to see the sun again. Any sun...

Maeve was interrupted by a sudden pained shout from Duaal. The young mage leapt to his feet, smashing his skull against the well-worn ceiling. But when Duaal fell to his knees, clutching his head and streaming tears down his cheeks, it didn't seem to be from the pain.

"Duaal?" Xia asked. She abandoned Maeve and grabbed Duaal by the shoulder. "What's wrong?"

"Tiberius!" the boy cried.

"What the hells?" Cerro asked. He put a heavy, reassuring hand on his nervously twitching falcon. "What's wrong with that boy?"

"He's kind of connected to Gavriel," Gripper answered. "Did you see something, Shimmer?"

"It's Tiberius. He fought Gavriel... and lost," Duaal said.

Cerro's scarred face went hard and he leaned over to the reinforced window.

"We're here," he announced. He spoke into the radio clipped to his shoulder. "Keep close and move fast. Our goal is the Waygate. Punch through and hold it. Go!"

"We have to get to Tiberius!" Duaal shouted over the clamor. "Find him!"

The Blue Phoenix crew nodded in agreement, and so did both Logan and Panna.

They were at the bottom of the rising moraine. The police van swerved and screeched to a stop beside a huge, empty hauler. Cerro shouted and kicked open the doors, throwing his falcon up into the gray fog. Thirty more cops poured out of the vans with guns held at the ready.

"Tiberius!"

Maeve heard Duaal's heart-wrenching shout before she could follow him out across the mountaintop. She jumped out of the van and ran past the cops toward the figure laying slumped in the snow. Maeve dropped her spear as she fell to her knees beside Tiberius. Xia and Gripper were close behind, followed by Logan.

Duaal skidded through the ice and snow to kneel over Tiberius, who lay in a spreading halo of red. There was another long line of blood in the snow behind him, leading back toward the ravine.

"Tiberius? Captain, can you hear me?" Xia asked.

A burn cut deeply into the old Prian's chest and his blackened right hand lay curled over the wound. Blood streaked his beard, but his blue eyes were open. Orphia perched on his boot, keening unhappily and pulling at the laces with her beak. Tiberius looked up at Cerro and managed a small nod.

"Captain," he wheezed.

Cerro inclined his head.

"Captain," he greeted the other man gravely.

"Behind you..." Tiberius said.

A wild-eyed man ran screaming out of the mist, a hatchet held over his head, and charged at Cerro. The Prian cop brought up his Talon-4 and put a lance of red laser through the Nihilist's knee. The zealot's scream rose in pitch and pain as he tumbled down into the slush. Another officer holding a shotgun at his hip rushed forward and cracked the matte black stock across the back of the cultist's head.

"Attention all members of the Cult of Nihil," Captain Cerro said into his com. His voice boomed from speakers bolted to the sides of the green and red vans. "You are all under arrest! If you lay down arms, you will be taken to Pylos Station Three to await trial. You–"

Shrieks of fury rang out through the gloom. Tattered shadows loomed up all around, closing quickly. Stones flew out of the fog at the police piling out of their vans, and then the Nihilist opened fire.

"Spread out! Make as many arrests as you're able, but we're not here for tea! We're going to stop this. Now fly!" Cerro ordered.

Twenty-nine cops fanned out around him and charged into the mist. Duaal had taken Tiberius' uninjured hand and held it in both of his. Tears shone on his cheeks as he stared at Xia.

"You can help him, right?" Duaal asked.

"There's no fixing this," Tiberius answered. He coughed, blood bubbling from his lips. "Gavriel's down there, at the Waygate! Go!"

Duaal's face paled and his jaw set in a hard line.

"You have to stop Gavriel," Tiberius said.

"The captain is right," Maeve agreed. Her voice caught. "I am a knight and know only a handful of simple charms, Duaal. You are the only true spell-singer among us. We must go."

Tiberius pulled his hand free and pushed at the boy's shoulder. He left a bloody handprint on Duaal's coat.

"Don't waste time, little hawk," Tiberius said. "Go!"

Duaal's eyes opened and he took a deep, cold breath. He stood and pushed his wet hair back from his face.

"Xia, do what you can for the captain. Stay with her, Gripper."

The Arboran sobbed and nodded. Rain and sleet dripped from his drooping ears. Panna had emerged from the van and stood staring, with hands pressed to her mouth in horror.

"You stay, too," Duaal told her. "All four of you should get into one of these vans and lock the doors."

The whine of lasers and the flat cracks of lead rounds pierced the thin mountain air. Maeve grabbed her spear from where it had fallen in the snow.

"They will manage," she said. "It is time to join the battle."

The police were spreading out in teams, moving forward in low crouches with weapons in hand. As the dark silhouettes of Nihilists came running and stumbling down the rocky slope, the Prians took careful aim and fired. Sharp whistles rang out as the cops called out attack commands to circling hawks and falcons. The sound of it was almost musical and reminded Maeve of the battle songs she had learned from Orthain.

Maeve's newly repaired glass spear caught the wan sunlight and sliced it into rainbow shards. She sprinted a few steps through the snow after the police and leapt into the sky, but something caught her wrist and she was pulled back to the ground.

"What do you think you're doing?" Logan asked.

Maeve found herself facing her hunter. The icy gaze that she knew so well, that had protected her memories from Gavriel's spells – for a time, at least – was gone now. Logan's blue eyes were wide and he looked... frightened. His metal fingers were locked around her wrist.

"Release me, Logan! I must find Gavriel," Maeve cried. "It is my memory he wields!"

"There are two hundred Nihilists up here. If you fly out ahead of the police, you're only going to get yourself shot," Logan said. His face resumed the cold mask Maeve knew so well. "You can't stop anyone if you're dead."

"I cannot remain and do nothing!"

"Then be smart," Logan said. "Let me go with you."

Slowly, Maeve nodded and folded her wings against her back again. She ran with Logan and Duaal to catch up with the cops. The two human men could have easily overtaken her with their longer legs, but they matched their strides to Maeve and remained close.

They picked out the lighter blue of Cerro's uniform and ran toward it. The Prian police hadn't made much progress up the slope.

"Captain! We must reach Gavriel and the Waygate," Maeve said when they were close. "There is no more important goal."

"I know," Cerro agreed. "But they're thick up ahead, and we've got Arcadians above us."

As if to prove his point, several Arcadians wheeled down from the clouds, black robes flapping in the rain and making them look more like bats than birds. Cerro whistled sharply. The smaller dark shape of his falcon flew out of the mist and intercepted the closest cultist. There was a splash of crimson blood and the Nihilist veered off course. With a sonorous cry of pain, he collided with the Arcadian beside him and they crashed together to the ground in a tangle of limbs and wings.

But that still left two more to fold their wings and dive at the police. Cerro fired at one of the falling fairies, who veered off and vanished into the stormy gray clouds again.

The remaining Arcadian slammed into the ground, landing in a low crouch. It was a woman, with lips skinned back from her teeth as she sang an angry battle chant. She flung herself at Cerro with a crooked nanoknife, but a larger foot came down on her heel and then a sharp blow across the back of her neck sent the Nihilist sprawling in the snow, wheezing shallowly. Cerro looked at Logan, who stood over the fallen Arcadian with his Talon in hand.

"Can you hold the southern end of the slope?" Cerro asked.

Logan scanned the shapes racing through the mist.

"Yes," he said.

"Good. Go and then we can break their ranks."

"In sixty," Logan said.

Cerro whistled and seven of the other cops darted with him toward the ravine. Maeve and Logan turned and sprinted through the slush along the southern edge of the flat moraine.

"Logan!" Maeve shouted.

Two Lyran Nihilists were scrambling through the snow, falling to all fours for better traction. They were closing fast. Maeve leapt, beating her wings as the paired Lyrans pounced. The cultists slid under her and she dove. Maeve fell on one of the wolfin Nihilists, driving her spear through their back. She landed and leveled her glass blade at the second, but Logan was already standing over the Lyran, a thread of steam rising from his laser.

"Fifteen seconds. We need to go," he said.

Logan spun and they dashed for the southern position. Maeve counted silently and right at fifteen, she heard a high, trilling whistle. From Cerro's position, she saw a group of police charge forward, red laserfire clearing the way.

But what was that flash of purple and gold? For the first time, Maeve realized that Duaal was no longer with them. The mage was following Cerro down into the Waygate ravine.

Duaal watched Maeve and Logan's departure in silence. They could handle things down to the south. When he made no move to follow, Captain Cerro looked over at Duaal.

"What's your plan, then?" he asked the young Hyzaari.

"Same as you. I'm getting down to that Waygate," Duaal said. His green eyes were dry now. "That's where Gavriel is."

Cerro nodded once and then whistled, first to his falcon and then again to the small squad of other cops. One of them was already limping on a badly wounded foot, but his attacker lay in a black-clothed heap nearby. A woman with a lined face checked the battery on her Talon.

Cerro looked at the other cops.

"Ready?" he asked.

"Yes, sir!" came the chorus of answers.

"Yes," Duaal said.

The fog was finally fading, torn apart by the wind and washed away by the rain. Cerro raised his hand. The ravine's edge was lined by Nihilists, like rows of diseased gargoyles. At least fifty of them were already caught in close, bloody combat with other squads of Prian police. There were far fewer cops than Nihilists, but each of the officers was of the toughest Prian stock and trained to fight beak and claw for their homeworld. All that the Cult of Nihil had were numbers, but they had those in abundance.

They spotted Duaal, Cerro and the Prians charging the line and turned to face the new threat. Duaal sprinted to keep up.

"Na illya ma'naari su!" he sang.

Blue-white lightning snapped out like a serpent's forked tongue, following Duaal's gesture, smaller than the jagged bolts jumping from cloud to cloud over the Kayton Mountains, but no less deadly. The curling electricity grounded on one of the Nihilists, who went ridged and fell twitching into the snow.

Imitating Cerro, the young mage ran in a low crouch. There was the occasional crack of a gun or the sizzling whine of a laser, but the Nihilists were armed mostly with simple clubs, knives, and an utter lack of regard for their own safety. They threw themselves at the advancing Prians with rapture on their reddened, disease-pocked faces.

A black shadow leapt at Duaal. The mage flexed his fingers into the symbol for fire, but before he could open his mouth to sing, the cultist collided with him. They fumbled on top of Duaal and raised a dagger, but a screaming falcon fell out of the sky and tore bright spurts of blood from the Nihilist's face. His dagger went flying and Captain Cerro appeared out of the rain, shooting the flailing cultist through the chest.

"We're clearing a path down to the ladder," said the Prian cop. "Come on!"

A sudden burst of laserfire from the south cut through the pack of cultists, forcing them to split their attention.

That must have been Logan and Maeve. Another pack of police hit the Nihilists from the north, two others harrying the Arcadian reinforcements swooping out of the clouds.

Cerro whistled. Duaal couldn't tell if it was a command for the birds or the police, but when the cops charged, he stayed close. A burly Prian took point, his shotgun held at waist level and booming continuously. Nihilists scattered before him, falling or retreating.

But one of the wounded cultists still clutched his own gun and returned fire. Duaal was close enough to hear the wet, meaty thuds and then the air whooshing from the officer's lungs as the bullets tore through him. The big cop wobbled, regained his balance and gave the Nihilist the death he wanted so much with a shotgun blast in the gut.

A howling human with an axe took the cop's arm and landed another deep blow into his ribs. With a roar of fury, the Prian staggered the final distance to the edge of the ravine and heaved himself forward. The cop reached out with his remaining arm as he slammed into the line of Nihilists, taking two of them down over the edge with him.

Duaal felt sick. The Prian police were just as relentless as the Cult of Nihil. And for now, at least, it had earned them control of the ravine. One of Cerro's men gave the reattached ladder a cursory check and then began climbing, but it would take far too long for thirty cops to make the descent that way. Cerro pulled bulky cylinders from their belts and fired pitons into the rocky ledge of the ravine with a pneumatic charge. Without hesitation, they leapt over the edge, down into the crevice.

"Move!" Cerro shouted to Duaal.

The mage swung his legs over the ladder and clambered down the wet rungs as fast as possible before the cultists above could regroup. By the time Duaal reached the ravine's uneven stone floor, Cerro and his remaining officers were hunkered together behind a heap of dig tailings. The rain had turned the ground into a sodden mire of mud. Duaal fell to his knees in the muck with Cerro and the rest of the police. Dirty rainwater soaked into his expensive clothes.

The Nihilists had gathered around the base of the Waygate to adore their leader, but then they spotted the invading police and turned together, swarming out toward Cerro's position. Duaal could just see two figures standing before the Waygate, on top of the great white ziggurat. One in ragged black and the other in perfect white. Gavriel and Xartasia.

Duaal didn't think. He just charged at the Waygate. He *had* to stop Gavriel. Tiberius had told him to.

An Arcadian pounced on him. The ragged fairy was too thin and dirty to make out any sign of gender, but it hissed at him in its own lyric language and swung a nail-spiked club clutched tightly in pale fingers. The mage jumped back, slipped in the mud and fell.

The Arcadian Nihilist swiped their club down at Duaal in an inexpert but still potentially lethal strike. Duaal rolled over onto his back and kicked up at his attacker. He hit, forcing the fairy to drop the weapon, but not before one of the nails gouged a ragged, bloody line into his boot and the foot beneath.

It wasn't a terrible wound, but it bled and it hurt. The Nihilists ran through Cerro's staccato shots and grabbed at Duaal, holding him as the Arcadian pulled a carving knife from their belt. With an effort, Duaal yanked his hands free and hooked his fingers, but couldn't seem to make his stiff, numb hands properly form the intricate spell symbols.

But the symbols weren't important, Duaal thought frantically. Maeve said that they were for children. Panna said they were just to help Duaal visualize what he needed to happen.

"*Ka li'ae avael!*" he said.

Red light smoldered sullenly for a moment in the misty afternoon, faltering and fading.

They were just symbols. Duaal concentrated and fire blazed out in a widening ring. The flames drove the Nihilists back, shouting and swatting at their burning robes. Duaal jumped to his feet and pressed forward again.

Gavriel stood haloed in the circle of the Waygate, hands raised over his head. His expression was exultant, victorious as he sang his stolen song. Xartasia stood at his side, a long-bladed glass dagger in her hand. She watched over Gavriel, like Maeve must have guarded her brother so many times. All around them, the lights of the Waygate swirled and pulsed.

Duaal felt Gavriel's magic echoing painfully back along his own thoughts, resonating like a plucked string. The boy dove under a clumsy punch from a stout Axial, and then he was on the oversized white stairs of the Waygate.

"*Na illya ma'naari su!*" Duaal sang out.

Xartasia's eyes snapped from Gavriel to Duaal and she held the glass knife out, singing a short counter-charm. The crooked line of electricity changed direction and arced into the ravine wall. Stone popped with a sharp retort and flung granite into the air. Distracted by the crack of lightning and the shower of rocks, Gavriel turned away from the Waygate, interrupting his spell.

For a moment, the entire ravine went still. And then the Waygate blazed with light. The pale colors flowing over the segmented ring turned suddenly an angry, fiery red and the Waygate hummed like a tuning fork. The note rose deafeningly, then broke and shattered into booming words.

"*T'sachka! Klova min hotek szo. Kreng vizizt gzdan k'mella. T'sachka, t'sachka! Klova min hotek szo. Kreng vizizt gzdan k'mella.*"

The voice was loud enough to make the mountain shiver under Duaal's feet, but it was flat and toneless. It overlapped with its own echoes and rebounded from the ravine walls. Gavriel's single eye blazed with fury.

"What are you doing, boy?" he shouted.

A dozen Nihilists turned away from the Prian cops and charged at Duaal.

"No! He's mine," Gavriel said. "You never should have stopped running from me, boy!"

The Nihilists parted, but they were't still. Black and the occasional red robe swarmed at the foot of the Waygate, locked in battle with the Prian police. The freezing wind reeked of ozone and gunpowder, heavy and metallic in Duaal's nose.

"*Ka li'ae avael!*" Gavriel sang in a voice only slightly less thunderous than that of the Waygate.

Flames filled the stairs and forced Duaal back, down to the cold, muddy ground. Gavriel descended the steps of the Waygate toward the boy as the frozen Prian wind whipped his black robes around him. Gavriel's pale, age-spotted skin was like an ancient shroud pulled over the long-dead skeleton beneath. But there was power there, confidence and certainty in every step, glowering there in his lone eye.

Xartasia stared and then spun to face the angrily pulsing Waygate. Gavriel stepped down from the final ivory stair and narrowed one eye at Duaal. The other wept red blood.

"You fled me and took my power with you," he said. "You were mine, boy. You belonged to me."

Duaal staggered back from Gavriel. He longed to say something, anything to the old man. To challenge the one who had taught him magic, who had taught him fear. Who hurt Tiberius. But Duaal's mouth was dry and every nerve in his body screamed at him to run, to get away.

Cerro was here somewhere. Wasn't it *his* job to save Prianus…?

"I'll kill you myself, boy," Gavriel said. "You deserve that much. And then I will finish what I began so long ago."

Duaal fell back another shaking step. Fear choked him and sent the whole world spinning. He was eight years old again, cowering before his master. Gavriel twisted his aged hands into the symbol for fire.

But Duaal wasn't a frightened little boy anymore.

Xia didn't think Duaal was a child... Gripper had mooned after her for years, but she chose Duaal. Xia had broken all her species' genetic purity taboos for him. Maeve was alive because of what Duaal had seen. *He* had saved her! Even Tiberius... Tiberius told Duaal to stop Gavriel. That only *he* could do it.

"*Ka li'ae imali!*" Duaal sang, the counter-spell to Gavriel's fire.

Smoke curled up around the ancient mage, but nothing more. Gavriel's long knobbed fingers spread and twisted.

"*Na illya ma'naari su!*" he chanted.

Duaal hesitated for an almost fatal instant as the air crackled. So many times he felt those same words echoing in his own skull, watching Gavriel's helpless victims writhe as the electricity seared through them.

"*Na illya ma'naari osa vue!*" Duaal answered barely in time.

He shifted the fork of blinding blue lightning away. It snapped into the wall of the ravine again, bringing down a miniature avalanche of ice and stone.

Gavriel held his ground while the rain and snow swirled around him. Flame billowed out from his hand, racing toward Duaal. The rain sizzled and the air rippled with heat. Duaal threw his hand up to shield his face from the heat as he countered again. The flame guttered and vanished into steam.

But... it hadn't just vanished, Duaal thought. Nothing just disappeared. The words to the song were *steal the fire's breath*. Breath. His spell removed the oxygen that fire needed to burn. Magic had rules, Panna said. Rules Duaal could understand.

Above, Xartasia stood with her wings and arms raised imploringly toward the portal. The Waygate's terrible voice came again.

"*Szo ghemma b'ho leng. Szo ghemma b'ho leng. Hotek mev khavvna tek vommen.*"

The flashing, swirling Waygate ring was no longer empty. Something dark moved in the vortex of light. Roiling black shadows were seeping out, low to the ground, like a heavy smoke.

"Lord Gavriel!" Xartasia called triumphantly. "The Devourers come!"

"What?" Duaal asked.

But he had interrupted the opening spell. Had Xartasia somehow completed it? No, only Maeve and Gavriel knew how. That was the whole point of the Cult of Nihil's work in Pylos. What the hells had happened?

The cultists abandoned their attack on the Prian cops and fell to their knees in the red-churned mud. Confused, the police lowered their weapons and began making arrests. The Nihilists didn't even seem to notice. Gavriel didn't turn his back on Duaal, either, but grinned like a child at the fair.

"It is done!" he shouted. "At long, long last..."

"No!" Duaal cried.

All around them, the Nihilists stared up at the growing shadows oozing from the Waygate. Even the police were still now, watching. A soft, sad song rose from the Arcadians. Loss and pain, all about to be ended...

"No, it's not over yet," Duaal said. He ran at Gavriel, singing and flinging fire. "We're not finished with this!"

Gavriel waved the flames aside, still smiling. "Death is coming through that door for you, boy. Yet you insist on meeting it early! Very well, I will give you oblivion."

He raised his fingers over his eyes like a spidery mask and sang in a powerful baritone.

"Anu'aa quai eru oraiva'i na!"

Gavriel was done playing games. Duaal twitched as the charge built in his brain, the electric spark that would trigger an aneurysm and kill him instantly. Duaal had only a fraction of a second, not nearly enough time to sing a counter-spell.

But the words... They were just symbols, too. Just a way for the Arcadians to create the memories, the thoughts that they needed.

Tools, symbols... No more necessary than the hand gestures or the arcanery Duaal used to wear.

With a thought, Duaal *pushed* and Gavriel's deadly spell discharged well short of its target, no more than a green zap of static. It was... easy.

Gavriel's eyes went wide in his lined face. He tried again, calling for fire and lightning and blinding light. But Duaal knew all of the old man's spells, all of those terrible songs that consumed the boy's mind years ago.

Sweating but silent, Duaal sucked all the air out of the billowing fireballs, grounded the lightning into the stone, soothed his nerves before Gavriel could finish the charm that set them ablaze with crippling pain. Gavriel grimaced with concentration.

Those were all the magic Gavriel knew. The spells that Xartasia taught him, the songs composed by the Arcadians thousands of years ago. Whatever trick Xartasia used to give Gavriel the clarity of mind, that blank screen upon which a mage could write their will... Gavriel still knew only the spells that she could teach him.

But magic could do so, so much more than this handful of rote charms. Duaal didn't know the words in Arcadian or even Aver to describe what he wanted, but he found that he could simply *see* it. Just as Panna said...

Duaal pointed at Gavriel. It was no more necessary than words or a song, but it felt good to level his finger at the old nightmare.

There you are, Gavriel. You're not a monster in the darkness, just a broken man singing in the rain.

The falling rain began to bead up on Gavriel's shoulders. The drops of water grew, merging and pooling across his sodden black robes. He raised his hands, splaying his fingers to rupture Duaal's brain once more, and saw the water along his sleeves. A wet film was building up, stubbornly refusing to soak in or run off as it was supposed to.

"What is this?" Gavriel asked.

He shook his arm and a few drops of water scattered into the air, but the surface tension held. The cloak of water grew thicker and heavier. Gavriel tried to sing out his spell, but Duaal sent the water flowing over the old man's face.

Gavriel choked and spluttered, his spell forgotten. He tried to swipe the water away, but couldn't raise his arms against its growing weight. The rain dragged Gavriel to his knees, unable to move in his liquid prison. Duaal stood over his old master.

I... I did it. I beat him...!

A pale blur of motion made Duaal look up. No longer singing in her vain attempt to control the Waygate, Xartasia had taken wing and landed behind Gavriel. She still held her glass dagger in one white-gloved hand.

Duaal shoved wet hair out of his face, ready to fight her, too. But Xartasia smiled dazzlingly as she slid the knife through the water and between Gavriel's ribs.

Shocked, Duaal lost control of his spell. The water broke and red-stained rain splashed down around Gavriel's feet. The old man tried to draw a breath to speak, but blood poured from his mouth and the only sound he managed was a strangled gasp.

"You wished so long for death, Gavriel," Xartasia said. "You have served your purpose. Now go."

Gavriel's body fell to the ground. Duaal stared, full of impossible questions, but Xartasia's unexpected betrayal wasn't the most important thing going on in the ravine.

Inky smoke had entirely obscured the Waygate and was now crawling in indistinct tendrils down the sides of the ziggurat. And then *something* stepped through the Waygate.

It was taller than even the biggest Hadrian that Duaal had ever seen, towering high over the mage. The thing had long legs and arms – two of each, like the Alliance species – but any other details were obscured by the faintly glittering black smoke that clung to the figure like clouds shrouding a mountain peak.

Every eye was on the blurry black shape as it slowly descended the white stairs and then stood wavering at the edge of the crowd. It raised one long, smoky black arm as though to greet the Nihilists, and then the darkness congealed into ebony claws. Without a word, the Devourer grabbed the closest cultist and sheared his arms off. Blood spurted up through the air and vanished into the midnight mist surrounding the alien creature.

The Nihilists' ecstatic moans turned into primal screams. The death that the Nihilists had waited for so long to greet, as eager as expectant lovers, had finally arrived... and it was terrible. More of the huge bipedal shapes surged from the Waygate. Smoke-turned-metal snaked out, sinking long spikes and barbed hooks into flesh, pulling the Nihilists into the spreading darkness. Duaal was desperately grateful that their gruesome deaths were hidden in the swirling black smoke.

"Don't just stand there!" he shouted to Cerro. "The Devourers are coming for Prianus!"

The cop bled from a dozen shallow wounds and stared up at the Devourers. But he shook himself and raised his gun.

"You heard him," Cerro called out. "You know your job and you do it here, now! These things don't go any further!"

The Prian police opened fire, pouring lead and lasers into the closest Devourer. The cloud swirled and hardened into something that looked like obsidian, but none of their weapons seemed to affect the great black monster at all.

"*Aercaidae a'na, ellu la wexalli! Marnavae eru sha'narii bae!*" Xartasia sang across the ravine. *My Arcadians, stand back from the aliens! Let them die first!*

All across the ravine, fairies spread their wings and took to the air, rising up into the rain. A dozen Devourers swarmed out through the ruined camp, grabbing Nihilists and police alike in claws and hooks. The crevasse was full of screams, but no blood or other gore. The Devourers left no remains.

Duaal fell swiftly back, but he slipped in a puddle and fell to the wet ground. Something hooked under his arms and pulled, but before he could lash out with summoned lightning or fire or anything else, he recognized Cerro's scarred face.

The police officer dragged Duaal back behind one of the tailings piles. There were only eight cops left. Duaal recognized the woman with the eyepatch he had seen in Pylos only days before. She cradled a bundle of feathers and blood to her chest. Tears ran from her intact eye.

"It won't take those Devourers long to finish this," Cerro panted.

He pointed back toward the Waygate, where the smoky monsters were still tearing apart kneeling and fleeing Nihilists. Cerro grabbed Duaal's shoulder.

"We don't have mainstream access down here," he said. "I need you to get up to the surface and call the station. Tell them what's happened. We'll hold this position, but it won't be for long."

Cerro was right. The screams of the Nihilists were rising up into a frenzied crescendo, but even that was beginning to fade out as they died. Two of the Devourers that had come through the Waygate were striding out into the ravine. Xartasia and many of the Arcadians perched high on the stony walls. The princess' eyes were wide, but she didn't look frightened. Her lips moved, but over the wind and screaming and the thundering voice of the Waygate, Duaal couldn't hear a word.

The black cloud that surrounded the Devourers billowed outward, rushing toward the Prian cops. The one-eyed officer dropped the corpse of her hawk and aimed her Talon. Her shots bit into the leading edge of the Devourer's fog, but merely struck deep black patches of smooth metal that vanished as quickly as they appeared. The strange smoke coiled into long tendrils, tipped with all-too-solid-looking blades.

The Devourer's smoky shroud wasn't limited to blades, though. Cylinders extended from the cloud, each as thick as Duaal's wrist.

Lasers burned out from them and swept the rocky heaps where the police took cover. Duaal threw himself to the ground.

When he lifted his face slowly out of the mud, the cop still knelt behind the tailings, both hands bracing her Talon, but her head was gone. Her blood sizzled and boiled as it dribbled through her cauterized jugular. Barbed obsidian hooks snapped out from the Devourer and yanked the still-twitching body away. Bones cracked and there were wet, tearing sounds.

"Get out of here!" Cerro bellowed. "Move!"

Duaal turned and ran again as Cerro and his remaining officers unloaded their guns into the Devourers. The alien monsters' own weapons answered loudly.

Duaal didn't look back, but bolted as fast as he could for the end of the ravine. The ladder hung precariously from the upper ledge, half dislodged by a stray shot. Duaal didn't like the idea of trying to climb it. If it didn't just fall off the wall, he would still make a slow-moving and exposed target for the Devourers. If only he could fly.

And why not...? We're all flying through space on the surface of this planet anyway. Just... forget the gravity for a moment, the force that holds me down to the ground.

Duaal jumped. The ground fell away, rose steeply and then he was landing on the top of the crevasse.

[36]

RED AND BLACK

"Inaction is itself a sort of action – a coward's action."

- DUAAL SINNAY, HYZAARI MAGE (233 PA)

Logan stood with his back against Maeve's soft wings. There were Nihilists everywhere, confused and frightened. Some were fleeing, others were fighting. He spun and thrust a kick into one charging cultist. Logan stepped aside to clear the path for Maeve's spear. It thrust under the man's ribs and withdrew as quickly as a striking snake.

A new shape vaulted up out of the ravine. But when he brought his Talon around, Logan found Duaal alighting on the wet stone, smeared with mud.

"Duaal? You... flew?" Maeve asked.

"It doesn't matter," the boy panted. "None of it matters now! I stopped Gavriel and... and Xartasia killed him! But the Devourers came through the Waygate anyway. Maeve, the Devourers are here!"

The inexorable voice of the Waygate still boomed across the mountain, a cold alien pronouncement of death. *"Szo ghemma b'ho leng. Hotek mev khavvna tek vommen."*

That wasn't Aver or any other language Logan had ever heard. The words meant nothing to him, but it did to Maeve. She turned away from the horror-struck Duaal with silver-gray eyes wide and full of tears.

"I have failed," Maeve said in a choked voice. "The Devourers have come again and they will tear the Alliance apart."

Logan could barely hear her over the shouts and shots, but he could read her lips and the despair on her face. He knew the story well enough to know what that meant, and Maeve well enough to know that she would go down fighting. Logan's fingers tightened on the grip of his gun. No, she would not die and he wouldn't make her watch another civilization fall. He grabbed Maeve's shoulder and made her look at him.

"These things *can* be killed, can't they?" he asked.

"Yes," Maeve answered. "But it is difficult. Orthain fought many, but killed only two. Even their own bodies do not remain after death, so we could never discover any frailty–"

A scream and a bolt of red laserfire sliced up from the Waygate ravine, cutting Maeve off. The Nihilists remaining on the surface were either fleeing in horror at the carnage below or flinging themselves over the edge, arms spread wide to embrace their death. Those who tried to run were not getting very far. The Devourers were fast, efficient and... Logan squinted down into the mist. Led by Xartasia, the Arcadian Nihilists were intercepting their coreworlder companions and pushing them back toward the Devourers.

Logan released Maeve's shoulder. The Raptor hunkered on the mountainside, cleaned of snow by the rain, and he ran toward it. Three Nihilists surrounded the ship, shouting and pulling at something underneath.

"The end has come!" laughed a man with ash on his face. "Time to go!"

Logan's shot burned through his shoulder from behind. The other two cultists – a scarred Hadrian and a Mirran with tattooed stripes – turned toward him and brandished their weapons. With a sing-song cry, Maeve fell on them from above like an avenging angel. Her glass spear-point slid into the neck of the Hadrian as her feet came down on the Mirran beside them. The force of her landing drove the Nihilist to their knees. She pulled her spear free of the Hadrian and leapt into the air once more. As Maeve landed, she slashed her spear through the kneeling Mirran's throat.

Even injured and drugged, Maeve moved with speed and grace. Logan felt a smile tug at the corners of his mouth. She was small, but so fierce. The fairy made something inside Logan blaze just like the Waygate, and it was no less dangerous. It was confusing, but he couldn't afford to be confused right now.

"What the hells took you so long?" growled a voice from under the Raptor.

Logan brought up his Talon and Maeve leveled her spear. Gruth crawled out from underneath the ship, dragging his blood-smeared leg behind him. Duaal ran over and held out his hand.

"What happened up here?" he asked.

"Up here...? What the hells is going on down *there*? What's all that noise about?" Gruth asked. He snarled and spat on one of the Nihilist corpses. "Where's Tiberius? He was supposed to come get this ugly thing!"

Logan ignored Gruth and climbed up onto the metal wing, then pried open the cockpit. The printlock wasn't working, but Logan jumped down into the pilot's seat.

"What are you doing?" Duaal asked.

"Taking off," Logan said. "Get out of the way."

He toggled a row of switches and the engines began cycling up. There was no time for a full pre-flight check, but he made sure that Gruth's tinkering hadn't taken down any of the Raptor's weapons. Logan would need those.

Gruth was trying to rise on his wounded leg. Duaal helped him stand and pointed to one of the police vans.

"We need to get you in there, with Panna and Xia," Duaal said. "They can help you. Once you're inside the van, radio down to the Pylos police. Tell them what's going on here and then get off the mountain!"

Maeve was watching Logan. He grabbed the interior handle of the canopy and yanked it down, sealing the cockpit. He pulled up on the stick and the Raptor rose steeply.

The mountain fell away beneath Logan, acceleration pressing him back into the seat. He yanked the Long Wings release handle and the Raptor surged into the sky as the weight of the extra engines fell away. The pod slammed into the rocky ground below and crumpled like a fizz can. At the peak of his climb, Logan rolled the Raptor over and let the nose fall.

The whole ravine looked as though it was burning, black smoke crawling unnaturally along the broken stone. Coldhand tightened his fingers on the triggers. Lasers swept the mouth of the narrow canyon, raking the smoke and whatever it concealed. The shots flashed as they hit something, sparking off of solid metal. The smoke was pulling inward, darkening and thickening. And then the lasers burned through whatever it was and the strange black clouds drifted apart like true smoke.

Maeve was right. These Devourers were tough and strong, but not invincible.

Logan dropped his Raptor into the ravine. He had to see what he was shooting, or else his weapon batteries were going to give out. Proximity indicators lit up a warning orange as his fighter slipped between the narrow fissure walls. Coldhand yawed the ship to one side to avoid an outcropping of stone, then pulled back hard as he grazed the ravine floor and came to a hovering stop.

The canyon was choked by black mist. It smoldered in a dozen individual clouds, roiling and churning, but never dispersing. The Devourers had noticed Logan's Raptor and were forming up into ranks. The huge Waygate rose over the sea of churning black fog, shining brightly in comparison. The lambent stones of the ring pulsed with angry red light in time with the voice ringing off of the ravine's walls.

"Szo ghemma b'ho leng. Hotek mev khavvna tek vommen."

Where were the bodies? There had been more than a hundred people down there. The Raptor's floodlight illuminated a Devourer tearing apart a body in the remains of a blue uniform with a pair of barbed hooks. A badge winked in the fragile light before it, too, was consumed – *Captain Cerro.*

A hot red laser beam fired up from one of the deep black clouds surrounding a towering Devourer and struck the underside of the Raptor. Logan rolled the fighter away before it could burn through the armor. When the Raptor leveled out, he flipped up the safeties on the missiles and jabbed his thumb down on the button. A flock of missiles sped from the launchers like angry falcons. The warheads fanned out and detonated around the foot of the Waygate. The concussion rebounded from the walls of the canyon, buffeting the Raptor. Logan held the fighter steady and fired another volley of missiles.

The Devourers' shrouds contracted into smaller black bubbles as the missiles exploded. Columns of true smoke began to rise from the cratered ravine floor and lasers flashed up to answer him. Logan held down the trigger of the Raptor's own lasers and raked them across the Devourers below.

The police fighter shook as it reached the side of the ravine and the wing impacted the rocky wall. Logan ignored the Raptor's shrill warnings and centered the targeting reticule on the Waygate. If he could destroy the gate, he could stop the Devourers from coming through. The missile launchers were nearly empty, but he intended to put the Waygate's invulnerability to the test.

Maeve covered Duaal as he helped Gruth limp down the slope to the van. The rain and fog were closing in again, turning the mountain into a nightmare island floating high over Prianus. Arcadians moved through the mist like ghosts, silent now. Maeve thought she saw Xartasia and called out, but the indistinct shape paid no attention and slid away, out of sight.

"Do you think Logan can destroy the Devourers and the Waygate?" Duaal asked.

"No," Maeve said.

The Waygates were millions of years old and had weathered the ages without a mark. Maeve doubted that even coreworld weapons could do much to the great monument. Duaal's lower lip trembled, but he nodded resolutely.

"Fine," he said. "So what can we do?"

"Logan will fight fiercely." Maeve gripped her spear so hard that her fingers trembled. Her hunter was down there alone with the Devourers. "I need to take advantage of the time that his weaponry will buy us. I must take control of the Waygate and close it."

"Like in Tamlin," Duaal said. "Hurry, Maeve."

Something cracked and thundered down in the ravine. Lasers whined and then Maeve heard the deeper, harder impacts of larger weapons. She ran to the edge of the ravine and jumped, spreading her wings and diving down. Her tattered clothes flapped against her cold, wet skin. Not for the first time, Maeve was grateful for Xia's medicines. There would be time for pain later, if anyone survived this.

Logan's Raptor shook again and sheered to the side, away from the wall. Something impacted hard against one wing and a long-limbed Devourer clung to the fibersteel. Logan couldn't see the alien's face – only more swirling, stormy black smoke.

He fought to keep the Raptor level as the cloud swelled and a pseudopod rose up. The smoke condensed into a dark metal axe and crashed down against the canopy. The glassteel cracked and Logan threw his cybernetic arm up to shield his face. The Devourer punched another hole into the Raptor's canopy and yanked, tearing the whole thing away.

Coldhand pulled his Talon-9 from its holster and fired at the thing's head. The cloud did its armoring trick again, presenting a solid shield. Logan's laser threw sparks from the black as it burned. He tried shooting around the edge of the hardened darkness, but the solidified cloud followed his fire.

It reacted to everything that Logan did, anticipating his attacks and responding. The Devourer's black smoke had to be some kind of nanomachinery. Like cleaning nanites swarming over a fresh stain, the cloud was always moving toward the next problem, the next threat. It made sense... The armor did look for all the worlds like smoke and one hundred years ago, the Arcadians of the White Kingdom had no knowledge of the tiny machines. They would have had no idea what they were fighting.

The glittering black nanite cloud was capable of much more than protection. The Devourer created a long tentacle, tipped in a sharp blade that rippled with oily, barely visible color up and down its length.

Just like Hallax's nanosword.

The tentacle slithered into the cockpit and Logan tried to dodge out of the way, but his harness held him in place. The Devourer slashed his shoulder and then buried itself deep in the seat back. The blade dissolved into a cloud and retreated, only to be replaced by another, poised to strike.

The Raptor was listing dangerously to the side, grinding the left wing hard against the ravine wall. Logan held down the trigger of his Talon-9, hoping a sustained burn could overwhelm the nanite cloud. The sharpened arm rose and aimed at Logan's heart.

A white-winged shape dove into the ravine and pounced on the Devourer. The inky cloud of nanites had pulled forward to deal with Logan and the Raptor, leaving the back only thinly protected. Maeve thrust her glass spear into the Devourer. Very familiar red blood splashed the wing of the Raptor and the Devourer turned to face the Arcadian, bladed armor coiled to strike.

Logan yanked the control stick and rolled the Raptor dizzyingly. Maeve and the Devourer slid along the wing and toppled down into the ravine. The Devourer plummeted to the ground and was swallowed by the black clouds of the other monsters as they spread out from the steps of the Waygate.

Maeve tumbled head over heels and Logan's heart skipped a beat. Then her wings unfurled and she swooped back up into the air, chased by barbed black hooks and searing lasers. Logan piloted the Raptor beneath Maeve as she soared past, placing himself between the princess and the Devourers. Their nanite clouds ripped into his armor plating and the instrument panels began to flicker red. One of the engines exploded. He fought to keep the Raptor aloft, but he was sinking beak-first toward the rocks.

Logan pulled the ejection handle. This low and in the narrow, rocky confines of the ravine, he would probably bounce off the walls and kill himself, but it was better than just letting himself fall into the nebulous black hands of the monsters below. The explosive bolts fired, but the Devourer had done too much damage. The seat whined and would not budge.

His Raptor continued its dying downward spiral, trembling as the Devourers fired into it again and again. Logan ripped the harness open and climbed laboriously to his feet. What now?

"Logan!"

The bounty hunter looked up at the sound of his name. Maeve dove at the Raptor again. Her spear was gone and her arms were open. The fairy touched down briefly on the edge of the cockpit, wrapped her arms around Logan's waist and then jumped.

———— • • • ————

Xia's medicine wasn't *that* good. Maeve groaned as she struggled to rise. Logan was laying on one of her wings. The bounty hunter was heavy, even for a human, and his metal hand dug into the sensitive skin of her back.

They had crash-landed to one side of the Waygate, just a wing-span away from the ravine's wall. The Raptor had crashed into the rock on the other side of the Waygate. Logan's fighter was a crumpled, torn pile of smoldering wreckage. Two Devourers jumped over the twisted metal and loped toward Maeve and Logan in long, easy strides.

Maeve shoved at Logan, but the bounty hunter's blond hair was streaked with blood and his eyes were shut. He had hit his head, but was still breathing.

"Logan! Wake up," she shouted. "I need you!"

The Prian's blue eyes fluttered and then snapped open. Maeve and Logan pulled themselves up as the Devourers stalked closer.

"I must close the Waygate," Maeve said. She looked up at Logan. "It will take all of my concentration."

"I'll cover you," her hunter promised. He wiped the blood out of his eyes.

Logan grabbed his Talon off the ground nearby and dashed with Maeve for the stairs of the Waygate. The steps vibrated under their feet as they climbed and the warning voice of the Waygate here was so loud that Maeve's ears ached.

"Szo ghemma b'ho leng. Hotek mev khavvna tek vommen."

Behind them, the Devourers broke into a loping run. Maeve's legs were heavy and tired. They were shorter than Logan's, too, and she tripped as she struggled to keep up. The hunter hooked his arm around her waist and helped her scale the oversized stairs, but the Devourers were closing quickly. They were tall enough to climb the stairs easily. Logan shoved Maeve away.

"Fly, Maeve. Go stop this," he told her. "I'll hold these things off until it's done."

Maeve spread her bruised and battered wings as Logan turned to face the Devourers. For a moment, he looked just like Orthain, shoulders squared against the faceless black demons coming for him and golden hair glinting in the fitful light as Maeve flew away. What had she ever done to earn the loyalty of such men...?

Maeve landed on top of the ziggurat. The Waygate yawned open before her. The sectioned ring was full of shadows and flashing red light, but she could see nothing beyond. How many Devourers had come through? No matter the answer, Maeve had little time. She felt it pressing in on her like a lead weight.

Gavriel hadn't finished even Maeve's botched spell. Could she close the Pylos Waygate the same way she had the one on Tamlin? Maybe not... but Maeve had no other ideas. She raised her dirty, shaking hands to the huge ring of burning light.

"No!"

In a swirl of angelic white, Xartasia landed in front of Maeve, holding a slim glass dagger with blood still bright red on the blade. Xartasia spun, dancing close, and sliced her blade against the inside of Maeve's wing. She took to the air again and landed on top of the Waygate.

Maeve tried to follow her cousin, but her injured wing buckled and would not bear her weight. She was confined to the ground, like any coreworlder. It was humiliating, but there was still work to do. Maeve turned back toward the Waygate and raised her hands again. From on high, Xartasia called out to her.

"Turn away, Maeve," she said in a ringing voice. "What I have done today, I have done for our home and our people. For Arcadia. Do not fight me!"

"You have told me that before, as Gavriel tortured me!" Maeve shouted. "You would have me lie down and die while you sew ruin through the stars!"

"Not ruin," Xartasia said, "but rebirth!"

Maeve couldn't listen anymore. There wasn't time. So she closed her eyes and struggled to recall the words she had sung a hundred years ago to seal the Tamlin Waygate. As Orthain fought, just like Logan did now. Yes, she remembered...

"*Ai'ae anna cellia bahn, senna eru vaen'na denno selequa'an...*" Maeve began.

Her voice was rough and cracked, but a sweet song didn't matter now. The Waygate seemed to hesitate. The ember light faded to a cautious orange.

"*Szo ghemma b'ho leng... leng... Leng zhoka,*" intoned the loud alien voice.

An impossible hope caught in Maeve's throat. She forced herself to continue singing. "*...Ellu oi'va scaeden sen eru'ma–*"

On her pinnacle perch, Xartasia spread her wings and began to sing, too. "*Alluna s'aelim wain'ii mae shassa keth am'avain!*"

Her song reverberated with certain authority as Xartasia fought to keep the Waygate open. The portal burned hellfire red again and throbbed with darkness.

"*Scennu varii lae ellu'da eira sessar,*" she sang. "*Qu'ii laess lai jaisha dii aes'ii soshin mae!*"

"*Aelex ferro mennal'ae. Aetrix dumma'ii!*" Maeve shouted back.

Xartasia slashed through the air with her glass dagger. "*Laennal emanuu shoda'aev ailina latam. Aetrix sumanni eleo ana va'an!*"

The Pylos Waygate glowered like an angry, sleepless eye.

Logan checked the charge on his Talon-9, ejected the battery and slapped in a new one. He had only one more, and then the hunter was down to his bare hands.

He could pick out individual Devourers now. The cloudy edges of their nanite armor overlapped and turned the aliens into a single seething mass... but it shifted in distinct patterns, with each swarm following the movements of single creatures inside. Logan counted sixteen Devourers remaining in the ravine. He could hear Maeve and Xartasia's warring songs at the apex of the Waygate. While they were battling for control, at least, nothing more seemed to be coming through. But if Xartasia won, how many more Devourers would descend on Prianus?

Five of the nightmares were charging the Waygate now. Maeve needed Logan to protect her while she sang. She *needed* him... It was a sweet, painful thought, but there was no time to wonder at it. The Devourers were on him.

The first one up the stairs stabbed a sharp tendril at him, black nanite cloud coalescing at the last moment into a wickedly curved blade. Logan threw himself against the banister. The nanite sword glanced off the edge of the step, actually slicing a deep wedge into what had seemed to be impenetrable white material.

The Devourers certainly possessed and knew how to use lasers, but they seemed to favor bladed or hooked melee weapons, Logan noted clinically. If they were eating the dead, maybe the Devourers didn't want to burn away any more flesh than they had to. It wasn't much, but it was something. Logan could stand up against swords a little longer than lasers.

He took aim at one of the Devourers and fired. Its nanite cloud reacted at once, condensing into a shield just like the one that had attacked him in the Raptor. More shots at the same target met with the same resistance. The hand-held Talon-9 wasn't as powerful as the Raptor's mounted lasers. By the time Logan could thin out the nanite cloud enough to score a meaningful hit, the others would be tearing Maeve apart.

So Logan changed tactics, shooting at the Devourer's wide chest instead of the smaller, more defensible head. But in mere fractions of a second, the nanites moved and hardened there, too. Whatever computer controlled the microscopic machines swiftly picked up on Logan's firing pattern and anticipated him, presenting a shield for each target even as he aimed.

The Devourers were closing in and Logan had to give ground, climbing up another tall step. There were four of them in range now, all reaching for the hunter. He held down the Talon's trigger and raked a hot line of red light across their indistinct bodies. The nanites hardened to take the fire and the Devourers didn't slow.

There was no room. If Logan stayed on the stairs, he was going to die. And then who would protect Maeve? Logan jumped and scrambled up onto the wide white balustrade, then leapt over a slice from an obsidian sword. The blade lengthened and arced after Logan as he slid down the wet, steep incline. He fired as he went, burning into the nanite armor over and over again. He had to keep their interest off of Maeve.

At the bottom of the stairs, the wreckage of his Raptor was still smoking. As Logan bolted away from the Devourers, they opened fire with their own lasers. Logan dove behind his crashed ship. It would never fly again, but at least its thick armor was still useful.

More of the Devourers took note of the scuffle at the foot of the Waygate. Nine... no, ten of the huge, dark aliens charged at Logan now. If he was going to keep them away from Maeve, he needed to figure out a way through the nanite armor.

The bounty hunter dashed out from behind cover and emptied the last of the Talon-9's battery into the encroaching Devourers. He aimed high, for the blurry lumps of their heads. One, two, three long burns and still it wasn't enough to get through.

The Devourers answered with a blazing inferno of return shots. Logan dove back behind the Raptor. The engines were designed to shut down when they had suffered this kind of damage and probably wouldn't explode. The heat had melted the last of the snow, though, and left bare, steaming stone.

Logan ejected the battery from his Talon-9 and then loaded his last one. As soon as the indicator glowed green again, Logan leaned over the Raptor's broken wings and opened fire on the Devourers again. They had closed most of the distance to the fighter's smoking wreckage and now sliced at the metal with sharp nanite weapons again.

The Devourers couldn't be operating the vast nanite swarms themselves. There were too many of the tiny machines. They had to be receiving instructions from a computer. As fast as Logan was, he wasn't faster than a computer... But computers were also stupid. They would analyze Logan's shots, predicting where the next ones would go and thickening the dark armor accordingly.

He shifted his aim, firing into the Devourer's cloud at random. They were clumsy shots, but chaotic enough to confuse the computers, making them hesitate. The Devourer howled in pain as one of Logan's shots struck. The black cloud pulled inwards and a dark patch covered the Devourer's leg where he had hit it. Administering medical attention? That meant fewer nanites dedicated to defense.

Logan poured laserfire into the black mass, always changing his target. The glittering nanites swirled in confusion, unable to calculate the Prian's pattern. The Devourer staggered and fell into the melting snow with a loud thump. The last wisps of smoky nanites swarmed furiously around the body. The corpse folded and shrank as the Devourer's own armor consumed it, leaving behind nothing but a greasy-looking smear on the ground.

The rest of the Devourers hissed in fury. They were all coming for Logan now.

The bounty hunter squinted. The cut on his scalp was sheeting blood again. Rather than fan out and surround him, the Devourers remained close together, their ashy armor reinforcing one another, but there were enough of them to circle Logan, and the ring was closing fast.

Even the overlapping black nanite clouds didn't seem to help their computers understand Logan's randomized attacks. A second Devourer fell and vanished, consumed by its own armor.

Two of the towering monsters spared nanites enough to create long, thin spears and jabbed them at Logan. He burned through one of them with a wide shot from his Talon, but the other needled through his pants, grazed the flesh beneath and pinned Logan against his Raptor.

Another giant of shadow was suddenly swinging a huge broadsword with a hooked tip. The Devourer spun and sliced at Logan. He threw himself down to the ground with a grunt, but his leg was still pinned and twisted awkwardly. The huge nanite sword missed, dissolved and formed again.

Logan struggled to rise, but could not get his feet under him. He splayed awkwardly on his back and held down the Talon's trigger. He would buy Maeve every second he could.

Sweat streamed down the back of Maeve's neck. She was getting sleepy, as Xia warned she might. A soft, heavy weight tugged at her, urging her to lie down. To just... stop. To stop fighting. Her eyelids drifted down and her song faltered.

Something hissed and there was a sharp crackle. Maeve jerked again as a Devourer reached for her from deep inside the Waygate. She jumped back and fumbled for the words of the closing charm.

"Aetrix dumma'ii!" she cried. *"Ma'an ae sua'nii vanni la shannoel vellius en assai!"*

The Waygate shivered again and the Devourer vanished into the hollow darkness of the huge ring, unable to pass through. Maeve was barring the door... but she couldn't seal it, not with Xartasia perched gloriously on high and crooning her own song. They were locked in a magical stalemate. At least until Maeve's already faltering strength finally failed her.

Logan was already doing all he could, more than she ever would have asked of him. Down below, the bounty hunter had his back against the ruins of his fighter and was surrounded by Devourers, each twice the Prian's not insignificant size. If he was to die, Maeve could at least ensure that his sacrifice wasn't in vain.

"A'allu sa–" She broke off the song suddenly, took a deep, cold breath and shouted. "Duaal! Help me!"

Duaal stood alone in the cloudy gray of the mountaintop, waiting. Waiting for salvation or damnation. It could only have been a few minutes since Maeve and Logan vanished into the ravine, but it seemed like an eternity.

Wind tugged at his torn and bloodstained coat, making it flutter behind him like the tattered banner in a losing war. The Waygate's deafening call filled his ears. It was alien, but Duaal didn't have to understand the words to know the message. Something was terribly wrong. The monotone thunder had faltered once, but not for long and resumed only seconds later.

But now... Duaal thought he heard his name. He squinted back down the rain-filled moraine, but no one was there. As he had told her to, Panna was driving the police van down the mountain, back toward Pylos. But there it was again. Duaal could *just* hear a frantic voice calling up from the red-lit fissure. It was Maeve, screaming for his help.

Duaal ran to the ravine's crumbling edge. It was full of seething smoke and flashing red light. The sharp-salty smell of blood filled Duaal's nose and he could just make out the tall, impossibly dark and shifting shapes of Devourers below. If he went down there... Duaal shuddered.

But Maeve would never ask for his help unless there was nothing else to be done. Duaal squinted through the gloom. There! He spotted a pair of white-winged figures at the Waygate – one dressed in perfect ivory and the other in tattered rags.

Duaal jumped. It was far easier to lighten gravity's touch than to completely ignore it. The mage fell through the crimson-lit smoke and landed lightly beside Maeve. Xartasia balanced lightly on the uppermost curve of the Waygate ring and stared at Duaal. Her song faltered, but Xartasia was too confident and too regal to be shaken for long.

Huge, angry shapes strained to push through the Waygate, but the portal was stuck halfway between open and closed. The vaguely humanoid shapes shoved and swirled like ink in a glass.

Maeve's already white skin was the color of ash on snow. She trembled and one of her wings was spattered in red. Her song was breathless and shook even harder than her body. Maeve turned her bloodshot gray eyes on Duaal.

"Help me..." she gasped between snatches of song, so quickly that Duaal almost couldn't catch the words. "*Su vaenna emmai'i* – Xartasia knows my spell too well – *Illuna mae kennuva eru fen* – She counters me too easily! *Hae enna ma jullen aetra'am'ii.*"

Metal clanged in a flat tone like a hellish gong. Below, Logan Coldhand was on the ground, his leg twisted up against the side of his smoking Raptor. He had parried aside a killing blow from one Devourer with his cybernetic hand and the black sword gouged a deep, rough furrow in the Raptor's hull. Coldhand answered with a bright bolt from his Talon-9 that drove the Devourer back, but two more closed in.

Logan couldn't hold out for much longer. The Devourers knew it, and a single human man – especially one full of metal – wasn't going to make much of a meal, Duaal guessed. Several of the black shapes separated themselves from the ring and billowed across the ravine, toward the Waygate. Maeve saw them and let out a low, raw moan of sorrow.

Xartasia sang. Her sweet voice cut through all other sound, as sharp as the dagger in her hand. She held the blade up, as though signaling the coming Devourers.

"You keep Xartasia fighting for control," Duaal told Maeve. "I'll close the Waygate."

The mage tried to sound brave, but his voice cracked. The Devourers were halfway up the stairs and would be on them soon.

Maeve nodded, still singing. Logan's Talon shrilled again, and then there was a snarl of pain from the bounty hunter. Tears rolled down Maeve's cheeks, joining the sweat and soaking the black hair plastered against her skin.

Duaal stared up at the glowing Waygate. It was... immense. Not just in size. He stood before a hole in the universe, connecting this mountain to... to wherever the Devourers were. This Waygate, this gap in space meant that distance was just an illusion, or at least a rule that could be bent and broken. The distance that separated Arcadia from the Alliance, Prianus from the deep core... None of that meant anything.

The Devourers had reached the top of the white stairs. Duaal heard Maeve's scream and felt the cold shadow of one of the monsters looming over him. He heard the grinding, buzzing sound of the black cloud reaching for him. So close... but even that distance was an illusion.

What was distance? The space between one atom and the next. But what did distance matter? Duaal found himself smiling. Had he lost his mind? But Maeve and Logan... Even when he had stopped hunting her, even when an entire galaxy separated them, they still found each other again.

Maeve was no longer singing as she fought for her life against a Devourer that had wrapped her in rattling chains. Xartasia's clear voice crescendoed in triumph as the Waygate rang and seethed, wreathed in scarlet light. The barrier was gone and the Devourers surged through again, a ravenous black storm of death that would rage across the whole galaxy.

A pair of Devourers grabbed Duaal by his outstretched arms. Claws bit painfully into his flesh and freed rivulets of blood that spattered the white ground. But Duaal didn't need his hands. He could feel the tight-strung power thrumming through the Waygate, thousands and thousands of strands of pure potential that linked the great ring to every other point in the universe. An axis, a center upon which all things could turn, if he would only give it a *push*.

Duaal closed his eyes and remembered the Waygate as it had been, slumbering in its veil of soft, pale light. Before any of this.

No more, he thought. *Go. Leave us in peace.*

And then everything stopped. The entire Waygate crevasse fell as still and silent as the void. When Duaal opened his eyes again, he was alone in the ravine with Maeve and Logan. They stared around in disbelief, amazed to still be alive.

Duaal laughed hysterically and then fell to his knees and began to cry. Tiberius had been right. He did it.

[37]

BY STARLIGHT

"Anyone who says facing your friends is worse than facing your enemies has never fought the Devourers. There is nothing more frightening. Unless, of course, the Devourers *are* your friends."

Maeve spent the next night under the watchful but often interrupted care of an overworked Prian doctor. But by the next evening, Xia moved her to the city of Pine Spire, back to the Blue Phoenix for observation. The Ixthian medic tended to Gruth, too, whose leg was still in bad shape. He would need a replacement and threatened to crawl back to Tynerion himself rather than face the prospect of a Prian cybernetic.

"I've seen that bounty hunter's hand," Gruth said. "No way."

Even with the Blue Phoenix's limited facilities – which were a little dusty from weeks of disuse – Xia was able to stabilize Gruth for the journey back to Tynerion and close the cuts in Maeve's skin. Her bones would take longer to knit, but the breaks were clean and Xia administered daily nutrient injections to help them heal faster.

Gruth spent most of his time asleep, medicated into unconsciousness against the pain of his ruined leg.

On the second morning after the battle for the Pylos Waygate, the newly promoted Captain Felsus made the journey to Pine Spire. He limped up from the skypad and into the Blue Phoenix. Panna brought him up to the mess, where Maeve, Duaal, Xia and Gripper sat around the table.

Panna took a seat across from Maeve. Her eyes were bloodshot and swollen from weeping. Duaal wasn't the only one to lose a beloved mentor. Captain Felsus' cybernetic leg whirred and clicked as he sat.

"I got my hands on the information that you were looking for," he said.

Xia was sitting beside Duaal and took his hand. She squeezed his fingers.

"Tiberius Myles had no will here on Prianus or in any Alliance records," Felsus said. He paused and looked at Duaal. "But he listed you as his only family – so it all passes to you, Mister Sinnay. Everything Tiberius had is now yours, including this ship."

Duaal closed his eyes and twin tracks of tears traced their way down his dark cheeks. He nodded. "Thank you, Captain Felsus. But I'm sure you didn't come all the way down to Pine Spire just to tell me that."

"No," Felsus agreed. He looked around the table. "Where is the bounty hunter?"

"Coldhand said he wanted to see what he can salvage from his Raptor," Gripper answered.

Felsus frowned. "He's not going to find anything. There's a lot we need to talk about, and one of them is the Waygate."

Panna rubbed at her eyes and sat up. "What's going to happen to it?"

"It's already been done," Felsus told her. "For the moment, that Waygate is far too dangerous to Pylos and the rest of Prianus. This morning, I had demolition charges set all along the ravine. We've collapsed the mountain back onto the Waygate."

Maeve released the breath she hadn't realized she was holding. The Pylos Waygate was finally gone, buried down in a stony grave. Panna wasn't happy about that fate, though.

"What...?" she asked. "What about Doctor Kemmer's discovery? All of Professor Xen's work?"

"Their data will be sent back to Tynerion, like Professor Andus requested. If Vostra Nor University can send new archeologists and enough CWAAF soldiers to protect Prianus against more of those creatures, we'll let them back into the site," Felsus said. "But until then, it stays buried. Miss Sul, I assume we can entrust the delivery of the professors' files and samples to you?"

"I can take them back to Tynerion, along with the... the bodies," Panna answered. She chewed her lip. "But I don't know if I'm going back right away."

"Why not, Sprite?" Gripper asked.

Panna smiled at the nickname he had finally chosen, but was still nervous. "Well, that depends on Xartasia and the Devourers. What's happened to them?"

"They're gone," Felsus said. He didn't look displeased about it... but not entirely pleased, either. "They've all vanished. Xartasia, too, along with all the Nihilists who flew off. According to your reports, many of them escaped the initial slaughter, but so far, we haven't found a single one in Pylos."

"Are they... gone? Really gone?" Gripper asked.

All eyes turned to Duaal, including Maeve's. She had never seen magic like what Duaal displayed in the ravine. At the head of the table, the young Hyzaari mage shook his head.

"I banished them all," Duaal said. "It wasn't the same spell that Maeve used on Orindell a hundred years ago. I don't know that one. What I did down there was a guess. I sent all of them away. The Devourers and the Cult of Nihil. Just... away."

"Where did they go?" Felsus asked.

"I don't know," Duaal admitted. "I had to choose a destination, a place I knew and remembered well. But I couldn't decide. The Devourers are a danger to any city on any planet that we've ever been to. I had only a moment and I was thinking of several worlds, trying to choose one. Xartasia could have ended up on any of them."

"What about the Waygate?" Gripper asked. He stopped chewing on his blunt claws and suddenly looked at Duaal. "It was saying all sorts of things. Did that have anything to do with it?"

Maeve started. "The voice of the Waygate? You understood it? I heard that voice before, in Tamlin, but could make no sense of it. I believed then that it was some result of my poor spell-weaving, but Gavriel never finished my song..."

"That Waygate wasn't speaking in Aver or Arcadian," Xia said. "Maeve, you told us once that the Nnyth know the Waygates best. Was that their language?"

"No," Maeve said. "They have no verbal language."

"It was kind of like... Arboran, I guess you could say," Gripper answered. "The language we use back home. It was different, but I understood some of the words."

"Can you tell us what it said?" Maeve asked.

"Um, sort of." Gripper thought for a moment. "*Error. Opening word* – that might have been *command* or maybe *story* – *has not been completed. Please select destination.*"

Maeve and Panna stared at each other.

"Are you sure?" Panna asked.

"Yeah. There's more," Gripper said. "*Gate* – or *door* – *operation interrupted. Technicians have been called to fix the problem.* I actually understand it better than I would have before I left home. We don't really have words for things like *technician*, but now I know ideas like that. It must have been a recording or something."

"Gods," Panna breathed. "It was an error message! It must have been triggered when Gavriel didn't finish the spell. He didn't need your memories at all, Maeve. All he had to do was fail to complete the opening ritual."

Gripper nodded. "The Waygate was just trying to contact its builders for technical support."

"The Devourers?" Maeve asked. "They built the Waygates?"

"I thought you said no one knew who created the Waygates," Xia said. "If this thing has recordings in Gripper's native language, doesn't that suggest that *his* people created them?"

Panna pursed her lips and gave Gripper a speculative look. "I'm not sure, but it's a fascinating question."

"It *is* interesting," Felsus said, tapping a closed fist on the top of the crowded table. "But what about this Xartasia woman and the Cult of Nihil?"

"She wasn't just following Gavriel's orders," Xia said. "Xartasia seemed to have some plan of her own. Maeve, do you know what it is?"

"Me?" Maeve asked. "No, I fear that I do not. I am as surprised as any that she turned on Gavriel."

"I suppose it would be too much to hope that Xartasia and those monsters were banished out into empty space?" Felsus asked.

"Afraid so," Duaal answered. "It had to be a place I knew. Space doesn't exactly have a lot of useful landmarks. They're somewhere in the core."

"That's not going to go unnoticed," Panna said. "The Alliance and CWAAF have to know what's going on."

"We sent word to Axis as soon as your call came in," Felsus said. "The only answer we've gotten is confirmation of transmission. As far as I know, they've seen not tail or talon of the Devourers."

"Whatever Xartasia's plan, it is nothing as simple as Gavriel's," Maeve said. "She wants something other than total destruction, or she would have let Gavriel do as he wished. There is more to this than we know and the Alliance must be warned. But Xartasia is of my own blood. I must fight her on this."

"Xartasia was willing to let a lot of people suffer and die," Duaal said. He stood up and circled the table to stand next to Maeve. "We haven't always gotten along and a crew this small doesn't really need a first mate, Maeve. You know nothing about managing a ship, or flying or even fixing it."

"No," Maeve agreed. After everything else, was she about to lose her home, too? Duaal was captain of the Blue Phoenix now and had the authority to send her away.

"But my ship and my crew are at your disposal, princess," Duaal said with a sad, satisfied little smile. "We'll take you wherever you need to go."

"I'm coming along, too," Panna told Maeve. She stood, as well, and bowed deeply. "If you'll let me, princess."

"It is not my place to permit or authorize anything," Maeve said quickly. "But... I would be grateful for any help offered to me. I do not know what Xartasia plans, but she is older, wiser and far more powerful than I am. I can refuse nothing and no one that may help me stop her."

"Good," Felsus said. He rose, too, with a mechanical creak. He didn't bow, but inclined his head to Maeve. "I hope you won't be offended when I say that I hope you leave soon, princess."

"No," Maeve answered. "You are right. We cannot afford to waste time here."

"We'll be gone after the funerals tomorrow," Duaal said.

Captain Felsus nodded. After heavy final farewells, he limped out of the Blue Phoenix.

Duaal stood in the cockpit. He traced the deep scratches in the back of the pilot's chair with one hand. Outside, the sun had long since set behind the Kayton Mountains. Only the faintest trace of violet twilight lingered between the high peaks.

"He was proud of you," Xia said from the door.

"I know."

Duaal sat down in Tiberius' chair. The ship had been untended for a long time while they were up in the mountains...

"It's getting late. Are you coming to bed?" Xia asked.

Duaal turned on the computer and screens flickered all through the cockpit.

"I've got a lot of work to do," he said. "There are a lot of checks and preflights to do before I even think about taking her back into the black. Go on to bed. Don't wait up for me."

Xia stood in the doorway and watched the young captain of the Blue Phoenix for a moment, then turned and made her way back to her own room.

Logan Coldhand stood on the Pine Spire skypad and stared up at the Blue Phoenix. It was late. He had assumed everyone would be asleep, but the cockpit remained lit. Someone was still awake. Was it Xia? Duaal?

Two days had done nothing to clear the hunter's head. Two days of wandering Pylos and then Pine Spire, even contemplating returning back home to Highwind. He could go back to Vorus, tell his teacher that he had been right all along.

But Vorus knows. He always did.

And then what? Felsus wasn't looking into the bounty hunter's identity, but how long would that last? Logan's crashed Raptor was gone, buried under tons of stone in the Kayton Mountains, along with the Pylos Waygate. He could get a ship – buy or steal one, if he had to – or pay the fare for one of the rare starliners leaving Prianus for the brighter lights of the core.

But he didn't want to leave.

No, that wasn't right... Logan didn't want to leave alone.

Everything ached: his mind, body and soul. Since waking up in the hospital room with a mechanical heart six years ago, all Logan wanted was to feel again. Anything. Pleasure or pain, joy or terror... And now he felt. He felt everything and it was too much. Logan had no idea what to do. The flood of feelings was too alien and strange.

The Blue Phoenix cargo airlock was closed, but Logan remembered the entry codes. No one had changed them. The thick fiber-steel door thunked open and Logan stepped through, then sealed it behind him. With any luck, whoever was still awake in the cockpit wouldn't have noticed the breach.

The ship hadn't changed much. The hold was empty of cargo and Gripper's suspended planter garden still hung from the ceiling, overgrown after weeks of inattention. There was a heap of null-field pallets along the wall, straps and webbing hanging from hooks, but none of the archeologists' equipment had been salvageable. It was all gone.

Logan climbed the fibersteel stairs and crept through the darkened Blue Phoenix. The only lights were the amber strips running along the floor on either side of the small corridor. System displays and network ports glowed green and blue in the bulkheads, but cast so little light that Logan couldn't see his own feet underneath him.

That was fine... He knew where he was going.

He was in the aft of the ship, in the corridor that ran between the bunkrooms. Tiberius had imprisoned the bounty hunter in one of these rooms, as the Blue Phoenix hurled itself into the corona of Axis' sun. But that wasn't Logan's destination now.

He touched the glowing orange sensor square next to another door and it slid open. More amber lightstrips ran around the edge of the bunkroom, along the joint of the floor and the walls.

Maeve was asleep in her bed, lying on one side with her wings tucked tightly against her back. Her sleep had been restless and her sheets were twisted around her knees. Maeve had certainly been through more than enough to give her nightmares for a lifetime, even a long Arcadian life.

Xia's work had erased most of the marks of the Nihilists' torture. There were white scars on her skin, but nothing livid or bleeding anymore. Maeve's long, sooty lashes rested against her high cheeks. Her black hair was much shorter than it had been on Stray and the inky locks lay softly across her small, fine-featured face.

The bounty hunter stood next to the fairy's bed, staring down at her. Maeve didn't stir. She was... what? Beautiful?

She is *beautiful. The most beautiful woman I've ever seen.*

Alone in her room and sealed away from the Prian cold, Maeve wasn't wearing much. Just the light, filmy dress of her temperate homeworld – a wisp of pale blue cloth tied around her narrow hips. Every smooth, svelte line of her slim body was bared to the hunter's gaze.

I don't know how to feel this way. I don't know how to feel at all.

But finding Maeve in Pylos had kindled something in Logan, a hot ember inside him that made the blood rush in his ears. He felt it even now. The sight of her, the memory of her kiss... It made the whole world feel tilted on its side and feel full of... of...

I can't do this anymore.

I need to be like I was. Something has to die again.

Logan slid his Talon-9 out of its holster. It was Maeve. It was always Maeve. She had been a mark, but she wasn't even that anymore. She was just some fairy woman. Why did she make him feel anything at all?

Somehow, Coldhand knew no one else would ever make him burn like Maeve Cavainna did. He pressed the barrel of the gun to her temple, just above one of her delicately pointed ears. It would be so easy. That was what Maeve had said back on Axis, as she held his gun and tore at his clothes. It would be easy. All he had to do was pull the trigger to remove this problem, this confusing and confounding woman.

His trembling finger tightened on the trigger. Kill her and it would be done. It would be easy, so much easier than feeling all of this pain and confusion.

But I don't want to... What do I want?

Logan's thoughts chased each other like moths around a flame, closer and closer to the bright, lovely danger. Logan dropped to one knee beside the bed. He still held the Talon against her temple, and pressed his lips to Maeve's. She tasted sweet, like honey or some rosy nectar. The ember inside Logan flared.

Maeve stirred in her sleep. Storm-gray eyes fluttered and then opened. Logan knew he should stop. This was a bad idea, an unwelcome advance, and beyond stupid. Logan pulled away, but even with the kiss broken, he still tasted Maeve's sweetness on his lips.

And then he felt her fingers curled around the back of his neck.

"I thought today that you had gone again," she whispered.

"I should have," Logan said in a rough voice. Everything seemed to rush and echo strangely inside his own head. "I can't do this. After what Hallax took from me... He killed me. But now... What I feel now burns me, Maeve. I want to rip my heart out, but I know it won't stop."

Logan's voice failed. His computer-regulated pulse was too hard, too fast. Had the mechanical pump broken? He pressed the gun against Maeve's head. Her staring silver eyes were as bright as stars and her fingers twined into his hair.

"I remembered you, my hunter," Maeve told him. Her soft lips brushed Logan's ear and a chill raced down his spine. When had she gotten so close? "In the darkness, when Gavriel tormented me, I armored myself with thoughts of you."

Logan's metal hand clenched, denting the bunk's welded frame.

"But Gavriel got exactly what he wanted from you," he said. "He hurt you, Maeve."

Her hand trailed along his tight jaw, down his throat and across his chest.

"I had to find you," Logan whispered so softly, as though trying to keep the secret even from himself. "I... I thought of you every day. I want... I need..."

"Illa enarri eru," Maeve sang under her breath. None of the delicate Arcadian words were ones that he knew. "I need you, Logan."

The fairy princess seized a fistful of his shirt and pulled Logan close again, kissing him deeply. The ember inside Logan burst into flame at her touch. His blood was on fire and his skin felt feverish. It was heaven, it was hell and he was burning. The Talon tumbled from Logan's nerveless fingers, forgotten.

Maeve's hands trembled as she grasped the hem of his shirt and pulled it up over his head. It wasn't cold in her room, but Logan shivered. The pale scar left by Hallax's sword stood out bright white even in the dim light. Maeve's feathered wings rustled, trembling in anticipation. Her fingers traced the line of the Prian's shoulders, down his tensed arms and the joint of metal and flesh just beneath Logan's left elbow. The sensation of her touch was suddenly distant. He started and pulled away.

"What have I done?" Maeve asked.

"There are parts of me that are gone. Forever." For the first time, Logan felt no anger or loss at his maiming, but shame. "I haven't been able to be with a woman since this happened. I don't know if I can do this."

Logan remained on his knees beside her bed with his unfeeling illonium hand curled uselessly at his side. Maeve stood. She was so small...! Even kneeling, Logan was almost eye-to-eye with her.

Maeve was naked to the waist and tugged once at the knot of her skirt, then even that fell away. The fairy raised her wings high. She stood proud, lovely and defiant before Logan.

"You are a whole man," Maeve told him. "And I will love every part of you until you never doubt your ability to feel again."

Maeve took both of his hands in hers and pressed them against her nude body. The cold metal of his left hand raised goosebumps on her pale skin, but her breath caught. Logan caressed the impossible silky perfection of her, trailing his fingertips over her belly and the gentle curve of her hips, then up her arched spine and between her wings. Maeve gasped and a rosy flush spread across her breasts.

She wants me to touch her...

And he wanted it, too, Logan realized. More than anything. He was on his feet in an instant, pressing the fairy back into her bed.

There was one last journey to be made into Pylos. Captain Felsus gave Duaal clearance to set the Blue Phoenix down in the Raptor landing field. Even Gruth limped down the cargo ramp, leaning heavily on a borrowed crutch and dressed in the best of his clothes that could be salvaged from the ruined camp.

North Pylos Police Station Three was just as crowded as before, but subdued. Word had spread about the events in the mountains and even the hardened Prian criminals seemed to retreat for the moment. Perhaps they were afraid, but Duaal liked to think that it was out of respect.

The funerals were held in a back lot behind the precinct station, where the cracked concrete was still wet from days of rain. The crew and passengers of the Blue Phoenix – including Logan Coldhand, Duaal couldn't help noticing – stood with the other black-clothed Prians, those families left behind by officers killed in the Waygate battle. Most of the hard eyes were sad but remained dry.

Of over thirty officers, only four had returned. Two more died of their wounds in the following days, leaving Felsus and a young female officer, Mell Savorse, as the sole survivors of Captain Cerro's force.

The bodies of the dead were wound in clean white cloth and lay atop twenty-four biers set up in a long line. Those claimed by the Devourers left no remains, but empty shrouds stitched with the fallen officer's names were folded neatly on the wood. Duaal and the others gathered at the end of the long line, where Tiberius' body rested on a pyre under a white-barked birch tree. Orphia sat in the branches above her master, keening softly.

An iron torch burned in a tall black stand. The red-gold flame jumped and sizzled in the rain, but did not go out. Uniformed officers snapped to attention as the tall, weathered Pylos police chief strode across the concrete to stand beside the torch. He squinted at the gathered mourners and raised a fist to the center of his chest in salute.

"Our lives are only the last sacrifice we make in the line of duty," he said. The wind whipped the torch flame dangerously close, but he didn't flinch. "The men and women of the Prian Police Force chose hard lives for themselves and their families, lives of honor and struggle in the face of overwhelming odds. There is no higher calling. We gather now to thank them for all they have done and bid them farewell. May God welcome them into the heavens as honored sons and daughters."

His short speech finished, the tall Prian lifted the torch from its sconce and lit each of the pyres in turn. When he reached Tiberius, he paused. His voice was quiet, only audible to those gathered around the bier.

"You made it all the way to retirement, only to come home and die. But we thank you, Tiberius Myles. You served and protected Prianus long after your due. God welcome you, brother."

He touched the torch to the wooden pyre and flames licked up all around the shrouded body. The Pylos chief nodded to Duaal and the rest before moving on to deliver curt condolences to stoic spouses and dark-clad children. There was warmer wetness on Duaal's cheeks than the Prian rain. He bowed his head beside Tiberius' pyre as smoke rose up into the clouds.

"He wasn't bad for a Prian," Gruth said. He shifted his weight on the crutch.

Panna wiped her eyes and then took a deep, shuddering breath. "Tiberius was the gentlest rough man I ever met. Professor Xen didn't think much of Prians, but he had the greatest respect for Captain Myles and it was well-earned."

Gripper's face was a mask of grief and he hiccuped with great, racking sobs. He tried several times to say something, but could only weep like a broken-hearted little boy. Xia took his big, clawed hand and stroked it comfortingly. Maeve stood beside the pyre, dressed all in the Arcadian's mourning gray, the wind tugging at her black hair and white wings.

"You welcomed a wounded and broken woman onto your ship, Tiberius. You gave to me a home when I had none and your friendship when I deserved none. Your grace and your loss will be remembered always." The fairy closed her eyes. She raised her face up to the sky and sang in a sweet, sad voice. *"En a vaellin saemma var'ii lae..."*

Maeve stopped and shook her head. Tears glittered in her dark eyelashes. "No, I will sing in your tongue, my captain, that you may know our sorrow...

"Above the raging storm, the stars burn ever on,
The light of those who came before and sing for us still.
Above the weeping storm, you fly forever on
Unto those silver lights and wait for me until.
That bright day when through the storm I soar,
And we may meet in blue skies once more."

Maeve opened her eyes again and the tears streaked down her pale face. She held one hand up to the flames of Tiberius' pyre.

"Farewell, my captain," Maeve told him. "You were one of the best men that I have ever known."

Logan stood beside Maeve. Not close enough to touch, but... close. Duaal had never seen the bounty hunter dressed in anything but the most utilitarian of clothes, but now he wore a clean, neat black suit – though his Talon-9 was still visible in an oiled leather holster at his hip. Logan stared into the bright, dancing flames.

"More men should be like you, Myles," he said.

Duaal stood at the foot of the pyre. They probably expected him to say something, but what was left to be said? Two men had been fathers to Duaal... one terrible and powerful, one brave and noble. Both Tiberius and Gavriel were gone now. One killed by the other and only one mourned.

I'm alone now.

Duaal's heart ached and his eyes were sore from crying. Gavriel killed Tiberius, but he had paid for that, if not at Duaal's hands. There was no one else to blame, and nothing to be gained by anger. Duaal looked up at Tiberius' pyre.

Is this what it means to grow up? he wondered. *Knowing the pain is there, but that nothing can be done about it? There's no one to run to anymore when I'm scared. There's no tantrum to throw, nothing that can bring Tiberius back. I just have to live with missing him.*

Duaal would miss Tiberius every day for the rest of his life, but there were other things to worry about now. Things that Tiberius would have seen to, but which now fell to Duaal.

"Xartasia is still out there. We fly within the hour," he said. "Are you ready?"

"Yes," Logan said.

Xia and Gripper were still crying, but they nodded. Panna did the same.

"No," Maeve answered. "I do not know that I ever will be. But it is time."

They all turned away, heading back to the Blue Phoenix. Duaal turned back once and called for Orphia, but the old hawk remained in the tree beside her master's pyre and would not leave.

[EPILOGUE]
SWORD OF DREAMS

"Time lost may never again be found. Or so it is said."

- TITANIA CAVAINNA, ARCADIAN MONARCH (234 PA)

Commander Dhozo stood at the edge of a withered field of dead grass. Something had changed. *Everything* had changed. What had been frozen stone and icy rain a moment before was now a heavy sky seething with dirty gray-brown clouds that obscured a pair of tiny, pathetic orange suns. Dhozo raised one huge fist. The hissing, buzzing swarm of his nanites clung close.

"Halt!" he called.

His squadron – just eighteen left of a twenty-one soldier squad hand-picked for this assignment – formed up around Dhozo. They weren't alone on the plain of crumbling grass.

A crowd of creatures, many with feathered wings and nearly all dressed in black clothes, stared in shocked wonder. They huddled behind a single woman. She was tiny, but with a regal bearing that defied her size.

"I know this place," the winged woman said. "This planet is Zeos, Gavriel's homeworld."

Dhozo's nanites translated the woman's words, sending signals back and forth to each other and their central computer, implanted at the base of his skull. A readout lit up at the edge of Dhozo's vision and he bared his sharp predator's teeth in sudden surprise. He thought he recognized the wings, the short, pointed ears... An aerad, a slave from the ancient feeding grounds.

Dhozo's soldiers moved toward her, but he ordered them back again. There was something important to be learned here. Something... unforeseen had happened. Hunger gnawed at his stomach, but the commander was more disciplined than hungry.

The little aerad woman stood as tall as she could, but was still half Dhozo's height.

"You will hear me, Devourer," she said in a clear, strong voice.

"Devourer?" Dhozo answered. His computer made an educated guess at the translation and repeated him in the aerad's language. "My species has been called by many names. Yours is not new or even very interesting. Why should I listen to you, slave?"

The last word made the woman's violet eyes blaze, but she only smiled. "My name is Xartasia. I can give you what you have lost. What is your name, Devourer?"

"I am Commander Dhozo, of the VSS Forge. What do you think you have to give us, Xartasia, besides the marrow in your bones? My people are hungry, and you are only a slave. We left your race to die long, long ago."

"You were as surprised by the Waygate's call as we. I have lore you also thought long gone," Xartasia said. "There is ancient knowledge that you have lost. I have sacrificed much to find it. But from you, I need only one secret. Let us trade our secrets, Commander Dhozo, to both our benefit."

"Talk holds little interest to me and my soldiers," Dhozo told her. "They are *very* hungry, little aerad."

Xartasia smiled again and gestured toward the huddle of aliens behind her.

"Let it not be said that I am a poor hostess. You may eat," she said, then held up a white-gloved finger. "But, even knowing your taste for them, you must not touch those with wings. The humans, Dailons, Ixthians and Lyrans are yours. They are happy to die."

All around him, Commander Dhozo's soldiers surged forward, nanites reflexively reaching in sharp, inky tendrils for the cowering creatures.

"Hold!" Dhozo ordered. "Not yet! There's too much we don't know. Take scans before you eat. Every one of them! And none of the aerads... for now."

With that, they lunged past Xartasia, who stood unflinching as the Devourers tore into their next meal. The creatures in tattered clothes couldn't run far on the open ground before Dhozo's people tore them apart, devouring skin and muscle, organs and bones. Dhozo's stomach rumbled fiercely, but he wasn't done with Xartasia yet. He stepped close to make himself heard over the screams of the dying.

"What do you want, little slave?" Dhozo asked.

"Show me your face, commander," Xartasia said. "Let me see to whom I speak."

Dhozo thought the command to his nanite swarm. It had been burned thin by the human in the fighter, but was still enough to tear Xartasia to bloody rags of skin within seconds, if he wanted to. And they would rebuild themselves, as soon as he could harvest the materials.

At Dhozo's command, the nanites coalesced against his skin. The layer of glistening black was thinner than his skin and was the only clothes he wore, concealing nothing and revealing all.

Dhozo knew how he looked to Xartasia, how his kind appeared to all aliens – huge monsters, beasts out of nightmare. Like her, Dhozo had two arms and legs, but no wings. His ears, too, came to points, but were much longer than Xartasia's. Where it was not covered by the nanites, his skin was smooth, hairless and dark gray over thick, corded muscles. His fingers ended in wickedly curved claws that matched the long, sharp fangs filling his wide mouth. His eyes were solid black over a broad, flat nose. Xartasia looked up at him, that secretive smile still on her lips.

"Fascinating," she said softly. A stale wind stirred the dead grass around them. "You look much like the creatures I met not so long ago in my search for you. The Arborans, as they are known."

The name meant nothing to Dhozo. He loomed over Xartasia, fanged mouth watering, but she did not bow or flinch. Strange. She didn't have the bearing of a slave at all.

But nothing was supposed to be alive at all in the old feeding grounds. They had been picked clean eons ago. But now there was so much to learn here... and to eat.

"Tell me about this deal you want to make," Dhozo growled.

LITTLE HAWK
[A story of Prianus]

"Why are you hurrying home? No one there for you!"

"Mum's working out late again, yeah? I got some work for her in my pants," said another one of Sullis' friends. The gap-toothed teen thrust his hips suggestively. "Her work comes cheap, don't it? Could probably keep her busy all night for ten cen!"

"Fly off!" Logan shouted.

He hurled himself at the nearest boy, not one of those who had spoken, but all of Sullis' gang were the same: bigger, meaner and stronger than scrawny ten-year-old Logan Centra. He bounced off the much larger boy and sprawled on the cracked pavement.

Sullis laughed. He was six or seven years older than Logan, but at least three times bigger, with broad shoulders and pocked skin. His gang tightened their circle around Logan. Sullis waggled his tongue insolently at the boy on the ground.

"Got something to say to your mum, Logan? Why don't you tell me?" he taunted. "I'll be seeing her later tonight. I'll take real good care of her, don't worry."

Logan's eyes burned with furious tears. He pulled his feet under him, but another one of Sullis' boys – a wiry, ruddy-faced young man – kicked Logan in the chest and sent him tumbling back to the grease-stained roadside. Cars raced and rattled by, their drivers taking no notice of the boys fighting just outside. Logan wheezed and tried to jump at Sullis again, swinging a poorly-aimed punch at the gang's leader. Sullis took a single step back, laughing again.

"You can't fight worth a turd," he said, then leered at Logan. "But then, what else you expect from the son of a whore? I bet you know how to ass about just fine. Gonna be a rental like your mum?"

"She's not a whore!" Logan cried.

He cast about for a suitable insult. His heart was racing so fast in his chest that he couldn't hear the individual beats anymore, just a thin hum like the pulse of a bird.

"But if she were, she would never work for you!" Logan shouted.

Logan could only see through one eye. The other was too swollen and he could only open it a crack. Even then, everything seemed muddy and red. Still, he knew the route home from school well enough that he could have made it with both eyes shut. Logan really hoped he wouldn't have to test that.

The sun was setting behind the steep mountains surrounding Highwind like a crown of great stone blades. The stars would come out before long, but it would be some hours more before they would shine with light enough to pierce the thick miasma of smoke and other pollutants that filled the city air.

Highwind looked not unlike a pile of old boxes, discarded but not empty. Like most Prian cities, the houses were cheap, mass produced as flimsy, barely habitable temporary shelters. They were only designed to last for a decade or two before being replaced, but most of the thin-walled cubes and squat apartment blocks were fifty years old or more. They had been patched and repaired so many times that the walls seemed quilted in blotchy rust, water-stained aluminum and flaking paint.

The roads of Highwind were just as cracked and piebald as the houses. The cars and pedestrians that traveled them were no less worn. Logan tripped a few times on the uneven concrete, nearly stumbling into a chem dealer lounging on the street corner. She glared at Logan through lank brown hair and prodded the boy onward with a boot against his backside. He hurried past without looking back.

Logan climbed the creaking stairs that zig-zagged across the face of his building until he reached the faded green door of his mother's apartment. For a panicked moment, he couldn't find his keys. Had they fallen out of his pocket when Sullis kicked him? But no, Logan found them a moment later in his back pocket. The old locks took some effort, but he muscled the door open with a grunt.

The small apartment was empty, of course. That much of Sullis' stupid taunt had been true – his mother was working late, as usual. Logan dropped his crack-screened school datadex on the couch and went to the kitchen for some ice. He broke a few cubes out of a tray in the freezer and wrapped them in a towel from beside the sink.

Back in the living room, Logan flopped down onto the threadbare couch. On the other end, his guitar twanged at the jostling as though gently admonishing its young owner. The boy considered playing, but his hands ached and his ribs hurt.

He closed his eyes, but he just couldn't sleep. Logan sat up and pulled the guitar into his lap, curling his stiff fingers around the worn wooden neck, and began to play.

"Oh my God! What happened?"

Logan looked up with a start. He had lost all track of time and now Lynn Centra stood in the doorway with her hands pressed to her mouth. Her cheeks were bloodlessly pale and a bag of groceries lay forgotten at her feet. Logan sat up, wincing. He touched his face and felt the crumbly crackle of dried blood.

Lynn ran to her son's side and snatched up the towel from the couch. The cloth was still damp from the melted ice and she caught Logan's chin in gentle fingers, turning him to face her.

"Oh, sweetheart. What happened?"

"Sullis," Logan mumbled. His lips felt stiffer and more swollen than before. The ice hadn't done a very good job, Logan decided. "He said things about you..."

"Shhh, it doesn't matter." His mother wiped lightly at the blood on Logan's split lip. "You shouldn't be fighting. It doesn't matter what the other boys say about me. They're just children."

"But they called you..." Logan couldn't even bring himself to say the word. It made him so angry just to think it. "It's not true!"

"No, sweetheart, it's not, but it wouldn't matter if it were," Lynn said. "It's just a job, you know, and not worth getting into fights over. If the older boys try to corner you, Logan, just run. It doesn't do any good to fight."

Her son muttered a noncommittal reply and didn't meet Lynn's eye. She sighed.

"Look at all this mess," Lynn said. "Why don't you go wash up while I get dinner ready?"

"Alright."

Logan showered quickly and put on cleaner clothes, then came back into the living room. Lynn was in the kitchen, warming a small bowl of noodles and some red sauce. She smiled at the boy and nodded to the cupboard.

"Are you intact enough to set the table?" she asked.

"Sure," Logan said.

"My brave little hawk." Lynn smiled at her son.

He opened the cupboard, doors wobbling on their tarnished, crooked hinges, and stood up on his toes to reach the bowls on the top shelf. Lynn owned only one set of dishes, four glass plates and four bowls with matching teacups and saucers. Those dishes were her pride and joy – after Logan, of course. Her mother's mother bought them many years ago from a Dailon who claimed they were antiques all the way from Axis. It probably wasn't true, but the glass was beautiful and delicate, finished in a rich blue like the evening sky.

Logan carried the bowls very carefully to the little table under the apartment's single window. Thick bars welded to the frame cut the view of the street outside into long slats like a paneled painting in one of the Union chapels. The sky was dark now, black like ink. There was only one moon out tonight, Unos. It hung in the darkness like a lopsided yellow grin, smirking down at the Prians scrabbling in the rocky dirt so far below.

Logan put out spoons and forks. He folded coarse paper towels under them and sat to wait for dinner. It was getting easier to open his left eye; the shower had helped. His mother stirred sauce into the pasta and carried it to the table. Logan scooped most of the noodles into his pretty blue bowl. He paused when the spoon scraped the bottom and flushed.

"Go ahead, eat up," his mother said. "You're a growing boy and you've got a lot of healing to do."

Reluctantly, Logan left only a little dinner for his mother. His stomach rumbled. He hadn't eaten since breakfast and that seemed an eternity ago. Lynn said a short grace over dinner and Logan dove into his food like a falcon on prey. His mother picked at her pasta, but ate very little. She was so thin, he thought, but still the strongest lady on Prianus. She looked worried and Logan hoped she wasn't worrying about him.

Logan couldn't avoid Sullis and his gang for long. They caught up with him a week later, after school. Logan was almost home and felt the first surge of relief at the sight of his building at the end of the street, but then he heard a voice behind him.

"Hey, whore-son!"

He turned just in time to see Sullis charging out from one of the drip-dens. The other people on the sidewalk parted, unwilling to get caught in yet another bout of gang violence. Sullis' eyes were glassy and dilated, his rough cheeks brightly flushed as some chemical coursed through his blood and set his heart racing.

Logan balled his small hands into fists, but remembered his mother's words – no shame and no fighting. As a dozen of Sullis' boys followed their leader out of the murky den and into the crowded street, Logan turned on his heels and ran.

"Where you off to?" they called out, chasing Logan and shouting to one another. "Come on back! We just want to give our best to your mum."

Logan reached the bottom of the stairs. His worn shoes rang on the rusted steel and he flung himself up the steps as quickly as his short legs would carry him. The staircase shuddered beneath him as Sullis and his cronies closed the gap. They were bigger than Logan and much faster. Would his head start be enough?

There was no time. Logan fell once, caught himself jarringly on his knees and jumped back to his feet, fumbling the keys from his pocket. One of the other boys was so close now that Logan could hear his labored breath sawing behind him. It wasn't Sullis, but one of his rangier and less chem-addled friends.

On the third story, Logan bolted the last few steps and jammed his key into the front door. He twisted as hard as he could. Sweat streamed down the back of his neck, cold as icemelt. With a jerk, Logan unlocked the door and ran inside, flinging the door shut behind him. He spun, reaching for the deadbolt, but the door had already bounced off a large foot thrust through the gap. Logan's pursuer bellowed in pain.

"You little bitch! I'm going to rip your skin off!"

The lanky boy lunged through the door and grabbed Logan. Sullis and the rest were close on his tail. They poured through the door and crowded into the small apartment. Someone slammed the door behind them. Sullis stepped forward, grinning at Logan. His lips seemed very thin and very dark.

"So this is where a rental lives." Sullis' words were slurred by drugs and he casually hooked Logan's legs out from under him, then cackled when the boy crumpled to the floor. "Not much, is it? But then, that's about what I expect from a cenmark whore."

His mother said there was no shame in sex work, but before Logan could debate the point with Sullis, the bigger boy drove a boot into his crotch.

"Well boys, let's make ourselves at home," Sullis said. "His mum rents her body easy enough. I doubt she'll mind sharing her place for a while. What's nice around here, Logan?"

Lynn Centra had to work even later than usual. Some drunk had knocked over a toy display, sending bits of broken plastic flying like the shrapnel of a grenade. It had taken an extra hour to collect the shards, once parts of model dinosaurs that were a favorite among those young Prian children whose parents could afford them.

She fished out a few last pieces from under a shelf and swept them into a dustpan. The plastic was molded on one side with a feathered pattern and painted in mottled blues and reds. Lynn emptied the mess into a waste bin and wondered if any of it was salvageable. If she could put the pieces back together, the toy dinosaur might make a good present for Logan. It would be his birthday soon and she didn't have any gifts. Lynn sighed and sealed off the garbage bag. Even if she could somehow piece together the broken model, Logan was already getting too old for such things. Children grew up so fast.

Finally finished, Lynn turned off the holographics and locked up the store. She ignored the listless catcalls from the whiskery old men lounging outside and hurried to her car. Highwind was no less filthy and dangerous by night, but at least the deep mountain shadow hid the worst of it away, out of sight.

A short Arcadian woman slouched outside the apartment block when Lynn arrived at home. She had pulled her dirty wings around her against the cold. Lynn felt a stab of pity, but then she caught the oily glint of a nanoblade in the alien's hand. She shuddered and decided to park on the other side of the building.

It was almost midnight by the time Lynn wearily pushed open her door and stepped inside. She heard sobbing. Lynn dropped her purse and turned on the lights. Something... everything was wrong.

The apartment was in ruins. All of the pictures had been torn off the walls, shredded into pieces and scattered across the floor. Lynn's clothes, too, were strewn across the tiny living room, some ripped or cut, some stained and soiled. The computer was gone from its corner desk and the sofa sliced open. The window was broken and shards of glass littered the worn carpet. Logan's guitar was smashed and lay like a dead pet in the corner of the room.

"Logan?" Lynn cried.

He was in the kitchen. The cupboards stood open and empty of food. The boy was covered in drying blood. There was a long cut on his temple that seemed to be the source of most of the red, but his lips were puffy and there were dark, terrible-looking bruises on his thin arms. Logan stood at the kitchen counter, cradling shards of blue glass in his hands and weeping broken-heartedly over them as he tried to glue them back together. Logan looked up at his mother's approach.

"They broke your plates," he whispered.

"My God," Lynn choked. She batted the broken glass out of his hands and held Logan close. "Oh my God! Are you alright? Did they hurt you?"

It was a stupid question. Of *course* they hurt him. Lynn scooped Logan into her arms and carried him out to the car. She needed to take him to the hospital. As she buckled him into the passenger seat, Logan began to cry again.

"I'm sorry, I'm sorry," he sobbed. "I couldn't stop them!"

"Logan, my little hawk, it doesn't matter. We just need to make sure you're alright."

"They said... and took... I'm sorry."

The rest was lost in tears.

"How're you feeling?"

Logan avoided his mother's gaze. He flexed his arm. It was stiff, but not too painful.

"Fine," he said. "All better."

"Good."

Lynn patted his shoulder gently and steered him across the hospital lobby, but a man cleared his throat. "Miss Centra?"

She sighed. "Logan, why don't you sit down for a minute?"

Lynn pointed to a row of white plastic chairs, each stamped with the words *Property of Highwind Municipal Hospital*. Logan nodded and padded across the scarred tile. He sat down beside a middle-aged woman who greeted him limply and then resumed her wet coughing.

Logan watched his mother. She spoke softly to the man, quietly so her son couldn't hear. But he knew what they were talking about: money, of course. It was expensive to see doctors on Prianus. Logan heard stories at school about other Alliance planets, closer to the galactic core where there were lots of the silver-skinned Ixthians who all but gave away their medical expertise to anyone, even criminals and the poor. But that was far away. There weren't many Ixthians on Prianus.

Logan kicked his legs. They didn't quite reach the floor. The woman in the next chair smiled, charmed by the cute display. But Logan wasn't trying to be cute. He was angry. His blood felt hot in his veins and seemed to burn behind his eyes. His legs were short and thin, knees still raw and red. He was weak, too weak to defend his mother's home and honor. If Logan was going to beat Sullis, he would need help. A lot of help.

Lynn Centra finished speaking with the receptionist and had signed something on a datadex screen that Logan was too far away to read. She gestured him over and offered the sullen boy a tight smile.

"Let's go home," she said. "You need your rest."

● ● ●

His mother had already gone to work by the time Logan woke the next morning. The broken cupboards were still empty, but she had left a candy bar and a small sleeve of crackers with a note: *I love you, my hawk. Have a good day in school.*

Logan stuffed the food into his mouth and left the little scrap of paper. He wasn't going to school today. He had more important things to take care of.

The rising sun pierced the thick haze of Highwind sky in silver-gray needles, sharp rays like impossibly slender nanoknives. The streets were busy, as always, full of the thick, noisy bustle. Though not many Prians could afford null-inertia vehicles, even the air was alive with traffic. Hawks and falcons flew through the sky and shrieked at one another as their paths crossed or even collided.

It was summer in Highwind, but the thin air remained bitterly cold. Logan cinched his wool coat tightly around him and began his hunt. None of the adults took any notice of the young boy shouldering past.

That was fine – Logan ignored them right back.

He stopped at the mouth of every alleyway and at the door of every dark bar and smoky drip-den. Heavy-set bouncers turned Logan away from many of these, but most simply ignored him or demanded entry fees, none of which the boy could pay. When he exhausted every place within walking range of his apartment, Logan took a bus deeper into Highwind and continued his search.

He stopped to stare through the window of a worn-looking palaestrum. Inside was a wood-floored gymnasium where a stout, balding man was practicing the Prian martial forms. A pair of women in loose-cut clothes studied the short man intently and tried to mimic his movements. Logan caught a reflection in the mirror and turned. A boy about his own age vanished into the shadowed alley that separated the palaestrum from the shop next door. Logan followed him through the narrow passage and behind the building.

Logan finally found what he was looking for – when he came around the crumbling brick corner, he was suddenly face-to-chest with a tall teenage boy. Behind him, Logan could see the younger one he had followed and seven or eight other boys. A pair of girls, little more than children – much like the boys – lounged against a door and watched as they rubbed runny red noses.

The boy in front of Logan didn't look anything like Sullis, but he didn't have to. He held himself with the same defensive, suspicious hunch. His breath carried the same reek of cheap rollers. He was exactly the same as Sullis.

"What do you want, you little prick?" he asked Logan.

"I want in. I want to fly with you and your boys."

"You've heard of Elson and my flock, eh? And you want a piece of the cuttings," said the boy, who must have been Elson.

"Yes," Logan answered simply.

Elson crossed his arms. His jacket had only one sleeve, showing off a sloppy falcon tattoo on the other bared bicep. Elson leaned in close to inspect Logan.

"You're a bit of a starling, aren't you? Got a piece? A knife or gun? No? Can't say you're impressing me much, little lark."

Logan didn't back away from the looming boy. "I've got even better. I live across town. There's another gang there, run by a boy called Sullis. Do you know him?"

"No," said Elson. "And why in the sooty hells should I care? *This* is my patch."

"They hit a house not very long ago. They stole some things. Some antiques from Axis. They're really expensive, worth a lot of colour."

The lie sat uneasily in Logan's stomach, as though he had swallowed a live snake. A poisonous one. Sullis had stolen some food and his mother's computer, but had been too stupid to recognize the real prize. He and his boys had smashed all of the pretty dishes one by one as they ignored Logan's pleas to stop. The memory of the shattered blue glass hardened his resolve.

Elson's almost colorless blond brows shot up. The girls shrieked at something and called for Elson's attention, but he just waved them off.

"You can show us where?" he asked.

"Yes. I know all their favorite places," Logan said.

"And what do *you* want, little lark? Just a cut... or something else?" Elson asked. He was a little sharper than he looked. He must have guessed that Logan wanted more than a few cen in stolen goods. "Something personal?"

"They said some things," Logan answered shortly. "They tried to shame my mother and they ruined her house. I don't want them to ever do it again."

"You want yourself some revenge?"

"Yes."

Elson grinned lazily, like a self-satisfied cat. "And that's why you want in. Alright, little lark. Even so, you can't just ask your way into Elson's flock, eh? You've got to prove yourself."

Logan frowned. "Fine. What do you want me to do?"

Elson gestured to one of his boys. "You got some paint on you? Yeah? Give it here."

The boy plucked a pressure-tube of lumapaint from his jacket pocket and tossed it to Elson, who held it out to Logan. He took the tube in his small hands, turning it over.

"What do you want me to do with it?" Logan asked.

"All this–" Elson swept his arms across the alleyway. "–is our nesting, isn't it? How about leaving a little reminder for all the other little pricks who want a piece?"

The alleyway was layered in graffiti of all colors and sizes, from insults to lewd pictures to any number of gang tags. Elson wasn't the only one to claim this area. Logan hefted the paint and flicked back the cap. He looked up at his new leader.

"My name," Elson said. "Big as you can, lark."

Behind Elson, the girls called out again as the rear door of the palaestrum banged open and a man stomped out into the alley. It was the same short, thick-bellied man Logan had seen inside. Elson turned to face him, forgetting Logan in an instant.

"What do you want, Vorus?" he snapped. "Tail it out of here, you wing-clipped sod."

"You seem to have missed the front door again," the old man answered almost pleasantly. "You can come in for classes any day, Elson. Why do you insist on vandalizing my back door instead?"

"Not interested," Elson spat. "Go away, you old stump!"

He prodded Vorus in his wide chest. With a sad-sounding sigh, Vorus caught Elson's wrist and twisted, driving the tall boy to his knees on the ground. Elson's gang drew back like frightened deer.

"You must learn respect, boy," Vorus said.

"Let go of me!" Elson shouted.

Vorus released the boy, who stumbled back a step. But instead of running, Elson pulled a snub-nosed laser pistol from his belt and waved it in the air.

"How dare you touch me, you mud-sucking old coot?" Elson shouted, leveling the gun at Vorus.

The old man lashed out with a surprisingly high, agile kick that cracked against Elson's hand. Elson dropped his laser with a howl and cradled his broken fingers to his chest. He staggered and ran, scattering his own gang in his haste to escape. The other boys fled down the alleyway, shouting and shrieking. Logan turned to follow, but Vorus grabbed his thin arm.

"No, not you," he said.

"I didn't do anything!" Logan protested.

Vorus looked at the tube of paint in his hand. "You were about to, weren't you?"

Logan dropped the lumapaint, but the old man didn't let go of him. Vorus hauled Logan easily through the open door and into the palaestrum. They were in a back room, not the one Logan had seen through the front window. There was a square table and a few chairs. Vorus pushed the boy down into one of these. A brown and black falcon perched on a stand under the window and chewed contentedly on his braided leash.

"What do you want?" Logan asked petulantly.

"What did you think you were doing out there? Why aren't you at school?"

Logan didn't answer.

Vorus sighed and dropped heavily into a chair across the table. He leaned back and rested scarred hands on his belly. "What's your name, little hawk?"

"Logan Centra."

"I heard you talking out there," Vorus said, "about your mother and another boy. Sullis? Is that his name?"

"Were you were spying on me?"

Logan bristled indignantly and jumped to his feet, but Vorus gave the table a sharp shove. Metal scraped loudly over the bare concrete floor and the table's edge hit Logan hard in the stomach.

He dropped back down into his chair, suddenly winded and a little nauseous.

"What did this Sullis kid say that made you come all the way across Highwind to join another gang?" Vorus asked.

"He... he called my mum a whore," Logan panted. "And said I should be ashamed. Then he came to our house and... and broke her things..."

He trailed off and looked down at his lap, hoping that Vorus couldn't see the angry tears that stung his eyes.

"He dishonored your mother and your home," Vorus said. He actually sounded like he agreed. Logan looked up again and found the old man nodding. "Tell me, little hawk, why did you want to take Elson and his boys to fight Sullis' gang? Was it out of revenge?"

"I... I just want Sullis to stop! I want him to leave me and my mother alone! He broke her favorite dishes and sent me to the hospital," Logan said hotly. He had found his breath again. "It was expensive and now she has to pay for it. It's not fair!"

"This boy, Sullis, is a criminal," Vorus said. "What he did was wrong and against Prian law."

"I know that!"

"Then what were *you* doing? If you defaced my palaestrum, if you joined Elson's gang, then you would be a criminal, too."

"But..." Logan protested.

Vorus furrowed his smooth, shiny brow.

"No. If you want to fight for honor, you must fight *with* honor, little hawk. Do you want to learn how?"

"I'm not very good at fighting," Logan replied sullenly.

"No, I can see that," Vorus said, eyes lingering on the boy's many bruises. "But you can be, if you work hard, practice every day and come to all of my classes."

"Your classes? Are you any good?"

Vorus laughed and slapped his hand on the table. "Me? Of course I'm good! I'm one of the best. I was a cop for most of my life.

You don't survive that unless you're a good fighter. I still teach police and anyone else who wants to fight for the right reasons."

"You think I could be any good?" Logan asked.

It was an intriguing idea.

"You need a lot of training. You're small and more than a little skinny, but when Sullis dishonored your mother, you went in search of allies and convinced them to do your work for you," said Vorus. He shook his finger at Logan. "It was a very bad idea, and an even worse one for a little boy."

"I'm not a little boy!"

"Yes, you are, but I think we can remedy that," Vorus said. "But I don't teach criminals, little hawk. Do you understand? I train men of honor and integrity. Are you a good man, Logan?"

"Welcome to my palaestrum, Miss Centra. I'm Arctan Vorus," he said, extending his hand. "I was hoping we could have a word about Logan."

"You stay the hells away from my son!"

Lynn Centra's face was pale. She was taller than Vorus, but still managed to look small and frightened. Her high heels clacked on the age-scarred wooden floor as she moved to leave.

"Please, Miss Centra..." Vorus put a gnarled hand on her shoulder. "Logan needs help."

"No, not from you!" Lynn said. She gripped her purse tightly against her knotting stomach. "I don't want you encouraging him, Master Vorus. Please, just leave him alone!"

"Logan's a fighter, Miss Centra. He's got fire in his heart and you should count yourself lucky that he's got something to fight for."

Lynn laughed shortly. The sound was sharp and unpleasant, full of bitter pain. "Whether you fight for something or nothing at all, you still end up dead."

"He's shown promise, Miss Centra. He's small for his age, but he'll get his growth. Logan's fast and he's clever. I think he has what it takes to be one of the best, maybe even good enough to join the force. Don't you want the best for him?"

"I don't want Logan to be a cop!"

Vorus frowned deeply. "The Prian police are a very thin, very fragile line between civilization and bloody anarchy here. Prianus needs good people."

"No! I wanted better for Logan. His father was a cop, too, and died before he could even hold his son." Lynn was still afraid, but her eyes took on the fierce, hard cast of a mother hawk defending her nest. "He left us alone. And for what? Honor?"

"I'm sorry, I didn't know. Logan never mentioned it."

"He doesn't know," Lynn said. She couldn't meet Vorus' gaze. "I don't want Logan to know. I don't want to lose my son, too."

"I found Logan in the alley out back, trying to join a gang. Is that any better? He wants to fight for you and he'll find a way to do it."

"He... he sings, you know," Lynn answered quietly. "And plays the guitar. He's amazing, really. I don't know where Logan gets it. Neither his father or I ever played. I always hoped that maybe he would get away from Prianus."

"And maybe he will. Or maybe he'll stay and fight for all of the people who can't or won't fight for themselves. That's not our decision. That's between Logan and God. I just want to teach him. What he does with the knowledge is up to him."

"What if he breaks his hand in your class?"

"Then he'll learn to play his guitar with crooked fingers."

Lynn sighed. "I can't pay for classes, Master Vorus."

"Then I won't charge. He can wash the mirrors and sweep the floors. We'll work it out."

She shook her head, scattering the tears that had gathered in her lashes. Vorus was right, no matter how much she hated it.

Lynn went to the palaestrum door and pushed it open. Logan jumped up from where he had been sitting against the wall outside. She brushed the grit from the seat of his pants and took a steadying breath.

"Logan, you can study fighting with Master Vorus. Pay attention and be sure to behave yourself," Lynn said. She smoothed her son's hair and smiled. "I'll see you tonight for dinner, my brave little hawk."

Logan kissed his mother on the cheek and then looked up to see Vorus waiting just inside the palaestrum door.

"Are you ready to begin?" the old man asked.

"Yes," Logan answered.

For more books by
Erica Lindquist & Aron Christensen,
visit us at **LLStories.com**